EDGE OF

SUNDOWN

Also from Chaosium

Lovecraftian Fiction

The Antarktos Cycle

Arkham Tales

Atomic Age Cthulhu (New)

The Book of Eibon

Cthulhu's Dark Cults

Eldritch Chrome

Frontier Cthulhu

The Hastur Cycle

The Innsmouth Cycle

The Ithaqua Cycle

The Klarkash-Ton Cycle

Madness on the
Orient Express (New)

The Necronomicon

The Nyarlathotep Cycle

Steampunk Cthulhu

The Strange Cases of Rudolph Pearson
by William Jones

Tales out of Innsmouth

The Tsathoggua Cycle

Once Upon an Apocalypse vol. 2
(Coming Soon)

The Xothic Legend Cycle

The Yith Cycle

Weird Fiction Collections

The Complete Pegana by Lord Dunsany

Eldritch Evolutions by Lois Gresh

Mysteries of the Worm
by Robert Bloch

The Terror & Other Stories
by Arthur Machen

The Three Impostors & Other Stories
by Arthur Machen

The White People & Other Stories
by Arthur Machen

The Yellow Sign and Other Stories
by Robert W. Chambers

Science Fiction

A Long Way Home

Extreme Planets

Horror

Once Upon an Apocalypse vol. 1

Undead & Unbound

Occult Texts

The Book of Dyzan

Edge of

Sundown

Edited by
Kevin Ross
and
Brian M. Sammons

CONTENTS

INTRODUCTION

SIX-GUNS AND SHADOWS

The western-horror story is far older than what most of us would even consider "the west". For generations the American Indians told dark tales of their own, of spider women, skin-walkers, cannibals, witches, and thunderbirds. When white men ventured into the west, they learned some of these nightmarish stories from the natives—and they brought or created their own as well: tales told around campfires of mournful ghosts and vengeful spirits and terrible monsters native to the wild new land west of the Mississippi.

The dime novels of the late 1800s spared little space for horror, save for the occasional mysterious hooded or masked rider. The weirdest of these early "pulps" instead opted for science fictional elements, more Jules Verne than Edgar Allan Poe: steam-driven mechanical men and wondrous flying machines rather than restless dead and bloodthirsty monsters.

It wasn't until the twentieth century pulps that the western horror story was born. There were pulps for everything in those days: sports, romance, oriental stories, adventure, boxing, horror, mystery/ detective, science fiction, and, of course, westerns. With such a broad range of story markets, it's no surprise that something as obvious as the western-horror combination came into being.

One of the first and foremost practitioners of the horror-western in the pulps was Robert E. Howard, whose heroic fantasy tales of Conan, Kull, Solomon Kane, and many others earned him a considerable following among the readership of *Weird Tales*. A full-blooded Texan with a love of history, Howard wrote and published several western tales, and given his knack for the weird, it was no surprise that he would eventually try his hand at mixing the two genres. Howard wrote tales of a Spanish vampire unwittingly released by a Texas rancher ("The Horror from the Mound"), a cowboy haunted by the black woman he murdered (the epistolary "The Dead Remember"), and a feuding Texan who stumbled upon a Lovecraftian race of subhuman reptile people ("The Valley of the Lost" AKA "The Secret of Lost Valley"), among others. Howard wasn't the only one writing horror-westerns, but he was probably the most prominent of his time. A few weird western films even popped up in those early days. *Riders of the Whistling Skull* seemed like a typical oater of the 1930s, with a trio of cleancut do-gooding heroes ("The Three Mesquiteers" -- groan), but it strayed into the outré when they stumbled upon a sinister Indian cult in a hidden mountain carved into the shape of a skull. There they encountered what appear to be cobweb-festooned Indian mummies. It's not as good as it sounds, but it sure must have been something different for its time! There were a few other offbeat oaters, mostly of the "old dark house" mystery school, where the masked or hooded killers lurking on ranches or in abandoned mines turned out to be just crooked ranchers or bankers in the end.

In 1948 park ranger Stan Powers wrote what would become the all-time horror western anthem, "Ghost Riders in the Sky", about ghostly cowboys forever cursed to chase the Devil's herd through the skies (a clever American take on the Wild Hunt of British folklore). Within the next year this eerie song was recorded by Vaughn Monroe, Burl Ives, and Spike Jones, and over the years it has been recorded by everyone from Frankie Lane to Johnny Cash, The Outlaws, and the western-horror-punk band Ghoultown; a version even appears in The *Blues Brothers 2000*.

Perhaps inspired by "Ghost Riders in the Sky", the comic book hero Ghost Rider was born in the early 1950s, originally as a non-supernatural masked hero, but later transformed into a ghostly avenger. The character remained a spectral western hero until the 1970s, when the Ghost Rider name was given to a demonic daredevil motorcyclist in the modern day(The western version had a cameo appearance alongside his modern counterpart in the 2007 film version of *Ghost Rider*).

For whatever reason, the horror-western really took off in the 1950s and 1960s, especially in the movies. *The Beast of Hollow Mountain* pitted rancher Guy Madison against an allosaurus with a ridiculously long tongue, while *Curse of the Undead* featured Eric Fleming (who played Clint Eastwood's trail-boss in the TV series *Rawhide*) as a preacher up against a gunslinging Mexican nobleman-vampire. In the 1960s William Beaudine gave the world *Billy the Kid vs. Dracula* and *Jesse James Meets Frankenstein's Daughter*, two of the most wretched westerns you'll ever see. At one point Billy the Kid empties his gun into Dracula (an obviously-slumming John Carradine), and then—honest to God—throws his gun at the vampire and knocks him out. The Italians (and Spaniards, technically) got into the act with the fine supernatural spaghetti western *Django the Bastard*, wherein the ghostly title character avenges himself on the officers who betrayed him and his men during the Civil War. (This film is frequently cited as the inspiration for Clint Eastwood's films *High Plains Drifter* and *Pale Rider*.) Ray Harryhausen's eye-popping *The Valley of Gwangi* had cowboys roping dinosaurs, including the rampant allosaurus of the title—a feast for dinosaur-loving kids, including your humble editor.

The 1970s and early 1980s saw a handful of western-horror comics, notably the Zorro-esque ghostly avenger El Diablo in DC Comics' *All-Star Western*, the character of Coffin from the black and white Warren comic magazine *Eerie*, and the Tex Arcana serial in the *Heavy Metal* magazine a few years later. El Diablo was a spirit that possessed wheelchair-bound Lazarus Lane and wreaked ruthless revenge on wrong-doers. "Coffin" was staked to an anthill, whose inhabitants ate half his face, then cursed by a dying Indian shaman to walk the west until he found redemption. The elaborately-illustrated Tex Arcana dealt with a western town's tongue-in-cheek adventures with vampires, werewolves, and demons, among other things.

The weird western film trend survived, albeit subdued, into the 70s and 80s, with films such as *The Shadow of Chikara*, *The White Buffalo*, and *Grim Prairie Tales*. *Chikara* had belligerent Confederate soldier Joe Don Baker and schoolteacher Ted Neely and their band hunting diamonds in the mountains of Arkansas, where they are killed off one by one by unseen Indian demons. (This eerie little film has to have set some record for the number of alternate titles it's known by: I have an original movie poster for it under the title *Wishbone Cutter*—the name of Baker's character, but I've seen video boxes with the *Chikara* title and *Diamond Mountain*, among others.) *The White Buffalo* is only tangentially supernatural, if at all, and despite some shabby mechanical buffalo effects, is an otherwise thoughtful story of Wild Bill Hickok (Charles Bronson) and Crazy Horse (Will Sampson) hunting for the title beast, which haunts their dreams. The much-later *Grim Prairie Tales* is an anthology of western horror stories told beside a lonely campfire by travelers Brad Dourif and James Earl Jones.

The 1980s and 1990s saw the horror-western making a comeback of sorts in fiction. Louis L'Amour published his modern science-fictional western *The Haunted Mesa*, and sf/horror legend Richard Matheson wrote no less than five westerns. Not surprisingly, one of these, *Shadow on the Sun*, featured a shape-changing Indian demon wreaking havoc on a small western town. This period also saw the rise of newcomers ("young guns?") like Joe R. Lansdale and Nancy Collins. Lansdale's *The Magic Wagon* displayed the remains of Bill Hickok, but otherwise wasn't very weird, unlike the full-tilt *Dead in the West*, which had a fallen preacher-gunslinger facing off against a zombie plague started by a vengeful Indian sorcerer. Collins also wrote several short novels and tales in this vein, including the Frankenstein-esque western novel *Lynch* (co-starring a mad doctor and his sasquatch assistant) and the Indian werewolf novel *Walking Wolf* (guest star: a vampire gunslinger). The 80s and 90s also saw the first weird western story anthology, *Razored Saddles*, edited by Lansdale and Pat Lobrutto, generally more weird, offbeat, or science fictional than strictly horror, though not without its dark moments.

The popularity of Lansdale's folksy, grim, gritty and grisly fiction led to his writing several comic miniseries in the 90s featuring DC Comics' western hero Jonah Hex. Created in the 1970s, with roots in the spaghetti western films, Hex was a ruthless bounty hunter with a horribly scarred face and an anti-social attitude to match. While definitely weird and at times even approaching a sort of "western gothic", the early Hex comics weren't supernatural. Lansdale changed that with *Jonah Hex: Two-Gun Mojo*, where Hex came up against a traveling medicine show run by a crazed wizard who was creating mindless zombie-like slaves—including, once again, Wild Bill Hickok. The series won a Bram Stoker Award for Lansdale and artist Tim Truman, and the follow-up *Riders of the Worm* and *Such* promised an even more blatantly horrific scenario: degenerate reptile people a la Robert E. Howard's "Worms of the Earth". Sadly, the story was derailed by singing cowboys, juvenile humor, and a corny science fictional lost race plot straight out of the old Gene Autry serial *The Phantom Empire*. The third series, *Shadows West*, contained fewer weird elements and was even more disappointing. Lansdale and Truman also took a decent shot at the Lone Ranger, with an enjoyable 4-issue miniseries entitled *It Crawls*, featuring a malevolent alien entity trapped in the body of an Aztec mummy.

The 1990s also saw the publication of the *Deadlands* roleplaying game, a wild mixture of western, horror, fantasy, steampunk, and martial arts elements set in an alternate America crawling with monsters and villains. The game spawned dozens of supplements, spin-off games, "dime novels" (part fiction and part game adventure), and a trio of weird western fiction anthologies set in the *Deadlands* game world.

The popularity of *Deadlands* led to another bumper crop of weird westerns in a variety of media around the dawn of the new millennium. Jeff Marriotte's sporadic horror-western comic Desperadoes dealt as much with racism, prejudice, and psychopathic villains as it did with the occasional supernatural being. The fiction anthology *Skull Full of Spurs* emphasized the horrific elements more than *Razored Saddles* had, but often flavored with humor and fantasy. Two different anthologies entitled *Weird Trails* appeared, one of western horror and fantasy stories edited by Mike Szymanski, the other a mock-1930s pulp magazine of weird western parodies edited by prolific author/ scholar Darrell Schweitzer.

Since then there has been a deluge of weird westerns, though little of any lasting substance. For every *Ravenous* or *The Burrowers* there have been a dozen direct to video western zombie and monster mashes, including the obligatory no-budget SyFy excretia with giant snake rampages and alien invasions in the old west.

The western-horror story may be alive, but we think it deserves better.

And that's where *The Edge of Sundown* comes in. We set out with one goal in mind: to gather together a collection of the best dead-serious western-horror fiction we could find. While there are other western-horror anthologies, and even some dark and entertaining ones, I have yet to find one that doesn't take the subject at least somewhat tongue-in-cheek, whether it's through tall tales, fantasy elements such as magic or steampunk, or slapstick (splat-stick?) humor. We were more interested in visiting the darker regions of the west, the places steeped in myth and legend—and blood. Meeting the men and women who lived there—the monsters within and without.

I have to admit, I expected to see a lot of grim gunslingers and vengeful Indian shamans—undead and otherwise—among the submissions for this anthology. Surprisingly, while there were a few of each, for the most part these stories steered away from the usual western clichés. Instead we've got a very diverse round-up of western horrors here. There are Chinese sorcerers, cannibals, ghouls, blood-sucking monsters, an honest-to-God living dinosaur, a wily buzzard, weird subhuman tribes, an animated skeleton with a purpose, a re-animated revolutionary, weird puppets, cursed guns, a couple of different lycanthropes, a vengeful Indian shaman (of course), a despicable voodoo practitioner, a Lovecraftian horror, and a card game with cosmic stakes.

Make no mistake, there are more than a few gun-throwing hardcases in these stories, but by and large our protagonists are ordinary folks caught up in very extraordinary circumstances. Most importantly, this is an anthology of western-HORROR tales, not western-fantasy. No tall tales here, no wink-and-a-nudge-as-it's-all-good-fun safe-betting. We're looking to give you the creeps, fair and square, no fooling around.

So right about now you should be checking to make sure your guns are loaded, that your holster is oiled, and you've got your hat cinched on tight.

Now—let's ride!

Kevin Ross
Outrider

THE CLAW SPURS

By John Shirley

T he moon was just like this'n," the Lone Hand said. "You see that, how there's that round hole through the clouds, that red ring around the moon...That's how it were that night..."

The cowboys looked up at the moon from where they squatted on haunches or sat Indian-like on blankets close by the campfire. One and then two of them nodded, seeing the red ring around the moon —and some other colors too, violet and a kind of blue with emerald mixed into it. But the red, they allowed, surely was the brightest ring. Old Partridge chirped up that there was no gainsaying the ring was the color of dried blood on dark blue fabric. It could not be denied.

It was the misty September of 1885, in Wyoming Territory, up in that region some folks called Montana. The drovers were engaged in a cattle drive. They had started from where the beef'd been fattening through the summer, on the Norther' Chaparrals, and were on their way down to the government buyer for the Cavalry at Fort Laramie. They were driving late in the month and there was anxiety that it might snow up in these piney hills, but there was only that thin scree of cloud over the moon.

The Lone Hand was called by this moniker because in the few days he had ridden with the outfit he had expressed a preference for working alone and, it was true, never failed to keep the cows that were his responsibility on the trail, needing no one to back him up. Now he broke off his story, musing to himself a moment, so that Kid Dreed

—a boy of scarcely eighteen—prompted him, "Go on and say, what 'tis that hoppen on a night like this. We got a tradichin here."

The Lone Hand was a lean sandy-haired man in a ragged duster and cracking black chaps. His black hat cupped his face in shadow as he nodded slowly, acknowledging young Dreed. "The tradition," he said, "of telling an adventure—true or untrue—on the drive around the fire of a night. Why, I am no man to buck tradition, boys, it's just that I do not quite know where to begin. This here story is one that has burned like the Consumption in my breast these many years, but I do not believe I have told it to anyone—and yet I know it well.

"It is like one of those Mexican saddles with the printings-on of horses and women and guns and, why, even volcanoes—so smartly worked into the leather that it's all one picture like a vine of ivy; a man doesn't know where it starts or finishes.

"Well now—I reck' that I will begin with that moon overhead. And I will tell you that this story is no windy. Regardless, boys, what you may suppose when you hear it, I swear this story is true... It began in the autumn of my fourteenth year, just fifteen years ago -- oh yes, boys, I'm younger than folks take me to be...That moon, now...."

I watched it most the way as I drove the buggy home (said the Lone Hand), on an early autumn night much like this one: that glaring moon, like a bullet punching the clouds; that ring of red, bleeding over on them thin clouds. I wished I had Consuela there to interpret: for as a boy I'd had a Mexican wetnurse, who fed me my breakfast some years after she ceased to suckle me, and it was she who taught me a respect for omens.

Well, I said to myself, if that red ring moon ain't an omen, then what is?

I traveled a rutty old trail, I remember, in the foothills of the Tetons —country not much different from this here, boys. I had failed to keep my eye on that treasonable old rut, nearly lettin' the horses stumble down the steep hillside, in my spooked distraction at the red glare of that moon. So it was that—cursing the team for hammer-heads, trying to regain control—I did not at first see the shine of fire in Crying Buck Hollow and was nearly upon our homestead before I knew that it was aflame.

Our house was no sod hut. The sod hut that we had begun in, it leaned out back and now was used for hanging meat and salting and the making of potations. The main house was of planed wood, fully two rooms and a loft, where I slept. There were two acres of corn and beans between the creek and the house and a pig wallow and a little lean-to barn. Most of my father's money was made through timber cutting taken right from that stand of trees on our land, for he was a woodworker. But we also sold some pigs and corn and venison, too, and did well enough.

Many days I felt a great comfort, standing with my father on this same hill, looking down into the hollow, contemplating our home-stead and how it had flourished. There was a sadness mingled in, for the graves of my mother and sister were visible from here too, in the daytime, in that hummock of higher ground along the creek, north of the house. Yet the house had sent its own reply to that sadness -- till now it had seemed to say, "You abide, still."

Now the comforting sight of that house was churning in gold and blue, such a prodigious fire that a single flame consumed all and only the house's skeleton was visible, black and red in the inferno.

Before I knew what I was doing, I had stood in the buggy and whipped the team down into the hollow, though they shied at approaching the fire. Could have been, however, the body of my father that spooked them for it was directly in our trail, about forty paces from the burning house. I jumped down from the buggy and ran to him, but somehow knew that he was dead before I found he was shot through the head, front to back, the back of his skull a wet ruin nor yet dried.

This and the vigor of the flame convinced me that the murderers could not be far gone. Weeping and shouting I knew not what, I took a burning brand in one hand and in the other my father's rifle -- which I found fallen not far from where he lay -- and searched in a widening circle around the fire.

I found the track of a shoeless horse, and not too heavy a mount. Only one. It could be the pony of an Indian; but there were also mountain men, in that territory, who rode their mounts shoeless, preferring to spend blacksmith money on whiskey and women when they came to town.

The tracks wound back onto the same trail I had come in on, then turned to follow a stream that crossed the way, a quarter-mile back. And there I lost it.

For a time I sat on a low, mossy boulder, contemplating the ringed moon coming and going in the stream's reflection, and pondering:

I had no doubt that the man who had killed my father was also the man who set our home afire. This was a sign of a completed vengeance in those places and at that time: you kill the man and you burn his cabin, too. If it was an act of vengeance, I could not be entirely surprised. My father was a good worker, but not altogether a good man. When he was in drink he gambled, and when he gambled he lost, and when he lost he grew surly and more than once had been obliged to spend a fortnight in the log jailhouse in Winslow for assaulting some tinhorn—or some man he asserted a tinhorn.

Losing my mother and sister to the smallpox had soured him, too, and given him over to drink and all that followed on drink.

Still, though he spoke rarely, he was not unkind to me. He had allowed me to go to school twice a week, and sometimes chose to set me to cutting wood till midnight as a punishment, when he might have beaten me for my boyish mischief. He liked to sit with me by the fire, while I read to him from almanacs and catalogues, and seemed proud of me when I explained to him the meaning of certain words. These were the memories I cherished; not the recollections of a drunken brutishness, or the loss of his poke, nor the time he had to take the mercury cure for the dirties some whore had given him, and how sick that made him, and what it done to his teeth.

"It may be," I said to that red robed moon in the water, "that my Pa done something he should not, and got his due for it. But here I sit, fed and clothed, lived to fourteen years old—nigh to fifteen—and that is his doing and none other. I will have revenge for him. I swear it on the blood of this ringed moon."

I went back to the homestead. The fire was burned down some, was them mean little blue flames, licking around the ruins of the house. I saw a wild dog or a wolf, I don't know which, beginning to tug at Papa's ankle, trying, maybe, to drag him back to its den. I shot at it and missed. I was never much of a shot. But the wolf showed its heels and fled into the darkness.

I remember noticing how much darker the woods seemed with Papa dead. Or maybe it was just the way the clouds had thickened up.

There were planks under a Conestoga tarp behind the house. It started to rain before I was done building his coffin. It wasn't as good as he would have built—he built many a coffin—but I was not ashamed of it. Lifting him into the box, I started bawling again. I made myself stop—it was almost like I heard his voice telling me to stop playing the crybaby—and I closed the lid, and didn't look at his face before I nailed the coffin shut. My only tintype of my father had charred up in the fire, and I regretted I could not have a camera-worker take a death picture of him, for remembrance pictures of the dead was all the rage in them days. But there was no time for that.

Mindful of that wild dog or wolf, I buried Papa deep, though the rain was making the grave fall in around my ankles by the time I was done.

Boys, it was a full two weeks before I knew who had done this thing to my father, for his fate was a year in the making.

I ranged in the buggy first to Winslow, but could find no one there who had a particular onus against the old man and the way people gossip I sure would've heard something. I feared the winter snows — even as we fear them now, boys—but even so I would not be dissuaded and drove the team up the mountains to Chokee, finding no word of him; and then down to the reservations near the border. For there was a power of gambling on them reservations, though every man knows it's as ruinous for an Indian to gamble as to drink. There I met an Indian named Broken Eye, a one-eyed Indian medicine man; he was a grizzled white haired old man who spoke a pretty good English, having endured the tender miseries of the missionaries as a boy. It was he who threw the seeing bones for me and said I was to look in a town to the north where there was much of the metals that white men killed for. I didn't know how Papa could have ranged so far, but I set out. I was nearly run through Papa's poke as well as what I got selling the pig, when I come to the silver-flush town of Parker.

Papa was a man with a cast in one eye and missing his teeth on that same side of his face. Any study of him at all impressed these traits on the memory. So it was that he was remembered in Parker as the man with a crooked eye who chewed on the other side of his mouth because of his teeth missing exactly from the middle to the left.

About eleven months earlier, he had gone to Parker, where he was unknown, perhaps fearing that the marshal in Winslow would be watching him with an unreasonable acuity. Seems he had heard that a silver strike, a day's ride north of Parker, had enriched the town entirely through the foolhardiness of the miners. For there were five gambling halls in Parker and little else.

I remembered the occasion as the time my father had gone to buy a plow mule, so he said, and was "robbed by highwaymen" on the way back. I had been skeptical even then.

In Parker he had run afoul of a fur trapping mountain man turned prospector. This was Elmore Jensen, son of "Swede" Jensen, the noted buffalo hunter. Papa had engaged in stud poker with this younger Jensen—thinking him a "lamb" to be led—and found him instead a cunning artist of the pasteboards, or at least not fool enough to drink whiskey while playing cards. Not to stretch it, Papa lost his all and, staggering drunk, he called Jensen a cheat. Jensen pulled his gun but misfired—for it was a damp night—and Papa, to his ironical misfortune, was able to fire his rifle first at near point blank range, shooting this younger Jensen through the breast. He did not die immediately, I am informed, but lingered the whole night calling for a messenger to bring his own father from the plains up North.

After conferring in private with the local constable and giving him his gold watch, Papa was able to persuade him that, though the other's gun had misfired, it was a fair fight as Jensen had drawn first. The constable made a noise about driving Papa out of town, but the short of it is he winked and let him go.

It was some six months before anyone ran into Swede Jensen and thought to give him the last request from his dying son. It was another three months before Swede judged it the time to begin his search for his son's killer and, so I surmised, two more before he found him. Swede rode an Indian pony, it was said, and always unshod. I was sure I had my man. Furthermore, I was told that Swede, on the way back, had fallen in with a great suety chunk of a lady procurer in Winslow and had taken to helping run her whores. So all the time I was searching for Papa's killer, he was warming his bone in a fat whore in Winslow, the nearest town to my home. I'd asked in Winslow first—but I had not asked Swede Jensen, nor his close associates, and only he and they knew he had killed a man ten miles away in Crying Buck Hollow.

It was the day of the first snow when I at last beheld Swede Jensen. I stood near the door of his establishment, in a ruck of melting snow and mud. It was difficult to see him, so thick was the smoke of pipes and twists in the Lady Day.

The establishment had pretensions to an elegance it had never completely accomplished. On one side of the room was a velvet settee; above it a portrait of dancing, scarcely clad maidens in the French style, the oil almost too big for the wall. A wind came in, sometimes, through knot-holes, and made the portrait jump, the ladies to truly dance. On the other side was the bar—which, by contrast, was just two raw planks over wooden barrels—and a shelf of bottles. Between bar and portrait were gaming tables, keno and poker tables, and a spin-the-wheel (as Papa had called it). The whores—in dirty gowns that had trailed in mud tracks, their hair greasy and their noses running —squeezed the men at the tables and whispered to them and often as not were back-handed for their trouble. Miss Day, the procurer, was not to be seen; it was said she usually lay abed upstairs with opium or laudanum. But Swede Jensen was immediately apparent. I had heard him described, and knew the man with the graying mane of blond hair, the flowing beard, the laughing blue eyes, and the brace of pistols in his coat, as my father's killer.

He was half sprawled on the settee, wearing a fur coat and a silken weskit, a tall whisky glass in one hand, on a thigh, his other not too far from the butt of a pistol slanted across his belly. He was laughing as a whore cursed a reluctant young farmhand for an "unmanly bastard".

I stood in the door and imagined what I might say before I did the deed. I would stand with my back to a wall, take a bead on his chest and shout, "O what a brave irony sir! You are a father who has avenged your son; I am a son who will avenge his father! I bid you goodbye—and let Satan bid you hello!"

And boom! I'd squeeze the trigger on the word hello and pray there would be no misfire.

But as I stood there, with my father's rifle cradled in my arms as if casual, Swede Jensen seemed to feel some malignancy toward himself and he turned his head, looking from one to the next, till his eyes met mine. He ceased to laugh, but the grin remained and his eyes were like ice coating granite. I saw a stillness in him then. Perhaps he saw in me a resemblance to my father; it could be he'd heard I'd been looking for him.

I knew for a certainty that if I threatened him, or even thought too hard about it, he would shoot me dead. He was known to be a fine shot and, in a contest up to Cheyenne, had come in second only to Bill

Hickok. He would shoot me dead of an instant and my father would never be avenged.

Of course I could backshoot him, and would not hesitate to do so, if that was the only way the business could be done. But looking at him, I saw an Indian charm around his neck; indeed, there were two and three of them on a thong. This and the preternatural fug of the man convinced me that he would know where I awaiting him in an alley, or in the trees by the trail. He had made some unsavory deal with the Indian spirits, I was sure, and could not be killed so easily.

As I reflect on it now, I'm sure the supernatural dread was my boyish imagination. Remember that I was only just fifteen years in the world, two days before.

But at the time I was as satisfied of his magical protection as the expectation of night following day.

So I turned away, puzzling out what I might do. I reasoned that, hoodoo or not, I was too much a boy to take on so powerful a man alone and if he was protected by Indian medicine, then I might seek out the same.

This put me in mind of Broken Eye.

It was to this Indian I now returned. I had to sell one of my horses and the buggy and rode on a folded blanket for a saddle back to the reservation. Along the way, I thought to glimpse a horseman, pacing me, a black silhouette against the sky, now and again. Was it Swede? The sight provoked me to rowel my old bay, till the horse was quivering with weariness.

It was a bone chilling dawn atop a treeless bluff when I found the medicine man just entering his sweat lodge. Broken Eye was not pleased to see me and asked me to come back in the new moon. I insisted on remaining and gave him most of what money remained to me. Told him I thought my Father's killer was after me and I had, anyway, sworn vengeance on this man.

Broken Eye said I must come into his sweat lodge, then, and wait till he was good and ready to speak. I followed him down stairs cut into the clay, into a kind of trench covered over with hide, and a smoldering darkness.

There followed a long day of hot, choking, stinking wretchedness, as we sat in the smokiest corner of the sweat lodge, both of us glossy wet, my eyes and lungs aching with the smoke of the acrid weeds he threw on the coals. The old man seeming unaffected, but only chanting to himself and swaying. At last when I, too, was swaying—but only because I was near to falling asleep or dead—he asked me, "Boy, when you swore to vengeance, what was the sky like that night?"

"I swore it under the red ringed moon, because it looked so like the blood on my father's forehead," I said.

"And this rider you seen followin' you, did you see what he wore or his face?"

"A droopy hat and a long coat is all I could make out. Maybe he was too thin to be Swede, but he could've been Swede's man."

"He was not. I have seen it. It was you yourself who summoned this rider. He is not Swede or Swede's Man. He is the one who wears the spurs of hawk claw and whose horse is mad and who should be long with his ancestors and is not. But go to him and ask him to do the deed and the deed will be done. There are warnings I should give you, but it is too late for them—just go, and take back your money. You will pay and pay enough."

Such was Broken Eye's speech to me. And I did not doubt him. He had about him a surety that said he knew things that others could not know. It was like the knowing of a tree, how it knows to grip the ground against the galestorm. It was a part of his substance.

So I set out on the trail again, riding slow now, and watching the hills. By and by I see the dark rider on the horizon, poised there and watching me. I lifted my hat and waved for him to come and then made camp under an oak tree, by a stream. Here there was only a little snow, in sickly patches, but the ground was frozen hard under me and I shivered where I squatted with my coffeepot and my weak little fire, waiting for him.

I fell asleep hunkered on my blanket, waiting, and only woke at the sound of horse's hooves—my own horse, pulling up its stake and running off, whinnying in fear.

I looked up to see him riding to a stop at the edge of the firelight. He seemed to have more darkness around him than the moonlit night should've allowed. I could see only his outline, unremarkable, rather like a circuit rider's shape. Maybe I was mistaken about this man, I thought, maybe he was just a wandering preacher.

"You called to me," came the voice, like a rustling of dry leaves.

"Are you the one the Indian spoke of?"

"That could be. Some will speak so. There is someone to kill, boy?"

I knew then who this was, and no mistake. The one the Indian had spoke of. "There is someone to kill," I said. "He is Swede Jensen, lately of the Lady Day in Winslow, who murdered my father. I have little enough to pay you, but I can fetch back my horse and give you him and you can have my land and I can owe you."

"Will you give me coffee?"

This surprised me, somehow, but I assented and he got off his horse, a black gelding so quiet it wasn't natural. The gunman came just close enough to the fire to take a tin cup, but not close enough to show his face, which was angled down under that drooping hat.

He took the cup in hands so dirty they were the color of a coal mine and his nails were almost as long as a woman's, but foul. I heard him make a loud slurping. His horse shied a little at the sound and lifted its head—the sight of this horse made me rock back on my haunches, boys, for I could've sworn that it had no eyes, but only holes crusted shut and its mouth streamed a red foam.

"Thankee," the stranger said, standing. I glimpsed a long barreled pistol stuck in his belt without a holster. "I could like to taste that coffee, so strong it was. I will take your case to this Swede."

"And the price?"

He paused and looked at the sky. I could not see his face. He said, "I have ridden too long and killed so much I can no longer feel the killing. I have been waiting for the right caller to give me rest and I believe I've found him. That is payment enough."

I did not understand him and would have said so but he strode away. When he swung onto his blind horse, I saw his spurs in the moonlight: they were neither iron like a cowboy's nor brass like a blue-leg's, but were made of hawk-claws fitted smartly into silver. Such spurs as I'd never seen nor heard of. Such as no respecter of horses would wear. He struck the scarred-up flanks of the horse with them hawk-claw spurs and the gelding screamed and blood ran down its patchy hide, and off he rode... toward Winslow.

No more could I sleep that night, so I searched along the creek bank till I found my horse and gentled him down and struck camp and set off for Winslow myself.

The next night I was riding up to the Lady Day, with a tingle in my neck, sensing that fate was bearing its fruit and not a minute more would pass without that apple plucked, and so it was. Swede was coming out into the muddy street, standing in the yellow light of the Lady

Day's doorway, laughing with a long-bearded companion—some fellow mountain man come to see him, I've since heard—when his laughter came up short in his throat, seeing a man step off his horse and approach him.

Now I had ridden up just seconds before and was thirty paces away, sitting my steed and watching, almost afraid for Swede, almost ready to call out a warning to him, though there was no sense in that at all.

If folks catch the smallpox and the blisters don't break but spread and something black is coughed up, why, it follows like the darkness of the moon that the sick one will die every time. I knew, for a surety, as I watched the hawk-spurred gunman step down from his horse and step once and twice toward Swede that death was in the offing, just as surely as seeing the finishing signs of smallpox.

"Swede Jensen," came the gunman's dried-out voice, "you have killed a man and left a boy without a father before the boy is ready. You have shot a man in vengeance and burned his home to the ground. Now is justice come to you, sir, and I bid you goodnight."

That was almost as good a speech as the one I'd had in mind and I felt my heart leap with joy as the gunman's pistol leapt into his hand —so it had looked, too, like it jumped to his hand and not the other way -- and though Swede was drawing too, cursing in Swedish, the fire leapt from the gunman's pistol first, fire the same color as the flame that had swallowed my home. Four times that pistol boomed and flamed and both men spun, Swede and his friend both, spinning in place for a moment, once around each as if to screw into the ground. Then they were fallen in the mud. There was screaming from the second floor window of the Lady Day, but no one showed their face and the gunman turned calmly and mounted his horse and rode off.

I went to look at Swede, to be sure. He was shot through the head, just like my father had been. Then I found myself riding after the gunman, though it was pure folly to do so. I had a hunger to thank him -- or perhaps it was out of fear, somehow, that I wanted to thank him. And something else was prodding me...

Yes, boys, there was something else. I wanted to see his face. It just didn't feel complete and done, till I knew the face of the man I had called to kill my father's murderer.

As I rode, I thought to myself that I should be going in the opposite direction. Consider, I says to myself, how you came to meet this man;

how he seemed to hear you call for vengeance; how the Indian said he come. Why go begging for further truck with the Devil?

But I could not help myself. I had to know.

So I found him on the trail—by that very boulder, near the spring where I had first sworn vengeance. I stopped my horse, and I tell you boys, I could hear my heart pounding like an Indian tom. But I had to know, I plain had to know.

The dark gunman sat still as a holstered gun on his mount, waiting for me. I spurred my horse closer—it had to be spurred hard, he did not want to approach the other mount or the rider neither. But, my horse rearing, I was at last close enough.

I fumbled in my coat and found a lucifer and struck its sulfur on my thumbnail and by the light of the match I saw his face.

A long lean face, gaunt and still. His skin seemed blue or yellow; maybe that was just the matchlight. His beard was as patchy as his horse's hide. His lips were papery-tight over his teeth. But it was his eyes, boys -- his eyes were glazed gray, like a snake's eyelid. They never blinked, though I raised the match close to that face. They were the eyes of a dead man. He looked out from those eyes, though—something way back behind them was looking out at me, though they never moved in their sockets. Could not move, I judged.

I cried out and dropped the match, and my horse reared and threw me. I fell heavily, lay dazed for a moment, one hand in the ice-cold creek.

At last I got to my feet, groaning with my bruises. I felt the loom of his horse over me.

"I'm glad you follered me," said the hawk-spur gunman. "I'm glad you come and seen my face. That's the last part of it, except for this--"

Then he kicked out, his spurs flashed in the starlight and he slashed me deep across the cheek with those hawk-claw spurs.

I screamed and fell to my knees, clutching my face. He got down off his horse and took my wrist and I felt something cold pressed into my hand—it was his six-gun.

"Now, you son of a bitch, you will pay me for what I done for you. You owe me for the killing of Swede Jensen and the avenging of your father."

I don't know how I understood what he was asking, but I did. Them cuts from the hawk-spur were burning on my face and some-way, once that happened, I seemed to know what to do. I lifted up that heavy pistol, with two hands, and shot him through the head and then his horse the same. I found some kerosene in his saddle bags, as if brought for this purpose. I set both bodies on fire and then once more I went in search of my horse.

Well boys, I drifted far from that territory, down to Texas, then out to Arizona territory. I spent some time around Tombstone; then up to Montana way. I learned to shoot straight and fast and for the first time learning the gun seemed to come easy to me. But I never killed another man till I was 19. A woman was dragged down and ruined by two saddletramps and she pleaded me her cause. I found them on the trail and shot them both, and that was the beginning of the life I lead now. Many times I've done that red and smoky work. You might've heard of Johnny Ringo—was me who shot him in the head, and set him in that forked treetrunk.

Then I come to a little town up north of here where some cowboys, not long ago, hurrahed Main Street. A man's wife was killed by one of those cowboys, who was only shooting at a lamp and never intended to kill that woman. But one of those cowboys killed her—and in all the promiscuous shooting no one was quite sure who. So the man says to me, don't do it here in town, but join their outfit, and up in the mountains... kill them all. Kill them all, and I will pay you well.

And saying those words, the Lone Hand stood and drew his pistol. Kid Dreed had guessed the Lone Hand's purpose and old Partridge and Jimmy D'onfrio, too, and were up and pulling, but it was too late —the Lone Hand was aiming and firing with never a misfire and every one of those cowboys went down, shot lethal.

There was another—the cook, an old man, a former schoolteacher, hiding under his chuckwagon—who had not been with the party hurrahing that town. The Lone Hand turned and regarded the frightened old man, and, thoughtfully reloading his gun, said, "You may live, if you swear to tell the tale I have told here tonight, for I would have it known as a warning to those who would otherwise cry for vengeance under the red ringed moon... and who might be cursed with a loneliness that's like what a man feels who dies forgotten in a cave that no one knew he crawled into."

The cook swore to tell it all at the next opportunity.

Then Kid Dreed, shot through the middle, squirmed and grunted and the Lone Hand saw that he was not quite dead. "Let me go," the boy sobbed, "I shot no one in that town, I swear it."

"Boy, you are gutshot and to kill you is a mercy or you will die in a pain you cannot imagine. But to tell you the truth..." He cocked his gun and aimed it. "I would kill you anyway, no matter what or how, since the man who paid me swore vengeance on all of you and it's my nature, you see, to kill in vengeance -- it has been my nature since that hawk-spur cut my cheek that night and will be my nature long after I'm dead."

So saying, he fired twice and the boy lay still forever after.

Then the Lone Hand found his mount and rode off under that brooding moon and, so it seemed to the cook, rode right up onto the bloody path the red-ringed moon made in the gathering mist and into places beyond.

CEMETERY MAN

BY SILVIA MORENO-GARCIA

She lay bleeding upon her cartridge belts. She could not stand up. The piercing pain in her stomach would not allow it.

Catalina raised her head, squinting.

A man with a long coat, shiny boots and a small leather case—the kind a doctor might use—approached her. Was that their surgeon? She didn't want them to cut her open.

The man paused before her, putting on his hat. She recognized him, all the stories hitting her like a *jicarazo* of icy water at dawn: the Cemetery Man.

Around the campfire, the *soldaderas* joked about the resurrected and the Cemetery Man. Catalina laughed with them. Well-known fighters like La Güera Carrasco, who loved to shoot her gun at the smallest provocation, or Margarita Neri, who was so infamous that the governor of Tabasco hid in a crate when he heard she was approaching his town, were not afraid of the resurrected. Catalina should not show any fear either. But alone, late at nights, she did not laugh. She thought of the resurrected lurching across the battlefield and the Cemetery Man, the shadow of his wide-brimmed hat falling upon a corpse.

Catalina wanted to raise her gun and blow his brains out, but her hands trembled and she was only able to scratch the dirt.

The man smiled.

Catalina woke to an annoying scraping noise and a sharp pain in her gut. Her head hurt and she winced.

She lay upon a narrow bed, in the darkness. Light filtered through gashes in some curtains.

Her hands felt numb as she flexed them, sluggish thoughts drifting through her brain. She was alive.

Alive... and where?

She pressed her hands against her belly, feeling the bandages beneath her gown.

The scraping returned, loud and irritating. She turned her head.

The resurrected stood in a cage. They had blown half his skull off but a metal plate had replaced the lost bones. The face was badly mangled, stitched together, and the skin was the color of milk curds. A few tufts of blond hair adhered in dirty clumps to its head. Its eyes were mismatched, shining bright.

The scraping was the sound of the chains against the floor as the creature moved.

Catalina started breathing fast.

"Easy, easy," the Cemetery Man said from behind her.

Catalina wanted to speak. The words lodged in her throat. She moved her tongue but could produce no sound.

"Calm down," he said reaching towards her and placing a hand on her shoulder.

"Don't touch me, you asshole," she slurred. "Damn necromancer."

His face lit up, as though he were mightily amused by her cursing.

"You're very lucky, do you know that? I've saved your life. We wouldn't want to ruin your stitches, would we?"

Catalina gritted her teeth. She did not deign to answer him. He grabbed her arm, tapped at a vein and produced a syringe.

"No," she said, twitching, but he held her arm firmly and slid the needle into her vein.

"Just a tad of morphine," he said. "It always helps to make things better."

He shifted her limbs, like a doll, pulling the covers up.

"You're going to feel much better soon."

"My head hurts."

"Why don't we go to sleep, huh?"

"No," she said, thinking of the resurrected in the corner of the room, staring at her from its cage. What if it broke out? She would not sleep.

Catalina shook her head, her eyes rolling back.

Wild dreams. Bizarre images, as if viewed through smoke and fire. The Cemetery Man's wide grin as he looked at her, sharp knife in hand. A pressure upon her skull, so she felt it must burst and she opened her mouth to scream. There was no sound.

Catalina shook, contorting in pain.

She woke up and vomited, half of the mess falling upon the bed and the other on the floor. Catalina sobbed into the pillow and did not attempt to move. Footsteps. Strong arms pulling her up.

"Come on, girl."

White, cold tiles against her feet. She saw a chain above her head. They were in the shower. Someone held her up. Someone pulled the chain and cold water rained down on her face. Catalina shivered as a nurse in a spotless white uniform scrubbed her.

Linen against her skin. Being carried again. She raised her head and saw that the Cemetery Man and a nurse were walking ahead of her. The person carrying her was the tall resurrected she'd seen in the cage.

The resurrected tore soldiers to pieces. They felt no pain. They had no thoughts. They were lumbering, idiotic, murderous machines. She remained perfectly still, not daring to twitch a muscle.

"Set her down."

Covers pulled.

The Cemetery Man brushed the hair from her face. He looked almost kind as he nodded. "Just a little nausea. A side-effect from the morphine."

The damn headache. It didn't cease. Catalina moaned. She muttered some gibberish that had no relation to real words.

"Damn it," the man muttered.

He drew his syringe.

No more, she wanted to say. *Oh, no more.*

"I want light."

He had been sitting by her side for a good five minutes, but she hadn't been able to bring herself to speak until now. Her throat felt raw and her body ached. The headache, although receding, was still like a splinter in her skull.

"There you are," the Cemetery Man said.

He drew the curtains. The tall windows let the morning sunlight in. He sat down next to her once more.

Catalina turned her head, to see if the resurrected was in its cage. It was. She looked away.

"How are you feeling this morning?"

"Where are we?" she asked.

"An abandoned typhus sanatorium, now my headquarters."

"In what town?"

"Barquilla."

Further than she thought, in the southern portion of the state. An area controlled by the Federales and far from her squadron. They must have traveled by rail. Catalina wondered how the hell she was supposed to make it back to the other *soldaderas*, wounded as she was, without a horse, nor weapons. The man grinned, as if he could read her thoughts.

"You wouldn't last long out there."

He leaned forward and began removing a bandage around her head, slowly taking off the gauze and applying a new one.

"I am Gabriel Mendoza. What's your name?"

He tossed the dirty gauze in a bowl. Catalina did not reply, her jaw set tight.

"I'll call you Adelita then," he said. "Like in the song. Have you heard it?"

"I know the fucking song," she said. "My name is Catalina."

"Cata."

"Catalina," she said.

"Surname?"

"Don't have one."

"Well, Catalina Don't Have One. How do you feel?"

"Great."

"Good. Maybe you'll have some real food today instead of mush," he said, gathering his things and heading towards the door.

"Hey," Catalina yelled, "you're not leaving me alone with that monster are you?"

"He's locked," Gabriel said with a shrug.

Catalina cursed him and the door slammed shut.

She tried not to look at the creature, but she did. It stood very still in its cage. He was even uglier and more malformed than she thought. She saw that half of his left hand was made of metal and there was another metal plate at his neck. She could picture the machine gun making dozens of holes in the poor bastard's body. Then she thought of Gabriel walking through the battlefield picking the pieces of guts and bone and muscle, sewing them back together and making them walk again.

She pressed her palms against her eyes to stop herself from looking at it.

One thing was sure: the Federales ate better than her squadron. It was tortillas with *chile* on most days for her. Gabriel brought chicken broth. With real chicken in it. Not just yellow, murky water with the faint flavor of chicken.

Catalina dipped her tortilla into the broth and chewed as fast as she could.

"Don't gorge yourself," he warned her.

"Fuck if I don't," she said.

"You're talking with your mouth open."

"Leave me alone."

He laughed. She thought of slamming the bowl of broth onto his face, but she was hungry. Catalina slurped and ate as quickly as she could.

"You're looking much better today," he said.

"When will I be able to walk?"

"Soon. Don't be thinking you'll run off now that those stitches are healing. There are many soldiers downstairs and they'd be itching to shoot a runaway prisoner."

"Can I sit by the window?"

"No."

Catalina shrugged, handing him her empty bowl and wiping her mouth with the sleeve of her gown.

"Where the hell did he come from?" she asked, staring at the resurrected man.

Poncho, the nurse, had brought her injection that day. Aside from the resurrected man and Gabriel, he was the only other person she'd seen since her arrival. Catalina did not know how many people worked with Gabriel, nor did she know how many Federales patrolled the building.

"Brehob?" he asked her.

"Is that its name?"

"Yes. He's a Canadian mercenary. Joined Villa. Gabriel picked him after a battle and brought him back. He thought he might be useful."

Once, on the battlefield, she'd seen a resurrected rip another *soldadera* open and pull her spleen out. Viscera showered the ground. Catalina shot the creature three times, but it didn't go down until a bullet hit its head. She'd developed a healthy fear of the resurrected since then.

She hated the creature, Brehob. The mangled body and the slack, stupid face, tongue lolling out. The thought of being torn to pieces crossed her mind at least once a day.

"He is disgusting. Ah, damn it," she muttered, pressing her closed fist against her forehead as it throbbed. "Hurry."

Poncho slid the needle into place. Catalina thanked God for the morphine. Without it, she feared her head might have split in two. She drifted into the velvet blackness of dreams, punctuated with flashes of red.

She dreamt of blood and the battlefield.

"Here. Idle hands belong to the devil," Gabriel said, dumping a book onto her lap.

Catalina stared at it as though it were a live, dangerous animal.

"You said you were bored."

"I said I wanted to sit close to the window."

"This is much better than staring at the sky. You can read and educate yourself."

"I only went to school 'til I was nine. I was a laundress. Not much reading is required."

"How did you end up in a squadron?"

"My dad joined the fight. I traveled with him."

"It seems like a scary proposition."

"I thought I'd be safer as a camp follower. There's money to be made from cooking or washing soldier's uniforms."

She didn't say she had been skilled with a Mauser since her childhood, when she went hunting with her father. She also didn't say the death of her mother had energized both her and her father, giving them the courage to join the fray. There were soldiers of fortune, of conviction and of circumstance. Catalina fell in the last category.

"But you were part of a female squadron. What happened to your father?"

"How'd you get in bed with the Federales, Cemetery Man?" she shot back.

"I really wish we'd go back to necromancer," he said, shaking his head. "It sounds so much better."

"I'm being polite. They call you El Zopilote, too."

He smiled, a bird of prey's look which seemed very appropriate considering that other nickname.

"How interesting," he said, pausing and rubbing his chin. "My story is very simple, Catalina. I am a scientist, despite the whisperings of the rabble who may claim otherwise. I was researching several interesting aspects of the human brain and body before the Revolution flared up. The conflict has allowed me to put some of my theories to good use."

"You're busy pecking carrion, you mean."

"I am not ashamed of what I do."

"Maybe you should be."

He patted her head, like one might do with a dog or a small child. She flinched.

"As interesting as this conversation is, I have my duties to attend to," he said, opening the book onto a random word. "There are some pictures. You might find it amusing."

Catalina frowned. There were big words in the thick tome.

"Zoology," she muttered, her finger upon the page.

Poncho set down the tray next to her and handed her a napkin.

"Why isn't the Cemetery Man here today?" she asked.

"He's busy."

The resurrected wasn't there either, though that was not unusual. Gabriel took him with him often. She preferred it that way. There was nothing more bone-chilling than feeling that monstrosity staring at her with stitched-together, mismatched eyes that seemed to know nothing. Flesh should not be made to shuffle upon earth like this again. Flesh should not give rise to such abominations.

"Is he coming at all?"

"Maybe later."

The door swung open. Another man in a nurse's uniform looked inside, a frenetic expression on his face.

"Poncho, come!"

Poncho did not pause to excuse himself. He rushed out, the door banging shut behind him.

Catalina smiled as she realized that in his haste he had not bothered turning the lock. The only time she'd left the room before was when the resurrected carried her to the showers. Not that she had been able to even attempt putting one foot out. But she was feeling much stronger and she had secretly been moving around the room even though Gabriel had warned her she might tear the wound open again.

She'd make some excuse if they found her outside. She'd say she'd had another migraine and went looking for help. They might be upset, but she couldn't miss this chance to inspect her surroundings.

Catalina padded towards the hallway, barefoot— they'd taken away her boots and clothes, the only thing she wore now was a nightgown. She poked her head out the doorway, fearing Poncho would walk back into the room, but the hallway was empty. If there were soldiers on the second floor where she slept, they were not patrolling that day.

Catalina headed down the hallway, glancing at empty rooms. It was very quiet. Very lonely.

The scream made her heart slam against her chest. It echoed down the hallway, eerie in the stillness of the building. Catalina considered retreating quietly to her room. But what if there was another wounded soldier there? Perhaps someone from her same squadron. Catalina inched forward until she reached a door with opaque, milky-blue glass panels. She heard Gabriel's irritated voice coming from inside.

"Didn't I say to gag her? Is it secure this time?"

"Yes, sir."

One of the glass panels was shattered. Catalina looked in.

A woman had been strapped to a bed, face down. Poncho, the nurse and the resurrected were there. She saw a table with odd tools. The smell of chemicals was thick in the air, mixed with the scent of blood.

Gabriel held up a pair of metallic instruments. Something wriggled, caught in the tip of the instruments: an ugly, large, white insect.

"Pull her head up," Gabriel said.

Poncho obeyed. Gabriel pressed the insect against the back of the woman's neck and the thing slipped inside, and under, her skin.

Gagged or not, the woman let out at inhuman howl which forced Catalina to cover her ears. She stepped back, eyes-wide. That was when Gabriel raised his head and saw her.

She ran.

Catalina knew running after you've had a bullet removed from your gut is not the best course of action, but she did not care. She was not going to let him put that thing inside her. Catalina was getting out of that damned sanatorium.

She reached a wide staircase and rushed down, much to the astonishment of a soldier, who stared at her in confusion. She hit him, slammed him against the wall with a loud crack, then kept running down. As soon as she stepped on the ground floor she heard the shots.

Bang! Bang!

Twice. Shot in the back this time.

Catalina fell down.

Catalina lay with her cheek pressed against the pillow, naked, as the Cemetery Man took out the bullets. Delicately, with the utmost care.

The bullets fell, clanging, into a metal dish.

She fell too, into the black maw of an insect.

"No!"

She jolted up and was surprised to find herself in bed. For a good minute she thought it had all been a nightmare. Then she felt the leather restraints around her wrists.

Catalina arched her back, groaning, feeling a new and fresh ache there.

"You've got a knack for getting hurt," Gabriel said.

"Somebody shot me!"

"And you broke a man's arm."

She recalled the soldier she'd shoved aside. Too bad.

"You keep monsters in this place. You're not putting them in me. You'll have to shoot me again and kill me this time, 'cause I ain't having that!"

"You've already died, you idiot," Gabriel grumbled, his face hovering close to hers.

She tugged at the leather straps, trying to sink her teeth into his neck, like a wild animal.

"Morphine," he demanded.

A nurse, stepping from behind him, handed him a syringe, while Poncho tried to hold her legs down. Poncho was strong, but she was stronger, and she kicked and flailed, sending Poncho stumbling back.

"Brehob!" Gabriel yelled.

The resurrected pinned her down. She stared into his face, his mouth opening and closing like a fish, while the needle slipped into her vein.

This wheelchair had leather straps at the ankles and legs, though they need not have bothered. Catalina sat quiet, staring at the wall.

"They say you are not eating."

She looked up at him.

Gabriel smiled. "We'll force-feed you, if we must."

"What have you done to me?"

"Ah, so you speak at last. Would you really like to know?"

"Yes."

Gabriel reached for the zoology book, flipped through the pages and showed her an illustration.

"*Cymothoa exigua.* A parasitic crustacean which attaches itself to a snapper's tongue. Eventually it causes the tongue to atrophy and replaces the tongue with its own body. I've developed a variation of this parasite. It now resides in your head."

Catalina wanted to scratch her scalp, fearing she could feel something stir beneath her skin. She controlled herself, her hands closing into fists, resting upon her lap.

"Why?"

"The resurrected are good for cannon fodder. They walk into the battle field, tear a few soldiers to pieces or serve as shields for us. But they can't think. They are strong, resistant and stupid. My most recent experiments focus on making them more intelligent. This parasite adheres to the patient's brain, allowing it to maintain its normal brain functions. It also accelerates your healing process. Think of what that means for a soldier: you always get to come back. Not only come back, but come back better."

Gabriel leaned down. "You should be grateful."

She bared her teeth at him. "I'll kill you."

"You can't. For the same reason that Brehob will never raise his hand at me. For the same reason I can walk by a field full of resurrected without fear: I made you. I own you."

He smiled, lifting her chin. His expression was almost fond.

"You're my best experiment so far," he said, a note of wonder in his voice.

Catalina wanted to bite his fingers and could not. She tasted bile in her mouth and swallowed.

She observed her body in wonder as it healed very quickly, even faster than the first time she'd been injured. Benefits of her new condition, Gabriel explained.

The parasite in her head gave her splitting headaches. They increased the morphine. A minor drawback, Gabriel said.

She had nightmares. She dreamt her skin split, pus oozed out, the stench of decay hit her nostrils.

Nothing of importance, just bad dreams that disappear with the morning, Gabriel pointed out.

He did not understand—did not even try to understand—what it meant to be her. What it meant to live and die and live again. The only one who might comprehend was Brehob in his cage, with his dull, empty eyes, staring at her.

It knew.

But she turned her head away from him.

She did not want to be like Brehob.

A man came to visit them. His hair was white and he leaned on a silver-tipped cane. He was small and frail, but Catalina noticed the way Gabriel spoke and moved around him and realized the Cemetery Man was intimidated. They spent some time in front of the resurrected's cage, then turned their attention to Catalina.

The old man, who until then had not spoken a word, opened his mouth when he saw her.

"What is your name, girl?" the man asked.

"Catalina," she said.

"How are you feeling today?"

"Fine."

"I've not seen one who can speak," the man said with a nod. "Is she the latest one?"

"Yes." Gabriel said. "She retains all her memories, all her personality. The parasite does subject her to some migraines, some degree of discomfort, but such things are minor. She is our most successful example," Gabriel said.

"But I hear you haven't been able to replicate this success."

Gabriel's face tensed, his eyes filled with an unpleasant sharpness.

"That is a gross simplification," Gabriel said.

"Armando Girat has also been conducting resurrection experiments. He has successfully produced six intelligent resurrected and assures me more can easily be created."

"Girat is not a scientist. His work is that of an amateur; a butcher."

"I have seen his work. It's comparable to yours, Gabriel. We need better soldiers. Soon Villa's rabble will find a resurrection formula for themselves. We cannot lose our edge."

"Villa does not have access to this technology."

"He's brought an American to do some research. A Mr. West. I hear good things about him. Bad for us. I think it would be best if your research were combined with Armando's."

"I will not consent to such a thing," Gabriel said. "I know what he'll do with her. That butcher will cut off her head, steal my parasite and then copy all my work. I'll be left with nothing."

She looked at Gabriel, so smooth and composed on all occasions, now turn ugly, brow frowned, an unpleasant grimace cutting his face.

The old man raised the tip of his cane, pressed it against Gabriel's chest. "I did not ask," he said. "I'll have the girl taken back with me. You'll soon follow, bringing your notes and equipment."

Two soldiers came for her in the morning. Poncho injected the morphine, waited a bit, then undid her restraints.

Catalina lay slack against the bed, like a dead fish.

"Let's get you dressed," Poncho said, helping her to sit up.

"Hey, we're running late," one of the soldiers said.

"It won't take long," Poncho muttered. "You think you can drag her around in a nightgown? I've got some clothes here."

"It won't matter one bit."

"Dr. Gabriel said--"

"Yeah, well--"

The soldier didn't have time to complete the sentence. Catalina jumped on top of him, sending him sprawling against the floor and twisted his head in one swift motion.

The other two men stared at her in surprise.

"The doses," Poncho muttered, his hands fluttering as he took a syringe from his coat pocket. "It must not be enough."

The soldier raised his gun at her. Catalina did not give him time to even start squeezing the trigger. She grabbed his arm, twisted it back, bones breaking. The soldier hollered, but she slammed his head against the floor, silencing his screams.

She turned and pointed the gun at Poncho.

"You don't want to die today, do you?" she asked.

He shook his head.

"Give me the needle."

He did. Catalina grabbed it, then hit Poncho on the head with the gun. Poncho blabbered, fell down, and grew silent.

Catalina found the clothes he'd brought for her: a blouse, a skirt and boots. She put them on and divested one of the soldiers from his jacket. She also took another gun, a leather holder and a belt.

Dressed and ready, she exited the room. The hallways were empty, just as before. Instead of heading down the main staircase as she'd done the previous time she moved in the opposite direction: there had to be service stairs. She found them after a little while and hurried down. She came out near the kitchen area and moved towards the stables.

The stables were large but there were only eight horses there. She saddled one horse and spotted a blanket that lay rolled upon a bench.

Catalina had the blanket and was heading back towards the horse when a tremendous blow sent her crashing against the floor. She blinked, stunned for a moment, the great outline of Brehob's body blocking the light.

He picked her up with one hand and Catalina tried to kick him, but her blows seemed to have little impact. He punched her in the face and Catalina tasted blood.

"Where do you think you are going?" Gabriel asked.

He was leaning against the stable wall, hands in his pockets.

"Back to my squadron, asshole," she muttered, spitting blood and saliva.

"I don't think you're going anywhere," he said.

Catalina tried to reach for one of the guns, but Brehob twisted her hand and she yelped, feeling the bones crunching.

"Come on, Catalina. It's not going to happen. All you're going to manage is to hurt yourself and then I'll have to put you back together again."

"Go to hell."

Brehob squeezed her hand and she felt the bones breaking.

"Stop it!"

"No, you stop it, Catalina! We both know you need me. You need me to take care of you and of your little parasite. You don't want to be like the resurrected in the battlefield, do you?"

She shook her head.

"Then be a nice girl and stop this."

Catalina ceased squirming. She held her breath.

"Give me her guns," Gabriel ordered. "Then let her go."

Brehob ripped off the holster she was wearing and tossed it to Gabriel. Gabriel held one of the guns and shrugged.

"How far do you think you'd have gotten with only this?" he asked, tossing the weapon to the floor, like a piece of rubbish. Who needed weapons when he had the resurrected to do his bidding?

Brehob set her down and Catalina held her mangled hand, wincing.

"I don't know."

"Not very far. Come here. Let's see what kind of damage we've made."

Catalina shuffled forward. He tilted her face up, brushing her lips, his thumb smeared with her blood.

"Nothing too awful," he muttered, then grabbed her injured hand, looking at the splayed fingers.

As he looked at the broken bones, Catalina raised her good hand and thrust the syringe into his throat. Gabriel opened his eyes wide.

"You can't hurt me," he croaked.

"I'm not hurting you. Just a tad of morphine," she said. "It always helps to make things better."

She pressed a hand against Gabriel's mouth to keep him from speaking and giving Brehob a command. He quickly relaxed against her body and she let him slide upon the floor.

Catalina picked up her gun and pointed it at the unconscious doctor. Her hand shook.

She could not kill him.

Catalina cursed.

She heard the creature moaning. It sounded eerily like a question.

Catalina looked up at its mangled face. The creature looked back at her with its odd eyes, opening its mouth as if it were to speak, but its tongue formed no words. Just the long moan, the clicking of a tongue.

She felt a pinch in her head. The creature opened its mouth in a wide o and all she could think about was that time one of them had killed a *soldadera*, and the viscera and the blood, and the stench, and how this thing was just the same kind of abomination.

Catalina squeezed the trigger. Brehob stumbled back and lay resting against a bench.

She moved closer and listened as the tongue kept clicking, words never coming and Brehob looked up at her.

"Bye," she whispered.

She pulled the trigger again, brain matter splattering her.

In the days after, when she rode in search of her squadron, she saw Brehob's face as she went to sleep. She'd killed people before, in battle. One more death was not what kept her up at nights.

She thought he was trying to say "please" when she shot him. She thought she'd seen tears in his eyes.

She lay wrapped in her blanket, staring at the stars. Her heavy gun lay next to her good hand. The bad hand was pressed against her chest.

She sensed the little parasite snug inside her skull, and she took a deep breath and she did not know why she'd bothered saying goodbye.

JIANG SHI IN CHINATOWN

BY KELDA CRICH

A brother and sister walked through the streets of San Francisco's Chinatown. Those who recognized them, those who remembered the old ways, made the sign of protection with their right hand, as they passed by. Unlike most of the residents of Chinatown, Goh Ming and Goh Kun were dressed in European fashion. But those who knew them knew that they were of the old country, the old China, the old ways that some of them had left China to escape.

"It's only been five years. Lien will be fine," said Ming. Her words were edged with the taint of self-conviction.

Her brother scowled. He was a tall, lean man. His face was marked with black tattoo sigils, marked with the writing of his calling. He said nothing as he scanned the ramshackle buildings of Chinatown.

All through the long journey from China his sister had kept her hope alive. They had booked a passage with the Pacific Mail Steamship Company and sailed to San Francisco on the steamboat *Ice Bird*. Ming had spent her time tending to the Chinese girls who made up part of the ship's lucrative cargo. Kun wondered why they had spent so much time fighting the spirit adversaries, when there was so much evil to be found here in the mundane world.

"It's my fault. I should have kept her with me," said Ming. This had been her constant lament for the last few years.

Kun was desperately worried about his sister. He glanced at her as she walked amongst the filth of the street. She was a finely-boned, elegant woman, incongruous in her European clothing. She should have been dressed in the softest of silk, the most exquisite of kimonos. She walked on, heedless of her tailored dress, the hem trailing in the filth of the street.

"A child could not have gone where we have been, these past few years," said Kun.

"But a child can come here, to this New World." Ming stopped in the street outside of a broken-down building. The wall to the building was faced with half a dozen doors. Each wooden door was locked and had a wire mesh at head height. At some mesh were faces. Ming walked over to the nearest door.

A girl's thin voice sang out, "One bit to look, two bits to touch, five bits for everything."

"Where are you from?" asked Ming, in Cantonese. The girl behind the mesh looked confused. She repeated her invitation, "One bit to look, two bits to touch, five bits for everything."

"An outrage," whispered Kun. He looked around the street and saw a group of men standing on the street corner. His fists clenched. He recognized them from their clothing and from the distinctive cut of their queues, the long pigtails that all of them wore. They were men from the impoverished Guangdong province. He glared at them and cried, "They take our children, for this. They are caged like animals. It is unspeakable."

The men's eyes slid away. They would not meet Kun's gaze.

"You. You allow this to happen?" shouted Kun. "Why are you here in this land? You came to look for gold. What have you found?" With an act of will Kun unclenched his fist and forced his anger to dissipate. To unleash his powers prematurely would be a mistake. He must appear to be what he claimed to be: a dealer of opium, in San Francisco to explore the opportunity of new business.

"It's all my fault," said Ming.

"Little Flower," said Kun, calling his sister by her family name, the name they had used in childhood. "You were not to know that the Sung Jing-Wei would betray us."

"I trusted her with my daughter, while I was elsewhere. I was protecting the world and yet I could not even protect my own daughter." Ming's eyes became vicious. "She said that she did not think I would return. She said that she thought I was a concubine looking to hide an unfortunate mistake. Sung Jing-Wei paid for her betrayal." Ming's face took on a faraway look, "I can hear her. She is still screaming."

Kun shook his head. It was his sister's duty to take revenge on the woman who had betrayed her, but he did not like how she relished that duty. "It is a pity that you did not let her speak before you punished her. We might have spent less time searching."

"I know this," replied Ming.

Their powers were limited in the mundane world. It had taken four years to follow the trail of Lien, sold like a commodity from person to person. The trail had led here: to the brothels of Chinatown.

Kun observed his sister. A calm had descended on Ming, and it chilled him. "You should return back to the hotel and rest, Ming. I think the search will be more effective if I undertake it alone."

Ming looked over to the Guangdong men at the street corner. They had resumed their stares. It was unusual to see such a finely dressed woman here. She nodded her assent, "I want my daughter, Kun. You will continue the search, and you will get her back for me." Ming glanced at the girl in the cage, who was still offering herself to the passersby. The smell of opium smoke was heavy in the air. "You must promise me that we will get her back."

He said nothing.

Ming and Kun were staying at the most exclusive hotel in the city. At first the clerk at the desk had been reluctant to register them, but Kun had needed no magic to persuade him, or rather, he had only needed the magic of gold. It seemed that the clerk was prepared to overlook the unfortunate color of their skin if it was overlaid with the cleansing touch of wealth.

Kun opened the door to their suite to see his sister pacing up and down in the over-furnished room. She had abandoned her uncomfortable gown for a costume he was used to seeing her in: her fighting tunic and trousers.

"Have you found her?" she asked.

"You must prepare yourself, Ming." Kun sat down at the writing desk.

"Speak then. Don't keep me in suspense."

"I have found her, but she is lost to us. She has been in a brothel for three years. Just like the one we saw this afternoon. I have seen her, and I have read her future. She will be dead in three days."

Ming's screams were the sound of an animal. They echoed throughout the hotel, and even through the sliding spirit-houses, where outlandish creatures paused at the sound of such rage in so powerful a sorceress.

Her brother tried to calm her, pulling her into his arms and murmuring soothing sounds.

"No. No. I will not accept it." Ming's mood turned, lightening quickly. Ming had been subject to these changes of mood ever since she learnt of the loss of Lien. These mood changes frightened Kun. He feared that his sister's mind might break under such pressure. Indeed, he feared that she might already be mad. Certainly she was no longer the competent woman who had fought beside him for so many years. "Lien will not die," said Ming with a calm certainty.

"I have told you, sister. I have read her future. In this world the fates are mapped out. She draws close to the end."

"Then I will change the future."

Kun's face paled. Use of magic needed a significant amount of control, lest the user be consumed by the forces they sought to wield. If Ming were to try to utilize her power, here in the mundane world, with her current state of mind, it would go badly indeed. He thought quickly, "There is only one certain way. Remember, Ming we are not in the spirit world. Our powers can be unpredictable here. We must seek help."

"It is true," said Ming. "You are suggesting that we ask the Earth God for his favor?"

"If that is what you decide. There will be a price."

"I will pay it."

Kun closed his eyes in thought. It seemed to him, that this could be a way forward for them both. But the price would be high. Ming would lose her powers, and be unable to continue in her fight against the malign spirits that sought to overwhelm the world. He would be alone. "Think carefully, Ming. Many others might be lost if you put aside your duty."

"I have fought for three decades. Now, I have another duty."

"Are you sure?"

"The Earth God has given us this choice. Without the choice we would be little more than slaves."

He bowed, "If you wish, but it will be hard without you."

Ming smiled softly, "I know, Kun, and I am sorry."

"I will prepare the incantation," said Kun.

The trance smoke rose in the fine San Francisco hotel. Old creatures formed within the mists. They prowled the corridors and entered the rooms and the minds of the customers.

An old lawman shuddered with unease as he remembered his first shooting. His life stripped back to that one moment, all the righteousness of justice, rendered irrelevant in the face of the eye blossoming on the chest of his first kill.

An aging beauty from Europe searching for American patrons, shivered as she saw into the unseen world. She glimpsed the underside of her yearnings, saw glittering aspects that would never fade away. She would always yearn for those old deep promises, buried beneath the fineries of her celebrated life.

A general saw the coyote smokes running through his mind. He chased them but they were always ahead of him. They led him onwards. When he tried to stop he found that he could not. His heart thudded into his chest as the coyotes led him further onwards, through the widening mountain passes and into the valley where he knew that many waited for him.

Kun took many hours to enter the state of cohesive dream. This was not the spirit world where reality was mutable and powers were tangible. He sat before the image of his Earth God. One of the ancient gods who had roiled in China's consciousness long before the new religions Buddhism, Confucianism, and Daoism took hold of the people.

Earth was one of the five core elements of reality. Kun and Ming had been pledged into his service to take part in the endless war circles which the gods have chosen as a means to indulge the endless prison of eternity. Sorcerers like Kun and Ming were tools to be used within these wars. They strove to maintain the balance between the elements, elsewise disharmony would tilt into the mundane world. Kun thought about the physical manifestations of imbalance which had manifested over the last fifty years: the devastating Opium Wars, the Taiping Rebellion; the millions dead, in flood, in disease, famine and war. It was Ming's choice to leave the battle. Kun felt envious. He, too, would love to put aside the duty which had defined them both for the last thirty years.

Ming walked through the dreams smokes, "Brother, I am ready" she nodded to Kun. "What must be done must be done."

Kun closed the ivory case which held the Earth God's image, "He has accepted your request. He will rewind the strands of your daughter's fate and re-spin them in honor of your service."

Relief washed over her face, "And the price?"

"It is as we expected. Earth will reabsorb your power. You will no longer fight the unseen war."

Kun wondered what the true price of this business would be. How would the loss of Ming impact on the harmony of the unseen? What would be the future of China over the next century?

Ming nodded. She pulled at the robe of her garment to reveal a small stone grown into her flesh. It was the totem of Earth. With her thin hands she pulled at the stone. Beads of sweat appeared on her face, as she pulled. Slowly the stone pulled away from her skin, until she held it in her hand, a bloody relic.

Kun held out his hand, "I will use this."

"For what?" asked Ming. Her face was as white as white silk.

"I will use it as part of our retribution," said Kun. "Remember that I am Lien's uncle."

Ming nodded.

"Go and rest now," said Kun. "The power will dissipate slowly."

Ming left the room and Kun focused on the stone symbol of his sister's power. It would be fitting to use this totem to bind the transgressors into their fate. He placed the stone in front of the Earth altar and began to sing. Slowly the soul stone began to change shape.

It was not unusual for a gentleman of quality to visit the brothels of Chinatown, but it was unusual for him to be accompanied by a lady.

Aaron Wallace narrowed his eyes, "You've got money?"

The tall, lean man nodded and opened his hand to show a handful of silver dollars. Aaron didn't like this man. He didn't like a Chinese man dressed like a gentleman. Aaron spat on the floor.

"I want an experienced lady," said Kun. "I want someone who has been with you for ten years or more."

"The girls never last longer than six years here," said Aaron. He laughed. He was pleased to be able to correct the gentleman.

"Then I will take the girl who has been here the longest."

"That'll be Lola," said Aaron. He frowned. "You don't want her, mister. She's all dried up. Why, there are some lovely girls, who just come out of the queen's place. Fresh off the boat."

"No," said Kun. Aaron could tell that the man was used to having his wishes gratified, quickly and without argument. "Lola is the one."

"It's your money," said Aaron. It was unusual, for sure, but the customer was paying for what he liked. He glanced at the lady, a small, elegant fine-boned Chinese lady, twisting her small hands together in an anxious motion. Aaron smiled again, revealing his mouth of baccy-stained teeth. "This way, mister," He led the gentleman and the lady through the corridors of the brothel. "Watch out for the big fella," he shouted as he saw a rat scurrying past. Aaron walked along the corridor until he reached the last door. "We keeps 'em in order," he explained. "Lola and Rose," he gestured to the room opposite. "They've been with us the longest. Just like you asked for, mister." Aaron unlocked the door to the room on the right hand side. "This is Lola, and she's been with us the longest, ain't you darlin'?"

Kun stepped quickly inside, ahead of his sister. He heard her moan when she caught sight of the half-starved girl chained to the iron bed. It was undoubtedly Lien. Kun smelled the taint of opium mingled with the animal scent of her unwashed body. Lien's body was defiled with burn marks. Worse than that, her mind was unhinged. She was drifting along the flowers of poppy smoke. Lien didn't lift her head when they entered. She was mumbling, but Kun couldn't make sense of her words. He saw a thin line of drool roll out of her mouth. Lien was clearly standing at the threshold of death. Kun glanced at his sister. He feared she would lose control to see her daughter in such a state of extreme degradation, but he saw that the stone mask was in place. Ming's face was rigid with determination. It was the face he had known of old, even though it was stripped of the glamour of youth. Now that her power had gone Ming would be subject to an ordinary lifespan. He looked at Lien, and a treacherous thought entered his mind. Was she worth it?

"This suit you, mister?" asked Aaron.

"She is acceptable," said Kun.

"Will your companion be staying?" asked Aaron turning to face Ming with a leer.

"She will," replied Kun. "We will both be staying all night."

Aaron was surprised. This was very unusual. Normally the punters were in and out within ten minutes or so. Aaron tried to calculate how much he could extract from this man, but Kun forestalled him by tossing him a silver dollar.

Aaron grinned, "Right then. I'll see that you're not disturbed, mister."

"See that you do," said Kun. As Aaron turned to leave Kun called him back, "Oh, one last thing. Who is the owner of this establishment? I would very much like to visit him. I have a business proposition for him."

"It's not a man, mister," said Aaron with a laugh. "Madam Sing-Song owns these cribs. She's Chinese like yourself. I'm surprised you don't know her."

"China is a large country," said Kun quietly. "I would, very much, like to meet her."

Aaron shrugged, he could see no harm in it. Madam Sing-Song always liked to meet the customers with money. "You'll find her boarding house on Priory Street, mister. You can't miss it, it's the fanciest house on the street. It's got dragons guarding the door."

"Thank you, you may go now."

Aaron saw that the lady had laid an ivory carrying case onto Lola's bed. She unlocked it with a small golden key. Aaron would have dearly loved to have known what was inside.

"What do you think of that Chinaman and woman comes in last night, all dressed up like gentleman and a lady?" Aaron asked his brother Dublin.

Dublin broke off a hunk of bread and poured out a generous slug of whiskey into his tin cup.

"I caught a glimpse of 'em when they came in," his brother sniffed. "They ain't no better than they ought to be, pretending to be something they're not. Shouldn't be allowed, heathens dressing up like good Christian folk."

"And you should have heard the way he talked to me, like I was nothing. He ought to know his place," said Aaron.

"Seems to me like America should be just for the whites. Seems to me like it's our destiny to be here, and seems to me that it's not right that the Chinese folk are making the money and we're not."

Aaron nodded, he'd often heard his brother talk about manifest destiny, seemed right to him. He'd heard a lot of talk about the Chinese, too.

His brother was a slow thinker, but he was deliberate, "Seems to me that anybody who's making money out of this business should be us. Take Madam Sing-Song for instance. We does all the dirty work for her, handling the girls and likewise, but we don't get much out of it."

Aaron looked thoughtfully into in his whiskey, "Maybe it's time we got out of this business, brother. Some of the other fellas look down on us, just because we work with the Chinese."

"Oh yes?" Dublin's eyes turned mean, but Aaron just kept on talking. "Heard some of them say that we was inferior just like the Chinese."

Dublin pulled out his Remington, "Who said that? I'll kill 'em. Ain't no call to be talking like that."

Aaron watched his brother's gun warily. Dublin had a vicious mean temper; it had gotten them into trouble, many, many times before. Aaron bitterly regretted saying anything. "Steady, steady, Dublin. It was just whiskey talk. You know I wouldn't let anyone talk disrespectful of you. We're family, ain't we?"

Dublin placed his gun on the table, "Yes, you've always looked out for me."

Aaron was keen to change the subject, "I'm keeping my mind on it. I've been hearing good things about Bodie. Maybe there's money to be made out there."

"Gold rush?"

"Some people makes their money there, why shouldn't it be us?"

"I dunno," said Dublin. "Seems to me like we got it easy here. Maybe we'll find our destiny here."

"Well think, on it, brother," said Aaron. "Well, better get the girls fed." He went over to the stove and ladled out cold rice from a pan into dishes.

Madam Sing-Song's house was, indeed, the most distinctive house on Priory Street. The front was painted with two inscribed panels. Kun quickly read the characters and was relieved to find that they were simple words of blessing with no real power. He frowned when he saw the stone dragons guarding the steps of the house. Whether by accident or design, Madam Sing-Song had afforded herself with a measure of protection. He touched the dragons to test the boundaries set up by the stone guardians and smiled. They were weak and corrupted. He only needed to establish an invitation from Madam Sing-Song to transgress the small protection they offered.

"Madam Sing-Song," Kun executed a bow to the woman who greeted him.

"I am honored that you have visited my home," replied Madam Sing-Song. "Please take a seat."

Kun sat down and observed the decor of the parlor. It was a distasteful mishmash of styles from various periods.

"Madam Sing-Song, that is an unusual name," he said.

Madam Sing-Song smiled, "Ah, my American friends do like to give sobriquets. It refers to my accent which the westerners find lyrical."

Kun knew that it referred to the plaintive sing-song cry of the women who worked in the Madam's Chinatown brothels.

"At my establishment you will find the finest that we have to offer in America and in China," said Madam Sing Song. She was speaking a very poor Mandarin. Kun was finding it difficult to understand her atrocious accent.

"So, I see," said Kun taking a drink from the young girl who served him. The girl kept her eyes down on the floor in a most respectful manner.

"I personally select the girls who live in my home, not just for their beauty but for their manner and fine deportment."

"They do you credit," said Kun.

Madam Sing-Song smiled, "I will be hosting a small party tonight. I will be pleased if you could join us."

"I'm afraid that I have a busy schedule while in this charming town."

"Not visiting my rivals, I hope," said Madam Sing-Song.

Kun stifled a grimace. This woman had lost all remnants of politeness, "No indeed, Madam. I am concerned with my sister who is unwell. She needs my care."

"Oh, I see. Well, I hope that you will give your sister my very best wishes."

"I am however," he consulted his notebook, "free in two days time."

"Oh yes, that would be most acceptable," said Madam Sing Song. "I will gather together the finest of entertainments, the best guests. In my home you will find the finest that America can offer."

"Yes, quite so." Kun stood to leave, "I will bring a few ladies of my acquaintance, if that is acceptable to you."

Madam Sing-Song frowned, "Ahem, it is not usual. If you think that my girls will not be suitable to your taste, then perhaps I could..."

"I have a small present for you," said Kun taking out a small, silk-lined box, "I hope you do not think it is impertinent."

"No, indeed," said Madam Sing-Song.

Kun held out a silk-lined box. Madam Sing-Song's eyes gleamed when she saw the jade stone that was nested within.

"Why, it's exquisite. Thank you."

"It is a representation of an ancient Earth God. You will accept it?" asked Kun. It was important to acquire her acceptance of the gift.

"Of course," said Madam Sing-Song, placing the ornament on the mantle.

"Well," said Kun, "I will take my leave. I look forward to meeting you again, in a few days time."

"Of course," said Madam Sing-Song. Her eyes flicked to the small jade stone. "Of course, your guests will be welcome in my home."

Kun smiled. He had the invitation he needed.

Aaron unlocked the door to Lien's room and shouted to his brother, "Hey, Dublin. Come and look at this. Old Lola looks like she's better."

Dublin entered the room. His eyes widened in amazement when he saw Lien sitting calmly on her bed, "Why, I thought she was due to go to the old hospital. That chinaman must have done her good."

Dublin placed his hand under Lien's chin and raised up her face, "Well, look at old Lola. I reckon she's good for another few months, after all."

Aaron was thoughtful, "Well, we've got a girl coming in, today. We need the room. Check on Rose, why dont'cha, brother."

Dublin crossed the corridor and unlocked, Rose's room. "You're right. She's not looking good," he shouted.

"Is she due a trip to the hospital?"

"I reckon so," replied his brother.

Aaron placed the dish of cold rice on Lien's bed, "You've had a lucky escape, my girl. Never mind, you'll be off to the hospital, soon enough."

He joined his brother in Rose's room, "What's she mumbling?" he asked.

A thin line of spit issued out of Rose's mouth. She waved her head from side to side, murmuring an incoherent litany.

"I don't know," said Dublin. "Who knows what they're saying in that heathen language of theirs."

"Ah well, let's get her to hospital," said Aaron.

Aaron unchained Rose from the bed. Each brother grabbed an arm and dragged Rose's un-protesting body out of her cell, through the corridor and out of the door. This was the first time that Rose had left her room in nearly three years. They dragged her through the overgrown garden where small turrets marked the ground and into a small shack the size of a privy.

Aaron gave her a cup of rice and a cup of water. In the room there was a rope.

"You're in the hospital, now," said Aaron. "You know what to do, Rose."

Aaron closed the door and locked the padlock.

"How long shall we leave her?" asked Dublin.

"She looked pretty frail. Couple of days should do it," answered his brother...

A brother and sister stood in Chinatown waiting for events to unfold. The man was tall and lean. His faced were marked with the sigils of his calling. The woman was petite and elegant. Her face was marked with the lines of age.

"It will be time, soon," said Kun.

"Five years I have waited for this day," replied his sister.

"You have no regrets?"

"No, brother. I am returning to life. My years of service to the Earth God already seems strange, like a dream, to me."

"There is still strangeness to come," said Kun.

"Yes," agreed Ming.

Two brothers sat inside a Chinatown brothel, drinking whiskey.

Aaron said, "I reckon we should go and check on Rose."

"Yep," said Dublin. "She should be about ready by now."

The two brothers walked through the garden.

In the street outside, Kun made a gesture of power with his hand, pushing through the veil of mortality and altering the balance, for a little time, at least.

Aaron opened the door and saw the body of Rose hanging from the joist. A rope was around her neck. Her tongue protruded from her mouth, long and black and obscene.

"Right then, let's get a grave dug for her."

Aaron cut the rope and let the body fall to the filthy mat. He leant over the corpse and grabbed its shoulder. The woman, who had been known as Rose, opened her eyes. She sat up slowly. Her movement threw Aaron off balance. He landed on the floor of the shack.

His brother started to laugh, "She's not dead. How did she manage that?" He drew out his Remington New Model Army revolver. "Ah, Rose, why did you have to make this harder on yourself?"

Rose rolled towards Aaron. Her head moved towards his throat. She made a keening noise.

Aaron shrieked, "Shoot her. For the Lord's sake, shoot her. She's gone mental."

Dublin, still laughing, raised his revolver and shot Rose. Dublin was an excellent shot. The bullet drilled into her chest and knocked her back against the wall.

Dublin reached out a hand to help his brother, "What was all that about?"

Rose's hand shot out and grabbed Aaron's leg. She started to pull him towards her.

Aaron screamed, "She's breaking my leg, shoot her again."

Dublin raised his revolver and fired again, but Rose was already positioned against the wall. The bullet pounded into her chest, but it did not stop her. She continued to pull Aaron towards her. When she had him in her embrace she bent her head towards his neck.

"Shoot her again! Again! Again!" shrieked Aaron.

Dublin fired until the revolver was empty. It made no difference. Rose continued with her leisurely feeding. When she had finished with Aaron she shoved his body aside and began to crawl towards Dublin. He wanted to run, he really did, but he was transfixed by the sight of her. Her lips were pulled into a rictus grin. As she crawled, the rope that was still fastened around her neck swung and brushed the floor.

"It's impossible," whispered Dublin. Rose seemed to smile at him, an impossible dead smile. Her hand snaked out, and snapped his leg. Dublin fell to the floor. As she reached for his neck he felt the touch of her fine, velvet, fungoid fur which grew all over her body. He felt the touch of her cold lips upon his neck. She licked his neck with her black tongue.

Dublin screamed as she consumed him. He felt the terrible sensation of being stretched endlessly thin. The moment stretched into screeching eternity as she fed off his life essence.

The creature that was once Rose crawled out of the death-house, a death-house that two brothers had chosen to call a hospital. She rose to her feet and awaited further instruction.

"She is awakened," whispered Kun. He moved his hands in the gestures of power. "Lien will return to you, soon."

Rose entered the brothel. She drew back her hands and smashed the locks which held the girls captive. She entered each cell and tore away the chains that tethered them to the beds.

She was recognized by some: "Jiang Shi."

The girls ran out into the street.

Ming called the girls to her. She sought out Lien and embraced her tightly. Mother and daughter reunited, at last.

"I will go now," said Ming to her brother.

"It is not finished," replied Kun.

Ming gestured to the girls, "This is enough for me. I have gold. I will return home. I will care for these girls. That is my duty."

Kun bowed. "Take care, sister. May your choice bring you peace."

He watched her lead the girls along the deserted streets of Chinatown.

When they had gone, Kun moved his hands to pierce the veil a second time.

Rose walked to the brothel's garden with her disjointed, hopping step. Within the garden small mounds of earth moved. Rose took a step forward. A keening lament issued from her throat. She called her sisters forward. The earth moved, like ocean swept by the ill-cast wind. An un-fleshed finger emerged from the soil, then another. A partially skinned hand reached upwards like an obscene flower reaching for the night sun.

One by one, the bodies emerged. The earth moved slowly, at first, then gathered speed to become a mound of churning dirt spawning its contents. The women who had been murdered in the brothers' death-house emerged to the sound of Rose's ancient song. They were the walking dead, the stiff-limbed, restless spirits, the Jiang Shi. They stepped forward, their heads lolling forward, their decayed faces looking in one direction.

Kun watched their slow shambling progression. They would find peace soon. It seemed to Kun as if they recognized each other. The ties that had bound them together in their pitiful life were driving them forward in death. They moved forward, lurching, hopping, seemingly falling forward in each other's embrace.

Kun followed the shambling progression as it made its way to Priory Street. Madame Sing-Song was hosting a party tonight. In her elegant boarding house would be many of San Francisco's finest citizens. Kun had secured the Jiang Shi their invitation. He had ensured that a totem stone resided on the mantle at Madam Sing-Song's boarding house. The innocent would be able to leave, but the guilty would be required to stay within the boundaries of the party.

The Jiang Shi walked on, their black tongues lolling from the death-grins of their mouths. They were hungry and tonight they would feast on the finest that San Francisco had to offer.

INNOCENTS ABROAD
BY DON WEBB

Miss Daisy Henshawe was astonished at the hustle and bustle of San Francisco. And a great deal of San Francisco was astonished by Miss Daisy Henshawe. Despite the severe fashions of her day, despite her unpainted face, despite the way her mother had told her to walk and talk and hold herself, Daisy Henshawe was beautiful. Her mother hated her for this. Daisy had golden hair, brown eyes, and (if you were fortunate enough to be behind her on a windy day) beautifully turned ankles. It required little imagination to presume that the rest was beautifully turned as well.

Daisy was nineteen. She had never spoken without first being spoken to. Since the ending of her schooling at age twelve, she had never been in public without her mother. And she had never, ever, been out of the city of Jamestown. And now her father was sending her and her mother to Paris to see that wondrous new structure the Eiffel Tower.

You could hear the winds in the sails for miles. Daisy felt that she would grow faint from excitement as the carriage made its way to the docks. She had stopped pointing out sights to Mother. Mother had been to San Francisco before. And Father merely looked worried.

All of Mrs. Gloria Henshawe's life she had wanted to go to Paris. Her father promised Paris if he could just find that claim. He always had a hunch. Just a little bit too late. Gloria never got out of California during her prime. Her father did, of course. Ran up to Alaska and died and Gloria married the first man who came along. An undertaker and coroner. Marriage seemed preferable to starvation. In the long years since she questioned her choice. Questioned her choice when he would come to her drunk and smelling of corpses, or when a hush would come over a crowd when she walked in. In the early days she had had to wash the dead while John built coffins. Thank God Daisy took over that job when she was done with schooling. John was prosperous now. He could've afforded help, but he stuck with Daisy. *He's only sending us to Paris as a gesture—to show everyone that he can rake in the money like any of the evil old men who run Jamestown.* In any event, Gloria Henshawe was going to Paris without her youth or her beauty. What was the purpose of Paris without youth or beauty?

The hansom stopped and John Henshawe and the driver began hustling baggage to the tars. John wasn't even going to go aboard with his wife and daughter. He might weaken in his reserve—call off the plan set in motion months before. This hurt in two vital areas: the pocket book and the heart. He hated to see his daughter go to Paris. He couldn't imagine her returning innocent. He pecked his daughter and wife on the cheek. The cab began climbing away from San Francisco Bay.

The Judge invited Henshawe to his poker game.

"You're looking right prosperous these days, Henshawe, seems only right we get a chance to fleece a little of that prosperity."

"I'm a hard man to fleece, Judge." Inside, his heart was pounding with pride. He had bathed twice today—as he had every day since his return from Frisco—to completely wash away the smell of dead men.

There were four men at the table (not counting Henshawe): Judge Sullivan Vian, whose presence upped sales of hemp rope considerably; Ralph Whelan, whose legal practice specialized in claim-jumping and will-breaking; Clem Larapallieur, who supplied laudanum and cannibus extract for all the town's aches and pains; and Clovis Durham, whose bank absorbed the miners' gold dust as surely as a black hole sucks in cosmic debris. Only the Judge was important. The Judge had started them all in their orbits and kept them there.

John Henshawe saw that the cards were greasy and spotted. Their patterns would be easy enough to learn—if you wanted to win the cash on the table. As a matter of fact, John expected to be taken in his first game. The redheaded barmaid in the green satin teddy put a double bourbon by him. The Judge passed the cards to Whelan and Whelan cut.

The Judge said, "Understand your fillies are doing a tiny bit of the grand tour. I ain't seen no rush of corpses at your mortuary."

It was a mediocre hand. John took two cards. Full house.

John said, "It's always seemed this way to me, Judge. If there ain't enough business you got to make some."

"Now son, I won't have you killing folks 'ceptin' greasers and niggers what don't count."

"No I just make use of what I got."

The Judge's full house beat John's.

"A couple of months ago, Chu Chi died from smokin' too much hop. You may all remember."

They all remembered, especially Clem, who had run the Chinese hop concession out of town to pick up their customers. Clem had sold the fatal cake to Chu.

"Daisy washed him up and I collected eighty dollars from the county for burying him. Then I dug him up and cut off his queue and twisted some feathers in his heathen hair. I took off his clothes and pressed a tomahawk in his hand—then I dropped the corpse out by Frijoles Creek."

Ralph interrupts. "I remember. Somebody brought the corpse to town and there was an inquest. They had to determine what tribe it was and how he died and where he should be buried."

"That's right. I got three hundred dollars for that one. The court ordered me to send the corpse to the Digger settlement to the North, but since I knew it weren't no Indian I just kept him. The sun had bleached him out considerable by then. I went down to Mrs. Murphy's boarding house. She always keeps the bags of tenants that skip out. I bought the bag of that Italian fellow that came through a year ago. Then I dressed the corpse up Italian style. I rode him out to the Phelan mine and I let him down on the well chain. Somebody pulled him up the next day looking for a drink of water and naturally there was an inquest. We decided that he was a European visitor who had met his death by misadventure viz falling into the Phelan well. I got ninety dollars from the county for the coroner's court and then I passed the hat around to take up for a decent burial, on account of he was a white man, and I got another thirty. Well I put up a stone and kept him in my back room. He was tolerable ripe by then so I decided to skelatize him. I put him in a barrel of quicklime. About that time a Mormon party passed through—European Mormons on their way to Utah via San Francisco.

I went by the hotel and pulled off one of their packing labels. I put the label on my barrel and toted the barrel to the stage depot. Well none of the Mormons loaded up the barrel since it weren't theirs. In a week the stage manager pried open the barrel and I was sent for. Well there was a big inquest on account of it looking like murder."

The Judge said, "I even had to extradite one of those Mormons and hang him for it."

"So I got two hundred dollars for the skeleton and fifty dollars for burying the Mormon and another fifty from his family for shipping him back to Salt Lake."

"You certainly got a lot of mileage from one body," said Ralph.

"I ain't finished my story. When I buried Joe MacKenzie his family paid me off with the rights to Split Pine Mine. Now the Split Pine weren't much 'count 'cause it had collapsed. So I took the skeleton apart and tossed some of the bones down what was left of the shaft. I got a pick and tapped the skull right here and then I put the skull on the lip of the shaft. Next day I ordered the county work force to excavate the mine on account of the skeleton, which was clear evidence of murder. They dug and dug and never found all the bones. So I held an inquest on what they did find—some poor miner—no doubt a slain partner of the late Joe MacKenzie. Eighty dollars for the inquest and I had a working mine. I sent my family to Paris on that one corpse and I ain't finished with it yet."

Clem dealt the tenth hand of the evening and John drew three aces.

Chu Chi woke. The last of the poppies had been blown away. It was his longest and best trip. Truly Clem Larapallieur sold good opium. He must work hard to buy some more. He had dreamt the most fantastic things. Chu Chi stood and his head fell off. This was most distressing even to a calm-tempered man like Chu Chi. He knelt in the darkness to feel for his head. His skeletal fingers passed through the empty eye sockets.

So, some of the things he had dreamt were true.

He fit his skull back in place. Someone had knocked a hole in it. Henshawe, he remembered Henshawe and his nagging wife and beautiful daughter. He could sense the objects of Henshawe's small back room: bathtub, winches, slab, saws. But he could not see them. He decided that if his current state continued he would research the phenomenology of perception. Also: philosophy, theology, and medical theory of death.

Chu Chi walked into the funeral parlor. Two miners, dead from tuberculosis, lay in their respective caskets. Chu Chi felt no communion with them. Only then did it occur to him that his might be a solitary state. That he could not play fan-tan or mah-jongg with the dead. There were no dead to share a pipe with.

Henshawe's greatcoat fit him—he might be able to pass for a scarecrow at a great distance. He lifted the latch and strolled into the California night.

The four men who ran Jamestown were buying John Henshawe's story. They thought it was all his doing—the scheming of his fine mind. They didn't know that Gloria had thought up the schemes, nagged him into doing them. They didn't even know that he was afraid of the dead men—haunted by superstitions that most morticians bury with their first body. He didn't need Gloria. He'd come to this poker game without Gloria. He took a swig of bourbon. He would show them.

"I've got the skeleton back in my shop right now. Tomorrow I'll hang some green goggles on his eyes and some leather straps on his chest. Then I'll take him down to Dead Man's Gulch and throw the parts in a Balm-of-Giliad tree. I'll hang some silk from Daisy's old bloomers on the thorns."

"What the hell's that supposed to be?"

"An aerialist. A balloon rider fell to earth."

They marveled at his invention. They drank. He lost more. He doesn't need Gloria. Just Daisy to wash the corpses.

The gold pieces were piling up in front of Clem Larapallieur. The five men had killed a fifth.

"Well, Clem, looks like you cleaned us out tonight."

"Aw, Judge, you'll get a chance to get it back. I'll see all of you in the morning when you come by for a hangover cure. Cures are on the house." Clem swept his gold into a small cotton bag which he placed inside his pants. The reassuring coldness of the gold steadied his drunken walk across the dark street.

LARAPALLIEUR
DRUGS & SUNDRIES

He went behind the counter. He was mixing up his hangover cure tonight. He dropped simple salts in a large glass, added water, and watched the foam. He was about to drink the concoction when he heard a scratching at his door. Perhaps one of his Chinese clients had crawled here in the throes of hop sickness. Perhaps it was Mrs. Murphy's cat. In either case it shouldn't be at the front door. He pulled his revolver. He threw open the door. No cat. Something white. A skeletal left arm. Maybe this was that drunken coroner's idea of a joke. He kicked the thing into the street.

The hangover remedy seemed a trifle bitter. He was halfway up the stairs when the spasms hit. First his gut then in hot painful waves through his body. He lost his grip and fell backwards. Just before the strychnine finished him he saw the one-armed skeleton of Chu Chi.

Chu Chi ventured into the deserted street to retrieve his lost arm. He knew he needed better covering if he was to pass in the world of men.

Even for a trapper like Chu Chi removing the skin of the druggist was not easy. It wasn't as tough as animal hide nor did the drugstore stock any adequate fleshing knives. So the skin broke and tore and broke. Getting into the thing was even more difficult. Chu removed his head to watch. He stuffed his body with cotton and charcoal. Then he stitched up the rents with fishing line. The druggist's clothes covered most of the stitching, and with the druggist's gold he could buy perfect clothes. The face hung slack on the skull. The new eyes barely functioned. Chu Chi found a pair of smoked glasses. With his eyes shielded he could get by with object-sense.

It was the first time Gloria Henshawe had been alone with her daughter. Truly alone away from John's interference. Daisy, my dear, there is something I must tell you. The reason we always keep you at home is that you are, well, plain. In fact Daisy you are ugly. You're a great disappointment to your father and me.

It was an eight-week voyage from San Francisco to France. They enjoyed excellent weather rounding South America. By the time of their arrival, Daisy couldn't look any man in the face. Even a priest.

Loud knocking broke John Henshawe's sleep. Nobody needs a coroner quickly. His trade is one of the few where the clients just lie there. He put his smoking jacket on. There was a Mexican at the door, his face hid by a large sombrero.

"I found a corpse on the road, *senor*. I have never seen anything like it."

"I'll get a lantern."

A skinless, eyeless body lay on the blood-soaked wagon bed.

"I do not think you will make much money from this corpse, *senor*." The figure had removed his sombrero. John saw himself reflected in the dark glasses. John made to throw the lantern, but Chu Chi caught his arm. The lantern fell into the wagon and shattered—scaring the horse and providing a bright, mobile funeral pyre for Clem Larapallieur. Chu Chi pulled the small knife he had used to skin the druggist. In the scuffle the knife found John's chest twice.

The aesthetic debate over the Eiffel Tower still raged. The introduction of glass-cage Otis elevators provided an excuse to visit the tower. After all the top of the tower was the one place you could see Paris without having your view spoiled by Monsieur Eiffel. The Henshawes came every day. Gloria wanted to absorb this view. If she could release a little bit of the view into her system every day, she might be able to survive Jamestown. Daisy watched the heights. If she could get her courage up, she would jump.

"Monsieur, are you blind?"

"Yes."

"So why do you want to ride to the top of the tower?"

"So I can smell Paris from a great height."

Everyone laughed. After all Americans are known for their eccentricities. The blind man walked toward two of his fellow countrymen —or perhaps countrywomen.

Moments later a screaming woman fell from the tower. Daisy and Chu Chi were already in the down elevator, arm-in-arm.

FORKED TONGUE
BY CODY GOODFELLOW

Just before sunrise, an hour before Cazador was to be hanged, a man came to his cell. He had filled his rusty mess kit with urine for the priest he knew would hector and crow on behalf of their pale god. The Apache war chief set the kit down when he saw the rangy Comanche half-breed with his long black hair plaited in a glossy black rope that lay over the broad left shoulder of an old Cavalry scout's tunic.

Cazador dropped the mess kit and dug a shard of brick from his straw bedding. Sharpened into a crude dagger, it would take more than luck to kill the cunning half-breed with it. But to have the life of the man who captured him and sold him to the Arizona territorial marshals, he would give much, and he had nothing to lose.

"Cazador de Cabezas," said the bounty hunter. "'Hunter of heads.' The Mexicans feared you more than Mangas. What's your Apache name?"

Cazador sneered, but his chest swelled with pride. "My Mexican name is good enough for you." Though he had been beaten by three jailers and burned with a branding iron last night, he showed only the steely pride of the unbeaten warrior.

"*Uzh-na-ti-che*," the bounty hunter said, perfectly croaking the difficult Apache name. He came closer to the bars. "Your name *will* be remembered, if that's what you were after. Your people will speak of you as the one who doomed them."

"*My* people were the Coyoteros of the White Mountain. We raided from Colorado to Mexico every season and knew no laws but our own. *My* people died when they settled for the sour land at San Carlos."

"They won't even have that, soon. You don't know what you did, do you?" There was no mockery in the half-breed's low, weary voice. His hands rolled a cigarette, but his piercing brown eyes pinned Cazador with the conviction of eleven elders. "I guess the courts don't have to explain their case at a hostile Indian's trial, do they? Your band killed everyone on that train and stole the Army payroll. Stagecoaches and stealing horses are more your line. Who put you up to it?"

Cazador laughed until something under his ribs seemed to burst. "Their war chief is dead. This land will never become one of their tame states. They will think twice before they—"

"They *always* think twice! That's why they always beat you. Even when you kill them, you serve them."

He turned away from the bars and let his voice drop to a whisper. "You've come to confuse me with circle talk. I don't know what you want..." *Draw him closer...* "Their greatest warrior is headless in Hell."

The bounty hunter came within reach of the bars. "One thing you should know about white chiefs... they *all* lie about their war records. Little white lies, they call them, even when they're big and black. Mortimer Babcock was the head of some kind of delegation sent out from Washington. Who told you he was a great warrior?"

Sharpened stone thirsty for blood, Cazador turned to face the bounty hunter, who leaned on the bars and offered Cazador the cigarette. With a good throwing knife, he could cut the murderer's throat from across the cell.

"Who told you to take that train? Who gave you those new Winchesters your braves had when they were all shot down at Agua Dulce?"

Cazador spat at the slur on the purity of his hatred. The bounty hunter set the cigarette on the bars, its sour smoke coiling up in a knot in the stifling heat.

"I had to ride you down and carry you back from the border, and I don't feel at all right about it."

"Give the money back."

"I'd rather earn it. Who paid you, Cazador?"

Slowly, as if walking on hot coals, Cazador came over to the bars. He snatched the tobacco and sucked it until his lungs filled with smoke, but he said nothing.

Reaching into a pocket, the bounty hunter produced a small bundle and began unwrapping it. "Your people said you wouldn't talk to me. But they said you might change your mind if you saw this..."

Cazador whispered a name under his smoky breath. The bounty hunter came closer to hear. Cazador caught his arm and jerked him off balance, slamming him into the bars. His other hand shot through the bars to stab the bounty hunter in the gut, but a faster hand trapped his and twisted two of his fingers until his hand went numb and lost the brick shard. Only then did he see the rattlesnake coiled round the half-breed's other hand.

Cazador released the arm with a high, high scream, but before he could retreat, he was struck.

The fangs slid deep into the webbing of his right hand, scraping the bone. When he jerked back with a shrill scream, they seemed to break off in his flesh.

The bounty hunter clutched the big bull rattler by the back of its skull. Thick as a forearm, its scaly gray-brown body dangled down to the brick floor. It hissed and drooled bloody venom from broken fangs. A white crescent was painted on the flat crown of its skull, between its slitted golden eyes.

Fiery agony raged up his arm, so overwhelming that he had to bite back a hot rush of vomit. Cazador retreated to the far corner of his cell with his head spinning. He dug in the wounds for the fangs, but he couldn't find them. He could feel them in his blood, inching closer to his death with every beat of his heart.

"Black-blood! Two-tongued witch!" Cazador cursed. "You tracked me for the white devils, now you kill me with snake medicine..."

The bounty hunter dropped the snake and let it coil at his feet. "I haven't touched you. Listen to me, *Uzh-na-ti-che*. You can still save your band from a worse place than San Carlos..."

Cazador shouted for the guards. The bounty hunter spat in disgust and stormed out of the stockade. His jailers emptied a slop bucket at him through the bars and laughed at his agony. They couldn't see the snake, couldn't hear the seething rasp of its eight-chambered rattle.

He remembered almost nothing of the stories the toothless old ones shared of the Father of Snakes, but he knew he was doomed.

He could feel the venom racing through his body like a thief putting out all the lights to bring the Great Dark even as his skin began to burn with a furious itching that didn't abate until he was bleeding... an itch like the growth of new skin beneath a wound.

Please, he begged any spirit who might hear, *let them not wait an hour to hang me...*

There seemed little point in staying to watch them hang Cazador de Cabezas. But the bounty hunter lingered at the back of the crowd when the troopers marched the last true war chief of the Coyoteros out of the adobe stockade and up to the scaffold. Cazador made no statement as they hooded him and drew taut the noose.

Cazador was hooded with a dirty cotton sack, and a brief declaration of the pertinent facts was made by a scar-faced territorial agent who looked like a ranch manager. Then the lever was pulled. Uzh-na-ti-che, alias Cazador de Cabezas of the White Mountain Coyotero Apaches, dropped to his slow and agonizing end. If the drunken hangman had simply misjudged the drop and let Cazador strangle rather than fall to a clean death, then he should not have smiled so to watch him twitch and dance for over three minutes.

Finally, the hangman, the agent and the deputy marshal ambled down from the scaffolding, leaving the Apache to twist in the morning breeze. Children threw rocks at the corpse. Only then did Inigo Hull turn to leave.

Truly, it was no better than Cazador de Cabezas deserved. A ferocious killer of women and children, he was only less infamous than Mangas Coloradas or Victorio because he lacked their head for strategy. Too hotheaded to run with any other chief for long, Cazador led his small splinter gang in messy, vicious raids from Colorado to the Gulf of California. The White Mountain Coyoteros were among the first bands to settle on the San Carlos reservation, but though they struggled to survive on bad rations and sad little ranches, they were all punished for the crimes of bad seeds like Cazador.

Still, it did nobody any good to let his corpse hang like a trophy in the middle of Fort Apache. Hull shouldered his rifle and shot the taut rope, heard the muted thud of the body hitting the hard sand beneath the gibbet.

A few infantrymen pointed their carbines at the mounted bounty hunter, but a sergeant who remembered Hull's service in the Indian Scouts told them to mind their own business.

Hull rode over to the trading post and found a couple boys to put Cazador de Cabezas into a pinewood box. He shouldn't squander any part of the bounty on the Apache's remains, but something about the job felt spoiled. The territorial authority had paid well for Cazador's return, but with no bonus for bringing him in alive.

The territorial agent smirked at Hull as he came out of the telegraph office and climbed onto his horse. When his ill-fitting coat slid back from his hip, Hull was surprised to see a bullwhip on his belt, alongside a Colt Army revolver.

Hull had visited the San Carlos reservation to learn from Cazador's people who else he ran with, and they had given Hull something to show him. They had said it would loosen his tongue. Then the old medicine men had laughed until Hull rode away. Hull did not believe he ever wanted to hear an Apache laugh again.

Snake medicine.

Hull wiped his hand on his buckskin dungarees where it had touched the painted scroll of crumbling snakeskin. He still puzzled over the way Cazador had spooked when he saw it. He was fast, and might've hurt Hull with his makeshift knife, if he hadn't balked just then, terrified.

Snakes were taboo for reasons that Hull had never been made to understand. The Apache would rather starve than eat turkeys or any other birds that might eat snakes. Superstitious fear at the back of it, but of what? Something far more powerful than a warning drove Cazador into a kind of shock when he saw the skin. And when he marched to the scaffold, had he not looked sicker than the fear of death would make a man, and holding his right hand in his left as if the arm were a dead thing?

Fool notions like this were how superstitions got started, and how superstitions became religions.

After he bought some supplies and listened to a dry goods trader who'd come from Las Cruces through hostile Indian country, Hull stepped back outside and found two of the boys looking for him.

"Someone took it away," they said.

"Who took it?" Hull looked around, but saw no grave detail. "Where's your friend?"

They looked at each other, then back at the scaffold. "He's still looking for it," one boy said, then they both ran away.

He heard screaming from the livery stables. A red Appaloosa mare bolted from the barn with a rider clinging to the terrified beast's neck as it stampeded over a straggling line of infantrymen on the parade ground and out the gate into the open field.

A stableboy came out shouldering the boy Hull hired to put away the corpse. His face was swollen and colored like a bruise, and he was vomiting on himself. The stableboy dropped him and commenced rolling in the dirt himself, screaming that he was burning.

The red-faced Irish brute who ran the trading post came out onto the walk and whistled. "Reckon they're gonna want their bounty back, boyo."

Hull shook his head. "They got their money's worth. Reckon they'll have to pay me twice for the same neck." Still wiping his hand on his leg, he spurred his horse after the cloud of dust.

Immediately outside the gate, Hull reined in and pivoted, but the wind was drawing the Appaloosa's dust westward, down the river valley. The insane sonofabitch was riding south towards the Agency, plunging down the slope to vanish into the cottonwoods that crowded the banks of the Black River.

Hull rode out on the ridge overlooking the river until he was several hundred yards off, with a clear view of Cazador riding like hell for the crossing.

Squinting down the sight on the rifle, he waited patiently until the Appaloosa dove into the sluggish current and began madly paddling. He could make out the rider's long black hair hiding his face, and the bloodstained gray of his shirt.

Hull had the Apache in his sights when his damned horse reared up under him. The shot went wild, the leaden roar of it echoing down the river valley. Hull tried to calm the yellow gelding. Wheeling and whinnying in utter unhinged terror, the horse had good cause to panic.

The ground all around them was rife with rattlesnakes. Braided tangles and writhing knots of young vipers boiling out of holes in the rocky soil. The rasping of their immature rattles was like a hundred beehives.

Hull snapped the reins and stood up in his stirrups to force the horse charge down the ridge towards the river, but the gelding's panic turned to agony as the snakes began to strike its legs. Singly and in rabid bunches, they clung to the horse's kicking, struggling legs. When Hull slapped the gelding's flank with the rifle stock, it lurched sideways and seemed to kick feebly to throw him out of the saddle.

Hull splayed out his arms and legs when he hit and rolled ass over teakettle down the rocky slope. He lay stunned on the ground, face up to the rising sun, for how long he did not know. When he got up, blood still flowed freely from a gash on his forehead. His horse lay dead amid the swarming rattlesnakes. He couldn't get to his saddle or his other gear, but it was a fair bet none of it would get stolen. Picking up the rifle, Hull stumbled down the slope to the reservation road where it joined with the wider river road that wound south around the agency about ninety miles to the provisional capitol in Tucson.

Dragging himself upright, Hull waved his hat at a cloud of dust that rose up from the road as if Cazador was returning with reinforcements. The dust parted to reveal a cavalry troop returning from patrol.

"D'you see an Apache on a red Appaloosa mare ride past you?" he shouted. The whole truth all at once would just slow things down. "Man they were fixing to hang escaped and was headed your way."

The 2nd lieutenant scowled at the dusty, bleeding half-breed blocking his way. "We haven't encountered anyone until we nearly ran you down. We're just returning from a long wild goose chase, and are in no wise receptive to nonsense..."

"Please, Lieutenant. I need a horse to catch Cazador de Cabezas, and I doubt anyone else can keep up with him going cross-country. He's hell on a fast horse, and he's headed for population."

"I'll thank you to get the devil out of our way--" the lieutenant started, but his sergeant, a leathery mustachioed man old enough to be his uncle, climbed down from his horse and passed the reins to Hull. In the beetle-browed stare the man cast his way, Hull saw recognition and a grudging gratitude, and knew he must've served on the bad patrol, when Hull saved the Sixth Cavalry from Mad Captain Ketrick and the Anasazi Circle Curse.

"Sergeant, I order you—"

"Beg pardon, sir, but I owe this man my life," the sergeant growled around a plug of tobacco, "and it's worth a damn sight more to me than a week in the stockade."

The fuming lieutenant looked to his men, who seemed powerfully preoccupied with the state of their tack, just then.

"Much obliged," Hull said.

The sergeant cracked his idea of a smile. "Mighty partial to this horse."

"Have it back to you directly," Hull answered, swinging into the saddle and putting his heels to the horse's ribs to send it pelting down the road.

The high-pitched squall of the officer's tirade faded behind him fast. The horse was worn but well fed and watered, and she seemed to cotton right away to the urgency of the matter.

Riding down the slope on the road with his eyes on the uphill side, he covered less than a mile before he spotted a broken branch on a tree in the mouth of a steep canyon that shadowed the road, running mostly south until it played out at Natanes Plateau. It would be slower than the road, but he'd already dodged a patrol. He wasn't headed for the reservation, at least. But where the hell was he going?

Predicting Cazador's next move would be a lot simpler if he knew for certain whether the Apache was alive or not. Whatever the Coyotero elders gave him to show Cazador must've had something to do with it. Whether it allowed him to somehow play possum and ride out the hanging or if it made him too sick to die honestly, he couldn't say. Hull had seen dead men do all kinds of things they weren't meant to in his time, but he knew of nothing that would make a dead man rise up and ride like a devil.

Best to stick to what he did know. Cazador was an outcast even among Apache warriors because he couldn't let go of a grudge. Hull had been sure someone had put Cazador onto the train raid, and he was certain the Apache would want to see someone pay for leading him on. Cazador kept mum because he didn't know, or cursed himself for a fool and so couldn't reveal who had backed him.

Cazador lived for revenge. The Apaches believed revenge was central to honor. They would want to see whoever shamed their tribe pay with more than just his life, if they could. But if Cazador wanted vengeance, he had only to turn around and ambush Hull. He had caught the Apache alive, denying him a warrior's death, and brought him back to be hanged. His last act before he was hanged was to try stabbing Hull.

A sneaking suspicion grew and began to iron out Hull's tangled brains. For all he knew, it was Hull himself who kindled this, when he told Cazador that the man he'd murdered had been no great white war chief. Whether or not he wanted to, whether or not he knew whom he was hunting, Cazador had been put on a warpath, and God help anyone who blundered into his way.

The trail ascended for nearly a mile before reaching a narrow notch between pillars of sandstone and granite. The sun had climbed over the mountain and shone full into the canyon, but Hull rode slower than even the rough terrain demanded, casting suspicious glances to and fro and even at the ground beneath his horse's hooves. By now, Cazador might not be alone. Geronimo was raiding pueblos in Mexico, Nana had regrouped after Victorio was slaughtered in Mexico, and no one knew where Mangas was. Plenty of impossible things had happened today, so the unlikely seemed almost inevitable.

Gaining the summit at last, Hull shaded his eyes and scanned the sharply descending mountainside. Nothing. He might have seen a plume of dust a few miles out on the open plain. Ranches and fenced grazing land began to crop up along the Gila. Rate Cazador was going, his horse would give out in a matter of hours. They were still about eighty miles from Tucson as the crow flew, and his own horse was lathered and panting.

He's only one unarmed Apache, his mind nagged at him. *He's no threat to anyone.* But Hull snapped the reins and drove the sorrel mare down the granite stepping-stones of the peak. No ambush awaited him that he could see, but he felt as if he was riding against a tide of dread that threatened to pull his guts out to flap in the wind. It was almost as strong as the certainty that this whole mess was more than a little bit his fault.

Hull nursed the horse down the steep slope, but she gave out just after sundown. Hull staked her near a patch of grama grass and fed her his canteen of water, then set out on foot. He'd return for her tomorrow or send someone to collect her, if he was unable. He had no bedroll and tired as he was, he couldn't sleep. He doubted Cazador would be making camp anywhere nearby.

Only an hour south, he found the red Appaloosa sprawled across the trail. He'd seen plenty of horses ridden to death by desperate men, but this was something else again. The mare's legs stood out stiff, and the head was contorted back as if the beast had tried to break its own neck in its convulsions. He almost touched it to see if it was still warm, but something made him draw his hand back as if from an unseen flame.

Its eyes were not right. The moon had not yet risen, but the stars afforded enough light to see that they had burst from their sockets. Its tongue had swelled to block its throat and the lathery flesh on its unsaddled back was a bed of weeping ulcers the size of hen's eggs.

Hull stepped back, scanning the ground for any sign of rattlers, but the brush was silent, devoid of life. A few clumps of black turned out to be vultures—about six of them, dead as doornails with their gizzards spilled out from their beaks.

This horse wasn't just exhausted. It was pumped full of venom, and it was worst wherever Cazador de Cabezas had touched it.

Backing away from the grisly scene, he found Cazador had left an unmistakable trail. His tattered, blood-stained shirt hung from a yucca branch; his pants lay on a rock beside the trail; and further ahead, he saw white, gauzy shreds flapping in the wind from the low branches and the boles of piñon pines. Running down the trail, Cazador seemed to have stripped and then shed his own skin.

Tired, parched and spent as he was, Inigo Hull found the strength to run, at least until he was far from the horse's carcass.

As the sun came up, Hull limped into the dooryard of a ranch house. It was a small, hundred-acre spread with no fulltime hands, only the one family, and he saw nobody. Sick certainty told him he wouldn't, for they must all be in the house, which was on fire.

The barn stood open. The horses shrieked and kicked the walls of their stalls, nearly kicked his brains out when he set them free. He chose the least hysterical riding horse and led it out by a lariat. After trying to bolt and kick him a few times, the slate-gray bronco took a bridle and saddle and took him on the road south.

Hull was ill at ease in any town with more than one street, and Tucson had almost a dozen. Since the territorial capitol was moved here only a decade before, the town had become a full-fledged city, with lawyers and politicians and other symptoms of civilization as thick in the streets as the bygone buffalo herds. Hull couldn't imagine the fugitive Apache could pass unnoticed in the town. He spotted two deputies on the steps of the capitol and a retinue of private guards escorting a carriage that parked before the capitol to a great stir among the lurkers on the sidewalk. The silver-haired but hale man who emerged from the carriage, Hull quickly gathered, must be John Anson Bowlund, the territorial governor. Another great war chief known for his bold campaigns to wipe out the Apache menace once and for all, waged with a pen from behind a desk.

Hull figured he should go see the Sheriff and try to get in front of Cazador before he did whatever it was he'd come to do. He felt lost and out of sorts until he saw a familiar face in the crowd.

The scarred territorial agent handed his reins to a stableboy and went up the steps but deliberately bypassed the crowd of reporters and other petitioners around the governor. Pausing at the top of the steps with a calfskin valise under one arm, he sneered over his shoulder at the crowd for just a moment, long enough for Hull to think he'd been spotted. The scar that seamed his face from eyebrow to chin pulled down his right eyelid, making him look sleepy, slow.

Hull swung down from the gray and tied it to a post across the street from the territorial legislature hall. Making his way across the street, he went through the open front doors and stepped behind a column to survey the politicians preening in the atrium. The agent went through a door at the end of the hall. Hull slipped smoothly and quietly through the knots of talking gentlemen, and cleared the door before the curiosity about his rough appearance touched off a small furor.

Hull found himself in a dim stairwell. Flattened against the wall, he heard footsteps going up, and stealthily followed. The hall was three stories tall, with hearing rooms, clerk's offices and a library above the room where the elected representatives for the counties into which the land had been carved up hatched their schemes to tame the last vestiges of Indian Arizona. He heard the agent's heavy boots climb to the top landing, and then heard a door open and close. Hull moved up to the next landing, but then froze when he saw movement on the landing. The agent had not left the stairwell, but had waited for someone else who came to meet him out of the public eye.

"Mr. Joyner, I have little time for—"

"Good news and bad, boss."

"On with it!"

"The Apache hanged yesterday morning like I said, but..."

"But what? He was a renegade, despised by his own tribe, you said as much. If there are more loose ends, sew them up. We've nothing to fear from the people of Arizona. When we become a state, they'll remember who settled the goddamned Indian question once and for all."

"But they sent another telegram right after, those idiots at Fort Apache. They said the Indian escaped on horseback."

"You said he was hanged!"

"I *saw* him hang, damn it. They've got their wires crossed. More likely, they just don't know one Indian from another."

"So he's *not* still at large? This only grows more confusing."

"No, I saw the right man hang. I'd know him, wouldn't I? He did you a bigger favor than any of your fatcat friends in Washington."

"I have no friends in Washington, but I won't need any, now. But this whole blamed mess... I can't be connected to it. If there's any trace, I'll—"

"You won't have to, boss. There was no hoopla back east, when Babcock came out. The President must've thought he'd spring it on you as a surprise."

"Backstabbing sonofabitch probably never figured I'd know he was sending that Indian-loving swine Babcock out here to take over. When they hear my speech today, they'll roll over and pretend they never cut the order."

Mr. Joyner gave a nasty little laugh. "Thought you'd like to have these for a keepsake."

"You imbecile, they should've been burned. Take them away. Even if he is somehow out there... we have nothing to fear from one man, do we?"

"One man who burned down your enemies and put you in the catbird seat, who I watched dance on the end of a rope yesterday? Oh no, sir, I wouldn't worry overmuch."

"See to it just the same, Joyner. I've got history to make."

The door opened and slammed shut. Hull slowly began to descend, when a thunderclap filled the stairwell and white fire consumed his arm. His revolver fell from spasming fingers. His head spun as he tried to see what the hell had hit him. Lightning struck again and a coil of rawhide encircled his neck and yanked him off his feet and over the railing.

"Thought I smelled a coyote," Joyner said. Jerking the bullwhip, he strangled Hull from ten feet away and nearly sent him plummeting to his death.

Through pulsating purple spots that filled his sight, Hull seized the whip and yanked back. Joyner snapped the whip taut even as he came charging down the stairs with a bowie knife up to drive it through Hull's breastbone.

Still choking, Hull staggered on the steps. The knife came down just as he flung himself under and inside its lethal sweep. Driving his head into the bigger man's gut, he took all of the falling weight onto his back, then pivoted and flung Joyner over the railing and down the stairwell.

Hull collapsed gagging onto the steps, prying the coiled bullwhip from his throat. He expected men to come pouring into the stairwell, but there must be a bigger noise somewhere else in the hall.

Working sensation painfully back into his arm, he likewise strained to get his head around what he'd heard.

This Babcock fellow was secretly picked by the President to replace the Governor. The hangman had hooded Cazador before Joyner ascended the scaffold to read the charges.

It would be a good enough case for a lynch mob, but Hull had no idea how such things were done in marble halls with chandeliers and statues of famous liars everywhere.

Lurching down the stairs to the bottom, he found Mr. Joyner even heavier in death than he'd been in life. The calfskin valise lay on the floor beside him, its mouth yawning open to let the corners of a sheaf of bone parchment papers stick out.

Somehow, his shock at the way white men ran things overcame his wonder at the black magic the Apache had wrought. *This is how they choose to run things, he thought with disgusted wonderment.*

Well, not today...

The Arizona territorial legislature had only just been called to order and made to stand for the entrance of Governor John Bowlund.

Though he appeared weighed down by a solemn burden, he wasted no time in mounting the podium and bellowing to the assembled representatives.

"Gentlemen, I come before you today not as the duly appointed executive of this great land that has given us all so much of its bounty, but as another outraged and frightened citizen, as one with the poorest among you, and sympathetic to the fears and anger of all our people. For while we have been engaged in the debate of the Indian question -- namely, of the consolidation of our many scattered and poorly managed reservations into one great community in the verdant southwest corner of our state, which would provide for the greater good of the Apache and the security of all this territory's citizens -- we have been continuously second-guessed by political interests clear across this great nation, who have seen fit to dictate how we should protect our homes and repay the incorrigible savagery of the hostile Apache nation within our borders.

"Only two scant weeks ago, another overseer was sent out from Washington to pick at our way of life, when he discovered the harsh realities of life—and death, I am sad to say—on the frontier. Killed by hostile Indian raiders while riding a train! It would seem to put the lie to any claims that order and felicity reign over all peoples in Arizona, or that the red man can be fully rehabilitated to join his white brothers in peace and harmony.

"A shameful blot upon our good name—until yesterday, when the last of the bloodthirsty band of killers who raided the train and slaughtered Mr. Babcock's delegation was hanged at Fort Apache, after having been apprehended by our good Arizona peace officers.

"The message sent back to Washington should be unmistakable. Order will not prevail in Arizona if it is to be governed from Washington. We, the citizen government of this territory, know how to settle the questions before us—"

The governor had them in the palm of his hand, those who were actually awake and sober. But his concentration wavered when a rain of paper came wafting down from the empty gallery at the back of the hall.

The governor sputtered and barked, but the spell was broken. A delegate grabbed a paper out of the air and studied it. Another one shouted, "This one's signed by the President!" Against the governor's strenuous commands, they began to compare pages.

Only the governor was looking up at the gallery when the other shoe dropped.

The body of Cort Joyner tumbled over the railing and fell to yank astonished screams from the assembled worthies below, only to jerk upright and swing from the bullwhip wrapped around his broken neck. His head sat askew on his shoulders, his drooping eyes seeming to glower accusingly at Governor Bowlund.

One of the few representatives not hiding under a desk demanded, "What's the meaning of this, John?"

"I have never... never seen this man..." The Governor's words came in halting fits and starts as he backed away from the podium and towards the door to his office suite at the back of the hall. "Have the marshals search that gallery! A murderous Apache renegade is somewhere nearby, it's the only—"

Hull broke through the cordon of deputies outside the hall and plunged down the aisle. "Governor Bowlund set up the Apache raid that killed a fellow the President picked to replace him."

"That's a damned lie! Arrest that man!" Governor Bowlund threw open the door to his office.

Hull was seized by two deputies and had to remind himself not to rough them up. Through the open door, he glimpsed something rising up from behind Bowlund's desk, a shadow backlit by sunlight pouring in the open windows. Before the governor could utter a sound, the silhouette engulfed Bowlund and stopped his gurgling whimper of horror with its own mouth in a gruesome kiss.

The door slammed shut. Chaos reigned. An oily gentleman pounded a gavel and hollered for order, but the legislature had become an outraged mob that shoved the deputies aside and crushed itself against the bolted, barred door until it gave way.

None could identify the extravagantly dead Apache warrior who lay across the governor's desk, a deflated, desiccated effigy with its jaw dislocated and hanging by one hinge from the monstrous ruin of its face. A long gray duster covered its naked body, which bore no identifying marks besides the noose around its neck.

The governor leaned back in his overstuffed rawhide chair, stunned and a good deal heavier than when he'd left the podium, only minutes before. His eyes stared through the august company of supporters and enemies united in confusion and horror. His hands clutched at his belly as if something he'd eaten had come back to haunt him.

Staring into the glassy eyes of the dead Indian on his desk, the governor seemed, for a change, totally at a loss for words. But then his lips parted and instead of a sound, there emerged no words... only a tongue.

Long and slender and black and forked, it vanished as quickly as it came. Bowlund's mouth sagged open, his jaw drooping to his chest and somehow coming off its hinges to allow a rattlesnake thicker than a strong man's bicep to slither up out of his throat. Its mottled brown scales were marked, just above its hooded golden eyes, with a white crescent.

Shock paralyzed the audience crowded into the office, but the territory's liberal stance upon the concealment of firearms meant that several men present shot the rattlesnake to bits before the entirety of its seven feet of length could pour out of the governor's body.

When answers were called for, it was discovered that the half-breed bounty hunter had used the confusion to take his leave. Many would later have cause to envy him, and none objected when a motion was introduced to the effect that the events of the day's legislative session be stricken from the record and any mixed or unmixed conversation.

A little white lie was the only way to preserve the dignity of that august governing body. Surely, they told themselves, that would be the end of that.

THE BUZZARD WOMEN
By Christine Morgan

They started in eating him well before he died.

With the part of his mind still capable of thought, Frank Fallon reckoned that was mighty unfair.

The rest was too taken up by bodily torments for much thinking.

At first, he'd cussed a blue streak, hollering how his captors had best kill him straightaway, because if they didn't, once he got loose it would be nine shades of hell the worse for them.

At first, yes, at first...

At first, he'd been more furious than anything else.

Who wouldn't be?

Waking in the middle of the night, waking with a head thumping like a bad tooth, a sick feeling in his stomach and a sour taste in his mouth... waking to wonder what in the world he'd been drinking...

Only to find himself tied spread-eagle on a damn rock!

Wrists and ankles outstretched... leather straps drawn down taut over his chest, waist and thighs... stripped mother-naked and staked out like some kind of he-didn't-know-what...

Humiliating and infuriating.

Not to mention cold!

Any heat from the day the rock might have held had dissipated by the time Frank opened his eyes to that black-crystal bowl of midnight sky more a-dazzle with stars than a showman's shirt was with rhinestones. The wind blew across every exposed inch of him.

The bonds had some initial give, and that struck him hopeful, until he realized the nature of them... the dampness that made the air's chill kiss all the chillier... the feel of the stuff... not straps of leather at all but strips of wetted rawhide...

At that, the fear commenced seeping in. He struggled until the bare skin of his back and buttocks scraped bloody against the coarse stone. To no avail.

In due time, the eastern horizon bloomed rose and gold, pink and yellow, but Frank was not impressed by the dawn's beauty.

Nor was he glad to see the sun rise in a brilliant ball of brightness. Glad for the warmth, yes, chasing away the cold... but as the sun got higher and the day got hotter, he'd be wishing for its absence.

His empty belly growled like a mean bear -- had he had supper? Damned if he could recall -- and the hunger was nothing next to his thirst. Didn't have to be whiskey... cider would do... hell, lemonade... water, for that matter...

The sun continued its steady climb. The sky turned the kind of blue that went on forever, nary a cloud to be seen in all directions. Morning headed toward a hot high noon.

The wetted rawhide began to dry out.

Hard to believe he'd spent half the night freezing and shivering, when before he knew it it was fair to baking. His arms and face were browned from the outdoors, but other areas didn't often get much sun and soon were going a painful red.

With slow but steady creaking sounds, the drying rawhide contracted. It pulled on Frank's wrists and ankles, rubbing his abraded back on the stone. The strips looped over his chest, waist and thighs also shrank and tightened as they dried.

And thirsty, good God was he ever! Water, just a sip! He had never been so parched, a word he'd used often but not fully understood the way he understood it now... his tongue a pad of dusty wool, his lips split and stinging, his tissues feeling the way the desert ground looked...

Such an aching in his shoulders now, too, there was... his arms extended full out, searing bolts of agony shooting through his muscles... one hip made a grating twinge as if the joint was about to pop from its socket...

At first, he'd hollered how they should have killed him.

Then he found himself wishing they would.

Better a fast death than this. Better a bullet, a knife or a noose. He may have earned those, but did he deserve this?

Frank Fallon, he was Frank Fallon. He'd gunned down four men in Utah and killed nine more since, most with a gun, two with a blade, and that one fellow he'd drowned in a pig-slop in Fresno City.

If that made him a bad man, so be it, but had he been on the run from the law all this while only to end up dying staked out on a rock? Thirsty and sun-blistering? Having his limbs wrenched like drumsticks on an overcooked Sunday chicken?

The shrinking rawhide digging tighter and tighter, pressing deep sore grooves into his flesh... blood already welling up dark and thick in places where the skin had broken...

Kill him, yes, in the name of mercy, kill him and make it quick, get it over with, put an end to this slow, unholy agony...

He'd gone from swearing to screaming at some point in there, he didn't know when. From raging to begging. From not wanting to die to being afraid he wouldn't. The terrors set in next, and the tears. He wailed like a child for his momma.

Lifting his head proved a monumental effort. It must've weighed a sandbag's worth. His eyes squinted glareblind at a landscape of wind-worn boulders, slanted slabs of stone, cliff faces and ravines. The harsh sun struck light-darts from flecks in the rock. Heat-shimmers rippled like puddles of quicksilver.

Wasn't there supposed to be a town? He thought he recalled a town. He'd been headed there... Vixby... had a friend there, wasn't that it?

A friend, yes... Simon... ol' Smiling Si, as they called him... Si, who'd got out of the gunfighter game after having most of his upper teeth and lip blasted off by that kid from Arizona... gone into business, Si had, opened his own place... told Frank how, if he ever needed somewhere to hide out and lay low for a while, to consider himself welcome.

He heard a rusty, screeching kind of cry. A bird-cry, but not of any bird he knew. Almost like a hawk, almost like a crow. Not like a buzzard, since buzzards had no voices—he'd learned that from the halfbreed who'd ridden with the Bodean gang—and the cry hadn't come from on high where a few of them wheeled black against the blue.

The cry came again, this time answered by others. There was a strange series of hisses and clicks, and a sort of rustling-flapping sound.

The smell hit him next. Sour and rancid, horrible, a rotting up-chuck stench that set his own gorge to lurching though there was nothing in him he could spew.

The rustling sounds and clicking closed in. Shadows fell across Frank as he strained in the rawhide's pull... hunched shadows, moving with a peculiar clumsy but fast kind of gait, almost hopping... feathered, stinking of picked-over carcasses... he saw cocked heads, stubbly-bald heads, scarlet faces... eager bright eyes over hooked beaks... big birdlike things nearly the size of grown men...

A blunt talon prodded at his ribs. It traced along the crusted blood-line that had run from where the rawhide cut into him. Other talons poked his outstretched—overstretched!—arms and legs.

Frank screamed. He writhed with such force that one of his shoulders finally dislocated with a gruesome wet snap. He screamed again, a scream like a lightning strike exploding from his throat.

The talons weren't sharp enough to slice, but the beaks were. Hooked points punched in like awls, pinch-gripped, and tugged Frank's skin into tent-peaks. He shrieked when the skin tore away in long peeling tatters like old wall-paper and blood flew in spattering sprays.

They started in eating him well before he died.

And it *was* mighty unfair; Frank knew it was.

Vixby... on his way to Vixby to lay low a while... saddlebag heavy with hard currency relieved from a bank... Vixby, and when he got there the town... the town was...

...dead horse on Main Street, gassy-bloated and flyblown... dog snarling from underneath a porch... unseen eyes watching through shutter-slats and from behind curtains...

He remembered the old man... the stumbling, cackling, insane old man with his tangles of hair and beard, wearing nothing but piss-stained drawers. He remembered the children, barefoot, dirty, who stuck out their tongues at him and then ran off, giggling.

And Si's place... Smiling Si's... the swinging wooden sign painted like a mouth with a wide silver-toothed smile... silver ones to replace the ones what the Arizona kid ruined... Si's place, Smiling Si, Silver Si... poker, dice, whiskey, women...

Now, there was only this.

Rawhide and blazing sun... their rancid carrion-stink... chunks of meat being gouged out of him, gulped down red and dripping...

That part of his mind still capable of thought held on a long damn time before letting itself be snuffed out.

"You're sure you know where we're going, Danny?" Lilah asked, shading her eyes beneath the brim of her bonnet. "I would hate to get lost out here in the middle of the desert."

"We ain't lost," Dan said, for what he could swear must have been the tenth time that day. "We ain't anywhere near lost."

And it hardly was the middle of the desert, not that he could convince Lilah of it. They rode through foothills of grass dotted with scrub, sagebrush, juniper, and wildflowers. Not sand dunes, scorpions, cactus and tumbleweed.

Ahead, the land climbed into steep mountains with a high treeline of dark green pines smudged by hazy distance. To their left and behind, it sloped away toward a long river valley of farms and pastures.

That was where Lilah peered, pretty face set in a worried frown. "You're sure, too, that nobody's following us?"

"We'd see them if they was."

"My pa, he's going to be powerful mad."

"Why else do you think I had us leave so early yesterday morning? We were miles away before he would've had any idea you was gone. 'Sides, they'd never think to look for us this way. They'd expect us to take the main road to Tully Springs. By the time they figure out we ain't there, it'll be too late."

To their right, a rugged rockface rose up, stone striated in bands of earthy color that glittered here and there in the sunshine with mica or fool's gold or possibly even something valuable.

The horses maintained a good steady pace despite being loaded down with half of what Lilah owned. Dan had drawn the line at her packing every-damn-thing including her ma's rocking chair; they would've needed a wagon. For a girl so eager to get away, she did want to bring it all with her.

"Didn't you say there was a shortcut?" she asked.

"There is." He pointed to a gap. "Straight on through the canyon. Little town on the other side. Vixby. I seen it on the map."

"Will we reach there by dark?"

"Doubt it. We'll make camp tonight."

"Camp? You mean, sleep outdoors?"

"Unless we can find ourselves another abandoned barn." He smiled, reaching to touch her stocking, where her skirt and petticoat had hiked up. "With another nice cozy hayloft."

"Danny!" She giggled, tugging the hem down over her knee.

"After Vixby, it's just a couple more days' ride to Leeds Junction, then we catch ourselves a train, and then we are on our way to San Monte! Wait 'til you see it, Lilah.. it's a right proper city, San Monte... they got the electric and piped water and all... I hear they even got *two* newspapers!"

He went on in that spirit as they reached the notch-shaped gap and proceeded into the canyon. The trail narrowed, wending between outcrops and around boulders. Pebbles crunched under their hooves. The rocks were wind-carved and rain-sculpted. Stubborn bushes struggled to keep a root-hold in the cracks.

The surrounding stone walls caught sound, bouncing it back. They caught the sun as well, and with the maze to baffle the breeze, it was warmer in the canyon than it'd been in the hills.

A few lizards scuttled for hiding at their approach. Once, a big brown hare bounded out of nowhere, briefly startling both horses and Lilah. High overhead, birds glided lazily on the updrafts.

"You're sure we'll be able to find work once we're there?" she asked.

It did often seem that every other sentence out of her mouth was another question starting with if he was sure, but Dan reckoned he couldn't hold her too at fault for it. She'd never been so far from home.

"Plenty of jobs in San Monte for a man like me," he said, hitching his hat to let his sweaty brow catch some cooling. "And you, Lilah... lordy... prettiest girl I've ever seen, with a voice like an angel? You'll be a famous singer in no time at all."

"Do you really think so?"

"'Course I do! Might have to start off small, in a saloon maybe, but once you get discovered it'll be the fancy theaters, nothing but steaks and French wine and the best hotels..."

"Really, Danny? You're sure?"

"Couldn't be more sure! You'll see. I got it all planned out."

"And we'll get married in Vixby?"

"Uh..." He felt himself heming and hawing, and coughed. "Well... we oughta... I was thinking we should..."

"What?"

"Hold off on that a bit... I mean..."

"Hold off? You mean, in case there's no preacher in Vixby?"

"Yeah! Yeah, that's it, there might not be a preacher in Vixby."

"Be one in the next town, though," she said. "If it's big enough to have a train station, it's got to have a church, at least one."

If he'd thought his brow was sweaty already... "We'll be in a rush and all to catch our train."

"We *are* getting married, aren't we, Danny?"

"Sure," he said. "Sure, just... I... you... no sense being hasty, is what I'm saying."

"Hasty?"

"See, now, if we held off some, saved up enough money... you deserve a real fine wedding, Lilah, with flowers and a lace dress and all, like you talked about..."

"I don't really need all that—"

"Got to have enough for a house, and—"

"I don't care about a house right away. A room's plenty, so long as we're together."

"Lilah—"

"Last night... why... I never... what we did last night... I never would have done if I didn't think we were going to be married soon!"

"Now, Lilah... dammit..."

"Don't you dammit at *me*, Daniel Winthrop!"

Their voices had risen, hers shrill and his in a kind of peevish whine that would have made his granny swat him upside the head and tell him to stop that sheep's bleating before he started growing wool. The horses flicked their ears, unhappy.

"Maybe my pa was right about you," she said, then burst into tears.

"Aw, hell..."

There was nothing for him to do but apologize until she was mollified enough to let him have a grudging forgiveness. Not mollified enough, however, to show much further enthusiasm for his talk of the high-life awaiting them in San Monte or respond to much of his conversational efforts. So, they rode along in a sort of sulky silence.

The shadows of the canyon walls began to stretch long and pool dark in the hollows. The sky above was still a faded denim blue, but it'd turn toward purple twilight soon enough and Dan reckoned they'd best stop.

Lilah continued not much speaking to him as they made camp—seeing to the horses, gathering sticks and branches for a fire, putting together a meal of corn-cakes and canned beans.

Then she did speak, to ask if he was sure they were safe. "I got a funny feeling on the back of my neck," she said, pulling her shawl around her shoulders and taking several quick glances up at the looming peaks and spires. "Like as if we're being watched."

Naturally, this made the hairs on the back of his neck prickle and stand on end, but Dan was damned if he'd admit it. "Ain't nothing," he said. "Nobody around here for miles, just us and the critters."

"Bandits?"

"Who's there to rob? Any bandit worth the name would pick a well-traveled path to lie in wait. Stagecoach route, maybe. Not way the tarnation out here."

While there was still some light left, he poured one half-filled canteen into the other and took the empty one looking for water. He did find some, a spring that gurgled from a cleft stone. It had a metallic kind of flavor that Lilah didn't care for.

"Tastes funny," she said. "Like sucking on an old penny."

"You're used to the well-water on your pa's farm, is all," Dan said. "This is bound to be different. Minerals and such."

She made a face, and pushed the canteen away. Dan shrugged and took that one for himself, letting her have the other. It did leave him with something of an oily sensation lingering on the roof of his mouth, which made him drink more to wash it away.

"I still have that watched feeling, too," Lilah said, later on as they finished up their meal and went about readying to bed down.

"And I told you, it ain't nothing."

"What about snakes? Or those buzzards we saw earlier? Oh, they are the ugliest things... what if they come after us while we sleep?"

"They won't." He put on his best smile, the one that had charmed her from the get-go. "And if they do, I'll be right here to protect you."

Lilah melted some at that, snuggling into his arms and lifting her lips to his for a kiss. When he made to slip a hand under her petticoat, however, she twisted out of his grasp. "I don't think we ought to."

"Lilah... but, last night--"

"Last night was last night and tonight is tonight," she said, lugging her bedroll clear to the other side of the fire from his. "I don't feel well, anyway. My head aches something fierce."

Dan rubbed his temples with his thumbs, smothering a groan. His head was commencing to ache, too, though he suspected not for the same reason.

"Maybe I'll feel better when we get there," Lilah continued, sugar-sweet on top and huffy as an offended hen underneath. "Once we're married and all."

She made a point of setting her back to him even from over there, and either fell asleep mighty fast or did a damn good job of pretending.

Finally, when the fire was about down to coals and embers, he did sleep. Not a good sleep, though... a restless tossing sleep of sick-to-his-stomach shakes and fever... he surfaced once long enough to wonder if maybe that water hadn't been as clean as he thought... sour, somehow... Tainted...

His head reeled like a half dollar spun on a tabletop, left to slow in swaying loops until it wobbled to a stop. He gazed blearily up at a skyful of stars that looked to be moving in a kind of pulsating swirled blur.

And... lordy, what *was* that smell?

The hotel in Leeds Junction wasn't fancy, but it was clean and cheap, and just across the road from the livery, where Jake Adams had already arranged to rent himself a horse for the remainder of his trip.

After days of train cars and stagecoaches, he found it irritating to be here in a room with a real bed, unable to sleep.

Worried, that was all. Worried about his sister. Closer he got, more he heard—or didn't hear, as the case may be—the more worried he became.

He had Emmaline's last letter, the one where she'd wrote out her plans and the reasons behind them, why she'd up and left Chicago. She was wearied of working in the textile mill, long hours for meager wages... that was part of it... but living with Aunt Martha more than likely made up the larger part.

Although where else besides family can a body turn to in their time of need, she had written, I can't but help feeling like an unwelcome burden, a charity case. I need to make my own way, dear brother. I need to get out of this crowded, noisy city.

This letter had reached him while he was in the stockade at Fort Bartlett, serving a stint for blacking the eye of a superior officer who'd been pilfering from the payroll. He was given his discharge papers once he got out -- and was lucky that was the extent of it; the officer had friends who could have seen him in front of a firing squad instead.

Their parents had passed the year after Jake joined the Army. Emmaline had little else to hold her to Chicago. So, like plenty others before her, she had struck out for the West. The wide, wild West with its bounty of opportunities.

I am not afraid of work and hardship, the letter had gone on to say. *And please do not think the less of me for it, Jake, but let us also be honest. My prospects here are rather lacking, to say the least. I am too tall by far and too sturdily-built to ever be a fashionable city lady. 'Handsome' is the kindest way I could be described, while you and I both know 'horse-faced' is much more the usual.*

Which was why his sister had signed on to be a mail-order bride. It appalled Jake, the idea of anybody agreeing to marry anybody unmet, through the post. He could not imagine picking a bride out of a catalog.

But, he did have to admit there might be something to it. There were many more lonely men in the West than there were eligible women. Here, they weren't so damn choosy over looks. Hell, a big strong gal like Emmaline would have the advantage over some delicate little thing. She'd make a fine wife for some rancher, farmer, miner, cowboy or soldier.

I will write to you again once I am settled, she'd finished. *All my love, your sister, Em.*

That had been over six months ago.

Six months with no further letters, not for him, not for Aunt Martha, not for the few friends she'd made in the textile mill.

Jake gave up trying to sleep. He dressed, buckled on his Colt more out of habit than concern, donned his hat and went downstairs.

Someone plunked away on a tinny-sounding piano. Two old-timers at the back made slow progress on a checkers game that might have been going on since the end of the War Between the States, two rail-men stood at the bar ignoring everything but their drinks, a busty past-her-prime woman with dyed-red hair talked to the piano-player, and a bearded man in buckskins sprawled face-down over a table.

"Whiskey," Jake told the barkeep.

"Comin' right up." The barkeep commenced the pouring, and looked Jake over. "You just in off the train?"

"I am."

"See more people leavin' here on the train than arrivin.'"

"Riding out tomorrow."

"Army?"

"Used to be." He tossed back the shot of whiskey.

"Not much call for soldierin' in these parts," the barkeep said.

"On my way to Vixby."

"Vixby?"

The music did not stop with a jangle, a sudden silence did not fall across the room, nobody edged away or brought their fingers to rest on gunbutts, but the barkeep's startled tone set Jake's nerves all on edge.

"You know the place?" he asked.

"Took me by surprise, is all. Damn near forgot about it. Ain't been nobody through here to or from Vixby in..." He paused, then called over to the woman, who'd been idly listening. "Rose! How long's it been?"

"Ages," she said, approaching the bar with a walk that made her upper stories jiggle like jellies on a plate. "Three, four months now?"

"Thought so," said the barkeep. "You know how it is with towns out here... sometimes they just dry up and blow away like tumbleweeds. All's it takes is a bad season for the crops... livestock sickness... claims go bust. First one business fails, then t'other. People drift off to try their luck elsewheres."

"One for the lady and one for yourself as well, if you're of a mind," Jake said.

The barkeep most definitely was of a mind. As he saw to it, Rose winked one overly-made-up eyelid at Jake. "Ain't you the nicest young man! I like him, Stanton."

Jake touched his hat brim to her. "I'd appreciate anything you could tell me about Vixby. I'm looking for my sister. Last I knew, she was headed there."

"Not much to tell," Stanton said. "Not much in Vixby to start with."

"That's where your sister was going?" asked Rose.

"So her letter said." He told them about Emmaline and her plan to become a mail-order bride, and how she'd not written to him since. "The man who runs it made the travel arrangements. She and some other women were to take the train here to Leeds Junction, then he'd pick them up and their husbands would meet them in Vixby."

Rose exchanged a look of distinct unease with the barkeep.

"I thought that, even if Emmaline had married and moved on, this Mr. Pine would know where she'd gone," Jake said, his worry reaching new levels of concern.

"Pine... Simon Pine? Smilin' fella with a mouthful of fancy silver teeth?" Stanton bared his own teeth, which were anything but fancy or silver.

"Em's letter didn't say. Why? Who is he?"

"Smilin' Si?" One of the men at the bar swiveled a bleary gaze in their direction. "Mail-order brides, is *that* what they be callin' it now?" He chuckled a sloppy, lewd chuckle and smacked his lips.

The temper that had landed his fist on his superior officer's eye and himself in the stockade flared up, and Jake had to wrestle it back under control. "Start talking."

And what he heard was indeed as bad as what he'd feared.

Simon Pine, better known as Smilin' Si, set up his "mail-order bride" business to bring in unsuspecting young women from back East. They thought they'd find husbands waiting for them, hopeful new lives like the one Emmaline had been after. Instead, the scheme was such that they'd be stuck far from home, far from the help of friends or relations. With nowhere else to turn, they'd then have little choice but to go to work for Smilin' Si's *real* business.

"A brothel?" Jake spoke through a clenched jaw, and though he had not yet put his hand to it, he was well aware of the good weight of the Colt at his hip "You're telling me this silver-toothed son of a bitch lured my sister out here with false pretenses and put her to whoring?"

The drunk at the bar was not so drunk as to be suicidal, and kept his mouth shut. The others averted their gazes from Jake.

He wrestled his temper back under control again. "Any of you here on good terms with Pine?"

Heads shook in the emphatic negative.

"Glad to know it," Jake said. He slapped down more money on the scuffed bartop. "In the meantime, drinks for the house."

Lilah tried not to cry for fear she would smother.

She couldn't breathe through her mouth on account of being gagged with her own bonnet, which had been spun into a calico twist-rope and tied around her head.

If she'd ever been so scared in all her born days, she couldn't think of when. She'd like to believe it was a bad dream, a nightmare brought on by that sour-tasting water and her argument with Danny, but it felt too real. Even if it made no sense, it felt too real to be a dream.

She'd woken to being seized and hauled out of her bedroll... dark shapes crowded around her... hissing and clicking... tight-pinching grips that weren't quite like hands and weren't quite like claws... scaly somehow, almost lizardy, but not... making her think of the pile of bird-feet left over after last autumn's turkey-slaughter... an awful reek, spoiled ham and unwashed bodies... a flappy rustling like too many chickens in a shed...

Then they'd pulled a sack over her head, coarse and itchy burlap, smelling of potato dirt, which was better than that other stink. Blind, blundering, hands bound behind her, she could only stumble along where they led her.

For how long?

She didn't know.

Her toes throbbed from stubbing against obstacles. The bottoms of her stockings had shredded clean away so that she was barefoot, not that the stockings had been much help against the rough scree of sharp rocks.

And Danny?

She'd heard him mumble and struggle, feeble-like, groggy, protesting. She'd heard a meaty thump and a grunt. After that? Nothing.

Was he dead? Had they killed him?

Why kill him and not her?

Did she really want to know the answer to that question?

Who were they? *What* were they? Where were they taking her? What were they going to do?

Did she really want any of those answers, either?

Eventually, after what felt like miles of walking, the sense of openness around her changed to a sense of enclosed space. A cave, she guessed. A warm, dry cave with a sandy floor that felt like a blessing to the poor bleeding soles of her feet. The stink was thicker here even through the earthy burlap, but other smells mixed with it -- wood-smoke, leather, root-cellar and pantry smells.

Those pinching bird-claw hands gave her a move-along shove so that she fell to her knees in a pile of straw. Lilah whimpered into the gag.

Now was when the real horrors would begin, she knew. Now was when they'd do terrible things to her.

Except they didn't.

They went off, rustling, hissing, and left her alone.

She curled on her side in the straw, still trying not to cry.

Sometime later, could have been hours or minutes, she heard someone approach.

"Ma'am? Can you hear me?" asked a female voice. "Nod if'n you do."

Lilah nodded.

"Gonna take that bag off, but you best stay calm. Understand me?"

Again, Lilah nodded.

Fresh air hit her face like a blessing after being stuck under that potato-sack for so long. There was light, too, the flicker of a tiny tallow-lamp that seemed a noonday blaze by comparison. Once her eyes accustomed to it, she squinted at the woman hunkered beside her.

Only she wasn't a woman, she was a girl no older than Lilah herself, a Negro girl with a serious expression. She wore a check-gingham dress that had seen better days over baggy too-big men's trousers, and a kerchief tied down snug over her head.

"I c'n untie your hands and take the gag out too, if you won't make a ruckus," the girl said, putting the tallow-lamp on a rock outcrop.

A third time and most emphatic, Lilah nodded.

"My name's Sophie." She worked the rolled bonnet free of Lilah's mouth and let it fall against her collarbones. "What's yours?"

After a few gasps, she said, "Lilah. Lilah DuPree."

"Well, Lilah DuPree, you are in one serious fix. Here."

The jug Sophie tipped to Lilah's lips sloshed with the same oily-tasting, copper-coin water as before. Lilah wanted to push it away but she was just too thirsty. She drank her fill, though it made her stomach swirl and her mind go dizzy.

"Where am I?"

"With the buzzard-women."

"The... what?" Still wishing she could convince herself this was a nightmare, Lilah cast a desperate look around.

It was indeed a cave. Strange drawings covered the stone walls, figures and animals, letters, symbols, done in charcoal or red and yellow ochre.

To the front was a living area of sorts, with a cook fire and crude furniture. There were racks of meat and fish, baskets of wild fruits and vegetables, bundles of herbs. Nearby was a cluttered disorder of crates, barrels, grain-sacks, jugs, dry-goods and other supplies. Over in a sleeping area, cots, mattresses and bed-pallets had been laid out, some with blankets hung up between them as partitions.

And there were hunched figures, some perched on stools and log benches... some moving... flapping... preening...

"Don't you scream, now," Sophie said. "They won't like that."

Bald-stubble heads darting about with quick jerks... scarlet faces, feverish eyes above wicked-hooked beaks... limbs ending in yellow talon-tipped hands and feet... feathered wings folded like musty, ragged ponchos... the grimy nakedness of womanly curves beneath... cawing and cackling at each other, making noises that almost might've been speech or laughter...

Buzzard-women.

"I said, don't you scream!" Sophie repeated.

A train-whistle whine escaped Lilah instead. She covered her eyes and rocked back and forth in the straw. "Are they gonna hurt me? Kill me? Please don't let them kill me. I don't want to die!"

"That's up to you, Lilah."

She broke down sobbing then for a while. When Sophie offered the jug again, she took it and drank without protest.

"Where's Danny?" she asked, sniffling. "What've they done with him?"

"That your fella? Your sweetheart?"

"Is he... dead?"

"Naw. You'll see him here in a bit."

"I will?" Relief fair sagged her bones. "Oh, good. We're headed for a town called Vixby, then--"

"We heard," Sophie said, waving it off with a hand. "Gonna get married and all?"

She faltered. "He... well... he said... he told me... he promised..."

"Uh-huh." Sophie's tone would have been enough even without the skeptical heft of an eyebrow and the way she crossed her arms under her bosom.

Lilah felt her cheeks heat up. Had Danny been stringing her? Taking advantage? Playing her for a fool?

The way he'd had everything so nice and planned out for their travel, their city plans... all planned out in order and detail... then as soon as she'd mentioned weddings and preachers...

What if they'd gotten to the city and it hadn't worked out like he said? What if some other gal came along, some prettier gal and...?

And their night in the hayloft... despite what Ma always cautioned her about how a man wouldn't likely buy the cow if he could get the milk for free... she'd brushed that advice aside, telling herself how this was different, Danny was different...

How could she have gone and been so stupid?

She did not just cover her eyes again, but covered her whole face with her hands.

"Make no mistake; your fella is gonna die," Sophie had said. "You, though, you got a hard decision to make, Lilah DuPree."

Not much in Vixby to start with, the barkeep had said, and he'd been right.

Jake did wonder, though, what Stanton would say if he could see the place now.

Dried up and blown away?

Hell. Died and not been given a decent burial.

That was Vixby, all right.

Dead and unburied as the skeletal remains of a horse in the middle of its dusty Main Street. Dead as the mangy tatters of fur and bone that must have once been someone's dog.

Shutters swung in a desultory breeze. Wisps of curtain fluttered through broken windowpanes. Weeds grew up through the gaps of the boardwalk and gardens were untended. A bristly drift of tumbleweeds had piled up against the wall of the general store.

And yet, as his own rented horse plodded into town, Jake had the distinct sensation that he was not alone. There were eyes watching him besides those of the crows along the fences and a solitary buzzard perched on the roofline of what could only be Smilin' Si's saloon.

"Hey, Vixby!" he called. "Anybody home?"

His voice rang hollow against the storefronts with their weathered, peeling paint. The crows startled up, scolding, then settled again. The buzzard did not so much as twitch. A skinny orange-stripe cat shot out from behind a waterin' trough and vanished under a decrepit shack.

He'd ridden hard all morning, much to the rented horse's displeasure, to find only this? Vixby was a sight worse off even than they'd reckoned in Leeds Junction.

From what he could see through open doors as he walked upstreet leading the horse by the reins, some folks had packed up what they could and left the rest to be scavenged by them as stayed behind. The store shelves had been looted down to a few odds and ends.

The waterin' trough, when he reached it, had just a silty, scummy puddle at the bottom. No matter how he worked the pump, all it earned him was a godawful rusty squeaking noise. The horse threw him a reproachful look.

"Heeeee-yah, not a drop!"

The sudden cry made him whirl gun-in-hand. It was only Providence kept him from blowing a hole through the scrawny old man with the long straggling hair and beard.

"Not a drop," this fella said again, seeming unawares of how close he'd brushed with a bullet. He'd emerged from between two houses, pig-filthy, in nothing but a pair of drawers that might not have been changed in months. His hands and head quivered as if with the palsies. "Not a drip, not a drippy-droppy-doo."

"What happened here?" Jake asked.

"Drought done struck. Only the crick. Only the crick, and see how well *that* went!" His jittering finger pointed more or less in the direction of the saloon. "Din't get me, though. Din't get Ol' Pete! Outfooled 'em, I did! Never touch it less'n from a bottle, ha!"

"Pete--"

The buzzard on the roofline launched itself flapping into the air. Ol' Pete, squealing like a girl, flung his scabbed arms over his head and took off running faster than Jake would have thought him capable of.

The Colt's barrel tracked the ugly bird across the sky. For a moment, Jake was sore tempted to shoot, to blow a hole in something on this crazy day in this crazy, forsaken town... but he didn't.

He made his way toward the saloon instead. Its sign, faded but legible, showed a mouth beaming a silver-toothed grin. Smaller signs advertised the services available, which made his jaw clench again.

That Emmaline ended up stuck somewheres like this, her hopes and plans all dashed to pieces by a no-good bastard preying on unsuspecting women...

Jake looped the reins over a hitching post. His bootheels clomped on the boards. He pushed through the batwings and stopped short at the sight that greeted him.

Where most places of this sort had a picture over the bar, a gilt-framed oil work of a woman nude in repose on a couch, this one had a dead man nailed up like some kind of whorehouse Jesus.

It was a wonder the corpse hadn't fallen from the nails, so badly was it decomposed. The shreds of what had begun as a fine suit seemed to be all that held the body together. Near as Jake could tell on the closest inspection he was willing to make, the man had been tortured. Had been cut, stabbed, burned, bludgeoned, and damn near everything but scalped. His mouth gaped open wider than seemed natural, until Jake realized it was because most of the teeth had been bashed out of his head.

The rest of the place was in a shambles. Furniture was overturned, curtains torn down, mirrors and lamps and glassware busted to smithereens, the fancy oak banister leading up to the second floor looking like someone took a hatchet to it...

The furtive scuttlings overhead were probably just rats. Jake did not want to go upstairs anyway, did not want to see the rooms where Em and the others had been made to ply their trade.

If she'd left anything behind... unsent letters, a diary... maybe some way of figuring where she'd gone...

He heard a new sound that wasn't scuttling from overhead but childish laughter from out back. Jake went down a hall past the kitchen and found an open door leading onto a field that sloped down to a rocky gully lined with spindly trees. Their leaves were yellow and sparse, but afforded some shade, and a creek trickled through them.

There were kids at the creek, three of them, two redheaded freckle-boys that had to be twins, and a brown-haired girl some younger.

They were raggedy-clothed and barefoot, giggling over something on the ground that one of the boys was prodding at with a stick.

"You, there," Jake said, pitching his tone gentle so as not to alarm them.

He needn't have worried. They turned to him without a trace of fear. He saw that the boy with the stick had been prodding a jackrabbit that lay shuddering on the creek-bank, its rear legs kicking spastically, sides heaving.

The children giggled again, and it unnerved him clear to the bone.

"Where's your folks?" he asked. "They around here?"

"They're gone," said the little girl. She dangled a naked dolly by one arm, its yarn hair cut off and tatty old chicken-feathers poked into its cloth body like pins in a pincushion.

"Buzzard-women got 'em," the boy without the stick said.

"Buzzard-women got our ma and pa," his brother added, and did another nudge to the jackrabbit.

"Got 'most ever'body." The little girl hugged her dolly, and giggled at Jake. "They'll get you, too, mister, if'n they find you."

The twins spoke in turns, which would have been right disturbing under the most normal of circumstances.

"Get you too."

"Take you away."

"Take you to the canyon."

"Kill you and eat you."

"Eat you all up."

"What buzzard-women? What are you talking about?" Gooseflesh had risen on his arms despite the heat of the day.

The trio giggled. The one with the stick jabbed it through the jackrabbit's ribs, skewering it.

"Kill you just like that!"

"Only not s'quick."

"And eat you!"

"Like this!" The second boy stooped, grabbed the still-spasming jackrabbit, and chomped into its furry belly. Blood gushed up like jam from a tart.

"The hell!" Jake cried. He took an instinctive backward step and almost fell on his rump.

The brothers' giggles became howls of laughter. They ran off together with their kill swinging between them.

"You best go 'way, mister," the girl said. "Afore'n they come."

"Wait, please, maybe you can help me," Jake said, reaching out. "I'm looking for someone. My sister. Emmaline, her name is. Have you seen her? I... I think she... worked here."

Her eyes went big and round. "That's the bad man's place."

"I know."

"They got him first."

"The... buzzard-women?"

"Got Pa and Billy, too." She raised the dolly to her ear as if listening to its whispers. "Not Granny, her's too old t'bother with... and not me... I's too little."

She ran after the boys before Jake could try again to stop her. He watched the children scramble under a fence, trying to make sense of what they'd said, and what he'd seen, and what was going on in this town.

The trickling of the creek reminded him that his horse would not be kindly disposed towards him if he let it stay thirsty, but as he got to the bank, he hesitated. The water had a peculiar sheen and smell to it, and where it lapped against the stones he saw it left a residue.

Drought done struck... only the crick... the scrawny old man's words echoed in Jake's mind.

That jackrabbit, the kids seemed to have found it already dying.

Sour-water, sick-water, poison?

Might explain some of it, but what about the rest? What about these buzzard-women who'd come and taken people away?

Take you to the canyon, the boy had said, gesturing off toward the rocky hills and badlands past the outskirts of town.

It was, Jake reckoned, as good a way as any to try next.

Tilted slabs and flat boulders covered the side of a ravine that dropped away at a steep, jagged angle toward a silvery thread of creek.

Dark shapes gathered on the ledges, shifting, rustling, perched like huge vultures. Or buzzards. The buzzard-women. Watching. Waiting.

More buzzards, real ones, glided in swoops and circles high above. Dozens of them, also watching, also waiting.

What Lilah had initially taken for wind-carved rock formations and tangles of sun-bleached branches were...

Bodies. Human bodies.

What was left of them.

Wasted carcasses, rotted and picked over... limbs twisted and stretched into grotesque postures... desiccated brown flesh like jerky clinging by sinews to sun-bleached bones, bones, not branches... scraps of leathery skin and stringy hair... gored-out hollows where eyes should have been... the stone beneath them stained with rusty maroon discolorations where blood had blotched and run... guts split open with loops of shriveled intestine hung out... big chunks torn away...

One of the bodies was recent. Whole. Fresh. Alive, even; stirring and groaning, tugging at the contracting strips of rawhide tying him down.

Danny.

Danny, tied naked to a rock in the harsh sun-glare.

A hard decision, but a simple choice, Sophie had said.

Did Danny die quick and with company, or slow and alone?

If Lilah loved him enough to kill him herself, and spare him the misery of what would otherwise be his fate, then she must love him enough to die along with him.

The eagle-claw knife was razor-sharp. It'd be fast and merciful.

But if she loved her own life more...

"Just don't get to thinking you can try anything clever," Sophie added. "Such as cutting his bonds, or turning that weapon against anyone else. Do that, girl, and you both end up going the long, painful way." Sophie'd pointed then, to a spot where two had been staked out side by side. "Like my Aunt Ruthanne and Uncle Buck."

If she wanted to live...

She'd have to join them.

She'd have to drink the water that welled up from the canyon's springs... she'd have to shave her head and paint her face with red ochre... eat like they ate... prey on travelers and unwary passers-by...

So, now, here she was. Standing with Sophie, neither of them having yet earned their feathered robes and masks, as the buzzard-women descended.

And Danny began to scream.

Jake could hardly believe his eyes and wasn't sure he wanted to.

Braced though he'd been for a grisly scene, hearing those screams and the wet ripping noises that accompanied them, he still hadn't been ready to witness some poor bastard being torn to pieces and eaten alive!

Then one of the buzzard-women saw him, and screeched in a way that turned his spine to ice.

They abandoned their feast to turn toward Jake.

"Not a move, not another step!" he shouted.

They moved much more than another step, advancing on him with their talon-tipped fingers curled.

His bootheels backpedaled on the hardpan. The Colt bucked in his fist, the report echoing off the cliffs like a thunderclap. He'd aimed high, the bullet lost off into the clear blue, in hopes of scaring them.

It worked—halted them in their tracks—but only briefly. After that, it served just to rile them further. They rushed him as a flock.

He fired again, dead on this time.

A buzzard-woman took it spang between the eyes. Her head split wide open.

The others halted again.

Jake about felt his heart plummet into his stomach.

Dear sweet Mary mother of God, he'd just killed a woman.

Sprawled in the grit, she looked barely more than a girl. Not a monster, but a girl, a thin girl in a shabby costume, and he'd put a chunk of lead through her skull.

Those nearest her, spackled with blood, brains and bone-chips, shrieked their outrage to the skies. If they'd been murderous before, they were savage now.

Retreating fast as he dared, hoping he wasn't about to go right off an edge, Jake plugged another of them in the leg. She fell, screaming, tripping up some of her sisters, slowing them into a jostling logjam.

Three more gunshots cracked loud. Two buzzard-women spun and fell in gouts of blood and feathers. A third, limber as a minx, sprang out of the way and only got grazed to the arm.

Then the Colt's hammer clacked on an empty chamber.

His back came up against a boulder. Jake risked a lightning-fast glance to each side and spotted an overhang, not much of a one but enough to give him some cover in preventing these mad bitch harpies from getting the above-drop on him. Three quick steps to the left and he was under it, reloading for all he was worth.

They closed in, hissing. He was cornered, surrounded, and they knew it. If they were outgunned, he was outnumbered, and they knew that, too. Might cost them dearly, but it was only a matter of time before he was theirs.

He opened up on them again. A buzzard-woman collapsed with her throat burst apart like an overripe fruit; the one behind her caught the bullet in the forehead. Gutshot for the next, doubling her over as if she'd been punched in the belly.

An eagle-claw knife whickered through the air. Unwieldy as it was, it never should have flown straight, but it slashed Jake's cheek to the bone. He staggered a few more sideways steps, that eye squeezed shut and gushing tears of both pain and gratitude to have not been gouged from its socket. Blood poured freely through his scruff of beard to splash all down his shirt.

He squeezed off a shot by reflex. It went wild, striking off a rock with a shriek of ricochet.

His face hurt like blue hell and the blood kept spilling from it. His shirt felt soaked, sodden. His right eye was useless.

Then one of them *did* get the drop on him. He'd lost the cover of the overhang without realizing it until the she-devil landed full on his shoulders. They tumbled to the rough ground together, her talon-finger gloves shredding his shirt, her beak-mask digging a ragged furrow across his brow.

Jake rolled but she held on like a bramble-burr. He wedged the Colt's barrel into her chest and pulled the trigger twice more, the shots muffled. Her body lurched and went limp, heavy deadweight sprawled atop him.

He thrashed his way out from under and got up. His breath labored. His torn face couldn't have been more of an agony to him if he'd buried it in hot coals.

The biggest of the buzzard-women pushed her way forward. She stood tall, broad-shouldered and sturdily-built, spreading out her arms wide, fully extending that buzzard-wing cape.

Underneath, she wore nothing but a rope belt decorated with feathers, claws and bones. Streaks of color like war-paint covered her naked skin -- red and yellow ochre, black charcoal, brown clay.

Around her neck, a cluster of silvery baubles glinted on a braided cord necklace made from human hair.

Silvery baubles that weren't nuggets or beads but teeth, silver teeth, silver teeth broken out of a bad man's jaw.

Jake stared at the scarlet-daubed features behind the hook-beak mask. They were the sort of strong features about which "handsome" would be the kindest description, and "horse-faced" likely the more usual.

"Em?" Stunned, he lowered the Colt.

Her wild eyes flashed.

"Emmaline, it's me. It's Jake."

His sister's head cocked to the side, the way a bird's did when something caught its attention.

Then she snapped her head forward and plunged her beak deep into his throat, even as he pulled the trigger one last time.

The man who ran the livery in Leeds Junction was none too pleased about the late return and sorry condition, but a generous bonus allayed his irritation.

Similar tactics were used to good effect on any nosy questions at the hotel and the train station.

The money, of course, had come courtesy of a saddlebag formerly belonging to a bank robber named Frank Fallon. It was a lot of hard currency for anybody to be lugging around, let alone two young women—one of them a Negro at that—traveling unescorted. Something, though, some look or manner, made even the foolhardiest ruffian think twice about bothering them.

"We're going to San Monte," the blonde announced. "I'm going to become a famous singer."

That evening, over coffee and pie, the barkeep Stanton mentioned how kind it was they'd brought back that horse all the way from Vixby on behalf of that soldier fella.

"I liked him," Rose said. "Did he ever find his sister?"

The girls glanced at one another.

"He did indeed, ma'am," Sophie said. "He did indeed."

THE
FLUTE PLAYERS
By Bruce L. Priddy

our people, three men, one girl, moved toward a homestead on the Nebraska prairie, nothing but a sod house and barn, two shocks of brown rising up from the endless green and gold. No other homes around, the closest people were an hour away by horse in Sundown, or in Fort Cottonwood, two hours further. Whoever lived here had not done much with the land, the grass not cleared, no fences raised. Two of the men walking toward the house were bounty-hunters, the other an unexpected captive. All four people had soaked through their clothes in the late summer heat, still hot despite the Sun drooping to the horizon. One man, by the name of Ashby, rode a horse. He wore a pair of trousers that, on a clear day, matched the prairie sky. His cotton shirt was once white, though it had taken a darker shade with his sweat. Another man, surname of Desmond, walked beside his own mount, leading it. For the most part bald, which he tried to cover with a dingy slouch hat, he sported a full beard. It seemed his hair was doing its damnedest to migrate to his mug. All of his hair looked oily, and upon meeting him, one would not be inclined to assign sole guilt to the Sun. The men were partners, but each wore his best friend on his hip.

Across the saddle of Desmond's horse lay the girl, unconscious, bloodied, dress torn and filthy. Blood stained her hair pink. Ashby and Desmond didn't know her name, didn't know for sure at least, but suspected she was a daughter of the Garland family, owners of the homestead.

Behind them walked a Cheyenne man, his hands bound. A rope tied to the horn of Ashby's saddle pulled him along. Ashby and Desmond didn't know who the Cheyenne man was. No exchange of names in their brief, brutal introduction. Ashby and Desmond had been to the homestead already today, found it empty except for a story of violence. The bounty-hunters had followed a trail of crimson-sullied grass stalks from the sod homestead, and when that expired, kept walking in the same direction. An hour later, they found a house. The Cheyenne man answered the door. Behind him, they saw the Garland girl, unconscious then as now, ruined and dirty. Ashby buffaloed the Cheyenne, split open his head, dropped him from waking. The native man's woman picked up a rifle to defend her home, but Desmond put holes in her heart and lungs. Blood oozed from the Cheyenne's head and knees. He had stumbled, but Ashby and Desmond could not be bothered to let him regain his feet. His leaking skull matted his black hair. A shirt once blue, a pair of trousers once brown lost their color to abuse and blood. Gnats were stuck in the wounds they came to lap.

Off where the sea of grass met the sky, clouds boiled black. The prairie danced in a wind that promised rain soon.

When this walk, his kidnapping, began, the Cheyenne man sobbed. He held the bound hands to his face, didn't want Ashby and Desmond to have the pleasure of seeing him weep. He prayed in a language his captors could not understand. Desmond barked at him several times to stop but the Cheyenne ignored him, praying louder each time, the words almost reaching a scream. When he finally decided he was fed up, Desmond shoved the dangerous end of a Remington revolver into the soft part of the Cheyenne's jaw, and said, "You don't stop disturbing my calm with that dirty pig-Latin, I'm going to make you leak like your squaw." A Kentucky drawl was thick in his voice, the beginning of every word hard, spoken around teeth in desperate want of a dentist.

"Not yet you're not," said Ashby. This man had a Kentucky drawl as well, but every word was annunciated, he being someone who worked hard to make his upbringing and what education he had evident in his voice. "We still need him." Desmond obeyed, though not before digging the barrel into the Cheyenne's skin.

After that, the Cheyenne fell silent, his demeanor as grim as the approaching storm.

When they reached the front of the house, Ashby dismounted from his horse, and nodded toward the Cheyenne. "Get him ready," he said to Desmond. The front door swung with every buffet of wind. At the front step lay what was left of a dog, too long dead to tell what killed it, body so dried the flies were no longer interested. As Desmond walked back to the native, Ashby took care of the Garland girl, gently resting her in the grass on a blanket retrieved from his horse. Both horses stomped and whined at the scent of the nearing storm.

Desmond stood behind the Cheyenne and kicked the man's knees from under him. As Ashby approached, Desmond buried a revolver in the man's hair, forcing his eyes to the ground. Ashby knelt in front of the Cheyenne. "Boy, you and me need to have a conversation."

"You sons of bitches killed my wife." The Cheyenne spit out the words. "I have nothing to say to you."

Ashby tried to lift the man's chin with a finger, but he jerked away. Ashby grabbed his face, pinched the cheeks together in one hand, and wagged a finger at him. "Careful. My partner doesn't like sudden movements, as we've all tragically learned today." Desmond blew an amused snort out of his nose. Ashby met the Cheyenne's enraged eyes and smiled.

"See, I think you have a lot to tell me. We have a warrant, signed by General Stephen G. Burbridge himself, military governor of the great Commonwealth of Kentucky, ordering the arrest and return of one Garland family to Louisville, along with the confiscation of all their wealth, to stand for charge of being traitors to Abraham Lincoln and the Union. The good general ordered every man to be put to the defense of Louisville, but Mr. Garland absquatulated with his family.

"My partner—I believe you two have become acquainted—and me tracked the Garlands for well over a month. Now, what I want to know is, why when we finally track them down here to this house, we find it empty of the Garlands but full of blood stains?" Ashby's voice dropped to a low whisper. "I want to know where the Garlands are, because there is a whole hell of a lot of money involved in this and I'd love to be paid. Think you could help me with that, boy?"

The Cheyenne growled. "I have no idea what you are talking about."

Ashby shook his head. "Lying to me isn't going to help either of us." He clapped with each word. The bounty-hunter brought a hand across the Cheyenne's face, drawing blood from his cheek. "You'd best tell me what blasphemous savage ritual you committed the Garlands to and where I can find their bodies, boy. Or things may go sideways from here."

"I'm a Christian!" As the Cheyenne spoke, blood ran from his mouth. "And I have a name. It's Henry. I took it upon my baptism."

Desmond laughed. "Savages don't take too well to the Word of the Lord."

Henry looked back over his shoulder. "The whites don't seem to have too well either." Then he turned his gaze back to Ashby. "Least not as well as the gray-backs have taken to your friend's beard."

Ashby held up a hand, cutting off Desmond before he could retaliate. "So, Savage Henry, you're claiming innocence?" asked Ashby. "Then perhaps you'd like to tell me how that you came to be in possession of the Garland girl."

"I found her on the prairie a couple days ago. On fire with fever and cut up like an animal got ahold of her," Henry said. "My wife and I were trying to nurse her back to health. But the girl didn't come to."

Desmond pushed at Henry with his revolver. "Betting you wish you'd just left the girl where you found her, huh?"

Henry pushed back. "I told you I was a Christian. Even if I wasn't, I'd never leave a child like that."

Ashby patted the cheek he'd slapped just a moment before. "What a noble soul." He chuckled and pointed a finger at Henry. "But Henry, I still think you're a liar. See, I can't shake the feel there's something you're not telling us."

Ashby grabbed Henry by the hair, pulled him up. "Take a walk with me." Henry struggled, tried to grab Ashby's wrist with his bound hands, kicked as he tried to get firm ground under his feet. Ashby held on, but had to use both hands to drag Henry through the tall grass. The stalks bent under the strengthening wind.

They came to a boulder half the size of a man. To judge by the weathering it was an ancient stone, older than the prairie where it made a home. Ashby shoved Henry to his hands and knees in front of the rock.

"I want you to tell me what that is." Ashby jabbed a finger toward the stone.

Painted in on the rock in red ochre was the silhouette of a hunchback with feathers or antennae growing from its head. A proboscis, short and thick, jutted from its face. The figure had the appearance of a flutist dancing to its own music, legs askew, hands to its proboscis.

"I have no idea what that is," said Henry. He brought himself up to his knees.

"I didn't tell you to get up." Ashby planted his boot heel between Henry's shoulder blades and kicked him back on to his hands. "There are a half-dozen other rocks around here, just like that one. Looks just like the kinds of scribblings savages make on rocks. But you're telling me you don't know anything about it." He chuckled.

"No," said Henry, "I'm not from here. I came to minister to the People that haven't been rounded up or killed by the cavalry men."

"Now see, Henry, you've gone and messed up." Ashby ground Henry's fingers between his boot heel and the dirt. "You know the savages around here. So, you know which of them is responsible for the unholy atrocity that befell the Garlands. You're going to tell me, no matter how many bones it takes."

Nearby, there was thunder. Henry's fingers cracked with the sky.

Desmond yelled for Ashby, but the wind ate most of the words. One hand trying to keep his hat planted on his head, Desmond pointed with the other at the blackened sky. Clouds swallowed what daylight remained.

Ashby lifted Henry by the collar. "Get walking," he said, with a shove.

Henry held his broken fingers to his chest. "By the end of this, I'll see the both of you dead," he said.

Ashby laughed. "Now, that's not very Christian of you. Desmond was right."

Before even reaching Desmond and the horses, Ashby was yelling orders. "Take the horses in the barn. We'll make diggings in the house."

Desmond waved his gun at Henry. "Come on, you."

Ashby yanked Henry back by the collar. "No, No. He's staying with us. We can't risk him running off before we finish our conversation." He shook Henry. "Not when we're becoming such good friends."

Desmond ushered the horses into the barn. The wind stole his hat and lost it to the grass. Ashby let Henry go with a warning he had no morals against shooting a running man in the back. He scooped up the Garland girl, wrapped her in the blanket. "Go on with you," he said to Henry, nodding his head to the house.

From the entrance, Henry could see the entirety of the small home, consisting only of a common room and two bedrooms. Violence had left no part of the house untouched. The Garlands had tried to make this a home, but something had destroyed that. What little furniture the common room had contained was so broken it was hard to tell what had once been chair and what had once been table. Vegetables, rotten to husks, still lay where they scattered from a pot fallen from a stove. Carmine stained white-washed floors and walls.

And in the stains, prints of hands, prints of feet. Henry was no tracker. Whatever story the prints could tell was lost on him. But, he could get a sense of who made them. Three adults, and a smaller set, probably made by the girl he found in the grass. Around and through these, dozens of prints so tiny, they could only have been made by an infant.

"Did these Garlands have a baby?" Henry asked as Ashby brought the girl in.

"I don't think so." Ashby kicked debris away from a spot against the back wall and laid the girl down. "I know what you're talking about, though. Anything you want to tell me about that?"

"No," Henry said. He eased himself to the floor beside the girl.

The sky began to fall on the house. Desmond came inside, had to fight against the wind to shut the door. With the end of his shirt, he wiped away the rain water his face and hair were in sore need of. A puddle formed at his feet.

"I hope your friends haven't been washed away," Henry said.

Desmond put a hand on his sidearm. "Keep making the chuckles, boy. We'll see what happens."

Ashby laughed. "I'm starting to like Henry." He motioned to Desmond. "Come on. Help me look for a lamp we can put a lucifer to."

Desmond shuffled past Ashby to a bedroom. "Maybe Garland kept some o'-be-joyful round here..."

Outside, a trilling, airy whistle played among the raindrops and was gone. Desmond paused in the doorway.

"What in the Hell was that?"

"It was a bird." Ashby swatted the question away. "Will you get to looking before it gets too dark to see?"

Desmond returned with an oil-lamp, a bit of sag in his shoulders. He handed the lamp to Ashby and said, "Looks like the Garlands believed in temperance."

The thunder and wind roared together.

Ashby lit the lamp. "Good. No need to get wallpapered tonight, anyhow." He sat the lamp on the stove but it did little to alleviate the growing dark. Shadows fell from the low ceiling, bunched together in the corners, distorted faces.

"Do you have any water?" Henry asked.

"We don't want a savage putting his dirty lips to our canteens," said Desmond.

"It's not for me," said Henry. "It's for the girl."

Desmond removed his canteen from his belt and put it to the girl's lips. Most of the water escaped from the corners of her mouth, ran down her cheeks.

Something tapped across the common-room window. Desmond started, the canteen dropped from his hands, emptying itself on the floor. Boards and bloodstains drank the water up.

"It's just the storm being a blowhard," said Ashby.

"Swear to Jesus Almighty I heard that damned bird again." Desmond looked out the window, tried to peer past his own reflection, saw nothing but rain. "What kind of stupid bird sings in the rain?" he asked his reflection.

"Stop worrying about the bird," said Ashby. "We got more important things to worry on, like getting paid." He walked over to Henry and knelt in front of him. We have a conversation to finish."

Desmond joined Ashby. "What do you say we do?"

"Well, that all depends on our friend Savage Henry here." Ashby patted Henry's leg. "What do you say? You ready to acknowledge the corn?"

Henry pulled his hands to his face, folded them as best he could, being bounded with broken fingers. He rocked with closed eyes and whispered.

"What's that?" asked Ashby. "You're going to have to speak up. No telling secrets."

"I'm praying," Henry said.

Desmond guffawed. "I'm thinking all that praying is worth a goober."

"I'm not asking for help," Henry said. He opened his eyes. Hot swells gathered in them. "I'm asking God to forgive my sins. And for my wife to not watch."

"You're a good man, Henry," said Ashby. "I'm almost sorry about what's going to happen."

Desmond grabbed Henry's wrists, tried to pull them to the floor. Henry struggled and the men wrestled, Henry screaming "No!" Desmond forced the Cheyenne down, straddled his back, and pinned his hands to the ground. Ashby picked up a broken chair-leg, lined the sharp corners up with Henry's good fingers.

"Anything you want to say?"

Henry set his jaw in a sneer. "Lord, I give myself to your mercy and ask for the strength to endure these cruel torments."

Ashby raised the chair-leg.

A long, pain-filled squeal invaded the house. Gooseflesh attacked all three men. Even the storm seemed silenced in fear for the briefest of moments. The sound stayed Ashby's hand.

"That was the horses," said Desmond. Each word shook.

"Go check on them." Ashby said through his teeth, to hide his own shaking words.

His partner chuckled, nervous. "In the dark? Alone? You must think me simple."

With a growl, Ashby threw the chair-leg against a wall. Using the Arkansas Toothpick from his belt, he cut Henry's bindings. Then he took the lamp from the stove and set it down beside the Cheyenne. "You still have a good hand. Make use of it."

Henry stayed on the floor. "No."

"Not a request." Ashby pulled out his revolver, cocked the hammer. "Get to stepping, or your worldly torments will be long and plenty before you're allowed to see your good wife and dear Lord."

Ashby waved Henry out the door. The bounty-hunters followed a step behind. Both held their Remingtons in front of them. Henry covered the lamp with his crippled hand. Buffets of rain pounded the broken digits, each brought a wince.

The walk around the house to the barn was slow. The lamplight could not penetrate more than a few feet into the rain. Desmond threatened every sound in the grass.

Another pain-wracked squeal from the barn tore through the night and storm. A yelp of terror escaped Desmond. He shoved his fist into his mouth to quiet himself. The lamplight quivered and swam with Henry's trembling hand. Rain could not scour away the stink of blood and fear-rich piss thickening as they approached the barn. Each surge of wind blew the stench into the men's faces.

The barn door was agape by inches. Inside, something sang in a trilling whistle. Ashby told Henry to wait then motioned for Desmond to open the door further. His partner had to fight against mud and the weight of sod to open the barn. The men gagged at the odor he released. With the barrel of his Remington, Ashby stared down whatever the dark barn hid. Henry crept to the doorway and exposed the black insides to the lamplight.

The horses lay on the ground, only their heads visible under the dozens of tiny creatures that covered both animals. Neither horse struggled against their attackers, but their pain was clear. Veins bulged. Nostrils flared, leaked discolored fluids. One horse rolled his eyes white. The critters were some mad god's insult to the human form, each the rough shape of a man, but hunchbacked, their hairless bodies a mottled gray, the color of spoiled chicken meat. A row of stiff quills ran from atop their head, down their spines. None could have been taller than a man's knees are high. Talons on human-like hands and feet dug into horses, held the creatures in place as they drained their prey through pink, pulsating proboscises. Blood seeped from the wounds. Some of the critters trilled as they fed, the barn transformed into an orchestra-house of depraved flutists.

"Dear Lord Jesus," Henry said a gasped whisper. He began to back away from the entrance. "I think I know what happened to the Garlands."

"Henry, I'm starting to have my suspicions that you're an innocent man," said Ashby.

The bounty-hunters aimed their revolvers at the monsters. "We ain't got enough hornets for this," Desmond said.

One of the critters raised its head, the proboscis detaching from the horse. Blood ran like mud from the sharp mouth. Compound eyes squinted at the three men, ommatidia glinted metallic in the lamplight.

The light! The light! Kill it! All three men heard the words as a coarse hissing between their eyes. More critters looked up from their meal. The men's heads filled with hisses.

The Remingtons made thunder. Every round that found a critter proved it mortal, punched through them, or removed head or limb from body. Still, more came, fulfilling Desmond's prediction. Henry smashed the lamp in the doorway. Burning oil splattered across dry hay, horses, and monsters, set them on fire. Screeches of pain and rage echoed in the men's skulls.

The men ran.

Exhausted from the forced march and his injuries, Henry was the last to reach the house. Desmond shut the door on his shoulder and foot. The Cheyenne screamed obscenities as Desmond pressed with his weight. Henry pushed with his back, hand and foot planted against the door-frame. The door came open, Henry stumbled in. Desmond grabbed him by the shirt, shoved him off his feet. As he fell, Henry grabbed the bounty-hunter's wrist. Both men landed in the mud and rain.

They rolled over each other, threw awkward blows. Ashby yelled something about more critters in the grass. Henry and Desmond ignored him. Desmond pulled himself on top, pinned Henry's broken fingers beneath a knee. Henry cried out. The bounty-hunter put his revolver to the Cheyenne's face.

"I'm sending you back to your squaw, boy," he said with a cock of the hammer.

Claws latched into Desmond's buttocks and sides. Desmond stood, cursing, tried to swat the monster from his back. The gun was flung from his hand, disappeared into the grass. A proboscis stabbed him beneath the ribs. He howled.

Henry scrambled on his good hand and both feet back to the door. Desmond lurched to the house, his movements stiff. His mouth begged for help. The words came out a dry gargle. He collapsed through the entrance. Henry shut the door, bolted it against the pounding monsters. The critter still clung to Desmond's back, the proboscis undulating as it drank him.

Ashby caved the critter's skull with the butt of his revolver. The blow tore the monster from Desmond, sent it into a wall. A hole opened in the critter's face where the proboscis had once been. The appendage remained in Desmond's back, flopped, poured dark red tissue.

A shriek cleaved into the men's skulls. Henry put his hands to his face, tried to pull out the sound. Ashby roared back at the critter, took it by the throat, beat it with his gun. Talons mauled Ashby's arm. He did not stop beating the critter or stop roaring until his weapon met floorboards. New bloodstains, consisting of the critter, Ashby, and Desmond, rewrote the old ones. The shriek expired with the monster.

Fire and storm fought over the barn. The battle lit the inside of the house in dark oranges and reds.

Ashby spit on the mash that once was the critter's head. He crawled over to his partner, pulled the severed proboscis from him. More tissue gushed from the wound. Desmond curled in on himself, limbs rigid, eyes bulged. His chest was still.

Ashby slumped back, popped the cylinder from his weapon, and threw it at the shadows. A replacement waited in his trouser pocket. Two tries were needed to drop the pre-loaded cylinder into the Remington. On the first, it slipped from his blood-slick fingers.

"Is he...?" asked Henry.

Ashby sprang from the floor, grabbed Henry by the face, pressed the barrel of the revolver to the Cheyenne's head.

Hoarse, hissing voices were a cacophony in their heads. Give us your friend. *We're hungry.* Claws tapped on the windows. *We're hungry. Let us eat.*

"Are you sure you can afford to spend a bullet on me?" asked Henry.

Ashby turned the gun to the door, put six holes in it. The critters made mocking, trilling hoots.

"That may not be the best use of them either," said Henry.

"I know," said Ashby. He knelt beside Desmond, checked his pockets for cylinders.

"Now what happens?" asked Henry.

Ashby sighed. "Seems these things don't like bright light." He refilled his revolver as he spoke. "So, we hold out 'til morning, then we go be on our merry ways."

Henry tapped the side of his head. "I think they know our plan."

"I don't care." Ashby stood and meet Henry's eyes. "Look, I mean what I said. We get out of this, we go our ways. I'm sorry about threatening to brain you. Desmond was stupid. He shouldn't have tried to shut you out. He put himself in the bootyard. And I'm sorry about your woman. That isn't much, I know. Safe bet says you've got a heart and mind for revenge. That's mighty understandable. But try anything... you'll be on your way to see your wife. Are we straight?" He offered his hand to Henry.

Henry looked at the hand, then back to Ashby's eyes. "Come tomorrow, no promises."

The bounty-hunter chuckled. "Fair enough. But let's worry about getting through tonight."

The girl let loose a high-pitch scream.

Ashby spun, weapon raised. Nerves almost pulled the trigger. The girl kept screaming, crawled back against the wall, tried to climb it. "You brought me back! You brought me back!" she wailed.

Henry ran to her, held her shoulder to restrain her. "It's okay. You're safe now." He tried stroking her hair to calm her.

She pointed at the dead critter. "They got in again!" Tears ran. "I didn't mean to do it! I wanna leave!"

"It is okay," said Henry. "They're outside, but we're in here. You'll be okay. My name's Henry. My wife..." he stumbled through the word, "and I found you in the grass and we took care of you. This... man... came to bring you home. What's your name?"

She made a few more convulsive sobs before she was calm enough to answer. "Hannah," she said into a dress-sleeve as she wiped it across her nose.

Ashby knelt beside them. "Miss Hannah, I'm Mister Ashby. What was it you didn't mean to do?"

"Old man in Sundown said we shouldn't build here, said a long time ago this plot belonged to an Indian tribe all the other Indians hated because they made their women take flies and fleas and mosquitos as husbands, and kept the children as pets. Then, the cavalrymen came from the fort and killed everyone in the tribe. But the pets were in hidey-holes deep under the grass and they escape. Papa didn't listen.

"And I didn't know the flute players were them, I swear it, Mister Ashby! They made such pretty music at night, playing in the grass. 'Til I saw them up close, I thought they were just kids. They'd talk in my head, said they wanted to play with me. So I let them in. Now mama, papa and sissy are all gone. I didn't mean to!" The sobs returned. She tried to burrow her face in Henry's rain-soaked shirt. "You're all wet," she said, in a matter-of-fact voice.

Ashby and Henry laughed.

"How did you get away?" Henry asked.

"I ran," she said. "One tried snatching me up. But I bit it. It tasted like dirt!" She skewed up her face. "Then I kept running, until I couldn't run no more."

Give her to us. We will let you leave.

"No!" she screamed. She bounced with fear.

"Hey," said Ashby, putting a hand on her back. "Don't listen to them. They're scary, but this is scarier." He held up his revolver. "So don't pay them any mind. You just listen to me and Savage Henry here, okay?" Hannah nodded, smiled.

"We'll talk about other things," he continued. "Now Miss Hannah, your daddy was a big bug with a lot of money. Some other big bugs want to know where that money is. President Lincoln needs it to help defend Louisville from the Seceshs. You know where your daddy's money is?"

"Oh, come off it, man," said Henry. "There are some more pressing concerns."

"I didn't come all this way, Desmond didn't die, just to see the elephant," Ashby snapped. He blew out a breath to calm himself. "Miss Hannah, you think you can help me?"

The girl shook her head. "No sir. He gave it all to charity before we left Kentucky."

Laughter put Henry on his behind. Outside, the critters hooted. Ashby tried to rub the frustration from his face.

"No matter," he said. "Come morning, we'll be going home."

"Home?" Hannah whimpered the question.

"Back to Louisville," Ashby said. "See, Miss Hannah, your daddy ran off when he wasn't supposed to. He didn't want to do his part for the Union, like some dirty copperhead."

"Stop it," Henry growled.

Ashby ignored him. "So, General Burbridge sent me to fetch you, your mommy, daddy and sister up. You've been through the mill. The general's going to want to hear all about it."

Hannah shook her head with panicked fury. "I don't want to see the Butcher!"

The general will make you a fancy girl for his dirty soldiers.

"No!" Hannah clawed at her forehead, tried to get at the words.

"Shut up!" Henry screamed at the critters.

He'll hang you from a lamp-post, swinging by your neck.

"I won't go!" Hannah tore from Henry. He grabbed at her dress. Fabric came away in his hand. She ran to the door, fought with the bolt. Ashby and Henry chased. Desmond's blood grabbed Henry's feet, pulled him to the floor. Ashby reached for Hannah, but was too late, caught nothing but an empty doorway.

Fear ran Hannah into the night and rain, into the critters. She became screams in the grass.

Ashby tried to throw the door closed. Critters were crushed between door and frame, left it agape. More spilled in. Ashby fired. He loosed only four rounds before claws and proboscises buckled him. His revolver clattered on the floor boards, skidded to Henry's feet.

Henry looked at Ashby beneath the devouring monsters. The bounty-hunter's head was the only part of him not covered in critters. His eyes bulged in pain, threatened to leave their sockets. "Help me," Ashby mouthed.

Henry held up his crippled fingers. "This is my shooting hand."

Henry ran to a bedroom, barricaded the door with his back. He prayed for sunrise, and forgiveness.

IN THUNDER'S SHADOW

By Edward M. Erdelac

September 25, 1876

To Professor O.C. Marsh, Yale College, New Haven, Connecticut
I have arrived in Delirium Tremens in Arizona Territory
and met with the Drucker & Dobbs Mining Co.'s geologist, Elvin
Planterbury, who contacted your office about the fossil he discovered in
their main copper shaft. Fortunately Mr. Planterbury was able to preserve
the specimen before it was broken up and sold off for the price of a few
drinks. It is, in my opinion, a tarsal fragment from a large pteranodon
(most probably longiceps). I have personally never seen a fossil so well
preserved. Work in the mine has necessarily not been halted to await my
arrival, and examination of the location at which the fragment was uncovered is impossible. I intend to survey the sedimentary substrate of the
upper area of the surrounding Huachuca Mountains. I have hopes that
should it prove fruitful, my work might warrant the assignment of a team
from the Geological Survey. I was able to purchase a quantity of dynamite
from the company as well as sufficient provisions and gear, but I shall likely
require more funds to ship any samples I find for your appraisal.

I was delayed in finding a guide. Most will not set foot in the Huachucas for fear of the Apache, but I have finally secured the assistance of a
local hunter named Neb Bukes. He tells me that "Huachuca" is Apachean
for "Thunder". We are to set out on the 28th.

This will be my last posted letter until my return.

Deferentially,
Calvin J. Pabodie

They hunched in a low tent in the dark desert, Pabodie and the old hunter, Neb, with a hissing lantern between them. It was raining every way but up. Outside, the pack mules shook their bristled manes and bowed their necks beneath the slanting silver drops.

Pabodie had his sketchpad on his knee. He was finishing up a drawing of a rattlesnake they'd seen curled on a rock along the trail earlier that day, aptly coaxing out the beaded patterns on its back with a stub of charcoal pinched between his blackened fingers, while the one-eyed hunter chewed jerky and sipped something hard smelling from a dented tin cup. Pabodie paused in stroking the narrow iris of the reptile to consider his companion, and caught him staring back with his one blue eye. The other had been lost in some long ago adventure. Its gaping socket was neither patched nor bandaged. Although the tenant eye was gone, the sagging lid still twitched and moved like a dutiful but deranged watchman keeping guard over a long dead charge.

"Pretty pitcher," Neb offered.

"Thank you," said Pabodie.

"So," said the older man, blowing out his gaunt cheeks and flecking his rusty beard with dried meat. "Lemme take a gander at this bone you're all fired up about."

Pabodie flipped his sketchbook shut and carefully lifted the fossil from his knapsack. It was only four or five inches long, but holding it made him catch his breath. With his fingers he was reaching back through the eons, touching a creature that had cast its shadow across a younger, wilder world. It was a world he had dreamed of seeing, ever since he was a small boy lying on his belly, staring at the strange creatures living and dying in the shallow tidal pools of his native Kingsport.

Old Neb wasn't nearly as taken with it.

He took the fossil in his hands and held it to the light, squinting at it like a man considering purchasing a lump of excrement from a swindler who swore it was priceless.

"*This* little thing?"

"Yes," said Pabodie irritably, as if one of his own children were being maligned. "Please be careful."

Neb screwed up his face, uncomprehending.

"What exactly am I lookin' at?"

"It's a fragment from the lower skeleton of a *pteranodon*."

"A *what?*"

"A huge prehistoric flying creature."

"Hell, Mr. Pabodie," Neb said, passing the fossil back (it swiftly disappeared into its swaddling in the cushioned depths of Pabodie's knapsack), "that thing's older'n I am. I figured it was fresh bones you was out after."

"Well," Pabodie said, allowing himself a snicker, "we'd be hard pressed to find fresh bones. I'm afraid this species died almost eighty million years ago."

"Naw," Neb said, waving his weathered hand and sipping his potion. "I seen one, couple 'o months back."

Pabodie smiled slowly.

"I hardly think..."

"I *said* I seen one," Neb said, plainly challenging him to doubt again.

Pabodie shook his head, but said nothing.

Neb set aside his cup and took out his tobacco and makings.

"Dan Spector down at the Moderado promised me fifty dollars gold if I could catch him a live bear for a bear garden he wanted to build out back of his place, on account of the Thursday night cockfights over at the Mexicans' down the street was cuttin' into his business. I'd heard tell of black bears high up in the Huachucas where the conifers grow, so I got me a cage and a string of goats. Spent a couple weeks up there till I got one."

Neb finished rolling a cigarette and lit it. The match glow shined in the hollow of his eye socket, but did not penetrate its depths. Pabodie's attention was drawn to it. It was like peering into the end of a gun. The wide black iris of his intact eye hardly looked any different. Pabodie knew then that he was sharing his fortunes with a madman, for this was no greening session; what the hunter told next, he sincerely believed.

"I'm hitchin' the bear cage up to my mules, when of a sudden, this big shadow comes up in front of the sun, cools everything down. Even the bear looks up. And the noise! Sounded like a hunnerd widows screamin' all at once in the belly of a lion."

He planted the cigarette in the corner of his lips and held out his arms for emphasis.

"Swooped down and picked up that bear, cage and all, just about ripped my mules out of their traces." He pantomimed a rifle shooting.

"I cut loose on it with old Mazeppa, but it took a high grain load like a buffalo cow takes note of a mosquito's peter. Flew way up, off over the mountains."

He threw up his hands and blew smoke.

"Cost me my gold and the price of the cage. Had to sell off my mules. Been lookin' for a way to get back up there and go after it. Then along you came, all providential like. What I figured was, it was a thunderbird like the 'Paches talk about. You call it a terra-whatsit, whatever you want, but," he shrugged, "same thing. You're welcome to all the bones we can carry back, Mister Pabodie. I want somethin' else..."

Pabodie's smirk had spread wider throughout the story. Neb presently noticed it and frowned deeply beneath his bushy mustache.

"You still disbelieve me."

"Well...," said Pabodie, not wanting to give offense and thinking swiftly of a placation. "What you saw was most likely some sort of condor. For instance, the California gymnogyps has a thirteen foot wingspan..."

"Its wings stretched fifty feet if they were an inch. You think I'm talkin' about some goddamned *buzzard*?" he exclaimed, the whiskey on his breath beating upon Pabodie like heat from an open furnace. "I ain't touched in the head, though by that smarmy goddamned look, you think so. Dan Spector gimme that look too. Him and all them goddamned drunkards in the Moderado, when I told 'em what happened. I been huntin' up and down this land for goin' on twenty years, Mister Pabodie. If I say I seen a goddamned thunderbird, who in the hell are you to..."

Neb's tirade was cut short by the sound of thunder like the reverberant crashing of a gargantuan washtub tumbling across the sky. Outside, Pabodie's horse and the mules screamed.

"They're afraid of the thunder?" Pabodie asked anxiously as Neb drew up his rifle case from the corner of the tent.

Neb threw open the case and bought out the big Sharps rifle he affectionately called Mazeppa.

"They're afraid of *somethin'*."

He pushed a long bullet into the breech of his rifle as lightning turned the tent walls blue. Another avalanche of thunder exploded over the empty land.

The rain jarringly ceased its incessant pattering on the canvas, as if someone had dammed up the flow in heaven. The animals outside whinnied their anxiety. One of the cries abruptly altered in pitch and rose above the rest. It was one of the mules, braying like Pabodie had never heard an animal do before. It was a prolonged, harsh sound, as of a woman being murdered slowly.

"One side!" shouted Neb.

He pushed past Pabodie and threw back the tent flap. The sounds of the screaming animals and the blowing storm filled their ears.

Pabodie stared as Neb jammed his battered hat on his head and went out into the silver flecked darkness. The lantern threw a shaft of light on the bucking animals. Pabodie's horse and the remaining pack mule strained against their tethers on the tall saguaro cactus to which they'd been tied, tripping in their hobbles to get away.

Of the second mule, there was no sign. Then Pabodie narrowed his bespectacled eyes and perceived the missing mule's braided tether still fastened around the trunk of the saguaro, pulled taut under its curved arms, trailing mysteriously into the dark sky like a Hindu rope trick.

The wind was tremendous, threatening to buckle their shelter. The rain was still driving all around. Yet it did not strike their tent, or the horses, or the ground encompassing their small camp, as if a great umbrella hung overhead.

Then there was a second tremulous flicker of lightning. The camp lit up like a photographer's studio.

Pabodie caught a glimpse of a massive shape suspended overhead, a huge, black shadow whose bulk shielded them from the rain like a tarpaulin. For a minute Pabodie thought that was just what it was—a large revival tent canvas uprooted by the tempest, hovering overhead by some unlikely trick of the converging winds. Dangling from the middle of the gigantic shadow was the missing pack mule, bugging out its eyes in terror.

Something clutched it by the spine. It hung limp as a kitten in its mother's mouth.

Even as the sky went dark again, Pabodie knew what it was. The Kingsport boy in him who had waded hip deep into the churning ocean imagining legendary beasts and cities beneath the waves with all the desperate faith of one born out of time let out an exultant scream that rang in his book and data scarred brain. Though that mature part of him that had attended two universities and sobered through the years as a teetotaler of wonder curled up in fear and bewilderment, the wide eyed boy in him gripped what he all too briefly beheld above the camp in both hands and guzzled the sight until drunk. This was something neither Marsh, nor Cope, nor any stodgy old ditch digging professor had ever seen. This was his alone.

It was without a doubt a *living pteranodon*, beating the rainy air with its tremendous wings, struggling to carry off the mule.

Pabodie crawled from the tent like a supplicant, heedless of the mud soaking his knees and hands, not daring to stand, desperate only to feel the wind of its wings, or to smell its breath and know it was real.

"I told you!" yelled the old man, whooping above the storm, his wild, red hair a ragged curtain across his ghost eye.

Neb primed his rifle as a new sound rose above it all. It was like the raw scream of an eagle many times amplified. The creature's call sent the animals into new frenzies. The lightning came again.

Pabodie pressed his spotted glasses to his eyes for fear they would slip from his face. He saw the long scissor bill and the gigantic, black, avian eyes. He treasured the glimpse of its curling, hooked talons sunk deep in the flanks of the kicking mule. As it shifted its grip, dark blood showered down on the other animals in random gouts between its tremendous knuckles. The lightning shone through its membranous wings. It sounded again, drowning his ears in noise. The cactus bent double as the creature beat its wings and tried again to pull away with its burden.

As the lightning flickered and died, Neb angled Mazeppa upward, dropped his cheek and fired. The captured mule disappeared in a fireball and a sound like an explosion of cannonade. The bullet had struck the pack containing the dynamite sticks.

Pabodie saw the color of the thing in the resulting flash. He saw the woody flesh curl and blacken. He saw the tan membrane of the bat-like wings; glowing like lampshades as they were engulfed in flame.

The creature gave a piercing cry. Pabodie saw Neb fly past him. The old man tumbled into the collapsing tent. Then something heavy as a cannonball slammed into Pabodie's skull and he fell face forward.

As his eyelids fluttered and stinging blood poured across his eyes, Pabodie's last sight was of a bright missile arcing into the vast, dark, rainy sky, trailing cinders and blue smoke like a rocket. The screaming of the *pteranodon* diminished and with it, so fled Pabodie's consciousness.

He was awakened by the back of Neb's hand cracking sharply against his cheek.

"Wake up, Mister Pabodie!"

He was pulled roughly up by his lapels to sit in the mud. All around him the storm was still raging. He was bitter cold.

"What the hell was in them packs?" Neb demanded to know.

"Dynamite," Pabodie answered. "In case we needed to blast."

"You damn fool! You should've told me!" Neb lifted him to his feet. "Help me get the tent back up!"

Pabodie wavered on unsteady legs and gingerly touched his forehead, feeling with his fingertips a perforation that had been washed clean by the rain.

"Something struck me."

"Mule's foot," Neb cackled, thrusting the tent pole into his hands and gesturing to an object lying nearby.

It was the foreleg of the mule, its severed end shredded, one splintered black bone jutting out.

"Lucky it didn't kick a window through your skull," Neb said. "Come on!"

It was hard work rebuilding the tent in the storm, and not much comfort when it was finished. They were already soaked to their skin.

The blast had killed the animals. They lay half-cooked where they'd fallen. A burnt fragment of the obliterated pack mule's tether danced where it hung from one broken arm of the ruined saguaro.

Neb managed to start a small fire, letting the smoke out through a hole he cut in the canvas with his big knife. They warmed themselves as best they could, Pabodie trembling with chill and excitement.

"I can hardly believe it," he stammered. "I mean, I've *seen* it, but I can hardly believe it."

"Well, if seein's believin' you're gonna be a whole lot more convinced tomorrow," Neb said. "We're gonna hike up into them mountains and find its carcass come first light."

"Oh, of course," Pabodie readily agreed. "Of course, we must! We must preserve what remains we can and port them back to town."

He thought briefly of provisions and water... did they have enough to trek up into the mountains and return? Could they salvage anything from the animals' packs? All these concerns fled in the face of his excitement.

The creature they had seen dwarfed the *longiceps* Marsh had discovered in Kansas. This was no dusty pit of calcified bones, but a fresh, cooling carcass they were after. It would be worth any risk. Would they find it before scavengers tore it to shreds? Did they have to wait until dawn?

"This is a discovery of the utmost importance," he managed, furiously wiping the spots from his glasses with a handkerchief. "There's... there's never been anything like it before..."

"Like I was sayin' before, you can pick your bones and whatever else you wanna box up and ship back east," Neb said. "I'll take you up there. Money don't matter so much, but you got to promise me one thing, Mister Pabodie. You got to let me have the heart."

Pabodie stared, his giddy, jumbled thoughts suddenly halted in their racing.

"What did you say?"

"I want its heart, if it ain't been blowed to mince by your Swedish blasting powder or gobbled up by some cussed varmint."

"Well... but why, on earth?"

The rain lessened outside. Neb listened for a bit before he sighed and answered.

"Mr. Pabodie, I been a hunter a long time. I hunted everything that ever walked, crawled, swam or flew. Men, even," he said, fastening a meaningful look on Pabodie. "They's a tradition 'mongst true hunters. You ask any Injin worth his blood and he'll tell you the same. Eat the heart of what you kill, and you add its strength to your own. It's true."

Pabodie said nothing. Neb stared across the little fire into his eyes for a long time.

"How old d'you think I am?"

Pabodie opened his mouth to answer, but Neb spoke, shaking his head.

"Never mind. You kin never guess. I got me the power of a million hunts. A million kills. I may look decrepit, but I'm twenty times stronger'n a yearling catamount. I got the spirits of fightin' bulls and killer eagles runnin' all through me. I kin twist off a bear's head with my own two hands," and he splayed and curled his knobby fingers over the fire. The flames seemed to retreat from him warily. "I kin run quicker'n a pint 'o whiskey through forty Irishmen, from dusk till the new day dawnin'. I been and done most everything in this world, and now I've given myself over to this; I want the thunderbird's heart, Mr. Pabodie... I believe it'll make me fly."

Pabodie could say nothing to that. He promised the old lunatic the creature's heart (what a feast that would be for a single man!) and prayed he would make it to the morning without feeling his whiskey breath in the night.

"Don't worry, Mister Pabodie," Neb said as they finally lay down across from each other. "I don't believe I'd gain a thing from eatin' you."

He laughed to himself and was snoring inside a minute.

Pabodie lay on his back and in a few hours, watched the canvas lighten.

At dawn they began their walk across the basin to the western foothills, packing only essentials. There was very little food, but their canteens had survived. Neb shouldered his Mazeppa. As Pabodie still fretted over the wild Apache of the country, he didn't object to adding the old man's lead and powder to his own portage.

The torrential downpour of the previous night had died somewhere before dawn. It was a harsh and vengeful sun that returned to wield its full ire against the rain washed desert like a raging cuckold against his wayward wife. The earth dried and cracked beneath their boots. It was as if the storm had never been.

At noon they clambered up the broken slopes, ascending the mountains via twisting trails that hardly deserved the name. These were empty gullies and furrows whose deceptive footholds often proved nothing more than shifting shale.

They said little. Neb only answered Pabodie's infrequent questions about their direction with a curse against the gall of all easterners and an assurance that he had marked the *pteranodon's* impact the night before.

When they turned a stone rise, Pabodie momentarily wondered if there was in fact some truth to Neb's mad bragging. Perhaps the old man might not have eaten the heart of an eagle and gained its uncanny sight. The huge carcass lay stretched out on its back before them. It was like the burned out ruin of a grand cathedral, all jutting angles and broken limbs like toppled spires.

Four coyotes scattered at their approach, emerging from the wounds laid open in the colossal torso. Its coiling innards were strewn about the stones, shriveled in a baste of drying blood, its thin tongue lolling half out of the canoe-like shell of its tapered bill.

Pabodie noticed the long maw was tooth-lined like that of the *pterodactyl* of Austria, not like Marsh's *longiceps* at all. The great eyes had been picked at. They looked like broken boulders of polished agate, their glistening surface besmirched with crusted blood.

Hordes of ants swirled at their feet in endless conveyance. A burst of winged insects of every sort lifted from the carcass as Neb anxiously laid aside Mazeppa and waded in the spilled and stinking guts of the thing up to his hips, pushing aside huge, jellied organs with his bare hands and making for its open chest cavity with lustful alacrity.

Pabodie leaned back against an up thrust boulder, took out his charcoal and hastily began to sketch the scene. He imagined himself standing before the College with... what? This drawing? What other proof could he bring them? Surely he could figure out how to bear some piece of the creature down to Delirium Tremens, something suitable for shipping back to Yale. Pabodie would single-handedly render the previous twenty years of paleontology practically obsolete with this discovery. To hell with Marsh and Cope and their silly bones, placing heads on the asses of dinosaurs and sabotaging each other's measly field digs.

How had this animal come to survive here? What was its food source? How did it live? How had it escaped discovery for so long? Well, that probably wasn't hard to surmise. The various Indian tribes of the region had spoken of creatures such as these in their pictographic and oral histories. The white man had never regarded them as anything other than folkloric traditions passed down from an earlier epoch. Who could have known these things actually existed in the modern world? What other animals thought long extinct might exist in some other desolate pocket of the world? The welcome onrush of forgotten possibilities thrilled him to his core.

"It's gone, goddammit!"

Pabodie had nearly forgotten his guide. Neb emerged from the depths of the creature like a wild man from a cave.

He was smeared from the crown of his hat to the heels of his boots in blood. Sinew and gore hung in chords from his shoulders. He shook off dribbling strands of it like a wet dog and scowled.

He reclaimed his rifle and bags. Then without a word or a look at Pabodie, he began to trek higher up the mountain.'

"Wait!" Pabodie called. He couldn't carry any sizable piece of the creature back to town on his own, and he certainly couldn't treat a hunk of its flesh for the journey without the hunter's expertise. His own skill lay in the preservation of dusty relics, not biological tissue. "Where are you going? We've got to save these remains!"

Neb kept walking.

"You've got to help me," Pabodie nearly screamed. "This is the find of the century, for God's sake! We can't just leave it!"

The old man paused on the incline and pointed to the dead animal with his rifle.

"The heart's been blowed to bits. It ain't worth nothin' to me."

"Now hang on just a minute!" Pabodie shouted. "I hired you! You work for me! Now you get back down here and help me carry some part of this back to town."

He observed the bloody old hunter's disapproving countenance and decided immediately to try a different approach.

"Look... you said nobody in town believed you when you told them about the thunderbird. Well, here's your proof right here. Now everybody down there will know you weren't lying."

"You think I care a whit about them jackasses?" Neb muttered. "Look here, boss. That buzzard's a female. Could be she's got a nest higher up she was tryin' to get back to. Nest means maybe eggs. Persevere a little with me. Might be you could get your hands on a nipper thunderbird to take back east. How'd that suit you and your professors?"

"Well," said Pabodie, looking reluctantly at the dead hulk drawing flies and putting his sketchbook in his coat pocket. "I guess that'd suit me fine."

Higher they went, following a trail only Neb could see. Just a scored white bone of a cow miles above the valley floor, or the tip of a broken conifer. Their food ran out on the third day. Neb assured

Pabodie there would be something to eat further on. He speculated just one of the eggs could probably feed a *jacal* full of Mexicans. They would save one for the road back.

Pabodie felt uneasy when they talked of it, and changed the subject. He remembered the casual way the old man had mentioned hunting men. The comment took on new meaning for him the tighter their bellies got.

The sun was cantankerous during the day. The old man stank, for he had not cleaned the guts from himself, and he'd been far from a rose before that. But it seemed the coat of dried slime protected his skin, whereas Pabodie's arms reddened and boiled into white headed blains that seared when his sleeves brushed against them.

They climbed forever, till the valley was a wispy dream half forgotten, and the San Pedro River nothing more than a thin dark slash bisecting an imaginary country.

The world lessened to needle points of hot stone now. They came to a place where the rocks were slick with viscid caps of white and black dung like curdled milk.

"There it is!" Neb declared, pointing to a natural pillar of sheer stone that pointed accusatorially at the blue sky.

It must have been forty feet up from where they stood, but capping the distant tip was a bulky, dark corona not unlike a desert bird's bramble nest, fashioned from twisted trees and God knew what else.

"It's too high," Pabodie said for the umpteenth time. "I can't go any further." He was past spent. In the course of his education he had certainly done his fair share of hiking in remote places, but this was the most arduous thing he had ever attempted in his life. He was sure he had reached his tolerance, fortune be damned.

Neb was not convinced. He angled the long barrel of his rifle nonchalantly towards him. "Oh, I believe you could, *boss*," he said.

Pabodie had thought the ascent up the mountain a trial, but it was nothing next to this lone climb, nails peeling back as he thrust his fingers into minute crevices and hung for panicked instants, swinging over a plunging death while his feet scrambled to find purchase. He didn't dare to look down at the rocky ground far below nor at the endless blue sky above for fear he would somehow fall into either one. He only pressed his face to the sun warm rock and confined his attentions to the next handhold, until a thick dry branch of long dead conifer brushed against the top of his head like a skeletal hand and sent his hat spiraling slowly down to Neb's feet.

Neb, who had shouted no encouragements, now turned his stained face to the sun and grinned.

"You're there, boss!"

Pabodie whimpered as he tested the overhanging branches of the nest with sore, bleeding fingers, and found them sturdy. He swung his weight onto them and slowly crawled up, finally wedging the toes of his boots into the knots of brambles. From there it was a relatively easy operation maneuvering up the latticework of interconnected branches and pulling himself over the edge to flop down gratefully into the deep, shaded center.

He tore his clothes tumbling down the side of the nest wall. His landing was not soft, as he had expected. A vast rick of bones lined the floor, which crackled and snapped and bit into him when he landed.

He felt a sharp sensation in his thigh and cried out.

"What's the matter?" Neb's booming voice called from below.

Pabodie lay on his side gasping. The pain did not abate, and totaled with all his labors of the day he resolved to rest here whether he could somehow manage the descent or no.

He shifted his weight and placed his back to the wall of the nest, feeling his pain double as he moved the offended leg. A splinter of foreign bone protruded from the side of his thigh. A sizable amount of blood was spreading down his pant leg.

"I've got a bone in my leg!" he shouted in answer to the old man, his voice cracking.

"What?"

"There's a bone stuck in my leg!" Shriller, he confirmed, "I'm bleeding!"

"Don't get hysterical!" the old man shouted, and Pabodie actually laughed to himself. "Tear off a piece of your shirt, pull it out, and tie it up tight!"

His shirt was in rags. Tearing it was no problem. But as he set to do so, he glanced about his surroundings, and his giddiness once more overtook him.

The bed of bones was of every shape and composition. Some scraps of flesh left to rot on the bleached bones gave him clues as to their origin. The mostly decomposed head of a buffalo bull regarded him from a corner, the hollow eye sockets reminding him of Neb.

His paleontologist's eye recognized specific bones; there were avian carpal joints in abundance, a pile of castoff pedicles from what looked to be a horse, and the jaw of a large cave bear. The remains were not solely animal. Necklaces and bijouterie of bright turquoise and scraps of crafted leather marked the skeletons of hapless Indians who had been taken away by the creature. Their attitudes suggested nothing of their deaths; they were scattered haphazardly about, mingled with their animal neighbors.

There were more remains than could be attributed to a single creature or its family. Pabodie suspected this was a kind of ancestral home which had seen more than one generation of the giant *pteranodon*.

He caught his breath. What bones might lie beneath this top layer? The nearly intact frameworks of ancient creatures and peoples and their crude implements filled this space, no doubt. Here was the treasure trove Marsh and Cope had waged a frantic war across the country to discover. Here was a bone picker's white El Dorado.

But these were the dreams of, in his mind, lesser men. He spotted what he'd come for. In the middle of the nest of deep black and blinding white, arrayed like pearls in the shade of the walls, a clutch of a half dozen speckled yellow eggs, each the size of a prize pumpkin.

His pain forgotten, he limped and stumbled across the bones to fall to one knee. He reached out and reverently touched one of the eggs with his hands, feeling the warm, smooth surface, thick as plaster.

He caressed it, as though his tactile gestures summoned it fully into being. To his delight, the egg responded with a slight shudder which he could feel in the webbing between his fingers, like an explosion far below ground. *Life!*

"Mister Pabodie!" called Neb.

But Pabodie was elsewhere. He was a boy pricking his fingertips on the spines of a sea urchin, full of wonder at the scope of creation and swept away by the notion of life so unlike his own.

He could almost feel the cool ocean air again.

And the air *was* cool. A shadow had fallen across the face of the hot sun.

Pabodie turned and looked up, thinking he would see a lingering storm cloud. What he saw caused the floor of his stomach to bottom out.

For a moment it was limned in fire, a demon wing intercepting the light of day. Pabodie knew what a mouse must feel as the fast shadow of a hawk falls across it—a curious euphoria, as if the suspension of the sun's murderous heat was a final gift from predator to prey to ease the coming terror and violence—a gust of refreshing coolness like an anesthetic preceding the sting of death.

It was the mate of the one they'd killed. A male. It was larger, and its cry broke the stillness and made his calf muscles lock. The father had spied a rat among its brood and was coming to remove the skulking pest.

Pabodie half turned, but where was there to go? The sharp shadow swept towards him... and was checked by a tremendous crash that sounded from down below and blew a decent sized hole in the creature's left wing.

It was Neb and his Mazeppa. She had blown the enraged father a kiss. Pabodie was spattered in its blood, but the diving *pteranodon* tilted and passed over the nest with a wind that made him stagger against the eggs.

Pabodie rushed to the wall, finding a hole in the branches. He peered down at Neb, who had mounted a high rock (not so high as the nest rock, but enough of a vantage to give him a clear shot with Mazeppa). He realized then that the canny hunter had suspected the existence of the bull all along, and had used him to bait it out. Though he burned momentarily at the old man's treachery, it didn't matter. They would both die now.

The big Sharps was smoking. There would be no time to prime a second shot. The male was arcing back and had spotted its inflictor. Another cry and it plunged towards him.

Neb flung aside his hat and the rifle, and when next his hands appeared, the big blade of his Bowie knife winked in the sun.

"Come on, you son of a bitch!" he screamed, and he uttered a bellow more animal than man, which the diving *pteranodon* answered in kind.

Neb did not shrink from that terrible attack, but bent his knees and sprung towards it, still yelling, leaping clear of the rock to meet it in a feat of agility that again made Pabodie question the nature and veracity of all the hunter's bizarre claims.

The spring took him nearly nine feet vertically. The colossal head of the bull darted with surprising speed, and its monstrous bill neatly transfixed the old man's body through the torso. Pabodie's last sight of Neb was of him clinging to the pteranodon's bill, one boot heel crammed in its nose hole, dragging himself like a determined Arthur up the length of the beak, stabbing the knife down again and again in a dying rage, as blood gushed from his roaring mouth.

This frenzied counterattack had confused the thunderbird; it bore its burden skyward, wheeled about, and flapped off to the south, screaming and turning and shaking its head, trying to dislodge the stinging pest.

Pabodie watched the winged horror become a black "W" in the distance, then wheel out of sight around the side of the mountain.

Neb had bought him time, but he knew it would be back. He could still survive if he could shinny down before it returned. He could scurry down the mountains, keeping close to the gullies and ditches and staying out of sight. He would go like a rat where the thing couldn't reach him. If only his punctured leg would support him.

He had no time to treat it now. Once he was relatively safe, he would turn attentions to it. For now he hastily spilled his effects from his knapsack. The trifle of a tarsal fragment fossil to which he had attached such foolish importance only days earlier tumbled out, becoming indistinguishable from the other bones. It was nothing now. He had to make room for the more precious cargo.

The egg.

He would take at least one of them. Bear it on his back down the mountain, back to town, back to Connecticut, back to Yale. Probably it would die on the journey, but it was still a treasure to risk bearing. It would surely warrant a further investigation by the Survey. He would be the appointed head of the expedition. It meant a meteoric career and early retirement. Books, and lectures around the world, a large, quiet home off campus—maybe overlooking the ocean back in Kingsport—and a generous pension for himself.

He'd be in the history texts, and who knew? Patents could follow. If he managed two eggs and lucked out with a male and a female, franchises. How many zoos would pay for live specimens for their collections? How many private citizens? What about possible military applications for these creatures? Why, they could provide an air borne cavalry if they could be brought to heel. He would change the face of everything if only he could make it back to town.

With the noise and spectacle of the thunderbird and Neb he had not heard the crackling behind him. Now he perceived the high pitched squeals and excited avian cries.

He turned, stupidly holding his empty knapsack as three of the black eyed, newly hatched *pteranodon*, who had instinctively redoubled their hatching efforts upon hearing the familiar cry of their father, poked out of their broken shells and regarded him. Smelling fresh blood so close, the squawking hatchlings swarmed him in a slicing confusion of sharp angles and slashing talons, scissor bills pecking wildly at his shocked face, easily punching through his spectacles to his succulent eyes. He fell shrieking and flailing, blind as they pounced upon him, claws tearing up his belly and thighs and ripping away his genitals. Naturally adept killers, they brought him down and fell to shredding him like a paper doll. His gargling, frantic screams echoed down the mountainside as their slim little tongues darted out to lap his blood.

By nightfall the wounded bull thunderbird returned, flying low, tired and scarred with a hard-won supper. The grim widower was puzzled when it found his hatchlings waging tug of war with the remains of an earlier repast.

SILVER WOLF
BY ANDREW KELLY

Big Jim had many dislikes, but only one thing he truly hated: Indians, the Menomonee tribe in particular, and an old renegade medicine man called Silver Wolf specifically. Nobody knew Wolf's true name; he was old, rumor said ancient, a medicine man, wolf-witch, skinwalker, shaman, wielder of dark Indian magic that could still make the red man dangerous. Rumor also had it that Wolf had once traveled dark paths with Misquamacus himself. All the nations feared and respected him; Big Jim hated him.

Wolf had led sporadic raids on white settlers; three years past he'd led a party that had attacked an isolated farm, slaughtering Jim's younger sister Hannah, her husband and five-year-old daughter. The army and bounty hunters always came up empty handed, most whispering that it was because of Wolf's "magic".

Big Jim lived on a small spread just outside of Progress with his woman, an ex-whore named Annabelle, and her eight-year-old bastard son Jake. Jim had been a wild one in his youth, but had settled comfortably into domestic life. Why, he even intended to marry Annabelle one of these years. Jim was happy with his life, until Hannah's murder. Since then he'd been filled with a fire sparked by the need for vengeance, to find and kill the old witch called Silver Wolf.

He followed leads and rumors, gossip and lies, tracing the renegade's movements, tracking old trails, always coming up short. With each failure his obsession and hatred grew. He persisted; his madness would not allow him to do otherwise, confident that sooner or later their paths would cross.

The old renegade was said to be traveling alone, which suited Big Jim just fine. He feared no Indian magic—he was a white man and

God was a white man—and he did not doubt that Silver Wolf was capable of every magic feat attributed to him, but his magic would not save him. Wolf was always on the run, always hunted, never daring to face Big Jim man to man. Jim had a reputation as well, one he had earned and kept: he was simply the biggest, baddest, meanest Indian hater there was, and when he died it would not be at the hands of a red man.

Jim remembered an incident that had happened the previous summer in the Red Peak district. He recalled a night that he'd sat at the fire, sipping coffee and stargazing. He'd seen a flash of silver eyes watching him from the forest. The eyes had slowly, cautiously moved toward him, revealing a huge gray wolf. It had sat and stared at him, mouth wide in a toothy, mocking grin, and Jim knew that he was looking into the eyes of Silver Wolf, the taunting witch challenging him. Much as he wanted to reach for his rifle he knew that it would be useless, that Silver Wolf would melt back into the forest before Jim could sight him in. Jim had pulled out his hunting knife and started toward the shaman. When Jim was only a few feet away and had raised the knife to meet Wolf's attack, the cowardly old witch had turned tail and disappeared into the dark forest.

Jim knew Wolf feared him; for all his magic Wolf was an old man, growing older and weaker, while Jim's hatred made him stronger. But the next day he could find no trace of Wolf, and the chase had ended the same as all the others had. The trail now cold, he headed back home, his lust for vengeance unappeased.

Desperate and frustrated, he did something that he hoped would never be necessary. Sympathizers and locals had kept him appraised of affairs on the reservation, and Big Jim found out that Silver Wolf had a twelve-year-old grandson living there. Jim camped out in the forest near the reservation, waiting and watching, scouting and planning.

One day the boy went hunting alone in the forest. When the boy did not reappear a party of braves searched the forest, and found what was left of him. What Jim had done to the boy was—by Indian belief —a monstrous sacrilege to the spirit.

Jim had left no evidence to accuse him, and none was needed. Word would get to Wolf, and Wolf would know who was responsible. No more chasing; if Wolf was the warrior he claimed to be, he would come to Jim.

But Wolf did not come to Jim. After a six month wait, Jim could wait no longer. Neighbors and army friends promised to keep an eye on Annabelle and Jake, so Jim rode hard that winter, looking for Wolf. Jim heard tell that he'd been given a nickname: Ahab. He had no idea what this meant, but he'd cave in the skull of anyone who said it to his face again.

Jim, in a foul mood, eventually gave up and headed home to Annabelle and Jake. He heard talk as he entered Progress, talk of Silver Wolf and Annabelle, and of an incident at Jim's place. He got the general details from the sheriff: Wolf, coward that he was, had waited for Jim to hit the trail, then had snuck out to Jim's ranch and had tried to kill Jake and Annabelle, but she'd got the jump on him and shot him dead. The army had claimed the body. Jim prodded his trail-weary horse into a gallop toward home. For the first time in a long time concern for his family came first.

That night over supper Annabelle told the tale. A week ago Jake came running into her room screaming that a red man had come in through his bedroom window. Annabelle had grabbed her rifle and ran to Jake's room; there in the moonlight stood Silver Wolf by the broken window, holding a knife out toward her, gesturing, moaning, trying to work dark magic against her. She shot him dead. He was old and weak and slow, had hesitated and died for it. Not a very impressive last raid for the legendary Silver Wolf.

Jim was unsettled by his first reaction to the story: hot rage and anger toward Annabelle. Wolf was meant to be *his* kill. Running himself ragged for years, Wolf had made a fool of him—in his own eyes, if not the eyes of others. Then Annabelle takes him out with a single shot inside his house.

The anger died quickly. He laughed heartily, grabbed her, pulled her into a rough embrace and kissed her. *His* woman had stopped the old witch. Annabelle reveled in her pride and Jim's approval, and she felt feelings for him that she hadn't felt in years.

It being a special occasion, Jim bathed that evening. Annabelle settled Jake into bed. She checked herself in her bedroom mirror, removed her garments, lay on the bed and waited for Jim.

Jim entered naked and wet from his bath, hard from the thought of her softness; it had been months since they'd lain together, and Annabelle was still a sight even after childbirth. She was ready for him. With a lusty growl he dropped on the bed and entered her before the mattress stopped bouncing. She wrapped her legs around his waist, dug her fingernails into his shoulders and squeezed him tight against her.

He looked into her eyes, wondering at the strange beauty of her dreamy smile and faraway look, directed not at him, but at something beyond him.

"He always enjoyed the chase, the sport of it," she breathed in his ear.

"No talk," he grunted. "Not now."

"But when you killed his blood, the game ended," she continued. "A child, Jim. Only a child."

He wondered how she could know about that. "How many children did *he* kill?" he snarled. "Annie, this isn't the time for this."

"So much power, more than any expected," she panted, thrusting her body up to meet his. "Not just to change form; his spirit can leave his body and claim another."

Her grip around him tightened. She locked her hands in the small of his back; her heels dug into his buttocks. He was pinned down in her embrace, arms at his sides, unable to move to gain leverage. Annabelle had always been a strong woman.

"He took Jake's body for his own and cast Jake's soul into his," she gasped. "How could Jake understand what was happening? He was reaching out to me for help, and I killed him! I am no longer of my own mind or thought, such is his power. His will is mine. His raids were indiscriminate, the hatred and killing general. This is personal."

He shrank inside her. He heard the door open behind him, and managed to turn his head enough to see Jake standing in the doorway, grinning, holding Silver Wolf's knife as if he knew how to use it—and intended to.

Big Jim bucked hard; Annabelle moaned and clung to him fiercely. "We both must die," she sobbed in his ear. "Such is the will of Silver Wolf."

Jake stepped closer; Big Jim looked into the boy's eyes and saw the eyes of another he recognized. He wanted to scream, but Annabelle smothered his lips with her own.

Silver Wolf was slow and skillful; Big Jim took a long time to die.

WHISPER
BY MARK ONSPAUGH

Johnny Ross was just telling Galen and Deke he'd sell his own mama for a drink of water when they came upon the first of the graves.

It was just after noon and the Nevada sun had bleached most of the color out of the day, leaving everything the look of burnished bronze. Their horses were dragging, and Galen knew they'd be walking soon if they didn't find water.

Deke, who couldn't summon up enough spit to swallow, kept thinking of the cold water he had splashed on his face just that morning. Hell, he'd like as not drink water from a stagnant pool or a filthy washtub at this moment.

The robbery had been a failure from the get-go, leaving their compadres Jack Mothershed and Bull Tanner bleeding out on the dusty boardwalk of Rusty Saw. The three of them had managed to kill the bank manager, a teller, two customers and the local sheriff for the princely sum of twenty dollars.

Johnny knew the others blamed him for the lean pickings at the bank. He had ventilated the manager, a scrawny little man with a grimy collar, before they had found the vault locked up tighter than a frog's ass. No one else knew the combination, something borne out by his ventilating one of the two tellers to get the other to own up.

They hadn't brought any dynamite; none of them had any experience with explosives. They'd probably blow themselves up before they did any real damage to the safe.

So they had ridden out of the town of Rusty Saw, a place far less colorful than its name. The three of them knew a posse would be looking for them, and that soon their likenesses would appear on posters all across the state.

Johnny wanted to head up into California, where the bustle of San Francisco would provide them with cover and many amusements. Galen had spat a thick glob of tobacco at his feet, the brown spatters matching the dried blood of Bull Tanner on Johnny's boots.

"How long you think we can hole up with twenty dollars, you pissant?"

"Long enough to find easier pickings, I reckon." Johnny Ross had answered.

Galen and Deke had looked at each other and shaken their heads. Johnny Ross hated when they did that, like they were so wise and he was just an ignorant sumbitch.

They were well into the graveyard before they noticed, because the markers on the outer graves had long fallen apart and were now covered with grit and scrub. Soon they were picking their way through dozens of markers, most made from rough planks scrawled with charcoal or carelessly carved with a pocket knife.

"This is about the sorriest sack of shit graveyard I've ever seen in my life," Johnny Ross muttered, and Galen had nodded solemnly. Deke had kept his mouth shut and his head still, lest he be thought of having some disrespect for the dead. They rode on, each hoping that the presence of a graveyard meant a settlement of the living, with food and water and maybe a whiskey before they went on their way.

The graveyard continued up a small hill. There were no flowers, not even mummified ones, and the scrub thinned out to nothing as they crested the hill.

There was a slight breeze on the hilltop, and they all felt it cool the rank sweat on their faces and necks. Johnny Ross kept hoping they'd find a horse trough. He'd jump into the damn thing clothes and all, even if it were green and redolent of pond scum.

Deke had nodded ahead as Galen spit, his missile desecrating the marker of someone named Cleve Hecklin.

About fifty feet in front of them was a clear spot roughly eighteen feet in diameter. In its center was a single grave, surrounded by a rusted iron fence. The fence showed great care and craftsmanship, its motif of twisting growths of vine and flowers culminating in a cherub in the center of the side visible to them. The cherub regarded them with wide and vacant eyes.

The headstone within the fence was large and made of marble, a slight pink and veined with purple and blue, like the limb of someone recently dead. Its shape seemed familiar to Galen, and he remembered reading accounts of Napoleon in Egypt. This marker was what they called an obelisk. It was a word he liked as a boy, but now it filled him with a vague sense of disquiet.

They dismounted and approached the iron fence, each curious about the strangeness and grandeur of the monument, which seemed more for the like of a king or a president than this sorry-ass boneyard.

The front of the obelisk had characters cut into it, carved with a quality of craftsmanship fitting its exotic and opulent nature.

The characters were like nothing they had ever seen. Even Galen, who had seen both Russian and Chinese in his travels, could not identify them. They seemed Oriental but had a cruder shape to them, missing many of the graceful swoops and curls of that other language. There was something in their starkness that made Galen uneasy.

"What do you reckon it says?" Johnny Ross asked in a whisper, his voice hoarse with thirst and possibly fear.

"Don't matter," Galen lied, "the occupant is dead like everyone else here, and of no use to us."

There was a moment then, when the world seemed to halt, and Galen felt a profound sense of vertigo. He grasped the wrought iron fence, which should have burned his hand, but felt as cool as stones in a mountain stream. It wasn't the feel of the metal that caused him alarm, however, but the sensation that he could hear something whispering nearby, something strange and needful.

Galen pulled his hands away from the fence and the whispering ceased.

He was about to tell the others they should ride like hell away from here when an old man rushed up from the far side of the hill, screaming at them in a full panic.

Before Galen could even process what he had said, both Deke and Johnny Ross had drawn their guns and shot the old man, three bullets bringing forth red blossoms on the billowing white shirt he wore.

The old man went down into the dust, his cries cut off with all the swiftness of a candle snuffed out by a quick breath.

Galen silently cursed the other two, vowing for the hundredth time that this was his last ride with them.

They turned the old man over, his wide staring eyes regarding them with pained surprise. His eyes were a deep blue, but quickly faded to the pink of an albino's. This caused Deke to cross himself, and Galen realized it was something he had never seen Deke do before, not in three years of hard riding, drinking and killing.

A stink rose from the dead man, but it was not the odor of loosed bowels. It was the stench of someone already several days dead. The pink eyes shriveled in their now cavernous sockets and fell away as the skin of the man began to constrict and expand, gas and rigor competing in some mad dance that was far too rapid for normal death and decay.

Both Galen and Deke stepped away from the body, Galen with the irrational fear that the body would balloon and explode into a mass of blood-red spiders, a nightmare he had had as a child.

"Something in here!" Johnny Ross called, and they turned to see him inside the fence of the grave. He was like a jaybird, Galen thought, easily distracted from the dead man by something new and shiny.

This turned out to be a more apt metaphor than he suspected, because Johnny Ross had caught a glimpse of silver under the sandy soil of the grave.

Galen wanted to tell the younger man to get out, that despoiling that grave might be the worst thing he could ever do, but his dried throat and morbid curiosity kept him silent, wondering just what mysteries the pink obelisk guarded.

Johnny Ross bent down and brushed the dirt away from the object hidden in the center of the grave. By the time he was finished, he had uncovered a silver object about twice the size of a large serving platter.

It's a shield, thought Galen, something belonging to a warlord.

Johnny Ross looked up at them, the unruly shock of blond hair that always hung in his eyes now damp with sweat.

"Look at it, boys," he crowed, "must be near a hundred pounds of silver!"

Galen knew it was nowhere near that much, perhaps twenty pounds or so, depending on its thickness. But what bothered him more than its presence in the grave was the fact that it showed no signs of tarnishing.

How is that possible, he wondered.

Johnny Ross started prying, trying to lift the thing from its resting place.

"Don't!" Deke cried out, all his fears of haints and hoodoos and God's own swift and brutal justice for the wicked and the unrighteous wrapped in that single word.

Johnny Ross just laughed and smoothed away some more dust, trying to determine what held his prize fast to the mysterious grave.

The shield was held in place by a grid of silver wires radiating out from the shield to the fence where they were tied to each upright of the wrought iron structure. Then someone had woven in concentric circles of silver connecting each strand.

The result was an enormous cobweb of silver wire, with the shield in the center.

But is the shield the spider or the fly, wondered Galen.

"You come out of there now, Johnny Ross," pleaded Deke, who had seen much more than he wanted to.

"You scared, big man?" Johnny Ross laughed, his youth and easy good looks giving him the bravado of so many of his age.

Deke looked at Galen, who decided this had gone far enough.

"Leave it be, Johnny Ross," Galen said, and his voice was little more than a whisper. Still, Johnny Ross made no jokes about Galen.

"This is worth more than most of the banks in the territory," Johnny Ross complained.

"Boy, only a fool would mess with something so tangled up with witchcraft and Lord knows what else."

"I thought you didn't believe in them things," Johnny Ross said.

"True enough, but a man who did died here, and that lends a certain weight to dark matters, if you catch my drift."

Johnny Ross looked at Galen blankly. It was almost as if he had forgotten that he and Deke had killed a man not ten minutes before.

Galen looked at the dead man, and was terrified but not surprised to see a collection of bones lying in the simple garments.

He just turned to dust while our backs were turned, thought Galen. How is that even possible?

"You come out of there now, Johnny Ross, or I will make sure you spend the rest of your days aching from a shattered knee cap."

Johnny Ross just laughed at this, and Galen knew he had overplayed his hand. The boy was his nephew, after all, and he could no more shoot him than he would his own sister. Blood was blood, a philosophy that caused more pain than it eased, he was sure.

There was a loud twang, like the breaking of a guitar string, and Galen saw that Johnny Ross had pulled his Bowie knife and begun cutting the shield free, each note like a plucked string on a devil's harp of bone and sinew.

The damage was done now, Galen knew, and still he and Deke just watched the boy, damning his bravado but envying it as well. Had they ever been this cocksure? Of course they had, and had lived to tell about it. God willing, Johnny Ross would, too.

The last of the sorrowful notes disturbed the stillness, then the boy tilted the shield up to face them. Now Galen could see Celtic knot-work around its border, a pattern he had seen in his Granddad's house. The old man had come over from Cork and had driven him crazy with tales of the old country. It was only when he was older that he had wished the old man was still around, because there had been magic and wonder in those tales he had been too callous to listen to.

In the center of the shield was the head of a great stag, and a working of flowers and leaves through its antlers.

Johnny Ross grinned at them, and then his gun was out and firing. A harsh bark from the pistol and Deke fell to the dust, his face full of dull surprise.

Galen turned on Johnny Ross in shock.

"What have you done?" Galen started to ask, and then felt the first of two bullets tear into his shoulder. The second hit him low in the gut and he was falling back into the hot, gritty dirt.

"Mine," Johnny Ross hissed. "Y'all thought you was better 'n' me, and now guess what? You're the ones who're gonna rot while I'm in San Francisco living like a king."

Johnny Ross hefted the silver shield over the iron fence and was fixing to vault it when something exploded up out of the grave in a hail of sand and rotted wood.

Johnny Ross had a sense of something in long, dark rags, something as swift and silent as sweat running down a man's back. It made for the old man they had recently killed.

Johnny Ross vaulted the fence, tearing a gash in his leg on one of the wrought iron spikes. Whereas before the fence had been as cool as morning grass, now it burned to the touch, and left his palms blistered.

He knew that, whatever had left the grave, it would not be done in by bullets. His only hope was to outrun the thing. Perhaps he could hide in the house until it went away.

Johnny Ross grunted as he lifted the shield, still trailing tendrils of wire like an immense silver jellyfish. Galen had been wrong, the thing weighed a good thirty pounds, enough to provide him with luxury over several lifetimes. He gripped it and began moving toward the house, giving the haint a wide berth.

There was a burning sting in his right hand, his gun hand, and he dropped the shield, thinking a scorpion or snake had bit him.

Galen lie nearby, smoking gun in hand. Not only was he not dead, the bastard had shot him! Johnny Ross tried to make his useless hand work for him.

It would not.

Another slug tore into the sand near his feet, raising a small puff of dust and grit that actually stung his fingers.

Johnny Ross stole a look at the haint, and saw with horror that it was turning his way. He struggled to pick up the shield but it was too heavy for one hand. With a terrified grunt he ran for his horse, hoping he could come back for his prize later.

The haint shrieked behind him, and Johnny Ross rode away, not daring to look back.

The creature made for Galen, but Galen had flung himself on the shield and gripped it tight, sensing it was some form of protection from the grave-thing.

It shrieked at him, its cavernous eyes filled with dozens of black motes like flies, its too-large mouth filled with broken and rotted teeth. The stench off it was so horrible it actually made Galen's gorge rise. He held his ground, though the wound in his shoulder was burning.

The creature suddenly turned and went for Deke. It picked up the dead man, and he flopped like a rag doll in its grip. Wailing, the thing dropped Deke to the ground and tore off into the badlands after Johnny Ross.

When he was sure it was gone, Galen put the shield aside and looked over his wounds.

Johnny Ross's first bullet had pierced his shoulder near the outer edge of the muscle. Galen felt the wound gingerly and determined that the bullet had gone clean through. He'd heal but had to get something to stave off infection.

The second bullet had struck him in the belt buckle, mangling the stout metal but leaving him only bruised. An inch up or down and he would either have a slug in his guts or be signing up as a soprano in the church choir.

Galen struggled to his feet and whistled for his horse. The big bay nickered softly and came to him. He tied the shield to his saddle, winding strands of wire to his saddle horn, and the animal bore the weight easily. Galen didn't feel strong enough to mount the animal, so he walked it away from the graveyard and up to the house.

The house had once been quite grand, a gothic affair with a wrap-around porch and a cross-gabled roof studded with lightning rods. Although the house must have been painted at one time, years of sun and sand had scrubbed it clean of its color, leaving wood the color of storm clouds.

There was a pump and trough in the dooryard, and Galen steered the horse to it eagerly. The trough had been empty a long time, its bottom filled with grit and the desiccated corpse of a scrub jay. Galen fished out the body of the bird and tossed it aside, then began to work the pump. It squealed at first, and he wished for some lubricating oil, but soon the action became smoother.

"I hope the goddamn well isn't dry," he thought, then realized that wasn't a prayer that the Lord would take kindly to. He kept pumping.

There was a throaty gurgling, then water gushed from the spout. Brown at first, it quickly cleared and pooled in the bottom of the trough. Galen got himself a couple of handfuls and then let the horse drink. He kept pumping, taking the time to fill the water-skin on his saddle. He wanted to be ready to leave in a hurry.

The front door was open; the old man had been in too much of a hurry to lock it. He must have seen them from an upstairs window and tried to prevent them from tampering with the grave.

Damn Johnny Ross.

Galen was about to call out but realized the house must be empty. Anyone who cared for the old man would have either cried out or taken a shot at them.

Cried out. Like the creature had done.

Galen didn't want to be far from the shield's protection but felt himself on the edge of collapse. He needed to tend to his wound and rest up. He walked the horse up the steps and through the front door, its hooves unnaturally loud in the vacant home.

Inside, the interior could almost be called spartan, were it not for the ceiling.

There was a single table and chair near a window, and a threadbare couch that had probably been old when the Sphinx was being built. There wasn't a single piece of furniture or decoration beyond these three pieces. Despite that, the floor was clean, as were the walls.

Again, the ceiling was another matter.

Protruding from overhead planks were inverted crosses and crucifixes of every size and type imaginable. From simple wooden crosses that looked as if they had been fashioned for a pet's grave to elaborate pieces of gold or silver, worthy of a cathedral. Unlike the shield, many of the crosses were tarnished or covered with rust or verdigris. In addition, a thick network of cobwebs formed skirts of dirty lace around each holy artifact.

Every cross inverted, and yet Galen did not think this was some sort of blasphemy. It was more like the person who had done it was channeling some sort of holy energy in. For a moment, he had the crazy idea that, if he went upstairs, he might find that the base of each cross had been wired to one of the lightning rods on the roof. When lightning struck the house, what sort of energy might be captured? Would it be the Eye of God?

Galen shook his head. He was getting delusional, and any moment he might collapse, leaving his wound to fester and possibly losing his arm or his life in the process.

He left the horse and shield in the entryway, feeling like some errant knight exploring a haunted castle.

In the kitchen he found an unopened bottle of whiskey in the cupboard. This and a lone can of beans seemed to be the only provisions in the house. It could be that the old man had needed to go to town for supplies, or...

The way he had aged outside, flopping like a fish as his body decayed to bone in minutes. Like Death had been waiting a long time to claim him.

Galen again shook his head, legends of bog witches and banshees appearing in his mind unbidden.

In a drawer he found some silverware, a shard of mirror and a page from an old Bible. It was a page from a family history, but none of the writing was legible. On the reverse someone had carefully written: "*Only beware of this, that thou eat not the blood, for the blood is for the soul: and therefore thou must not eat the soul with the flesh: But thou shalt pour it upon the earth as water.*" It seemed like a reference to the creature, but wasn't very illuminating.

Using the mirror Galen was able to tell that the bullet had indeed exited cleanly. He took a slug of the whiskey and then poured it liberally on the wound. The pain was like pouring hot metal into his shoulder. He hissed through his teeth, and tears welled up in his eyes.

He bound the wound with a dishtowel and went back to the main room. He tied his horse to the sofa, wrapping the reins around one arm. He untied the shield and leaned it against the couch, then stretched out, intending only to rest for an hour or so. Then hopefully he could ride off before either a posse caught up or the creature returned.

When Galen woke, it was night, and the house was cloaked in a darkness so profound that, for a moment, he thought he had been buried alive. He sprang up and his horse whinnied softly. He touched the flank of the bay, and its warmth and familiarity anchored him. The throb in his shoulder was a dull ache, and further served to orient him to his surroundings.

Pale moonlight was spilling in through the open front door and the windows, bathing everything in a spectral, silver light. Galen got up, his back protesting from his hours on the old couch.

His stomach rumbled, and he thought of the can of beans in the kitchen, and the splash or two of whiskey left. He could have done with a steak and some strong coffee, but those meager provisions would have to do.

There was no wood for the stove, which wasn't surprising. He figured the old man hadn't required warmth or food in some time. Galen retrieved a spoon from the drawer and opened the can with his knife. He devoured the beans, trying to will himself to go easy, so that he might keep it down. When he had scraped the last morsel from the can he ran his index finger around the inside of the can and licked the sauce from it.

He drank the last of the whiskey and placed the bottle and the empty bean can in a wash bucket with the fork. His mother had always impressed upon him that a gentleman cleans up after himself, and Galen had tried, in this way at least, to follow her teachings.

The sky was beginning to lighten and Galen knew he should ride before the heat of the day was too much for him. Still, a tiny part of him loathed the idea of going outside in anything less than daylight.

And there was the upstairs.

Whatever else he might have been, Galen O'Connor was a curious man. He had gotten that from his mother as well, a librarian back in New York who had insisted he learned to read. He had hated it at first, until he had discovered serialized stories in the newspaper and penny dreadfuls. The exotic richness of those stories, overflowing with both charm and dread had filled him with longings to travel and explore. But traveling in style to exotic ports was for the rich, and Galen had neither the patience nor the inspiration to become a wealthy man, save through being a good shot and a better rider. So he had taken to robbing small banks and merchants, never quite securing enough to give it up. When his Aunt Bess had died Johnny Ross had come looking for him, and Galen had taken him in.

Now both he and the boy had to pay for that lapse in judgment.

Galen took the stairway carefully, not wanting to end his adventure with a broken leg in this ancient house.

The upstairs was not clean like the downstairs, and Galen suddenly had a vision of the old man spending his days sweeping the downstairs or sitting by the window. The image was so strong it almost seemed a memory, and Galen was mystified at the intensity of the vision. How could a man engage in the most tedious of pastimes continuously without going mad?

His boots left tracks in the thick dust, and more than once he had to brush away shreds of cobweb that stroked his face and hands like silken fingers.

There were portraits on the wall, paintings, daguerreotypes and photographs of dour people gazing out unhappily from the grimy walls, the long tatters of faded wallpaper hanging down like funeral garments long decayed. The slight breeze of his passing caused the graying strips to flutter like moths trapped to a specimen board.

There were three bedrooms upstairs. The first held an enormous bed, the covers folded back. Its linens were thick with dust, and a mummified woman lay on one side. The air smelled slightly like cinnamon. The corpse did not startle Galen, he had half expected to find someone dead up here. And the corpse itself wasn't much different than some of the Dia de los Muertos sculptures he had seen down in Mexico. This one could have easily been papier-mâché as well, just not as brightly colored.

The room itself was richly appointed, with furniture as old as the house. A large vanity sat against one wall, its mirror gone and replaced by a painting of Christ in the Garden of Gethsemane. The anguish on the face of Christ was so cunningly done that Galen made a small whimpering sound in his throat before he was even aware of it. He saw then a spectral figure had been painted whispering into the ear of the Savior. The figure looked like the creature.

Galen felt a ripple of gooseflesh up his spine and willed himself to remain calm. Panic led to disaster, like men needlessly killed in a botched holdup.

He checked the other rooms, and found beds still carrying the impressions of former occupants, whose only remains were piles of gray powder.

Galen startled himself once, catching his reflection in a small window. He looked haggard, spent. His black hair hung in greasy ringlets and his gray eyes were almost lost in deep shadows. He longed for a bath, but didn't think he could bear to stay in this place any longer. Better to find a town, get his wound tended and sleep in a proper bed.

He started down the stairs, and some sixth sense caused him to ease his gun out of its worn leather holster. Galen moved slowly, trying to be as silent as the ancient steps would allow.

Johnny Ross sat by the window.

The creature was bent down beside the boy, whispering in his ear.

Galen approached slowly, but the creature did not turn. Johnny Ross's face bore an eerie resemblance to the portrait of Christ upstairs. The agony on his face had twisted and shaped it into a caricature, more a Grecian tragedy mask than something human. Johnny Ross's once-hazel eyes had rolled back in his head, and Galen saw with horror that the boy was weeping tears of blood.

Galen drew just a little closer, and realized that the long spectral fingers of the creature disappeared into the boy's shoulders. It was there to stay.

He caught some of the whispering, then, hushed tones that would rise to a maddening buzz like a hornet's nest just out of reach, then quiet to a hissing that was full of urgency and need.

How long might a man listen to such a sound before going mad?

Galen aimed his gun, then stopped. If Johnny Ross died, then wouldn't the thing come for him? And if he were to quickly kill himself, then mightn't it search the countryside for someone, someone who would listen?

Galen reluctantly holstered his gun. He hated leaving the boy like this, but the young man had wantonly courted coupling with this thing with his first step inside the fencing around the grave. No suitor with a bouquet of flowers on a young woman's porch had done more to secure a lasting union.

Galen retrieved his horse and left the house. His last act was to secure the shield across the doorway. The stag gazed at him, neither praising nor condemning him. Galen felt sure it would keep the creature inside the house, and said a silent prayer for the doomed boy within.

Galen wanted to bury Deke, but there was no shovel to be found, a curious thing in light of so many graves. He could have buried his friend under the pink obelisk, but didn't think the big man would rest easy there. Besides, he could sense the presence of the creature and Johnny Ross at the window, and it made him feel ill.

He could hear the whispering, the constant buzz of a creature too long without companionship.

Galen said a prayer for Deke, and left him for the coyotes and the buzzards. As terrible as that was, it might be that Deke would have the most peaceful fate of the three of them.

Galen rode away swiftly, and gradually the whisper faded from his ears.

Even when Galen was out of range of that terrible sound he continued to hurry, until the obelisk and the old house and Johnny Ross were all far behind, and a new town beckoned with color and noise and life.

THE DARK CELL

BY JEFFREY THOMAS

You're mighty young," Rose said to the newcomer. She didn't really want to start up a conversation, but one of them had to. She was being polite to mask her resentment. She hadn't been hoping for company, and this pretty but surly-looking Mexican girl didn't appear enthusiastic about the prospect of making new friends, either.

The girl looked out through the cell's door, as if she hoped the guard who had locked it only a minute earlier might have a change of heart and come back to release her. "I'm sixteen," she mumbled.

At least the girl understood English. Rose said, "Sixteen, huh? Lord almighty. Twenty-eight, here. I'm Rose."

"Yeah?" the girl said. But after several moments, without looking around, she said, "Maria."

Maria. Well, Rose felt that was enough of an effort on her part. She didn't want to ask what a sixteen-year-old girl had done to be sentenced here—lest Maria ask her, in turn, what her own crime had been.

At the time of her arrival at the Yuma Territorial Prison, on October 22nd, 1899, Rose had been given the designation 1551. This number was worn on the front of her respectable blouse with its puffed sleeves and cinched waist, which also bore a tight pattern of thin horizontal lines—a demure and apologetic indication of her status—unlike the men's uniforms, striped with broader bands of black and white. There were more than three thousand male inmates at the Yuma Territorial Prison, but at this time only eleven females were incarcerated. Their small group, as of today, increased by one.

The men were stacked six to a cell with one chamber pot between them, but Rose had been fortunate to have a cell to herself these past nine months. (*Nine months... nine months... she could have carried a child in that time, and yet it was only the start of a thirty year sentence.*) "Fortunate" was a relative consideration, however. The prison was located in the Sonoran Desert, atop a bluff overlooking the Colorado River, and on summer days like this the temperature could reach 120 degrees. Rose had no window in her cell. And she hadn't truly been alone these past nine months, when one considered the company of lice, bedbugs, and cockroaches. But she had had the luxury of suffering her indignities alone. She had been able to deal with that suffering by sending her mind away, sending it afar, into memories of good times from her childhood and dreams of good times that had never happened. Now, she felt her privacy had been compromised. Now, after having found a way to adapt to her situation, acclimate to it—to accept this existence as her life—she was experiencing an acute sense of punishment all over again. It was as though she, Rose, were the new prisoner, not Maria.

"I killed my brother Emilio," Maria muttered with her back to Rose, as if talking to someone out in the hallway. "He called me a whore." At last she turned around so that Rose, seated on the edge of her bunk, could see that pretty but surly face again. "What about you?"

Rose hesitated only a second. This had been inevitable, hadn't it? Best to get it over with. "I killed my husband... William."

Maria grinned then. The toothy grin didn't make her look more pretty; in fact, Rose preferred her looking unhappy.

Rose decided she hated her.

Conditions at the prison were unavoidably harsh, owing to the heat and overcrowding, but efforts had been made to enrich the lives of the inmates and one of those efforts was the library. The staff kept the male and female prisoners separate, and so presently the only inmates using the library were women. Rose sat at one of the tables that ran through the center of the room in a long row, while framed portraits of Thomas Jefferson, George Washington and Abraham Lincoln watched over her like benign guardians. She had been hunched over the book spread before her—its subject being the marvels of natural history, her favorite book in the library—losing herself in strange untamed lands, open vistas without cages, without men holding guns, when someone sat down on her right so close that their arms touched. She looked up into Maria's face with its sneering smile... a smile that curled her lip up and exposed her gums, like an animal baring its fangs.

"So how did you do it, *hermosa Rosa*? How did you kill your husband?"

Rose returned her gaze to the book, but could no longer walk within its pages, tread upon distant soil. The book was once more a closed window. "That's none of your business. I told you all I'm going to say on that."

"You didn't tell me nothing more than his name. *William.*" Maria drew out the name with mock wistfulness. "Come on now, Rosa," she purred, "don't you want me to tell you how I killed my brother Emilio?"

"No." Rose didn't look up. "I don't want to hear that."

"We're stuck in a cell together, the two of us. Don't you think you ought to be polite to me?"

"If you want polite, be polite to me, and don't ask me about my husband again."

Peripherally Rose saw Maria sit back a little in her chair, felt the girl's glare burn on her skin like the hellish sun that baked them in this oven of adobe and stone. "Maybe I'll just ask the other girls what they know about it, then."

"You do that. I can't stop you. But you won't be hearing anything about it from me."

Rose continued flipping through the book, feigning nonchalance, waiting for her cellmate to move to another chair to strike up a conversation with someone else. But she didn't. Maria was now staring down at the book, also, and Rose thought she could sense the anger circulating through the girl's veins without release. A turned page: picture of a leopard. Another page: cougar.

"Ah!" Maria said when Rose turned the next page. She reached in front of Rose to tap the black and white illustration with a fingernail. "*Tigre.*"

"Jaguar," Rose said.

"We say *tigre.*"

The densely detailed engraving portrayed a wild-eyed, startled jaguar apparently in the act of clambering up a tree. Rose knew that —though their numbers were diminishing, owing to the guns of man —jaguars could still be found in Mexico and as far north as Arizona. Rose's husband had had a friend who claimed to have shot one, once, and sold its gorgeous pelt with its camouflage of intricate rosettes. "But you get a black one sometimes," William had told Rose. He had been drinking when he related this story about his friend, and had reached out suddenly to take Rose's chin and jerk her head around to face him. "Just like I got me a black one right here. All beautiful on the outside... but a black soul inside."

Rose broke free of the memory with a little start. This was not the way she had hoped to be transported when she cracked this book open today.

"Tepeyollotl," Maria whispered, as if speaking only to herself, still staring at the jaguar. "He is the god who looks like el *tigre*. He is the heart of the mountain... the god of dark caves and echoes."

Rose didn't meet her eyes but asked, "Why echoes?"

"I don't know. Maybe a long time ago, people didn't understand who it was talked back to you when you were talking alone."

"This is the stuff you Mexicans believe?"

"The Aztec people. You ever read about them in your books, Rosa?"

"No... I haven't."

"That's where we come from. A magic people. But the only magic you believe is *Jesús Cristo*. That magic... and the magic of *love*. You loved your William so much, huh? That's why we kill people, right, Rosa? Because we love them too much, or we hate them too much. You... I think it was love."

"You don't know a goddamned thing about me, little girl. What I'd love is for you to go bother somebody else right now."

As if she hadn't heard her, Maria went on, "I hated Emilio. Always hated him, because he thought I was nothing. He couldn't see inside of me. I'm not just this raggedy little girl people think they see." She thumped her breastbone, thrusting out her jaw defiantly. "I don't like it when people see me as nothing, Rosa. I hope you don't make that mistake, too."

Rose finally cranked her head up slowly to regard the girl. "Why can't you leave me alone?"

Maria leaned her face in close. "Because you ain't alone, pretty Rosa. I'm like your echo."

"Get away from me," Rose said in a barely audible voice.

"Can't."

Rose broke their gaze, looked down to close the book -- like a barred door clanging shut, locking her out -- and maybe Maria felt Rose was dismissing her, saw her as nothing, because that was when the Mexican girl picked up another heavy book from the table and swung it in both hands against the side of Rose's head.

The guard who walked alongside Rose had hold of her arm, but not roughly; it was more that he was helping to hold her up. She seemed to hurt all over at once, as if every nerve were a glowing hot wire. Fistfuls of hair had been pulled out of her scalp, her cheeks were plowed with long claw marks, and her muscles felt deeply compressed where Maria had bitten her in the side of the neck. In the prison infirmary they had wound gauze around her throat.

"That wasn't smart, Rose," the guard said. His name was John and he was tall, husky like her William had been, but his voice was soft and more regretful than accusing. "It ain't often we got to put you ladies in the Dark Cell."

"It's her you ought to be throwing in the hole, John, not me," she mumbled through her purple, swollen lips.

"She's already there, Rose."

Rose turned toward him as they walked. "You can't put the both of us in there!"

"The both of you were fighting... the both of you have got to pay. People get put in the Dark Cell for less. I'm sorry, but it ain't up to me."

"I was only protecting myself! Look what she did to me!"

"You gave her some, too, Rose. You closed up both her eyes pretty good. Busted her lip, bloodied her nose. Her face was red from eyes to chin. Course, it wasn't all her blood. That girl's an animal, I'll give you that."

"Do you know how she killed her brother?"

"Don't know much about that story. Just heard that she made a god-awful mess of him."

They were coming close to the chamber they called the Dark Cell. Because it was near to the women's cells and the library, Rose knew its location well enough, though she herself had never been inside it before. She had heard troublemakers might spend anywhere from one day to a few weeks in the Dark Cell, but she'd also heard of one inmate who had spent over a hundred straight days in there.

To change the topic of conversation, or maybe to somehow make Rose thankful that she was secure on the inside rather than outside these walls, John said, "Hey, you should see the dust storm moving in out there, Rose. Looks like a solid wall rolling across the world, tall as a mountain. A mountain made of cotton." He struggled to convey it. "Can't see past it. Must be quite a thunderstorm stirring up all that dust, pushing in behind it."

"Seen them before," Rose said bitterly.

"Well, I'm sure you have."

"John... I'll take the blame for the fight. It was all my fault, all right? I'll do my time in the hole myself, all alone. But you can't put me in that little cage with that girl."

The big guard stopped walking, and thus so did she. Looking down at her with sincere concern etched on his face, he said, "Rose, like I told you, it ain't up to me. Look, I don't think that little senorita will go at you again no matter how loco she is... nobody wants to do any more time in the Dark Cell than they have to."

Rose sighed, and then asked, "You have a wife, John?"

"Yes, I have. Married twelve years."

"You love her good?"

"Good as I can."

"I reckon she's a lucky lady." She gave him a tremulous smile.

"You'd have to ask her that." He took her arm again gently. "Come on, Rose... let's get this over with." And they resumed their march.

Only a little further along they came to their destination, its entrance gated by a door of riveted metal bands. Like the women's cells and the library, the Dark Cell had been carved directly into the rock face of Caliche Hill. Another guard, Martin, stood waiting for them outside the metal door, carrying a Winchester loosely in both hands. John nodded at the rifle and asked, "What's that for, Marty?"

"Heard stories about that little Mexican girl," and he tipped his chin meaningfully toward Rose's marred face, "but she didn't give me no trouble. Bob helped me lock her in, but he's gone back to his post."

Martin returned his attention to Rose as he stepped aside to unlock the door.

"We emptied eight men out of the cage before their time to make room for you, Miss Rose. Don't that make you feel better? Maybe they'll say a prayer for you tonight."

Beside Martin's boot was a kerosene lantern. John squatted by this to light it, and when he straightened he carried it before him.

The gate screeched as John pushed it open, and he ventured first into the narrow passage with its rough, leprous walls. Rose followed, with Martin behind cradling his rifle. At the end of the little tunnel, a room opened up like a hollow pocket in the granite, about fifteen feet by fifteen feet. And in the center of this room was a cage fashioned from metal bands, like the gate. Aside from the shifting glow cast by the lantern, only a miserly portion of light leaked into the cell through a small air vent in the stone ceiling.

The restless lantern light caused a crosshatched pattern of shadows to move across the cage's sole occupant, who was crouched down in one corner because the cage was only five feet in height. Through the shadowy stripes on her face, Maria glared out at the trio. No, Rose knew, glared at *her*. Even in this insufficient light, though, Rose could see that the young girl's eyes were swollen almost shut from the blows she had landed in self defense. Maria's contused eyes put Rose in mind of a drowned man she had once seen fished out of the river, dead in the water for days, his face bloated and monstrous... transformed into something inhuman.

Having set his lantern on the floor, John bent forward to unlock the cage's door. As he did so, he said, "You got three days in here, ladies. I suggest you don't add to that. It would be a good idea for you to use this time to talk out whatever it was got you so fired up in the first place."

"Bread and water every day," Martin added. "That's it. No blankets, no pillows, and you see that grate?" The grate formed the floor of the cage. "That there is where you'll be taking care of your business." But he hadn't needed to explain that part; the hot, boxed-in air reeked of urine and excrement.

Rose thought of the man who had spent over a hundred days in this room, in this cage, and shuddered. The door of the cage squealed open, and then Martin was giving her a nudge forward with the length of his gun. For one hallucinatory moment—a disorienting fragment of memory, like a suddenly remembered nightmare—Rose thought it was her William behind her, pushing her with that shotgun of his. And then she was bending down to step into the cage. Too cruelly small, she thought, even for an animal.

The wind howled past the air vent in the ceiling of the Dark Cell, like ghostly lips blowing into the mouthpiece of some hellish instrument. An ululating wail, rising and falling as the gusts rolled past like the titanic phantoms of dead gods in an otherworldly procession. Though evening had not yet fallen, the dust storm had blotted out whatever meager light the vent offered. The man-made cave might have been the bottom of a well filled with inky water.

Rose could even feel the desert sand sifting into the cell, a gritty pollen against her face in a nearly imperceptible caress. It got into her nose, her mouth. She became conscious of how thirsty she already was. When would they bring them water, as Martin had said they would?

Pitch black. Had Rose ever known such a blackness? A person could not close their eyes to approximate this profundity of darkness... unless perhaps they did so in a room at night with all lights extinguished, curtains drawn, but Rose thought even that might not approach this total lack of light. Perhaps if one's eyes were burned out with a heated poker. Perhaps then. Perhaps if a person floated in the heavens after the last star had burned out.

But she was not alone in the void. Though she could not see her, not the slightest reflected glistening of an eye, she knew Maria was still there squatting on her haunches in the far corner of the cage. In lulls between the wind's banshee cries, she could just barely hear the girl's raspy breathing. Sometimes, the faintest tinkle of metal links as she shifted her position slightly. The two of them had had shackles affixed to the ankles of both legs, their shackles chained to opposite walls of the cage.

Yet the cage was small, and Rose knew that Maria could reach her if she wanted to.

Rose sat with her arms wrapped around her knees, her skirts doing little to cushion her behind against the hard grate of the floor. She wanted to change positions, to try lying on her side with her arm as a pillow, but feared the sound of her own chains moving might startle Maria into action. And she was afraid that if she reclined, she might fall asleep.

Three days. Could she go without sleeping for three days? Of course not. Well, if she did sleep, how would Maria know the difference? But then, though she had never heard it herself, Rose remembered William complaining about how she snored at night. In the early days—before the drinking had got bad, before the pain of the toothaches that he said were demons excavating their own little hell inside his head—he had teased her about her snoring in a good-natured way. Later, however, he would elbow her awake irritably. Tell her the sound she made was so loud and ugly it gave him nightmares. "My Daddy used to snore," he said, "and it always scared me at night. I didn't know what the hell that was. I thought it was some animal outside the house... or in the house, prowling around." And he said, "I swear some night I'm going to wake up and grab my shotgun to shut you up for good."

Then, without really planning to, Rose said aloud into the darkness, "I don't want any more trouble." She heard her voice echo. It sounded like a ghost imitating her, mocking her. "I'll tell you about William... about me and William... if that's what you need to hear."

She waited for some kind of response or acknowledgement, even a grunt, but there was nothing. Could the girl have fallen asleep? No... no... even through the blackness between them, Rose could still feel that unabated glare boring into her.

She resumed then, and told the silent spot where she figured Maria to be how handsome William had been when she had first met him at a church dance. How sweet he had been, or seemed to be. But after their marriage the drinking had escalated, in response to the pain in his jaws that he could at least put a name to, and the pain in his mind or soul he could never articulate to her, and perhaps not even to himself. "He hit me time to time," Rose related. "Afterwards, when he was sober, he'd say, 'I'm sorry, Rose.' Course, he'd just do it again. And then it was, 'I'm sorry, Rose' again. Well, I took it. But I had some pets. I had me a cat named Tom and a dog named Rascal, and a horse. I always loved animals, ever since I was a child. I brought home birds with broken wings, pollywogs in a bowl of water. One time our family cat even knocked a snake cold, batting it with her paws, so I took that snake and put it in a bureau drawer until it came to and could move around again, and then I took it outside and let it go, and my Momma was never the wiser. I felt closer to animals than I did to people. I felt connected to them. See, animals ain't evil like people are. The harm they do each other... well, it ain't like the sins we do. They only kill to feed themselves. Or to protect themselves."

Only the echo answered. Only the banshee song. But still she went on.

"Sometimes William would give Rascal a kick. Most times I bit my tongue about it, and other times I spoke up, but of course then he'd turn that anger on me. Which was probably what he wanted to happen, anyway. But one day he saw Tom sitting on the kitchen table and he picked him up and threw him right against the wall. Then he stomped on over to Tom and gave him a kick. Such a kick." Rose paused for a moment to contain the emotion that threatened to seep out and stain her words. "Well, he killed him with that kick. And so I went at him. I pushed him away and slapped him in the face. Slapped him good and hard right across his jaw full of pain down deep in the bone, and I didn't care.

"But then he went in the other room and got his Spencer twelve gauge."

A slight jingle of metal chains. Rose paused in her story, waiting tensely, but the sound was not repeated. Still wary, at last she continued.

"Rascal was outside, so William stomped out into the yard and called him, and when the dog came around the corner of the house William shot him. Then he walked right on past what was left of my Rascal, walked straight to the barn, with me chasing after and crying and screaming. And before I could get my hands on him to try to pull him away, he shot my horse.

"When I tried to hit him again, he turned around and struck me right in the chest with the butt of his gun. Knocked me onto the ground. And he stood over me and pointed that precious pump-action of his right down at my face..."

A new sound caused Rose to pause again. It was not the shifting of chains, but another sound, at first barely heard until a momentary ebb in the roaring dust storm exposed it for what it was.

Tiny, whispery giggling... coming from some uncertain point in the utter blackness.

The surprised anger that welled up in Rose left her speechless. Fury had knotted in her throat, even as it sent electric currents crackling through every nerve in her body.

She did not finish her story.

In the dream, Rose had taken shelter in a cave in a mountain side to escape the pummeling of a monsoon rain. For several moments she stood at the edge of the cavern's opening, watching the torrents punish the jungle canopy below her, before turning away and following a passageway eroded by time through the mountain's flank.

When she came to a hollow chamber in the rock, she crouched down with the granite wall pressed against her back for a sense of security, wet and shivering and hugging her knees for warmth. She would wait out the storm. Wait for many long years if she had to, before she could emerge free into sunlight again.

But slowly she became aware that she was not alone in the Stygian darkness. She did not hear the beast that sheltered in this cave, did not even smell it, but simply sensed its presence as if the savage blood in its veins radiated heat through its hide. Sensed its feral eyes—which she knew could see her clearly, even though she couldn't see her own hand in front of her face—summing her up cunningly, as the beast waited for just the right moment to spring.

"Don't do this," she said to the black beast camouflaged in the darkness, her own voice echoing back to her. "Go back to sleep... please..."

She thought the beast replied with a low growl, rumbling deep in its throat, but it was difficult to tell as the sound of the rainstorm drumming against the mountain side swelled in intensity... became deafening...

The crackling sound that had awakened Rose was so loud that for a moment or two it made her think a fire raged all around her, cooking her alive. She was wildly disoriented by both the strange sound and the impenetrable darkness, not aware of when she might have fallen asleep or for how long. She was sure she had let out a gasp or unintelligible exclamation upon coming awake. As far as the darkness was concerned, she might have believed she was a spirit without a body drifting through oblivion were it not for the pain in her bottom and back from the pressure of the metal bands, like a giant waffle iron, against her.

The tangible contact of the cage at least helped ground her thoughts, gave her mind a handhold, and she remembered where she was—but what was that ungodly sound? Now it put her in mind of a vast audience clapping their hands, as if the Dark Cell might be filled impossibly with countless people, all applauding her punishment... but that wasn't the cause of the great clamor, either.

Then something like a pebble thrown in the darkness ticked her thumb, stinging her skin, and she drew her hand back as if bitten by a scorpion. While she had heard scorpions did indeed venture into the Dark Cell, and occasionally snakes too, she realized that what had struck her hand was a piece of ice. Hail stones the size of bird shot were finding their way in through the little vent in the ceiling, but the clicking sound of their impact was drowned out by the thunderous onslaught of frozen pellets against the roof of rock above. The dry hot dust storm, whipped up by the rain storm behind it, had moved on and been replaced incongruously by this.

Had night fallen while she dozed? Again, there was no way to gauge the passage of time. Rose once more recalled that one prisoner had spent over a hundred days in this cell. She wondered who he was, and if the experience had driven him to madness.

But more important right now was a different prisoner: the one who was chained across from her in this cramped box. Did Maria realize that Rose had fallen asleep... been vulnerable? Perhaps she herself had drifted off. Well, the girl certainly couldn't be sleeping now, not with this cacophony raging above their heads.

Rose arched her back, stretching her aching muscles, and repositioned her legs to one side so that she sat on the outside of her left buttock. This series of movements caused her chains, unavoidably, to clatter across the grated floor.

Immediately, she heard a sound that seemed to be a reaction to her movements. It was hard to distinguish over the skeleton dance of the hail—and might she even have imagined it?—but she thought she'd heard a deep throaty rumble.

Rose froze like a startled deer, breath clenched in her lungs' tight fists. The sound, real or imagined, had been less than human... *bestial*... and it made her recall Maria touching the engraving in the natural history book and evoking the name of Tepeyollotl, the jaguar god of a magical people.

It was easy to believe in magic in the absolute absence of light. Easy to believe in magic when it sounded like the sky outside had split asunder, the fabric of reality ripped wide open and all the tumult of the universe pouring in through the rift. The four elements all cascading through the fissure in a chaotic state, raw material to remake this sad little world... to *transform* it...

Again, a deep bass growl, maybe not so much heard as transmitted through the metal bands of the cage, like a vibration through a tuning fork. The warning growl of an animal that feels threatened... or hungry.

"I know you," Rose whispered so softly that she couldn't even hear the words herself. "I know who you are."

Somewhere in the darkness, the rattle of chain links as they dragged across the floor grate, like a delayed echo of her own movements.

"You've killed before," Rose said, louder this time, maybe loud enough to be heard above the hail storm. "But you don't have to do this again. Please don't do this again."

A different kind of sound then, veiled by the hail, veiled by the dark, but it still cut straight to the heart of Rose. It was that giggling laughter again, though closer this time. And on the tail of it, a voice croaked, "Poor Rosa." Once more, mockingly: "Poor Rosa."

Then, she flinched when an unseen hand touched her cheek, as if in a tender caress. "I'm sorry, Rosa," that voice said, near and intimate. But it was a lie... his love was a lie... and the beast roared.

John and another guard, named Bob, arrived at the entrance to the Dark Cell at a run. Bob had drawn his Remington revolver when he came within sight of its gated door—which unsettlingly stood open and unattended—but John stopped his companion from plunging into the passageway until he could light the kerosene lantern he'd brought with him.

The men found their fellow guard Martin standing at the end of the passageway staring into the cell, just short of its threshold, as if he had never quite entered the room—or as if he had retreated from it.

"What did you do, Martin?" John asked, smelling the gunpowder that still hung in the confined air. "What in God's name did you do?"

The fusillade of hail had ceased, leaving an unearthly stillness in its wake. Though the storm had passed on, evening had descended and no light shone through the vent in the Dark Cell's ceiling. Martin had brought his own kerosene lantern, however, and it rested on the floor in front of his feet. Between its wavering light and the illumination cast from John's lamp, the three men could see enough of the two prisoners chained inside the cage at the center of the room to know that they were both dead.

"I thought it was something else," Martin said in a weak, stunned voice. "What I saw... I didn't know how it got in there, but it had a hold of the girl's neck..."

John squeezed past Martin into the chamber, pushing down the barrel of his Winchester rifle as he did so, to get a better look at the bodies. He held his lantern up higher, and hissed, "Dear God."

"It looked like something else," Martin repeated, as if he stood before a doubtful jury. "I swear it did. It wasn't a person, John. It was some kind of... animal. But after I shot it... after the smoke cleared..."

The sixteen-year-old named Maria lay on her back, eyes gazing emptily at the vent in the ceiling as if her spirit might have ascended through it. Her tightly striped blouse was saturated with blood from the ragged wound where her throat had been torn out, the larynx exposed and carotid artery chewed through.

Chewed was the word John thought, when he saw how blood was smeared thickly across Rose's nose and lower face. But it was Rose lying there across Maria's body, Rose with three bullets fired into her back, not some animal as Martin claimed to have witnessed.

"Look what she done to that girl," Bob said, wagging his head. "Just like I heard she done to her husband."

"It wasn't Rose," Martin insisted, and he was beginning to quake with sobs now. "I swear it wasn't, boys!"

Gently, Bob took the rifle from the other man's hands. "She was killing that Mexican girl, Marty. You did what you had to do."

"But what I *saw*, Bob!" Marty cried.

"It was dark, Marty," Bob reassured him. "It was dark."

John couldn't take his eyes from Rose. Couldn't stop thinking about their conversation when he had been escorting her to the Dark Cell.

"She was afraid to be put in there with Maria," he said. "I thought it was Maria she was scared of. But now I think maybe she was scared of herself."

He thought of Rose asking him if he loved his wife, and there was a deep contraction in his chest. He reminded himself that her punishment hadn't been up to him... and there was nothing he could have done to change it... and that there was no denying the woman had been both dangerous and mad...

And yet he couldn't help but murmur, "I'm sorry, Rose."

THE TWO OF GUNS
BY JOHN F.D. TAFF

Dust.

Dust and heat dominated the desert stretched before Gus without an end in sight. The frisky bay he'd stolen had slowed some miles before, as the land ahead began to look exactly like the land behind.

Gus reined in the horse amid a cloud of dust. He produced a frayed bandana from his shirt pocket, mopped sweat and dust from his balding head. He rubbed his eyes and scanned the horizon.

To the northeast, through a shimmering curtain of heat, he saw a small tail of brown dust wagging in the afternoon sky.

Sheriff Holloran and his posse.

Not getting closer, but certainly not falling behind.

He'd left Wilson Ridge in a hurry after shooting a man in the bar following an exchange of pleasantries concerning each others' questionable family lineage and dubious personal habits. He didn't remember what brought it on, didn't even know if he'd killed the man, though the posse chasing him was a good indication that funeral arrangements were pending. He had left so quickly that he dropped his gun on the way out of town and didn't turn back to get it. Doing the two-step at the end of a rope didn't appeal too much to Gus, no sir.

The horse neighed in impatience. He yanked the reins, slapped the horse on the rump. The bay took off with a slight, disapproving whinny and a skitter of hardscrabble.

He leaned over in the saddle to spit, but thought better of it. He might be out here long enough to curse every mouthful of liquid he had spat without care into the dust. He swallowed carefully, gave the horse a sharp spur.

He rode for another hour before he caught sight of something moving up ahead. After a couple of minutes, Gus was able to tell that it was a wagon; not a homesteader's wagon, but a salesman's wagon. The heat haze made estimating distances in the desert tricky, but he guessed another half an hour would bring him to the wagon—and its contents.

To cheer himself as he rode, he thought of all of the things he would do once he got to the next town. He'd stay at the best flophouse, maybe get a whore. And, of course, a gun. After the last few hours, he deserved it.

When he snapped out of his daydream, he was perhaps a half-mile behind the wagon. Through the dust its rickety wheels threw into the air, Gus could see the wagon was painted a bright red. Ornate woodwork covered its body, stenciled in gold and green.

A snake-oil man, Gus thought with pleasure. He'd be sure to have a whole heap of money.

As he drew alongside the wagon, Gus saw the words "The Incredible Dr. Alatryx" painted onto it in tall, sky-blue letters. "Egypt, India, The Orient, Persia."

"Hello," said the driver, drawing the two horses in with a tug on the reins, and jumping from the front of the wagon. He was dressed in a dusty black suit, a black hat and polished snakeskin boots. Easterner, Gus snorted to himself. Gus noticed that the driver limped a bit, favoring his left foot as he walked toward him, hand outstretched.

Gus dismounted and took the man's gloved hand. "Pleased to meet you."

He grimaced at the man's limp handshake, took his hand back quickly.

"And I, friend, am pleased to meet you," the man said, removing his hat and wiping his forehead with an immaculate white silk handkerchief. "I'm Dr. Alatryx, and I am at your service." He made a deep bow, bending crisply at the waist. "How can I help?"

"Well, a drink'd be good."

Dr. Alatryx looked at him, and Gus noticed that his eyes were a strange reddish-violet. They were intense, giving his face an otherworldly cast, as if he *did* hold some mysterious power to cure what mortal doctors could not.

"Then, friend, we shall share what I have." He walked past Gus toward the back entrance of the wagon. His unworried, unafraid demeanor confounded Gus.

Dr. Alatryx inserted an ornate silver key into a lock on the wagon's rear door, drew it open with a low creak. He ducked into the wagon's dark recesses, and Gus heard the sound of many things being moved here and there inside.

The doctor reappeared with a bottle of amber fluid and two clear, crystal glasses. "Here we are," he said, handing a glass to Gus. He uncorked the bottle, poured a generous shot into Gus' glass, then his.

The label on the bottle read, "Dr. Alatryx's Mysterious Persian Cure. Good For ALL AILMENTS! Indigestion! Headaches! Tooth Pain! Gout! Piles!"

Gus didn't wait for the doctor to fill his own glass. The whiskey's fire cut through the dirt, dust and dryness. Saliva sprang inside his mouth like a gusher, following the whiskey down his throat. Gus moistened his lips with his newly wet tongue, and laughed a little at the "Mysterious Persian Cure" before taking another draught.

Dr. Alatryx watched Gus with amusement, then took a small drink from his own glass. "Where are you heading, friend?"

"Whatever town'll have me," Gus laughed, finished the whiskey in his glass. Dr. Alatryx refilled it for him. Gus stared into the whiskey as he swirled it in the glass.

"Trouble?"

Gus jerked his head up and looked at the doctor. "What business is that of yours?"

"None at all, friend. But if there were trouble, I have in my wagon things that could help you."

Gus took another drink, his eyes staring at Dr. Alatryx over the rim of the glass, his brow a map of frustration and interest. "What makes you think I'm in any trouble, stranger?"

"What makes a man ride through the desert in the middle of the day with no water, no hat?" he mused. "What makes a man flag down an ordinary patent-medicine salesman in the middle of said desert? *What makes a man travel alone without a gun?*"

Gus started. "What makes you think I don't have a gun?"

Dr. Alatryx laughed and set his glass of whiskey onto the step leading to the wagon's door. "A man like you would carry his gun for all to see. Since I see no gun, you must not have one." He leaned forward, dropped his voice to a conspiratorial whisper.

"*Therefore, friend, you must need one.*"

Gus turned away from the doctor's gaze. His stolen bay cropped at a small clump of weeds it had found.

He didn't like the way the word *friend* spilled from this man's lips.

"'Spose I do need a gun? You got any?"

"Do I 'got' any?" he asked and laughed again. "Sir, Dr. Alatryx has been around the world. He has seen the mysteries of ancient Egypt. He has talked to the wizards of Persia. He has been privy to the secrets of the Orient. Just like the wagon says." He limped to the top step of the wagon, tapped its side and turned back to Gus. "You can read, can't you?"

"I can read," Gus said defensively. Dr. Alatryx disappeared again into the wagon. Gus leaned over to make sure he was preoccupied, then grabbed the bottle and filled his glass to the rim.

More sounds of things being moved, tossed and dragged around issued from the wagon's interior. "Yes, the Orient," came his voice. "Did you know that the Chinese invented gunpowder?"

Dr. Alatryx returned holding a wooden case. "The Chinese are a strange and wondrous people." He set the plain, polished wood box down on the wagon's last step and opened it. Inside, nestled in crushed red velvet, was a gun. Gus recognized it as a .44 caliber Remington No. 3. A six-shooter. Pretty good gun, though it had to be nearly seven years old.

The Remington's wooden grips had been replaced with grips of a dull black material that had strange carvings on them. On the case's opposite side was an impression in the velvet where a second gun had been.

"This is a special gun, the last of its kind," said Dr. Alatryx, drawing it reverently from its resting place. The black grips were highly polished, yet reflected little light.

"What's so special about a '75 Remington?" Gus asked. He was beginning to worry. This was taking too long. What if the posse was catching up with him? He knew Sheriff Holloran from previous encounters. He'd hang him out here from anything they could throw a rope over.

"Friend, this gun never misses."

"How's that?" asked Gus.

"This gun not only never misses, it can't miss. Do you hear what I'm saying, friend? It cannot miss. *Ever.*"

He handed the gun to Gus.

Gus turned the gun over in his hands. Other than the strange, carved grips, the gun looked like an ordinary Remington.

"Can't miss, huh?" asked Gus with aggravated disbelief.

"Correct."

Gus pointed the gun into the air. "So, if I wanted to shoot my horse, I could point the gun in the air and shoot, and the horse'd drop dead."

"Deader than a nail," said the doctor. His eyes were narrowed, and his mouth was drawn in a fierce smile. "But, friend, I should warn you..."

The gun went off with a crack, and Gus' arm jumped with the kick of the first bullet.

From the front of the wagon came a loud whinny and the sound of a horse falling to the ground. Gus' smirk faltered, and he stood in shock for a moment.

Dr. Alatryx smiled, his perfect white teeth showing.

Gus sprinted to the front of the wagon and found the bay sprawled amidst the ragged plants it had been eating. There was a large hole through the back of its head, and blood beaded on the horse's smooth flanks.

It was, as Dr. Alatryx had predicted, deader than a nail.

Gus looked dumbly at the gun held in his hand. He had fired the gun into the air and had killed a horse standing more than 50 yards in front of him *on the ground.* As the implication of this seeped into his sun-baked brain, Dr. Alatryx came to stand beside him.

"You didn't let me finish. The gun's cylinder cannot be removed. The six bullets in the gun are the only six bullets it will ever fire. Well, I should say five now, though I suppose one bullet to prove its accuracy is one bullet well spent."

"How in the hell...? I mean, what kind of gun is this, anyhow?" sputtered Gus.

"As I said, friend, it is a special gun, the last of its kind. After its remaining five bullets are spent, there will be no more like it in the world," said the doctor.

"How much?" asked Gus, with no intention of buying it.

Dr. Alatryx drew a silver pocket watch out of his vest. He snapped it open. "Noon. Well, my friend, let's say we have a sale on this rare and potent weapon. For you, today, I'll sell it for $50."

Gus turned away and smiled, holding the gun pointed at the ground. The gun barked once, and the second bullet sped to its target.

Dr. Alatryx lay stretched on the ground. His hat had fallen off, and a spill of black hair swept the dust. A single red spot grew, spread along the whiteness of his shirt. His violet eyes remained open. Gus prodded him with his foot.

"Deader than a nail... and dumber, too," he laughed. He bent and pulled the silver watch from the doctor's dead hand. The thin chain holding it to his suit parted. Gus looked at the watch, stuffed it into his pocket.

He walked back to the rear of the wagon and picked up his drink. Draining it, he climbed the stairs and entered the wagon's cramped, hot interior.

Dr. Alatryx, as it happened, turned out to have everything Gus wanted. Everything, that is, except for the whore... and the gun's mate. He even searched Dr. Alatryx's body for the second gun. The doctor carried no weapon. Damn fool, thought Gus.

He dressed himself in a dark brown suit of fine material, just his size. He found a new brown bowler in a box under reams and reams of oriental-looking cloth. He found and took more than $500 in gold, hidden inexpertly in a leather bag behind a loose plank in the wagon's wall.

In thirty minutes, as his new watch told him, he stood outside the wagon again, swallowing another glass of the late doctor's miracle cure. He threw the empty glass into the desert and put the bottle into his saddlebag, which now hung from the back of one of the doctor's beautiful black stallions. It was, Gus mused, the prettiest horse he'd ever stolen.

He climbed into the saddle, the horse unaware or uncaring of the fact that he had shot its owner. He turned to look in the direction of the pursuing posse.

The cat's tail wagged a lot closer than it had the last time he checked.

Smiling, Gus drew the gun from its new holster on his hip, looked at it quizzically. He turned in the saddle, pointed the gun approximately in the direction of the cat's tail and fired.

"The devil take ya, Holloran!"

The horse, frightened by the noise, pranced nervously, upsetting his lazy aim. Another time, another place, another gun, Gus would have been angry at the animal. Now, he only laughed as he put his new spurs to the horse's sides and galloped away.

About seven miles west of Gus, the posse had paused so its nine members could drink from their canteens. A tall, bearded man took a long draught, wiped his mouth with the back of his sleeve.

"Gettin' closer boys. I expect we'll have him before dinner," said the man, capping his canteen and replacing it in his saddlebag. The other men, taking their lead from him, finished their drinks and repacked their canteens.

"In a couple miles, we'll split up. Mike, you, Jimmy and Matt'll go north. Me, Lou, Joe and..." The man grasped his chest, flipped violently backward in his saddle, tumbled to the ground behind his horse. The other men dismounted quickly, drew and cocked their guns, and approached him.

When they turned him over, they scanned the desert warily. For on Sheriff Timothy Holloran's chest, just below and to the right of his silver badge, another badge had appeared, red and wet and more meaningful than anything he had ever worn in his life.

Gus dismounted from the black horse, tied it to a railing in front of the Esmeralda Hotel in the small town of Gasping Gulch. The name fit, for Gus noticed that the town barely held back the desert. Dry tumbleweeds blew along the streets, and dust devils spun into existence, twirling away like phantom dancers.

He removed his saddlebag from the horse with some difficulty, his new-found property weighing it more than he was accustomed. He climbed the creaking steps to the Esmeralda, and pushed through its doors.

Several men looked up from card games, drinks or women to see who had entered. Almost in unison, a wrinkle of disgust passed across their faces.

For a moment, Gus wondered at why he merited this sort of reception. Then, he realized. The clothes he was wearing. Everyone took him for an Easterner.

He walked through a side door in the bar and stopped at the hotel's front desk. No one was there, so he rang the bell.

From the same door he entered came a man he assumed to be the owner of the hotel. "Yeah?" he asked. "What can I do for you, stranger?"

"I'd like a hot meal, your best room and your prettiest woman for the night. In that order."

The man looked at him with mild disgust. Gus reached into his pocket and drew out $50 in gold coins. He plunked them on the counter.

"I reckon this'll cover it."

The man picked up a coin, examined it. "I'll be damned. You'll get the best room, the best meal and the best girl, I'll see to that, mister. Just why are you in this godforsaken place anyway?" He slid the money into his waiting hands, deposited it into a pocket behind his apron.

"Just passing through," said Gus.

"Sure, I understand. Betty!" he yelled. A couple of seconds later an attractive, if worn, brunette woman walked through the door from the bar. She wore a short, frilly red dress, a garter on her thigh and a tattered feather in her hair.

"Yeah?" She eyed Gus from foot to crown.

"The gentleman here will be staying with us for a few days, and he'd like a friend. So, why don't you help him upstairs and be real friendly-like to him?"

"Sure," she said, sidling up to Gus and putting her arm through his. "What's your name?"

"Gus," he croaked. He smelled whiskey on her breath and smoke in her hair, but he was excited.

"Well, Gus, how'd you like for me to get you outta these fancy duds and give you a bath?" she asked, giggling as she led him up the stairs to his room.

Four-twenty five on the silver pocket watch.

Gus put himself back into his stolen clothes, adjusted them, looked at Betty sleeping in his bed. She'd been worth the money. He strapped on his gun belt, drew the gun from its holster. The carvings deep in the black grips looked like foreign writing. Maybe German, Gus thought.

He closed the door softly, crept down the narrow corridor to the staircase, his new shoes creaking more than the dry floorboards.

In the bar, every head turned to him, as they'd done before. But this time, their faces wore expressions of interest, curiosity and, on some, avarice. Obviously, the innkeeper had been regaling them with talk of the new guest and his ready finances. Gus would have to be on guard against men wanting to take advantage of this situation–*men like him.*

Gus strode to an empty table and sat, all eyes on him. He looked around the room, and the innkeeper took this as a sign that he was needed.

"Yes, sir, can I help?"

"Yeah, I think I'll have me some dinner now," Gus replied. "Beef-steak, some potatoes, some bread and butter, and some pie, any kind'd be fine. Oh, and some whiskey, too. Best in the house."

"Of course," said the man. He leaned close to Gus, nudged him with an elbow. "Work up an appetite, huh?"

"Yeah, I guess you could say that."

The innkeeper came back with a whiskey bottle and a glass. In due course, the steak, a baked potato, a warm loaf of new bread, butter and a half an apple pie followed. Gus pounced on the food, tucking pieces of steak in as quickly as he could chew and swallow. Everybody still watched, but what the hell, he thought. Let 'em.

He was comforted by the weight of the strange, cold gun strapped to his thigh.

He continued to cut, chew, drink and swallow until he had eaten it all. His head swam with the half-bottle of whiskey he had used to wash it all down. He pulled the pie tin to him and started on its contents.

As he pushed an aromatic fork-full of the apple pie into his mouth, however, a hand came down on his. It pulled the fork from his mouth and sent it clattering across the wooden floor.

"Wha...?" Gus mumbled around a mouthful of pie. He turned, half expecting to see Sheriff Holloran. His hand dropped to his gun belt.

"I wouldn't."

Gus stood, froze when he saw who it was.

He looked a little worse for wear, but it was him, right down to the piercing red-violet eyes. He wore a different hat and a long, tan oilskin coat that swung around his knees. One of his hands pushed the coat aside at waist level, then rested firmly on his hip to reveal a gun.

Oh, no. Oh, shit, no.

Carved deeply into its dull, black grips were a series of lines, shapes and seemingly meaningless squiggles.

"You're dead," was the only thing he could think of to say.

"I don't know what you're talking about," said Dr. Alatryx. He pulled out a seat, sat at the table. "Sit, friend, we have business to discuss."

Gus sat, looked around. People were watching, trying hard to pretend that they weren't.

"Dressing and living well on my money, I see. Oh well, no matter. What's done is done, friend," the doctor said. But, this time the word friend was sneered. "There is, however, the small matter of payment."

"Okay. Fair is fair," whispered Gus. "I'll pay you a hundred and fifty dollars for the gun and everything."

"Do you take me for a fool? You stole the money from me along with everything else," laughed Dr. Alatryx. "No, what I want is something that you cannot welsh on. Something infinitely more valuable.

"You."

Gus blinked.

"What the hell's that mean?" he asked.

"Tomorrow at noon. Just you and me. We've each got one of the guns, so it depends merely on who is fastest."

"What if I say no?"

"Then, friend, I will shoot you where you sit with my last bullet."

"Tomorrow at noon?" asked Gus. "No funny business?"

"None. I give my word. Shake?" he asked, and he held out a gloved hand.

Gus took the doctor's limp hand in his with a grimace of distaste.

Dr. Alatryx stood. "I would get plenty of rest were I you." He turned and took two steps toward the bar's street exit. "Oh, and don't think about leaving town," he said turning back to Gus. "I've taken the liberty of shooting your—I mean *my*—horse. Good night."

And he left the bar.

Gus sat for a minute, stunned. He eyed the pie and realized his appetite had left him. In fact, he felt decidedly queasy. He stood and left the bar. When he got to his room, Betty was gone, but that was just as well. He slipped out of his clothes and got into bed. He placed the gun under his pillow and, surprisingly, went straight to sleep.

He awoke with the sun in his eyes. The white linen curtains flapped in the breeze from the open window. He swung his legs over the edge of the bed, sat for a few minutes. Standing, he walked to the chest of drawers near the door. A porcelain basin and a china pitcher sat on the chest. He poured some of the water from the pitcher into the basin and washed his face. The water was tepid and oily.

It was early, and it seemed as if the town had not yet risen. He thought about what he was going to do today: leave or stay another day or two and impress the locals. And risk capture.

Then he remembered what had happened last night, and he flopped onto the bed. He had a gunfight to attend this morning, and he could see no way of getting out of it.

Gus stared bleakly at the strange gun hanging in its belt from the back of a chair.

"Well, shit," he said aloud, jumping to his feet. "It don't matter none that my horse is dead. I've got money! I can buy another horse and get outta here!"

He clambered into his clothes, packed his belongings into his saddlebag, hefted it quietly into the hotel's corridor. He crept down the steps, past the front desk and into the bar. The innkeeper was busy cleaning, preparing for the day's business.

"Mornin'," he said when he saw Gus heading for the front door.

"Howdy," Gus said softly. "You reckon anyone in town is awake and can sell me a horse?"

The innkeeper looked at Gus with mild interest. "Sure, Billy down at the blacksmith's shop has a couple, and he's probably awake by now. You fixin' to leave?"

"That's right."

"I don't give no refunds."

"Keep the goddamned money," said Gus, turning toward the door and leaving the innkeeper to smile at his unexpected good fortune.

Once outside, he chose to walk on the dirt street rather than the plank sidewalks so as not to make noise and attract attention. Looking both ways along the street, he saw the blacksmith shop about four buildings to his right. He walked quickly toward it.

He came to the shop's big stable doors and was about to knock.

"Going somewhere, friend?"

Gus turned, and there he was... *again*. He no longer wore the coat that covered his gun belt; the holster rested empty against his hip. The gun was in his pale hand, the muzzle pointing unwaveringly at Gus.

"Just checkin' to see if there was a horse for sale... for after our business," Gus blurted.

Dr. Alatryx smiled. "Confidence is a charming quality. Overconfidence is a deadly one," he said. "Should we attend to our business, friend?"

Gus sighed and dropped his saddlebag to the ground. He frowned slightly and said yes, his hand dropping nonchalantly to the gun in his own holster.

Dr. Alatryx cocked his gun in warning.

Gus squeezed the trigger without taking his gun from its holster. As he pulled it, he heard Dr. Alatryx's gun click in front of him.

Jammed.

Gus' gun boomed, echoing across the wooden canyons of the town.

His fourth bullet crashed into a surprised Dr. Alatryx's chest, shoving him backwards, his arms pin wheeling, the gun torn from his hand. A gout of blood and gore splashed the dusty red wall of the blacksmith shop. Dr. Alatryx slumped against the wall and lay there.

Gus shook with the rush of fear that swept through his body.

"Shit," he whispered. He knelt near Dr. Alatryx and examined the wound. The son of a bitch had to be dead now. He stood and prodded the body with his foot.

Nothing.

He bent, lifted the gun Dr. Alatryx had dropped. He was careful to point it away from himself.

As if it mattered.

Dr. Alatryx's last bullet unjammed itself and roared from the barrel, lifting a thick patch of hair and scalp from the top of Gus' head, matted with whitish-red clots, and slapping it against the rough wooden wall near the doctor's bloodstain.

Gus' body stood for a moment as if not understanding that it was dead before collapsing in a heap next to the doctor.

Gus' stolen brown bowler bounced down the dusty street on its rim, joining a herd of desiccated tumbleweeds as they rolled out of town.

A bucket of water splashed against the wall, and the gore mixed with the dust to form a foul-colored paste. The sheriff, also the town's general store owner, hooked his arms under Gus' body, which hung limply from under the bed sheet the innkeeper had brought. A deputy took Gus' feet, and the two carried the body to the sheriff's office, where they laid it on a pallet inside one of the empty cells.

"Are you sure there's no other bodies?" asked the sheriff. "People are sayin' they heard two shots. And there were two stains on the wall. But that poor bastard's only got one wound. Not that it weren't enough."

"No, sir, I checked all over," the young deputy answered. The sheriff took the answer at face value, but knew he'd be spending the better part of his day searching the town anyway.

The office door rattled, and two men walked in. The sheriff caught a brief glimpse of a crowd.

Let 'em wait. I'll show the body later.

The first man was the innkeeper. "Must be our lucky day," he said. "Sheriff, this here man's an undertaker makin' his way to California. He said he'd be glad to help."

The second man was dressed in black, a tall hat crowned his head, and two streamers of black crepe flowed down from the top of the silk hat and covered his face. A long coat protected his suit from the dust.

"Pleased to meet you, friend," said the undertaker, offering his hand to the sheriff, who took it and released it quickly, a glimmer of disgust crossing his features.

"Well, sir, seein' as how this man has plenty of money, we've got gold to pay you," said the sheriff as the undertaker bent, uncovered the body.

"Dead as a nail," clucked the undertaker.

He reached into Gus' vest, drew out the silver pocket watch. It opened with a snap, and he smiled. "This will be all the payment I require."

"Fine. There's a cemetery about two miles outside town," said the sheriff.

"When I finish my business, I will take him there. It's the least I can do for my payment." The undertaker closed the watch, slipped it into his vest.

As the undertaker stood, the folds of his coat parted to reveal two black guns strapped across his hips, each with intricately carved ebony handles.

"That's the most heavily armed undertaker I've ever seen," whispered the sheriff to the innkeeper.

The innkeeper, however, was lost in thought, trying hard to remember exactly where he had seen a gun like those before.

RED SHADOWS IN TERROR CANYON
By Lawrence Berry

Tracks In Red Sand...

Spur Hardesty followed the woman's trail through the aspen forest at the base of Purgatory Mesa, bowing his head as he rode through the glossy leaves. Her horse had tired in the long run from Durango and the hoof prints in the soft loam showed stumbles and missteps.

Perhaps Miss Pierce would accept being rounded up without too much disagreement. Her father, and the fiancé, Chester Plummer, had predicted she'd have to be brought back tied to her saddle.

He rode out of the aspen saplings onto a dry riverbed. Half-buried tree trunks littered the wash, left by flash floods from the gorge to the east. The riven mesa rose like a scarlet citadel against the morning sky.

Something about it picked at his memory. Then he realized that they'd traveled much further than he had thought and had come to Terror Canyon.

The legends surrounding it began when a trapper brought a wagon into Durango, minus the family that owned it, a casualty of something that lived in the gorge. Dried blood had soaked into the weathered wood, leaving little doubt as to the family's fate. A cavalry patrol went out to make a search and didn't return. A larger, well-armed force was sent and they found a regiment hat. The horse soldiers rode the full length, camped, and traveled back over their trail the next day with no further discoveries.

It was as haunted and hungry a chasm as existed in the San Juan badlands—and Nancy Pierce was riding directly toward it.

Spur gave Sainglend a nudge and they followed the trail through the broken trees.

Private Justice...

A woman sobbed somewhere ahead, her cries echoing in the tight walls of sandstone. Spur rode toward the sound, finding Nancy Pierce weeping over her horse. She whirled at his approach, wiping her face.

He eased down from Sainglend, his Arabian curious about the fallen mount. Spur nodded to Nancy Pierce and went to her bay. The animal's knees were swollen from the hard trek and he'd gone too far without water. White streaks showed around his mouth where he breathed out his salt.

"Nancy, would you lead Sainglend back a ways?"

"You know my name."

Spur dug his card from his gun belt and handed it to her.

"Private justice," she said. "That's you?"

"I'm Spur Hardesty—private justice is what I provide."

She turned the card over, reading the note from her fiancé. Spur found him a fussy man, with a peevish attitude. He argued about the fee, which was standard, even though his beloved bride-to-be was riding into the San Juan desolation, in the spring, when the flash floods were at their worst. If she got herself swept up in a torrent, the only thing Spur would find would be her intestines. Interior parts tended to catch on the boulders and unravel like party streamers.

"Chester paid you?" she asked, raising her face to him, sullen with anger.

"Yes, to bring you back." Despite the week in the saddle, the weather and sun, she was beautiful. Long black hair ran over slim shoulders, moving with the breeze. She was like Sainglend in her fineness.

"My father wants me to marry him."

"I met your father, Nancy, and he's plenty worried."

"Father needs money," she said, hell in her voice.

"*Ira furor brevis est.*"

"A gunman who fancies Latin, now that is a precious thing. Anger is a short madness?"

"It should be, in my opinion. Your father is sorry, which in another reason I'm here. To tell you he regrets making the arrangement." Spur gestured toward her horse, not wanting to be unkind. Durango would take care of itself.

"What if I get on that big stud of yours and ride off?"

"Sainglend wouldn't allow that."

"I'm not going back to Chester Plummer," she said, and stormed away, pulling the Arabian into a trot.

Spur heard a whisper high up in the gorge, traveling toward him in broken echoes. He looked to see what made it, finding nothing but long vines moving against the cinnamon stone. The mesa wind wasn't strong enough to shake them, and didn't have sufficient force to scatter the curious foulness that tended to gather in the air.

The cliff face remained unchanged, unchanging. The vines ceased to move and hung still.

Nancy's bay tried to gather his legs under him and stand, a forlorn attempt that came to nothing.

Spur knelt beside the gelding and spoke to him tenderly, rubbing his head. He was a good horse, but only an Arabian, or an appaloosa, could survive long, continuous travel in this part of the badlands due to the dragging weight of the sand. Its death was certain the moment she set out.

He drew his pistol and shot the horse behind the ear, putting the bullet into the base of its brain. The same odd whisper drifted down, a susurrus of lost spirits, following the crash of the gun shot.

Late afternoon sun and scarlet stone conspired to create sanguine bars of shadow on the heights and nothing moved within them. He remembered the feeling of being close to a death that couldn't be seen from his cavalry days and this was not a comfort.

He had suffered the same unease on the hunt for Looking Glass, on the day the War Chief finally went to ground, grown tired of pursuit by the horse soldiers. The Indians used an Apache trick, smearing pine resin on teepee leather so it would hold the local soil and plant life, blending themselves perfectly into the terrain.

Ten men died in as many minutes, seemingly destroyed by the wilderness itself.

The Nez Perce believed three kinds of death inhabited the badlands—the one you saw, the one you didn't, and the one that killed you.

Cannibal Nightmare...

Nancy had walked Sainglend far enough back to blunt the shot, but not so far that the stallion would throw a fit, showing good horse sense.

She hadn't touched his canteen and he swore under his breath, knowing he should have given her water immediately. She was standing up on sheer willpower alone.

Spur pulled the canteen free. "Give me your hand."

"Why?"

"We'll try a little water, but it may go down hard. Spit some out first so you get your mouth wet, and then try a small sip."

She opened her fist, stained with dust and leather. Spur poured water into her palm. She spit as he had asked, then sipped at the water, thirst in her face strong as a fever.

Looking Glass let Spur's unit find him a second time and killed most of the remaining soldiers, using the same ploy. Captain Roth had led them a full day past their water supply and Arturo Rodriguez cut the big vein on a pack horse's leg at sunset to remedy the problem. They drank its blood, filled their canteens, and rode for their lives when night fell.

When he saw thirst now, he thought of horse blood.

"What're you going to do with me?"

"Take you home."

"You might as well shoot me right here then. I won't marry that weasel, Papa be boiled in vinegar."

Spur lifted his hat and raked his hair back. "Think about it this way. Your horse is dead, your water is gone, and I happened along to help you."

"Would you bring all this chivalry to bear if you weren't being paid?"

She was mocking him. "Let's get you on Sainglend and I'll walk you out." Spur heard the whispers again, coming from different places in the cliff face, and the fine hair stiffened on his arms and neck.

"I thought I told you to shoot me, get it over with," she said.

Spur had the advantage of regular food and water. He tossed her into the saddle before she could put up a fight. They needed to get moving. He felt it right down to his boot heels.

She kicked him in the ribs with the point of her boot.

It was a moment before he could find wind to speak, but he was determined to carry on with logic. "It will be easier for us all if you ride and I don't have to tie you to the leather."

"A decent man would want to know what this is all about."

"I am sure you're going to tell me."

Sainglend neighed and Spur spoke to the stallion, soothing its worry, getting the horse moving. The whispers traveled with them, paring away the distance. When he first heard the faint voices, they almost seemed to come from the sky, above the rim. Now the sounds came from a source much lower and considerably nearer, closing at an alarming rate of speed.

Spur turned, walking backward. He saw a flicker of movement as something crawled across the cliff face, skittering along so fast it seemed to fly. He passed Nancy the reins and loosened his pistols, thinking about taking the Winchesters off the saddle. The hand guns were faster, however, and shot on line with his instinct. Whatever lived in Terror Canyon was quick as starlight.

"What are you doing?"

"I think we have company."

Something massive unfolded out of the cliff face and arced down toward them, using one of the vines as a rope.

Spur pulled his guns and put two shots in the huge shape, aiming and firing the right, then the left, hoping to hit the wide chest, wanting to be sure his bullets found flesh. Ragged, unkempt hair whipped around the creature's head as it lost its hold on the vine and fell, its body writhing in panic. It hit with mortal impact, the bones in its back snapping from the force.

Whatever it was, he'd never seen one before. The thing was more human than animal, from a race he didn't recognize. The features on its wide, heavy face were crudely formed, and showed the mistakes of too common a nature in its breeding. It wore a twist of leather around its loins that bore a regiment tattoo and Spur sucked in his breath, raising his eyes from the cannibal nightmare at his feet.

Nothing moved along the walls, but his belly and his heart told him it wasn't over. They sent one of their slow ones, an old one, to test his meddle.

He glanced at Nancy, who looked back in shock. This was a long canter from high tea at the Stater Hotel in Durango. He began backing up, trailing after Sainglend.

The cliff face erupted with movement and the battle was on. The canyon people had skin the color of the cliff walls and could trick the eye, merging into the sandstone as if they were part of it. They moved over the rock following handholds carved into the rock, fast as deer in flight, taking to the vines, sailing toward him out of the shadows.

He let his hands go, firing at motion he felt more than saw, grinning at the howls of agony that followed the barrel flashes.

Nancy screamed as she was pulled out of the saddle by a young bull hidden in the wash. Spur turned to fire on it, and then checked his guns, Nancy's body flinging back and forth over its shoulder as it scaled the gorge at an incredible pace.

Spur swung into the saddle and sent Sainglend running.

The Arabian bent into a gallup that made the walls of Terror Canyon blur. Spur lay flat against the horse's neck and held on, shadows cutting lines across floor of the gorge as the people of the canyon tried to catch them.

The largest creature he had yet seen waited on the ridge cap at the canyon's entrance, a monster the size of a Grizzly bear. It threw its body out into space and caught one of the vines, flying down with massive grace.

Spur's Colt pistols were dry and it would take too long to pull a rifle.

He reached back and gave Sainglend an urgent slap, something he'd done only once before in both their lives. The stallion, who had come to him from halfway around the world, gift of a magician that lived on an island of jade, stretched out and ran as an arrow flies, through the canyon, out into the riverbed, more eagle than horse.

The monster landed behind them with the force of an earthquake, a heartbeat slow from smashing them to ground.

But then it had the woman, and perhaps it didn't really care.

A Game Of Blood...

Spur freed his spyglass from his saddle bag and studied the canyon walls, seeing half a dozen hulking shapes ranged along the rim, watching the scarred river bed. A rounded peak rose in the distance, far back in the interior. The spire was too far away to make out any worthwhile details, but he sensed movement around it the way he sometimes sensed a hawk flying too high up to be seen.

There wasn't any sane way to go after Nancy without riding back up Purgatory Mesa and around, keeping out of view of the scouts, and staying well back from the entrance. The canyon itself was killing ground and had been since the dawn of the last age. It was also true they probably had a somewhat wider territory than was apparent and he'd have to stay far back from their scrutiny. In the end it would be a gamble, taking the battle to them, because he'd have to depend on surprise.

Spur grudged the time it would take, but one well-executed ambush deserved another. This retaliatory equation had been his final gift to Looking Glass in that long-passed war, a season of hate that still felt new to him in his heart. Maybe you could never kill some enemies enough, no single death provided adequate satiation.

Spur knew himself to be a killer—cousin, son, and father to Looking Glass, and about as alien as a lizard to good, competent, steady Captain Roth. This was a game of blood now, and a hell-spun part of his soul rose to it.

A Coming Storm...

The aspen forest made Spur ride higher, and go further down country, than he wished. Night had fallen when he stopped a mile from the deeper ink that marked the opening in the canyon wall.

Sainglend would wait without a hobble, grazing and listening for his whistle.

Spur slung his two Winchesters, tied his boots to his belt, and made the ascent. He'd been scaling canyon walls since he could walk and it wasn't a hard climb, even though the breeze had risen to a gale and he could smell rain in the air.

He strung rope as he went up, preparing for a fast descent on his return.

He could feel the might of a spring storm when he made the top the canyon, sage brush bouncing past him in the surging wind. Pinpricks of light showed in the darkness, half a mile into the mesa. He headed toward them, forcing his body through the push of the blow.

Skulls In The Moonlight...

Spur hadn't gone far when he found a shallow arroyo and decided to use this as a passage. He sensed the presence of his adversaries on the higher ground, most likely watching the approaches out of habit;

this, too, reminded Spur of Looking Glass, who saw everything, everywhere around him, even his own death.

He came to an obstruction that blocked the way ahead, shining like old snow in the moonlight. He scrambled around the blockage and stopped in horror. A mountain of skulls had jammed in the cleft, carried by seasons of melting snow. Ivory jaws and midnight eyes grinned up at the stars.

Evil lived here.

Evil reigned and ruled over this lost sea of red stone.

But that was going to end.

Winchester Holocaust...

The walls of the arroyo shrank to nothing and disappeared. Spur crouched behind a lonely scrub oak, considering the eroded peak that was his destination. It was pitted with caverns that gaped in the flux of the storm light, many carrying the remnants of cook fires, testament to the use the people of the canyon had found for the dead bay. Only they weren't caverns exactly, they were more like the mouths of tunnels, with well-engineered arches worn down by heat and weather.

Nancy stirred and he saw her, staked to a sandstone pillar that widened into a platform at its top, supporting a carven god unlike anything Spur had seen in native American encampments. It was hideous, and repellently sexual, with a head like a nest of snakes—a composite creature that was part sea creature, something not of this earth or time.

Insanity hung over the city like a demonic aura.

The tunnels led to what pits? What hideous abnormalities lay below his feet? Did they mean to feed on Nancy's flesh, or sacrifice her to some malignant throwback crawled out of an abyss deep in the mesa?

The foulness here was beyond Spur's comprehension and fed the hatred growing in his heart.

The people of the canyon had a much larger fire at the top of the peak, partially shielded by an outcropping of stone. He could see the turn and flash of flames, and wild movement against it, but their city was empty of life. Everyone was at the picnic.

Spur tied his knife to his arm with rawhide and set out. The wind raged with greater force and he could see a near-constant blaze of tiny lightning strike ten miles away. All the rain in the world was coming down there.

Shadows grew and fell with the cloud cover, by turns hiding and revealing the uneven surface of the mesa. It could have been an illusory sea from hell he traveled across, a black ocean of false promises.

Nancy lifted her head, hearing the click of his boots.

Spur cut the vine they'd bound her with, a tough weave made of cactus fiber, one of the things they hadn't forgotten in the ruin of the ages, a wisdom not yet lost.

"You shouldn't have come," she said, green eyes glistening in the flashes of moonlight.

"I can see you have them where you want them." Spur lifted her to her feet, her legs unsteady.

A whisper drifted over the mesa. One of the watchers had seen him.

"We have a chance here, if you can reload the guns when I need you to."

She looked at the rifles as if they were willful children. "Show me."

"These are handmade Winchester rifles, the best in the world. They take a .44-70 cartridge and will blow holes in anything I hit." He put his hat in her hands, filling it with bullets from the carrier on his belt. Spur pushed a cartridge part way in the receiver. "Nothing complicated here. Slide six bullets into the magazine supplying the shorter barrel with your thumb, eight in the long rifle. Hand it back to me."

"Why are they different?"

"When you're hunting a man in heavy brush, a twenty-inch barrel can be of worthwhile benefit, but it carries less ammunition. The person with the last cartridge tends to come out on top in most contests of this kind, so it's good and bad. The twenty-six inch rifle is better for distance because the site radius is longer."

Nancy shook her head at the import of something he'd said, turning from private reservations. "I can do this, Spur."

The canyon people were coming now in streams, moving quickly down the ramps that linked the tunnels. Spur waited until the first ones reached open ground, Winchester at the ready. He began firing when they attacked, flame gushing from the barrel as residual gunpowder burned. The sun-brilliant muzzle flashes, and the instant falls into wind-ripped night, made the slaughter an elegant play of face cards, each printed with shattered skulls and rent flesh.

Spur cut them down the way he once saw wheat felled in Kansas, at harvest time—their bodies made dark sheaves and black blood followed the ripples in the sandstone, flowing away into the mesa.

He ran the first rifle empty and took up the second gun. The killing became a slaughter, the slaughter a Winchester holocaust, and all the savage darkness in his nature rose like hunger, like red thirst.

A great slithering cry, different than the whispers he'd heard before, rose above the shriek of the wind, calling the people of the canyon back from destruction. They faded up the naked stone, into the tunnels.

Gun-smoke swirled and tossed, a silver fury in the spectral glow.

Spur hated their stink, their viciousness, their very existence. He didn't think he could kill a sufficient number of them to sate his gun lust, yet mercy stilled his hands. Enough of them had died in this place where they made their home to render a sort of justice. He had fed the skulls in the arroyo the blood of monsters and set the balance sheet to rights.

Spur slung the rifles and left the field, carrying Nancy with him, angling directly for the rope passage down the cliff face.

The lightning in the clouds painted a stark illumination over the mesa and the smell of rain had grown overpowering. The full measure of the storm was minutes away.

They had good fortune and went to the descent, without having to search along the rim for the rope tie. Spur lowered Nancy using an improvised hoist, and followed her at speed.

He didn't smell the canyon people, or see them, but he felt them, out in the electric darkness, a kind of giant anger kindling into rage.

Terror Canyon...

Spur whistled for Sainglend, the horse running to him. He threw Nancy in the saddle, slamming the rifles in their scabbards, and got on behind her, turning the horse toward Purgatory Mesa.

The ground began to jump under Sainglend's hooves and Terror Canyon gave voice to a titanic roar. At first it seemed as if a deeper, more pure night flowed out of the gorge, then this swelled into a forty foot wave, exploding over the wash in a fury of ivory foam. The black water bristled with boulders and smashed pine trees, eating everything in its path.

Sainglend made the crossing and drove for higher ground, following the rise into the aspen forest. The soft earth slid away beneath him, churning into the current. Spur twisted off the saddle and put his shoulder into Sainglend's hind leg, giving the stallion support to work against. Black water swirled to his waist, then rose to his chest, pulling him into the flood. Nancy grabbed his wrist and yanked him back with desperate strength.

Sainglend would not relent and charged again and again into the slick mud until his hooves caught buried granite and gained purchase. He heaved his massive body out of the roaring water, dragging Spur and Nancy with him.

A dozen steps took them to the trail Spur had followed earlier that day, lifetimes ago, and they labored up the treacherous slope to a rain-whipped meadow, safe from the water tearing away the bank.

Spur wiped his eyes so he could see.

A massive wave raced down the center of the ancient channel, acres of earth caving in before it. The canyon people were halfway across the riverbed, driven by hatred and desire, led by their monster chieftain.

The flashing obsidian crest swept them up and rolled them under, the white spume turning red.

A Dry Blanket And Good Whiskey...

Nancy found his hand and pressed his fingers, tender and tired. She had held to the saddle when all was lost. No more could be asked of any man or woman, this side of the grave.

She'd need water, a fire, a dry blanket, and good whiskey, if she was going to see Durango alive.

Sainglend stirred, restless, wanting his rub down and his feed bag, ridden half to death this long day. Spur gave him his head, trusting the horse to lead them to shelter.

FEAST OF FAMINE

BY BRIAN M. SAMMONS

"First time in Mexico?" the man said to the woman at his side.

The two had just left the southernmost train station in the country, the end of the line as far as civilized gringos were concerned. Now the odd pair was sitting in a sun-bleached buckboard wagon heading farther South, while the smoke-belching train, after taking on precious water for the boiler, was returning to the North. The old wagon creaked as it was slowly pulled by a swaybacked mare the word 'nag' didn't do did justice to. The wagon rattled down a single dirt trail that passed for a road, in these parts, with the man at the reins.

He was short but well-muscled, dressed as a peasant farmer, and his yellow-tinged eyes not only reflected his battle with jaundice but also a good nature. The smile on his face was easy and relaxed as he gazed out at the wide open nothingness all around them. The well-used scatter gun that sat between the pair was a reminder that even in the middle of desolation, you could never be too careful.

The woman, actually riding shotgun, was his opposite in almost every way. She was tall and thin with bright scarlet hair tucked up under a man's bowler hat. Her green eyes were all but unreadable behind thick glasses that perched on the end of her nose and she had her lips pressed into a tight grimace. Where the man was dark by nature, and made darker still by a life outdoors, she was paler than most gringos that came to Mexico. If he had not seen her step off the train with his own eyes, Arcadio might have guessed she had eaten or drank something down here that did not agree with her. Many from up North just didn't have the stomach for Mexican food, let alone the water.

"Yes." The woman's said simply.

"So, you're a reporter? Here to do a story about the famine?" Arcadio asked, looking to help pass the long ride with a little conversation. His words were heavily accented and tinged with a hint of incredulity. He had never imagined that the reporter he had been sent to bring back would be a woman. He was sure no one at the mission had guessed that either. Such an idea was just crazy, but then Arcadio had heard that gringo ladies were more uppity and demanding than the Mexican women he was used to. The fact that she wore men's trousers, jacket, and hat increased her foreignness to him.

"Yes." The woman repeated. She then took a moment to really look at her surroundings for the first time. "Everything here is still green and growing, it's hard to believe that there's a drought."

"Oh where I'm taking you is still far away, we won't get there until late tomorrow. But yes, here it is green and living, there everything is brown and dead. But that is Mexico for you. Things here can change, just like that." The man snapped his fingers to punctuate his sentence.

"Not just in Mexico." The woman said quietly, almost to herself. She absently rubbed her hands together. She wore thin leather gloves that seemed out of place in this scorching heat. However she did not wear them for warmth or even for fashion, but to hide the three missing fingers on her left hand.

A hand spotted black where flesh had died to frostbite, pulled the large stone out of the bank next to the near frozen river. Round and thick on one end, narrow and sharp at the other, it would make a good weapon. Suddenly from behind came the sound of footfalls crunching through snow. The stone was quickly stuffed into a pocket of a jacket too thin for the freezing weather and, soon after, three people were standing by the icy river.

"Day four and it's still snowing." Constance said bitterly, stating the obvious to the others. As time stretched on, the obvious was all that was left to talk about. This was the third and longest blizzard they had suffered through since becoming snowbound over a month ago.

Constance bent at the knees and removed her burlap mask that she had made out of a long empty potato sack. While the mask was comical to look at, it worked well and so far her good looks had been spared the disfiguring touch of Jack Frost. She reached for one of the waterskins freshly filled with icy water, only to drop it with a pained wince. Her hands had not fared as well as her face in the bitter cold. Already one of her pinky fingers was almost completely black and a number of other digits were also on their way to becoming lost.

"Here, let me help." Abigale said. The other woman had the good fortune to have packed some light gloves for the long journey. While not ideal for the bitter cold, they were better than nothing.

"Let's get the water back to the camp. There's still enough daylight left so that I can check the traps." John said. He had his hands shoved into pockets of his beaver fur jacket, easily the best garment any of them had to combat the cold. However John sure wasn't any gentleman and he jealously hoarded his fur coat. He had even beaten poor McGillis half to death in a fight over it five days past. Two nights ago the unrelenting cold had finished what John had started, bringing the number of settlers down to just the three of them.

"Why bother? They ain't never caught nothing." Constance whined, carefully using her good hand to pull her hood back over her head.

Abigale's stomach growled loudly as if to echo Constance's statement. It had been two days since anyone had eaten anything. Even then, their last meal had been two frozen carrots, the very last of their provisions, and a few mouthfuls each of the last of the horse meat.

"We might get lucky, you can never know." John said as the three of them walked back to their camp somewhere deep in Canada's Northwest Territory.

"We never should have listened to Captain Holsten. He clearly lied to us when he claimed to have lead folks out this way. We started off too late, move too slowly. Mr. Pearsons was right; we should have stayed at that last town," Constance said, the madness of monotony breeding repetition as she had said that very thing now six ways to Sunday.

"What do you think happened to him and the others?" Abigale asked.

"No tellin'. With the snows this bad, they could be hunkerin' down too, waitin' on it to move on out. Or maybe they made it back to that town and are now on their way back with help."

"Or maybe the Indians got to them first." Constance added. The woman's American born fear of the natives had caused her to keep looking over her shoulder all during their long trek West.

"Yep, that could have happened too, but I doubt it. Any Injuns in this snow will have their own problems to contend with. They won't go addin' to them by killin' any white folk they come across." John said.

"Would the Indians help us if they found us?" Abigale asked, desperate to pick at any frayed thread of hope.

"No Ma'am, they wouldn't do that neither. Probably just go around us, leavin' us to our fate, and we'd never know they were even there."

As the trio trudged through the thigh-high snow, the ever constant wind seemed to pick up. It could be accurately called howling, but to one of the three survivors, it was whispering. Over and over again for the better part of a week the wind had been calling out, muttering a single word. To the one that could hear it, the wind was whispering their name. As they continued to listen to it, their icy fingers caressed a concealed rock in a pocket. Their mind began to wander with thoughts of blood and their belly growled with a gnawing hunger.

"Senorita Anderson, You're the American reporter, yes?" the doctor in the blood splattered apron asked, his accent rich, his voice deep, his eyes surprised.

"Yes, and you are?"

"Dr. Madaleno Gutierrez, at your service." The middle-aged man said through a weary smile. "I'm sorry if I seem taken aback at seeing you, but when you wrote to us you only used your first initial of M. I - we all just assumed that you would be a man."

"That's exactly why I only use my initial for my byline. Many men don't think a woman has anything of value to say, so why should they read what one writes?"

"Ah yes, this is true," Dr. Gutierrez said and then quickly added, "Oh, but not that I agree with it. I love women. No, I mean I respect women. And woman or no, any help your stories can do for us down here would be wonderful."

The white woman smiled a bit wanly, "Well that's why I'm here."

"And you really think that if rich Americans hear about all the troubles we are having that they will send us money, medicine, or food?"

"We Americans can often be generous."

At that, Arcadio snorted a bit too loudly from where he stood with his hat in his hands in a corner of the Spanish mission turned makeshift hospital. When the American and the doctor looked his way, he bowed his head, mumbled an apology, and wandered to another corner of the room, one farther away.

"But isn't your country still rebuilding after their Civil War? The Great Reconstruction, yes?" The doctor asked.

"That was some years back, but what help I can do for you won't come from the government, but from individuals, good Christian families of means who will read about your plight down here and will want to help in some way."

"That is good news. Any help these poor souls can get would be very welcome," the doctor beamed. "Oh, may I ask what the 'M' stands for?"

The woman paused for perhaps a second longer than Madaleno thought would be necessary to answer such a simple question before saying "Mary." Then she quickly asked, "Just out of surgery?" She pointed at the bloody leather apron the doctor wore.

"Unfortunately yes. As hunger grows people get desperate, do stupid, violent things. Someone shot a man and his wife then, we think, stole what little food they had hidden away. The senora died but I was able to save the husband." The doctor then added grimly, "He had already lost his daughter to starvation and now he has lost his wife and his leg. Sometimes the cruelty of life can be too much."

"That is dreadful. I do hope my words can do some good for these poor people."

"As do I." After a moment of silence, the doctor asked, "Did Arcadio show you your tent?"

"Yes, thank you."

"I wish we had better accommodations, but again, we did not think you would be a lady, so..."

"A tent is fine," the American said briskly. "I don't want to keep you from your patients, so can you point me in the direction of the worst of the famine victims so I can report on their suffering first hand?"

"Certainly. Well then, it was lovely to meet you. I'm sure I'll see you from time to time. Arcadio!" the Doctor called out and the yellow-eyed man walked forward.

"Would you please take Senorita Anderson and show her some of the starving?"

"Yes, of course. Senorita, you haven't eaten yet, would you like to get some food before I take you?" Arcadio asked.

"No, no I'm not hungry."

Arcadio's eyes narrowed slightly and he smiled nervously. "Are you sure? I noticed you hardly ate anything yesterday when we stopped for the night and you must have been on that train for a long time before that."

"Yes, Senorita Anderson there's no point to you starving yourself." Dr. Gutierrez said. "When people come here for the first time, they sometimes feel guilty about eating with so many suffering close by, but you'll do no one any good if you join their ranks."

The woman put on a strained smile and said, "You're right, both of you. Yes I guess I could use something to eat. Where can I go for that?"

Arcadio gave her instructions to the mess tent and then told her that he would join her shortly. After she walked away, he shot the older doctor a questioning look.

"Yes, I can see what you were saying, there's something odd about her." Madaleno said.

"Maybe she's sick?" Arcadio asked. "She seems so pale and sweaty, even for a gringo."

"She didn't act like it. Keep an eye on her for me. Let me know if she shows other signs of illness. Last thing these people need, on top of everything else, is to catch something from her."

Arcadio nodded and started after the woman, then stopped and turned back to the doctor. "That was the first time I saw her eyes without her spectacles. The first time I really looked into them, you know?"

"Yes?"

"She has the eyes of a hunter."

"What?" the doctor said with a chuckle.

Arcadio looked at the other man in all seriousness. "She's looking for something or someone. Of that I am certain."

"Maybe." Madaleno said. He then removed his bloody apron and called over a boy to take it out back and give it a 'dry wash' with dirt and stones as water was too precious to waste. The child limped over, shirtless, with every bone in his torso clearly visible under his skin. "Well if she's looking for hell, she found a good place to start."

"There is no way I'm eating that," Constance said with a grimace.

"We all said we'd do this, it's the only way. None of us have had anythin' to eat in days and who knows how long it will be before we're rescued. And if'n that don't come and we have to walk out of this come spring, we ain't gonna make it that long on just tree bark and whatever shoe leather we got left to boil." John said as he held out a chunk of charred meat to the cringing woman.

"Maybe check the traps again?"

"Those traps are bullshit. They ain't never caught nothin'. And honestly, I didn't know what I was doin' when I set them. I'm a farmer, not a trapper or a wild man. I don't even really know how to use this." John said and nodded to the revolver and gun belt that he wore.

"And before you ask, we tried spear fishin' again and you know how well that went. All we got for our troubles was more frostbite."

"But I can't eat a person, it's…" Constance's voice faded away as she eyed the offered meat in front of her. Her words were soon replaced by a loud rumble from her belly.

"Don't think of it as a person. He's dead. He's just meat now and we need to eat if we're going to live through this. Look, Abby is eating." John said and nodded to the other woman on the other side of their meager fire.

Abigale looked up from her own portion of sliced homesteader thigh. "It's not bad if you just don't think about it."

"Oh God," Constance whispered as she took the meat with a trembling hand.

"It's the only way, you know that," John said as he sliced another serving off of the leg spitted over the flames. "And when we get out of here, we don't tell this to no one. Not ever."

Constance put the meat gingerly into her mouth, took the smallest of possible bites, chewed a couple of times and then spit the burnt flesh out.

"I can't, I won't become a God damn cannibal!" Constance shouted as she stood up and ran out of the shelter made from wood salvaged from wagons whose owners were long past caring. She quickly disappeared into the howling winds and flying snow outside.

"Constance, come back." John called after her and began to rise.

"She'll come around, she just needs time." Abigale said with her mouth full.

John looked down at the eating woman and was about to tell her to shut the hell up when his empty stomach painfully cramped up. He dropped to one knee and gritted his teeth.

Abigale kicked the piece of cooked leg that Constance had spat out towards him.

Without a word John sat, picked up the meat, and began to eat.

Outside the shelter the winds continued to howl, and for one of the three caught in that frozen hell, it whispered of dark and secret things.

It had been four days since the American woman had come to the refugee camp, and true to his word, Arcadio had kept an eye on her. He knew she spent most of her time at the east end of the once tiny town that was now overrun with the starving. The east end of the now sprawling city of tents and hastily hobbled together shanties was where the most malnourished of the famine's victims were housed. The gringo woman spent long hours there talking with the slowly dying people, chronicling their miseries.

The white woman also appeared to have finally adjusted to Mexico. Gone were her sweats and pallid complexion. She also seemed less edgy and more at peace. The haunted, hunting look in her eyes was gone. Arcadio thought that she might have found whatever it was she had been looking for.

Maybe she just needed to help others? Some people are like that, He thought to himself as he walked down the dusty path towards the reporter's tent.

Just like you, right? A nagging voice inside Arcadio's head said.

Arcadio shook it off and when he made it to the tent, he stopped outside of it and called out, "Senorita Anderson, are you there?"

Arcadio waited for a moment and then called out again. After still no reply he lifted the tent flap and went inside to escape the scorching Sun. He removed his dirty hat and pulled a cloth from his pocket to mop his brow while looking about. Seeing everything neat and tidy, the man decided to wait for a few minutes in case the reporter turned up. He certainly didn't intend to snoop, at least not on a conscious level, but when he spied one of the woman's bags peeking out from underneath her cot, his curiosity got the better of him.

Kneeling, Arcadio pulled the battered suitcase out and found it unfastened. Opening it, he expected to find clothes and frilly lady things, but instead he discovered a new looking book, a worn leather-bound journal, a lady's handbag, and a bundle of some sort of animal hide in a roll and tied with a ribbon. This discovery only fueled his inquisitiveness, so after a look over his shoulder at the tent's flaps, he picked up the book.

As he could not read Spanish, let alone English, he just quickly thumbed through it. He saw that nearly every page had parts underlined or notes written in the margins in the same fine hand. He was compelled to stop and look at a number of illustrations done in black ink, and was shocked at what he saw. Each and every picture showed people killing and eating other people. One had black-skinned savages with spears stabbing and cooking white men. Another showed large men in skirts with odd designs drawn on their faces and wielding wicked looking clubs dancing around a fire that had a human torso spitted over it. One picture Arcadio recognized as the people before his people, the Aztecs, by the stepped pyramid in the drawing and the jaguar headdress the man in the illustration wore as he cut out another man's heart with a stone knife. There was even a picture of a white man, down on all fours like a beast, with a small child clutched in his jaws.

Who would own such a book? Arcadio wondered. *What man or woman would want to see and read about such things?*

Arcadio next opened the journal with trepidation, afraid of what else he may see. However his fears were unfounded as there were no illustrations in what he assumed was the gringo's private book. There were just words, lots and lots of words, and dates for each entry. The earliest was from 1851 and the latest was from two days ago. Never before had Arcadio so badly wished he could read. While the images in the awful book had sickened him, he desperately wanted to know what was going on inside the woman's head and he knew this book could tell him.

Maybe I should take it to Dr. Gutierrez? Surely he can read English, Arcadio thought and set the journal aside on the cot.

Next he picked up the flowery woman's handbag. Arcadio undid the clasp and pulled out of it many papers with official marks and stamps on them. Some of the papers had the seal of the eagle of America, others the crown of Canada, and one even had the stars and bars of the Confederate States that were no more. Although he never had one, the Mexican man knew they were identification papers of some sort. He had seen them a few times before, especially when he had worked for a short time on the docs of Tampico. It was because of that knowledge that Arcadio knew where on the papers a person's name was usually written and even though he could not read them, he recognized that every identification paper had a different name on it.

"What are you doing?" a voice asked from behind Arcadio. He turned to see the woman he knew as Mary Anderson standing at the tent's flaps, looking at him, but after what he had just found, he wasn't sure who she really was.

"What are *you* doing?" Arcadio said. He picked up three of the woman's identity papers and showed them to her.

"You're going through my things?"

"Yes, books on people eating people and papers in different names. Who are you? Who are you really and why are you here?"

The white woman was silent and Arcadio couldn't tell if she was concocting a lie or dredging up a buried truth, so he turned back to the open suitcase and pulled out the hide bundle.

"Let's see what this is, no?" He said and noticed that she flinched as he undid the ribbon that held the bundle together.

To his surprise the bundle held nothing, so he examined the skin itself. One side was covered in thick gray and white fur that he recognized as belonging to a wolf. The other side was cured and tanned and had once been brightly painted, but untold years had dulled the image and caused the natural pigments to fade. There were three figures painted on the hide and Arcadio recognized the trio as Indians from America because of their dress and the feathers in their hair. They were probably meant to be a family as there was a man, woman, and small child of undeterminable sex, however what the man had done to the others, no father would ever do. The Indian had killed his wife and child, they lay in red pools and a bloody axe was still in one of the man's hands. His other hand held the severed arm of his child up to his mouth where long, sharp teeth tore into the meat. There was a wild, feral look on the man's face as he ate and his eyes, instead of the brown all Indians had, were a pale, ghostly blue.

"More sick things." Arcadio said and tossed the grotesque painting into the woman's bag, then turned back to her. "So speak up, Senorita, why do you have such horrible things?

"I'm looking for…something. I first encountered it years ago in Canada and I've been following it ever since." She said.

"What *thing*?"

"It's hard to describe. It's a power, a force…you've seen the book?" Mary asked, pointing to her suitcase.

"Yes, people eating people."

"Many people over many years have believed that evil spirits and even ancient gods could make people become cannibals."

"What is, *cannibals*?" Arcadio asked.

The woman smiled, "People who eat people."

"So you think ghosts and spirits make people do that?"

"No," she said, "I think it's just one spirit, ancient and powerful and known by many names by many people all over the world."

Arcadio said nothing and just looked dubiously at her.

"Akua, Baxbakualanuchsiwae, Rakshasa, Ithaqua, Kishi. The Indians up north called it Wendigo and your own people have a name for it, Xixim. It has been both worshiped as a god and feared as a demon over many years. It is very real, and it is here now."

"Why is it here, if all this is even true?" Arcadio said.

"Because of the famine, it is drawn to such things, or it causes them, I'm not sure. It feeds off of the slow death by starvation and causes people to turn on each other in desperation. Misery is what it craves. For it, a famine would be a feast."

"Yes, but this famine has been going on for a long time and I have seen no *cannibals* or anything like what's in your awful book."

The white woman took out a small bundle from under her arm and it was the first time Arcadio noticed it. She opened the burlap sack, reached inside, and pulled out a bone. It was a femur, a human leg bone, and it was charred black and one of its knobby ends was broken off. It was also far too small to have come from an adult.

"I found this and more like it in the east end of the camp. This bone has been burnt from cooking and there are gnaw marks on it. It has also been cracked open so that whomever ate the meat off of it could get at the marrow. I've been asking around and most there won't talk to me, but there was one old woman. All she would say is that people are disappearing and she mentioned the Xixim."

Arcadio stared in silence, his stomach turning and mind racing. What he had just been told was simply too much to take in. He was used to death and horror, he had seen his first dead man at the age of eight, had killed his own when he was eleven and living on the streets of Mexico City. He had been a young soldier with Santa Anna during his last days of blood and fire before he was exiled. He had used what the army taught him to become a *vaquero* and had used the gun to defend his herds from both beast and man. Before finding Jesus and being saved, he had done his share of bad things he'd like to forget and witnessed even worse done by others, but this? The evils of man he believed in, but spirits?

"So if this evil spirit is real why do you chase it? Aren't you afraid of it?"

"It took something from me…" The woman said and then trailed off into silence.

"Your fingers?"

The woman's eyes widened with surprise and she looked at her maimed hand still within the leather glove.

"You hide it well, but I noticed it the second day you were here by the way you hold things." Arcadio said. "Did someone do that to you?"

"No, I lost something else to it…"

Constance was a whore, a fact known to all who knew her, and assumed by anyone who looked at her. She had a pretty face, a busty body, and not much else, so she did what she had to do to make her way in the world. While she wished things might have been different for her, she didn't lament her life or lose a wink of sleep over it. The world was a hard place and you had to become a hard bitch to survive it and if that meant renting her body to drunken, foul smelling fools for a few moments at a time, then that's what Constance would do. But even as an unrepentant whore, Constance had principles that she would not compromise, no matter what. She alone did not eat the dead while the other two survivors gave in to their appetites. She was proud of that.

But holding onto principles always seem to come at a price, and for Constance, going so long without food had sapped her strength. She had burrowed into a small pile of coats and clothes stripped from the frozen dead like an animal looking to hibernate. While she could do nothing to alleviate the hunger, she had at least escaped the cold. Now in the warm, dark silence, her mind wandered. She had no idea if it was day or night, when she last ate, or even if she was awake or just dreaming she was awake. Her principles also cost Constance every ounce of her strength, so when the hungry thing came for her, she could not do a thing about it.

With her senses dulled by exhaustion she didn't even notice that something was digging down through the pile of frost covered rags to reach her until the last suit coat was pulled away. Even then she thought it might be a dream because of the soft hands upon her. Not clawing or hurried but slow and caressing. They were the hands of a lover. When Constance at last opened her eyes and saw who it was touching her, she smiled. She recognized the person slowly undoing her layers to reach inside to cup her breasts. And why wouldn't she? They had traveled together for months, heading towards the West for the promise of something better. They had even been lovers while on the long trek, although that had been kept secret lest the others in the wagon train take offense. But this wasn't a visit from an old love looking to rekindle something lost. This was something else, entirely.

Maybe it was the way the fingers pinched at her flesh, or the drool that leaked out from between chapped, blue lips? Perhaps it was the low growling the hungry thing made, or the mad look in its eyes? No, it was the smile that finally caught Constance's drowsy attention, or more specifically the teeth behind the withered lips. There were just too many teeth for a person to have and they were all impossibly long and sharp.

A single tear began to pool in Constance's left eye as her sleepy mind began to put things together. She tried to make words, but only "Wh...wh...wh" escaped her.

"Ssshhh," the hungry thing hissed, "Far too late for that."

"Wh...why?" Constance managed, at last, but then quickly bit her lip in pain. The hands that had been pinching her breasts were now slicing through her undershirt with long claws. As the talons lightly scraped the flesh beneath the shredding garment, Constance felt an incredible cold coming from them so deep that it burned.

"Why?" it mocked. "Because I'm hungry. So very hungry."

"Pa...puh...please..."

"Ssshhh," the thing wearing the face of Constance's one time lover whispered again. It took one hand away from the trembling woman's body to caress her blonde hair. The touch was surprisingly gentle and that made it even worse. After a few seconds, it stopped, reached into a pocket of a jacket it wore, and pulled out a large, sharp rock.

"I'll make it quick for old time's sake." The hungry thing grinned.

Constance tried to lift her hands to protect her face but her arms felt like lead. She looked around for something, anything, any sort of hope, and then remembered one thing that might save her.

"Wha…what about…" she began, but the thing straddling her cut her off by pressing a freezing claw to her lips.

"Ssshhh," it said, "I'm saving them for later."

And then the rock came down.

Arcadio had listened to the gringo's unbelievable tale. It was a story of snowbound settlers in the wilds and of a man turning into a monster. That monster, she had called it a *wendigo*, ate her friend and had tried to do the same to her. She told him about running blindly from the beast after finding the remains of her friend until she lost it, and herself, in the dark woods. There she wandered cold, alone, and starving, for days before chancing upon a group of surprised fur trappers from a nearby town. She even confessed that she had to do unspeakable things in order to survive, something Arcadio could relate to.

"So if you…ate of the dead, why did you not become a monster?" He asked at the end of her story.

"I don't know. I've asked myself that very question a hundred times. Maybe I didn't eat as much as him, or something inside me was stronger than what was in John. Maybe the thing just wanted him. All I know is that I want to find that thing, that wendigo or xixim or whatever it is. I've been looking for it for years, from Canada, through America, and now down here, and this is the closest I've ever been to it since that winter long ago."

Arcadio believed her. He wasn't sure he believed all the rest, but he had known from the start that she was a hunter.

"So you think your John is here, in the camp somewhere?"

"Oh yes, the wendigo is here." She held up the gnawed bone again. "And it's eating well."

When Arcadio had hung up his gun three years back he swore his days of living selfishly were over. He had come to the refugee camp at the start of the famine to seek penance for his wicked years. Through helping these poor people he had found a measure of happiness and peace and he would be damned if he was going to give that up. It had taken him too long to find it. So while he had promised the Lord he would kill no more, if the woman's wendigo devil was real, he hoped that God would not mind him sending it back to Hell.

"Show me where you found the bone." He said.

"You'll help me?"

"Yes, but first, we must stop by my tent."

The pair left the woman's tent, who said her real name was Abigale, and crossed over to his. Once there Arcadio blew the dust off of an old trunk, unlocked it, and pulled out an old gunnysack. Inside the bag was a cracked and sun-bleached belt trailing a loop holster that held an old Colt Army revolver. He pulled the gun belt out and cinched it around his waist. The familiarity of the rig's weight was like meeting an old friend after far too long, and Arcadio hated that feeling. He pulled the revolver, checked the action, loaded the cylinder, and then replaced it in the well-worn holster. He then told Abigale to step outside and wait for him for a moment, which she did. After he was done praying, he joined her outside and told her to lead on.

The two made their way through the overcrowded town towards the East where the dusty tents and crude shanties crowded closest together. There was a clear but unmarked line where the east side began as the throngs of skeletal people vanished from the streets, but the moans and cries coming from inside humble dwellings increased, as did the stench of death. They saw only the sporadic starving child or withered old woman as they went, but Arcadio could always feel eyes watching him. Occasionally he would hear faint whispers of 'Xixim' or muttered prayers to the saints who appeared not to be listening.

"Over there, that shack," Abigale said and pointed with her good hand.

Arcadio moved slowly to the shanty, pulling his Colt from its holster and thumbing the hammer back. He kicked the door open.

The slaughterhouse stench hit him first.

Then came the sound of buzzing of flies.

Lastly, he saw mangled human shapes on the ground and, in the shadows of one corner of the room, movement.

Not wanting to, but helpless to stop himself, Arcadio took a couple of steps into the blood stained shack with Abigale close behind him.

He pointed his pistol towards where he had seen movement. A hiss came from the corner that sounded like a scalded cat. Standing his ground and waiting for his eyes to adjust to the gloom, he eventually saw what it was.

It was a girl, no more than ten-years-old, naked and caked in drying blood running from her mouth down to her immature chest. She was hissing through needle-like teeth and slashing at the air between them with long, dark claws at the end of her small fingers.

"*Ay Dios mio*" Arcadio whispered.

"No," he heard a voice say from behind him. It was a low growl that could scarcely be called human. "Only my God is here."

Turning, he saw a flash of motion and then his hand exploded in pain. Before he began to scream he was dimly aware that his gun, and two of his fingers, had hit the dirt floor. Then a cold, strong hand grabbed him by the throat, lifted him off his feet, and threw him to the ground where the wind was knocked out of him. The filthy child-thing scuttled from the corner, hissing as it came, and grabbed both of his wrists and pinned them to the earth with strength far beyond her tiny frame. The little girl's touch was scalding hot and blisters rose on Arcadio's flesh.

As the man tried to catch his breath, Abigale straddled him like she had done years ago to a terrified woman in northwest Canada. She smiled down at Arcadio, revealing her own mouthful of deadly fangs.

"Sorry, but I lied a little bit in my story." She said, huffing out frigid air between her now blue lips.

As if on cue, a back door to the shack opened and others began to pile into the small, hot room. They were all Mexicans, dangerously thin, and possessed claws and fangs like the two beasts that were already upon Arcadio.

"What?" Was all the trapped man could think to say.

The hungry thing inside Abigale chuckled again, "Ssshhh, always with the questions when it comes to this. I told the truth when I said I was searching for something. I wanted to find the one that called out to me all those years ago. He changed me, made me feel powerful. But when He left me after that winter I felt hollow, empty. You see, he *did* take something from me and I've been trying for years to get that feeling back."

The other famished nightmares formed a circle around Arcadio, knelt down, and reached for him. With burning claws they began to cut through his cloths, and when a nail would cut him in the process, that thing would stop to lick his blood from its steaming talons.

Abigale leaned down close to the trapped man and breathed a winter's chill into his face. "I've tried feasting on others many times, in many ways, but without Him there, it was meaningless. Just bloody meat, nothing more. But now I can feel Him again. He is here and I can hear Him calling my name once more. He is inside me right now."

The hungry thing stopped for a moment and shuddered in ecstasy, a line of drool falling from her lips. It then looked at him with coldly glowing blue eyes and said, "I pity you. Not for what is about to happen to you, but because you'll never know what it is like to be this close to a God."

Abigale stretched out on top of the terrified man and began to writhe around, dragging her long red hair across his dark skin. The movements might have been sensual if not for the terrible cold that poured out of her.

"But enough of questions and answers. You are beautiful, young, and strong. That strength will go into us, and through us, into Him. You not only nourish us this day, but also a God. You should feel honored."

The Abigale-thing then sat up and cast a sweeping gaze about the others that stared down at Arcadio with hungry eyes.

"Brothers and sisters, let the feast begin."

SON OF THE WILD MOON

By Michael G. Szymanski

The homestead had been reduced to a collection of scattered wreckage, closer now in appearance to the ruins of a battlefield than the aftermath of a common Indian raid. The Comanche would make off with what they could carry and burn what they could not, but the destruction wrought upon this lonely huddle of structures had been deliberate, systematic, and complete. Not only had the wooden house and attendant sheds been burned to the ground, but a stone outbuilding in the northeast corner of the compound had been demolished to the foundations, its components strewn in a wide arc across the primitive settlement; even the split rail fence that had surrounded a modest corral had been reduced to far-flung splinters. Of the settlers, there was no trace.

Sergeant Joshua Dark stood in the barnyard surveying this scene, sweating in the heat of the noonday sun as it roasted the dark blue fabric of his cavalry uniform. He was unaware of the discomfort, and of the trickle of salty moisture seeping down from beneath his wide-brimmed hat, intent as he was he on an attempt at comprehending the scope of the violence evidenced by his surroundings.

He had joined service quite near the end of the war between the states, but still had witnessed death and destruction on a scale of such horrific magnitude that his mind remained unable to encompass it, inclining him to shy away from those terrible memories for fear that they might consume him. This, though, was more chilling in a manner he could not readily define. The wrathful violence and totality of the destruction was beyond rational understanding. What could these people have done to engender such hatred in the hearts of the raiders?

One answer sauntered toward Joshua from the remains of the cabin, the smile on his face as greasy as the lanky black strands oozing limply from beneath a filthy, battered hat that had fared no better than the rest of his uniform. Corporal Deke Calder hawked up a gob of snot and spat into the sand just short of Joshua's boots. He did not salute, just began speaking in a tone ripe to bursting with disrespect.

"Ain't nothing in the cabin; fire burnt it all up."

"Any sign of the homesteaders?" Joshua could not force his regard to encompass the man and so subject himself to the open mockery that smoldered in his heavy-lidded eyes.

"Nah, just like the others. These folks is either slaves or dead; either way, they cain't tell us nothing." Without waiting to be dismissed Calder strolled off to inspect the barn, leaving Joshua to stew in his continuing shame.

This was his reward for doing the right thing, the end result of his honest though admittedly naïve desire to see justice done. When he'd reported his commanding officer for running guns to renegade Indians he had been so imprudent as to discount the terrible power and petty vindictiveness of military politics. Said commander had been found guilty and summarily relieved of duty, and from that day Joshua was looked on as a disloyal cur no less deserving of punishment than the actual criminal he'd exposed. By way of retaliation his superiors had vengefully assigned him to K Troop.

They were the dregs of the service, criminals before the war, most assuredly during and very likely after. They were unwanted troublemakers and miscreants whom no other commanding officer would find the least acceptable, so they had been thrown into this sorry excuse of a unit, there to await some suicide mission that would rid the army of their embarrassing presence once and for all. Now Joshua's fate had become inexorably entwined with theirs.

Red Dog, a shifty half breed who served as the troop's guide, scout and interpreter, slumped out of the woods behind the smoldering cabin. He kept to himself for the most part and rarely spoke beyond the requirements of his duties, yet of all the men around him, Joshua trusted him the most, and knew to keep his peace until the guide had worked around to what needed saying.

"I found tracks," he said at last, then paused again for reasons Joshua could not identify but had come to anticipate in his conversations with the man. "They are old and not clear. They are the tracks of one man on foot."

"How could one man have done all *this*?" Joshua gestured to the carnage surrounding them.

Red Dog shrugged. "One man left this place, heading for the mountains. One man."

He should be thankful, Joshua knew. This was the first time since they'd begun their pursuit of the raiders that they had left behind the slightest trace of themselves. Yet it surpassed belief that a single man could have wreaked such havoc as had been demonstrated over these past weeks, and so the mystery was deepened by Red Dog's discovery. At least they now had a clear direction for their hunt; towards the snow-capped mountains looming on the western horizon.

Their camp that night was, as always, a slovenly and disordered affair with only two sentries walking a picket line, that pair displaying obvious signs of drunkenness. Joshua allowed this transgression to pass, electing to choose the battles he fought. He was not unaware that his authority over these men was minimal at best, and that if he were to force every issue of military discipline as they occurred he would undoubtedly find himself the victim of an unfortunate and surely fatal accident. So he ignored these relatively minor infractions, concentrating instead upon the completion of his mission.

To that end he applied himself to the map of the territory into which that mission had brought them. It was a sketchy effort to depict a vast stretch of wilderness comprised of dense pine forest, innumerable lakes, streams and, dominating all, that range of ragged peaks delineating the western boundary of the tract. All told, he was considering an area of over 3000 square miles, most of which remained wholly ignorant of the tread of Man.

A handful of settlers had filtered into the region over the previous three years, the rich soil and plentiful water offering the promise of assured success and escalating prosperity to any who were willing to work for it. The approximate locations of these homesteads were indicated on the map, a red circle now drawn around those that had been attacked; seven to date, and now Joshua encircled the eighth by the flickering light of his campfire.

The morbid task complete, he studied the parchment, attempting to divine some pattern in the arrangement of hand-drawn circles that represented the brutal end of dreams and worse, the end of lives. Some small interval later he became aware of a presence beside him, arrived without sound or the slightest disturbance to announce itself, those conditions thereby identifying his visitor.

"What do you see in your map, Fancy Knife?" Red Dog asked. Fancy Knife was Joshua's Indian name, which referenced the ornate saber he carried at his side, a gift from his father upon his promotion to sergeant. It was an elegant, finely crafted blade etched with delicate filigrees along its entire length, and though more suited to ceremonial purposes, his father in his pride had insisted Joshua wear it at all times, as it was a "blade worthy of your current rank and future aspirations".

Joshua replied to Red Dog's inquiry. "Chaos. Death. Madness. A trail of hatred and evil that gives nothing away of its source."

Red Dog grunted. "I see a map with circles on it."

Joshua allowed a bitter laugh to escape his lips. "You are a pragmatic and practical man, Red Dog."

"I see what is there and do not look for what is not."

"And what else is there that you see here?" He tapped the surface of the parchment.

Red Dog did not answer immediately, either considering the words he would say, or determining whether or not he should utter them at all. He reached his decision. "I see an animal marking its territory."

Joshua was taken off guard by the remark. "But we are searching for men, are we not?"

"Are men not beasts?" He jutted his chin to the troopers at the far side of the campfire by way of demonstration.

A rueful smile crept onto Joshua's sharply handsome features. "I would be a fool to argue *that* point." He reconsidered the map. The destroyed homesteads did in fact delineate a rough semicircle around the foothills of the mountains. Perhaps the raiders *were* clearing out anyone who might point the way to their hidden stronghold. Joshua traced the arc of circles with his finger; if Red Dog was correct and the pattern held true, then the next attack would come...

"There." At first Joshua assumed Red Dog was referring to the map, but when he looked up the guide's attention was focused beyond the trees at the far side of the camp. He followed the scout's gaze and saw it immediately; a shimmering red glow in the sky that signaled only one circumstance.

"Fire, and of some considerable size." Red Dog nodded grimly. "We are close enough to catch those devils in the act this time. Corporal Calder!" he called to his second in command, who was lounging by another fire exchanging a bottle of whiskey with three other men. "Get the men ready to ride with as much weaponry as they can carry!"

The corporal was slow to respond, whiskey and inherent laziness delaying his reaction, but when he saw the glow in the sky he threw the bottle away and leapt to his feet, driving the men around him to do likewise. If anything could incite this troop to activity it was the prospect of a fight, and more specifically the opportunity to kill.

Joshua strapped on his revolver and saber as Calder barked orders and cursed the men who were slow to respond. Grabbing his Winchester and two boxes of cartridges he trotted back out of his tent and across the camp to his horse, which Red Dog had saddled for him. No sooner had Joshua taken the reins than the scout had faded into the forest in the direction of the burning homestead. The men were mounted but their formation was, as always, disordered and unruly. Joshua took no notice of this, spurring his mount to the north and into the trees.

"Let's get them sumbitches!" Calder shouted out behind him, and the ground shook with the thunder of hooves following after him, one pack of vicious animals racing through the night to face another, anticipating the bloody conflict to come.

They were too late to save any lives; he'd known they would be the moment he'd seen the firelight. What frustrated him now was the realization that they would also be unable to exact the least measure of retribution for the barbarous act whose aftermath they were riding into.

The three buildings comprising this homestead were engulfed by raging sheets of flame, which leapt over 20 feet into the air and threw showers of sparks even higher into the chill evening sky. Two horses vanished into the night as the troop arrived, but they were riderless and without saddle. They most likely had belonged to the settlers and had bolted in fear of the flames. Two men, Dunbar and Lang, spurred their mounts after the steeds and quickly vanished into the night. Of the raiders themselves, there was again no sign.

Joshua's focus turned to something on the ground some hundred feet before him as he reined his mount to a halt. He endeavored to sort out what he was seeing there, then recoiled in horror when he at last succeeded.

A young woman, hardly more than a child, lay on the grassy sward in front of the cabin, her slender body possessed of a profound stillness that was coldly, implacably eternal. Something crouched over her, and at first glance Joshua thought it to be the family dog mourning the loss of its mistress. But it was no dog, and it was not grieving.

A black wolf, the largest Joshua had ever seen, raised its massive blood-smeared snout from the girl's chest cavity where it had been feeding, met Joshua's gaze with its baleful, glowing yellow eyes and snarled, though to Joshua's fear-soaked mind the utterance possessed more in the nature of a contemptuous, sneering *laugh*. A ropey length of dripping intestine trailed from its jaws back down into the girl's body and without taking its eyes from Joshua the beast jerked its head, snapped the steaming length in half and gobbled down the portion it retained.

Joshua sat frozen, barely able to think. It was only when the wolf languidly licked the blood and ichor from its snout that the spell of horror was broken. Anger and outrage flushed through him in a flash flood of righteous indignation. With no conscious thought to direct his actions, Joshua retrieved his rifle from its saddle sheath, brought it to bear on the vile animal and fired all in a single, fluid motion.

The bullet struck slightly off center of the wolf's chest, but instead of collapsing from the surely mortal wound, the beast reared up on its hind legs, spun about and loped off into the forest, evincing no discernable manifestation of injury. And the sound it had made when the bullet struck; a roar of pain and unadulterated rage, a cry of such base and carnal frustration such as no mere animal should have been capable of producing. That fearsome outcry was more stunning than the initial sight of the animal, and before Joshua could recover the beast was gone from sight.

Three men rode past in pursuit, laughing and joking with one another like children let out early from school, anticipating the retrieval of a fine new pelt. He should have called them back, but there had been something unsavory about that wolf and its treatment of the dead girl that caused Joshua to desire its demise most fervently. In such a state of mind he turned to find Calder beside him, regarding the torn body before them with a grin on his face that could only be described as... wolfish.

"Pretty girl, she was," he observed. "Shameful waste of such a sweet..."

"Finish that thought and you are a dead man," Joshua growled through clenched teeth as he fought to hold his wrath at bay.

Calder expelled a derisive snort but otherwise remained silent as he nudged his mount forward toward the burning homestead. Joshua fought the sudden impulse to raise his rifle and put a bullet between the vile bastard's shoulder blades. This was no company of men he so marginally led; it was a pack of animals no less primal and voracious than the one he had just run off.

Again, the destruction of the homestead was total; nothing remained to identify the family that had been massacred there, nor could any trace of the raiders be found despite the loamy soil around the cabin and barn. Peppered amongst the complaints from the men as to the dearth of salvageable items from the homestead were crudely phrased criticisms of Red Dog's tracking abilities, which the fellow bore in his usual stoic silence.

Joshua knew, though, that if there *had* been tracks to be found, the scout would surely have found them. So how then had the raiders staged their attack, executed it with such efficiency and removed themselves with such alacrity, all while leaving behind no trace of themselves? The question disturbed him as much as the second, which he voiced to no one, not even Red Dog: how had that wolf gotten to the bodies that quickly? His thoughts were interrupted by a call from Hastings, a gaunt, shifty-eyed fellow who had gone to check the corral.

"Hey Sarge, you want to see this."

In point of fact he did not. A dairy cow lay on its side, one glassy, terror-filled eye staring sightlessly at the pale full moon. The wretched creature's flanks had been slashed to the bone and it had been completely eviscerated, it's still steaming entrails spread out around it in a sickening display of blood and gore. Worse yet, even Joshua's untrained eyes could not help but see that portions of the cow's flesh and innards had been torn away and eaten.

"What the hell you suppose did *that*?" Hastings wondered in a whisper.

"I have no idea," Joshua replied, turning away from the sight. "Some animal, most likely."

"Like that wolf we run off? Could be there were more of 'em we didn't see?" Hastings blinked as he realized something. "Hey, where are them boys that took out after that critter? They should've been back by now, one way or another."

"Get five other men, mount up and be ready to ride." Joshua barked the order as he strode for his horse, a feeling of dread already gnawing at the pit of his stomach.

They followed the tracks of the horses into a dense forest of pines, many of which were nearly two feet thick and possessed of such height and span of limb that they blotted out the moon's silvery illumination. They were forced to light lanterns so as not to fall prey to some dangerous, possibly fatal mishap, or simply lose the tracks they were following.

Joshua sorely missed the presence of Red Dog, but the scout could not be readily located and he had felt the urgent press of time. Besides, it required no great skill to follow after the hunters, as they had made no effort to conceal their tracks in their headlong pursuit of the wolf. It was only when they entered a small clearing overhung by thick branches that those tracks became difficult to read, obscured as they were by the churned soil therein.

"They must've stopped here for a while," Hastings speculated. "Could be they met up with some of them raiders and had out with 'em here."

"But we heard no shots fired, and we surely would have at such close proximity." Joshua scoured the ground, searching for tracks leading out of the clearing.

He had just spotted them when another trooper, Richards, complained: "Can we move this along? I don't like being out here much, and now it's commenced to rain."

"What're you talking about?" Hastings snapped. "It ain't raining at all."

"Sure as hell is," Richards threw back. "I can feel it on my face right now."

Hastings pushed out an exasperated growl as he spun about to throw the light of his lantern on Richards. He froze, face draining of color, his lips pulling back in a rictus grin that was a mirror image of Joshua's own expression. Richards had indeed felt moisture striking his face, but it was *not* rainwater.

The trooper's face was streaked with thick crimson that had traced a sluggish path from his temples over his cheeks and down to his chin. Even as the other troopers realized what they were seeing another thick ruby droplet fell from the darkness overhead to land with a sickening *splot* on Richards' forehead. He quickly rubbed it off, looked at his fingers, and gagged. It was blood; he was standing in a slow shower of blood.

They trained the light of their lanterns upward and every man, veterans of the bloodiest battles of the war, cried out in fear and dismay at what they beheld there. Richards fell backwards from his horse, unaware that he had vomited on himself, and for his part, Joshua sat paralyzed in the saddle, staring up into the trees at what had been left for them there.

The entrails and internal organs of the three men who'd set out after the wolf festooned the lower branches of the surrounding pines, grisly decorations bearing no resemblance to anything of a man, save in the copious amounts of thick red blood that dripped down from the remains and onto the still living men below. *Could a man contain that much viscera?* Joshua wondered in a moment of madness before chaos broke, shattering the spell.

"*Jesus Christ!*" Richards exclaimed as he worked furiously to wipe his face clean of congealing blood, while at the same moment Hastings muttered, "What the hell," as he threw himself from his mount to land in a crouch, rifle cocked and at the ready. Horses and men milled about in confusion, the men cursing or gagging, as their constitutions dictated.

"Hold together, men!" Joshua commanded, unsure whether he still maintained sufficient authority over these men to assure their obedience. Difficult to command such obedience when he himself desired nothing more than to bolt from that ensanguined clearing and never look back, or ever think of it again.

Rucker, the youngest of the troop, staggered backwards into the surrounding trees, his light briefly illuminating what waited there for him an instant before he bumped into it. He turned, saw what he'd blundered into, and screamed until all the breath in his body had fled.

One of the three troopers hung impaled upon a pine branch so thick it had nearly split the man in half, rupturing his chest and spewing its contents onto the ground at his feet. Those portions of his body that remained intact were ravaged by rents and slashes so deep that bloodied bone showed clearly in the lantern light. Joshua could not tell which of his troopers the man might have been, for his entire face, along with his scalp, had been torn from his skull and was not to be seen amongst the carnage.

Before anyone could form some reaction to all this, something large and of considerable bulk crashed down through the branches overhead. All but Joshua and Rucker reacted with hair trigger instinct, filling the clearing with the thunder of gunfire and the sharp tang of burnt powder. Their target pounded into the ground with a sickening *squelch* and lay still, as still as it must've been even before the bullets had struck it.

The third missing trooper gazed up at them with eyes that had surely taken a vision of purest horror into eternity, bulging from a face that was slashed, torn and *bitten* by some frenzied beast whose nature could only be wildly imagined. Or perhaps not.

As though in response to that unuttered thought, the howl of the wolf pierced the tumult of the men's panicked disorder. It was powerful and close at hand; *very* close at hand. It was the cry of a wild animal, yet Joshua could not escape the impression that within the animalistic vocalization there lurked the taint of twisted human mockery.

"What're we gonna do?" Rucker demanded, voice high and still heavily laced with hysteria though they'd returned to the homestead nearly twenty minutes before. "Did you see what was done to them men? What're we gonna *do*?"

"We calm ourselves and formulate a plan of action," Joshua replied, hoping to quiet the man's fear with a calm confidence he did not in fact possess. The tactic had just the opposite effect.

"*Plan of action*? What the hell are you talking about, plan of action? You were there, you saw; them men were ripped apart in next to no time without a sound heard from any of 'em. I suppose you want to chase after what done it? That's damn crazy! What ambushed them three wasn't no man, wasn't even *human!*"

"Horse shit," Calder spit into the churned earth. "Shut your yap and get a hold of yourself. These raiders are trying to throw a scare into us and that's all. They don't want people settling around here, so they're making sure them as are here already think real hard about staying."

"You go look at them three men whose parts is scattered over the trees back there and tell me that was done by men!"

"I'll do that, and what I see won't be any worse than what I saw in the war. Hell, I've most likely done worse myself. And I'll tell you this, boy, if you're still whining like a little girl when I get back I'll put a bullet in you and shut you up for good."

"That's enough for the both of you," Joshua forced himself into the argument. "Three men died needlessly because they went off on their own and that will *not* happen again. From now on we move as a unit and fight as a unit. Is that *clear*?" A surly silence met his question. "Is that clear?" he inquired more forcefully.

"Yes *sir*," Calder growled. "So long as we don't wind up dying as a unit." He stomped off toward a group of men huddled in conversation by another fire and, after a moment, Rucker trailed after.

Again, Joshua felt the familiar presence beside him. "I'd wondered where you'd gotten to."

"Following tracks," Red Dog pointed at the mountains looming over them. "They go there."

"So these raiders have a lair nearby."

"No raiders; there is only one."

Joshua shook his head, disbelieving. "No one man could achieve the carnage we've seen."

"It is no man."

"What? Do you mean the wolf?"

Red Dog nodded. "It is a wolf, and it is not."

"It is a predator and a scavenger; it could not have perpetrated such atrocities on those men."

"Part of it could; the part that is a man."

Joshua was dumbfounded, and his face must have reflected that. "We call him Son of the Wild Moon," Red Dog continued. "In daylight he walks as a man, but when the moon is full he walks as a wolf, hunts like a wolf, but with the evil of the man in its heart. He kills only to bring death and fear, and he will not stop 'til he gets what he wants."

"That is crazy talk, a legend of your tribe most likely used to frighten children into obedience. How can you expect either me or these men to believe such a fantasy?"

"Do you believe that men did what was done to your troopers? Men who move like the wind and leave no tracks? Men who butcher other men so quick, and with no sound?"

"Easier that than what you propose. We both know that my authority over these men is tenuous at best; were I to present them with such a story, even that small measure would vanish in a flash."

Red Dog shrugged. "Believe or not, what is true will stay true."

"Assuming for a moment that you are right, what motive would such a creature harbor for such rapacity?"

"Like I told you; it marks its territory, and does not want people living here."

"It would be an extremely methodical beast, then, since it is wiping out these homesteads in sequence..." Joshua broke off, pounding the heel of his hand against the hilt of his saber. "I'm a fool," he hissed. "I should have seen this sooner." He turned to the scout. "If our quarry continues as it has, we can anticipate where they, or it, will strike next, but this time we shall arrive *before* the attack and be ready for it. We move out at once; there's no time to waste."

Joshua strode off to issue his orders and spur his command into motion, but the specter of Red Dog's thoughtful scowl hung over him like a dark cloud redolent with a manner of doom that might well prove to be inescapable.

The next homestead was sadly reminiscent of those Joshua had previously observed; a tight cluster of log and sod structures, and a large barn with adjoining corral, all seemingly designed for the express purpose of being indefensible. The only difference here was that all remained intact, the inhabitants alive and, for the moment, safe.

Joshua led his troop up to the main cabin where a tall, bearded man in his third decade stepped out onto the porch, a Winchester rifle cradled in his arms in what seemed a casual manner. While the men did not appear hostile he was most certainly wary, and Joshua could understand why; movement behind the curtains hung from windows on either side of the door gave away the presence of a family that required constant protection in this wild frontier.

"Good evening sir," Joshua spoke as he brought his mount to a halt before the porch. "I am Sergeant Joshua Dark of K Troop, assigned to patrol this region in search of a band of raiders that has been attacking homesteads."

"Charles Forsythe," the man responded in the blunt manner of the distrusting. "Saw firelight from the McCandles place." He gestured in the direction from which the troop had ridden in. "What happened there?"

"The raiders struck before we could reach them. There were no survivors, I am sorry to report."

Forsythe frowned and studied his boots. "Figured as much. They were good people. Had a daughter near Samuel's age; figured maybe one day... But that's done now. It's coming here next, ain't it?"

Joshua realized the implication hidden within that question but did not respond to it; the men were on a razor's edge as it was, and any discussion along those lines would surely precipitate them over the edge into open rebellion and most likely mass desertion.

"We feel certain this homestead is next to be targeted. There has been a single attack tonight, and the hour is not late. But if not tonight, then very soon."

Again Forsythe frowned. "It'll be tonight, all right. The moon won't stand for it any other night for a month. I expect you have a plan?" Though it was a hopeful question, the tone of its delivery was weighed down by a sense of defeatism so powerful as to possess near physical mass.

"Yes I do, and I would appreciate a few moments of your time in which to discuss it."

"Better come on in, then." Forsythe turned and shuffled back into the cabin, his posture akin to that of a broken man. He knew something, Joshua was certain of it, and in this strangest of circumstances the slightest bit of intelligence might prove invaluable.

Joshua dismounted, signaling Red Dog to do the same. Instinct told him the scout would prove of value to him in this conversation. To Calder he said, "Deploy the men as we discussed, and conceal the horses in the barn so they do not give us away."

"Yes *sir*," Calder acknowledged in that mocking tone he favored. Without saluting, he turned and began ordering the men into position. Yet again and for the sake of expediency, Joshua ignored the disrespect and proceeded into the cabin.

The interior was an efficient use of space; a story and a half high, bedroom for the parents on the first floor along with an open living area dominated by a stone fireplace and bracketed by cozy lofts where the children slept. All was neat, clean and in good repair, clear testament to the determination of this hardy pioneer family.

There were six of them in all; husband, wife and four children, two sons and two daughters. Eleanor Forsythe was a handsome, understandably work-worn woman who spoke with quiet confidence despite the evident fear mirrored in her pale blue eyes. The children, ages ranging from six to fourteen, were pale blonde and quietly inquisitive. They were introduced in descending order of age as Toby, Angela, Kate and Samuel.

Niceties observed, Eleanor bundled the children off into the lower bedroom so the adults could speak freely, though Joshua doubted they would have been cognizant of a single word had they remained. They had never before encountered an Indian in such close proximity and stood transfixed by the sight of Red Dog in all his buckskin glory. So intent was their wide-eyed regard upon the scout that his stern mien of unflappable calm was fractured by an infinitesimal measure that only someone who knew him could ever discern. It brought the faintest flicker of a smile to Joshua's lips to realize that Red Dog was embarrassed by so much attention directed at him.

When the children had gone, Charles offered them seats at the dining table while Eleanor set about brewing coffee, though it was clear she was as much a part of the conversation as any of the men, what little of it there was to begin with. Charles spoke first.

"You have any idea what you're up against here?"

Joshua threw a furtive glance at Red Dog, but the stoic rider of the plains had returned and the man was unreadable as a stone. "We... suspect, though we have been unable to confirm our suspicions."

"So you've got no idea," Charles grunted.

"Charles," his wife cautioned.

"No time to beat around the bush, Ellie," Charles countered. "It could be out there right this minute, scouting the place, figuring out where we're weakest."

"You said '*it*,'" Joshua interjected. "By which I take it you mean... the wolf." There, it was out in the open now, a burden lifted from his shoulders.

Charles scratched absently at his chin. "If that's what you want to call it."

Ellie stepped to the table and poured coffee. "It comes only on the night of the full moon; thank God for that, or there'd be none of us left by now. First were the Voelkers, then the Hagmans; Indian raids, we thought then, until the following month when the Koenigs and the Fleischmans were attacked and... *remains* were found."

Charles resumed the narrative. "The bodies we found were cut bad, with stone knives, we would have figured, but it was clear right off those folks had been butchered and *eaten*; one maybe while he was still alive. Now it looks to be our turn."

"Charles, don't say that!" Ellie hissed, fingers digging into the flesh of his forearm like the talons of a bird of prey.

"When I heard that wretched baying tonight I knew our turn had come. I was ready to sell our lives dearly, but wouldn't have Voelker and the others have done the same, for all the good it did them? I could not; we *will* not allow that to happen to my family. Before you showed up I'd lost hope. Now you're here... I don't know."

"Can you stop this abomination, Sergeant?" Ellie wanted to know, clearly desperate for assurance.

"Between the firepower at our command and Red Dog's knowledge of the beast, I think that we can."

"Bullets won't hurt it much," Charles said. "It doesn't seem to..." His words were cut short by the staccato patter of gunfire, punctuated by the voices of K Troop raised in panic.

They rushed to the windows to see several troopers with torches providing illumination for a larger number of men armed with rifles, which they were firing into the corral, or rather at something within the corral. Even as a second volley broke the preternatural silence of the night something large and blacker than the midnight darkness leapt over the fence of the corral and was swallowed by moon shadow.

"It's here," Charles whispered flatly in the tones of a man preparing for battle—or death.

"And we've lost the element of surprise," Joshua growled his frustration. Why couldn't this lot of unruly, unprincipled miscreants execute even the simplest of strategies without making a complete bungle of it? The answer was, of course, that it was because they were unruly, unprincipled miscreants of the first order, which was how they had found their way into K Troop. But this was life and death now, and by *damn* those men would listen and obey. To Charles he said, "Perhaps they've wounded the creature; fatally so, or at the least sufficiently to drive it off."

Charles was not hopeful. "We're all crack shots out here and we've put over a dozen bullets into that godless thing since it first showed itself; six of them at least were kill shots, but none so much as slowed the beast." Joshua recalled his own shot, square in the animal's chest, and its utter lack of result. His hope for a swift resolution to their situation withered and died under the harsh assault of grim reality.

Calder swiftly herded the men back to their hiding place, himself standing watch just inside the double doors of the barn. Now that his own hide was at risk it seemed the disrespectful reprobate had discovered a newfound enthusiasm for the success of their mission. Joshua prayed that his enthusiasm was infectious, and did not come too late.

"I suggest you both arm yourselves," Joshua told the homesteaders. "We may not be able to kill the beast but we may discomfort it sufficiently to drive it off for the remainder of the night."

"Toby and Angeline are better shots than me," Charles offered. "Kate and Samuel are fair, but they can reload a rifle right quick."

Joshua was uncertain. "I would not wish to put the children at risk..." he began.

"Sergeant," Ellie cut him off with quiet dignity. "They deserve the right to fight for their lives, don't you think?"

A moment's hesitation and Joshua gave in to the steadfast determination in the woman's eyes and the iron in her spine. The children were called out, given their tasks and assigned their positions around the cabin. They moved briskly and without question to their posts; Joshua thought ruefully that his own troop could learn something of military discipline from these brave young ones.

The next assault was over before they were aware it had begun. First came a splintering of wood followed a heartbeat after by a scream of mortal agony, then the single bark of a rifle. Deathly silence reclaimed the homestead for a few eternal seconds after the shot was fired.

The door of the privy, a cramped little shanty situated near the barn, burst open and ripped from its makeshift hinges, allowing Private O'Connell, who had positioned himself inside, to stagger forward into the moonlight. Eyes wide and mouth gaping, he took only three shuffling steps away from the privy before a thick gout of blood welled up from between his lips as he collapsed face forward onto the ground.

The man's back had been ripped open from shoulders to hip, the cavity of his torso having been completely hollowed out. Copious amounts of blood flowed rapidly into the gory hollow thus excavated, quickly filling it to overflowing. The ruby spillage soaked into the earth around the body, making of the vicinity a most abominable mud hole.

Gunfire erupted from the barn, all of it concentrated on the privy, which was quickly reduced to splinters. Those in the cabin made to join the filicide, but Red Dog called out for them to desist.

"No good shooting at what is not there," he told them.

The gunfire from the barn tapered off to nothing, and as if that were a signal, a howling filled the air, a chilling sound that seemed to come at them from all directions at once. Then, adding to the horror of it that howl degenerated, or perhaps evolved into peels of harsh, cruel and gloating laughter, unmistakable and unquestionably possessed of the same source as the howling.

The last shred of doubt was torn from Joshua by that guttural, throaty expulsion of blackest mirth, and he now fully accepted that what they faced was no animal but a supernatural creature that was also, at least in part, a demented human being of wicked nature and black intent.

"If we hold it off until morning," he repeated his hope, "we can evacuate the remaining settlers and apply for reinforcements..."

Red Dog shook his head once, a gesture of grim finality. "It will not let that happen. We must kill it tonight, or it will kill us."

Joshua did not argue; instinct told him that the scout was correct in his assessment. The beast was cunning, and certainly would not desire the revelation of its existence to reach the outside world, there to bring a literal army down on its head. And even if they survived the night, would not the creature simply vanish into the trackless forest, moving on to another fringe of human civilization, there to unleash its depredations upon another group of unsuspecting innocents?

There was also the all too real possibility that Joshua simply would not be believed, whether from genuine skepticism or in recognition of an opportunity to be rid of a troublesome and unpopular officer in a manner that would brand him a disgrace and a failure. His hand drifted to the hilt of his saber, all his tension and frustration transferred into his grip upon that silly, pretentious martial bauble.

Something drew his eyes back to the barn, some change in the quality of light that he could not at first identify. A steadily increasing, flickering illumination silhouetted the structure, and realization struck as a low curse escaped Charles' lips. "It's set fire to the barn!"

He did not wonder how such a thing could be possible; the all too real tongues of flame licking around the corners of the barn made eloquent reply to any such question. Gunfire erupted again, this time from within the barn, and yells of alarm were quickly transformed into cries of fear and mortal agony, which increased to a furious level, as did the gunfire. Joshua could do nothing but curse his helplessness.

Private Rucker, Joshua thought, leapt from the small second floor opening into the hayloft. His arms were outstretched before him so that he could ensnare a thick rope looped over a large pulley above the opening, used to convey bales of hay up to the loft. Having obtained possession of the rope, the boy began to slide down its length to the relative safety of the barnyard.

He had not descended far when the rope was suddenly and violently wrenched upwards and into the barn. Rucker's unexpected ascent was as swift as it was brief, terminating abruptly as his hands were drawn into the pulley and crushed into its confines. The snapping of bones could be heard clearly by those in the cabin.

Rucker's screams of agony took on the sharp tinge of abject terror as an enormous lupine head emerged from the darkness of the loft. All three men in the cabin raised rifle to shoulder, but none could achieve a line of sight on the beast that would not involve fatal injury to Rucker. A moment later that objective was rendered moot.

Jaws gaping wide, the thing lunged forward to bury its snout in the trooper's stomach. Rucker's screams reached a terrible crescendo as the thing shook its head with violent energy, boring deeper and deeper into the trooper's body. Satisfied that it could progress no further, the hell-spawned beast jerked his head violently downward.

Rucker, still screaming, fell, but behind him now trailed two ropes; one of dark, weathered hemp, the other the blood-moist pink thread of the young man's intestines, which were of sufficient length to follow him all the way to the hard earth below. Above, the creature clenched its jaws, severing the intestine and allowing it to fall in slick coils over the bloody remains of its erstwhile owner.

The beast turned, its gaze focused on the cabin, focused on Joshua, he was certain of it. Its jaws gaped wide and he expected to be assailed by yet another ear piercing howl, but it was worse -- much worse -- than that. The creature *laughed*. To hear it was one thing, but to see that animal visage contorted into a hideous mockery of devilish mirth was another matter entirely. Cold terror coursed through Joshua's veins at the sight of that impossibly human expression displayed upon the lupine features of his unnatural adversary.

Gratefully, the repugnant visage retreated into the darkness of the barn, the retreat merely set the stage for yet another shock. Though his body lay in a broken heap in the barnyard, Rucker's *hands* remained still wedged securely within the pulley mechanism overhead, having been torn from the trooper's arms by the supernatural force of the creature's thrashings.

Flames now engulfed the entire rear face of the barn, fiery tongues licking greedily at the edges of the roof. The great commotion inside continued in diminished form due to the decimation of the occupants therein. Joshua felt helpless and ineffectual; he should be in there with his men, fighting alongside them, and most likely dying with them. What sort of leader was he to cringe in relative safety while his command was systematically wiped out to the last man?

Not entirely to the last man, as it transpired.

At the height of whatever manner of battle was taking place within the barn, the double doors facing the yard were thrown open with such violence that they slammed into the rough planks of the siding and rebounded several feet as a massive cloud of thick gray smoke billowed forth from the gap their absence had created.

From the depths of that cloud charged perhaps a dozen wild-eyed and panicked horses who scattered into the questionable safety of the night. In the dust of their passage raced two men, desperate and quite obviously fleeing the barn for their very lives. Leading the way was Corporal Calder, followed closely by a badly lacerated Private Richards, whose forward momentum was severely impaired by a pronounced and obviously painful limp.

"Unbar the door!" Joshua shouted as he raised his rifle to cover the fleeing men. "Be ready to let them in!"

Angeline and young Samuel temporarily abandoned their posts to comply, while the adults made ready their weapons to provide what covering fire they could.

The two fugitives were halfway across the yard when the beast launched itself from the smoke, instantly drawing fire from the defenders inside the cabin. What must it have been like for Angeline and Samuel, standing exposed in the open doorway as a creature from the darkest corner of hell bore down on them with rapacious intent?

In two great bounds the thing was upon Richards, paws larger than horses' hooves slamming into his back and driving him to the ground. Richards *bulged*, swelling like a bladder being tightly squeezed as blood erupted from his nose and mouth, drowning any scream of pain he might have attempted. His left eye was expelled from its socket when the beast leapt from his back, sending shreds of cloth and lumps of torn flesh spewing out behind it.

It was in midair when Calder flung himself through the doorway. The instant his feet cleared the opening Samuel slammed the door shut and Angeline dropped the bar back into place, pulling back just in time to avoid having her fingers crushed as a tremendous weight slammed into the sturdy portal.

Calder was on his feet in a flash, pistol shakily aimed at the still shuddering door. "Jesus *Christ*! What the hell is that thing?"

"Something we've never encountered before," Joshua told him. "Something we may not be able to defend against."

"Shit! What's that supposed to mean?"

"Mind your language, Calder; there are women and children present."

"What? What?" Calder spun around to take in the room, fear and confusion at war in his dark soul.

"It is gone for now," Red Dog informed from the window, all of which were thankfully too small to permit the beast's egress. "It will return. It must."

"And what do we do then?" Calder wanted to know. "That bastard ripped us apart in the barn and we couldn't even put a scratch on it. It set the place on fire, Dark. How could it even know to do that?"

"Because inside it is a man," said Red Dog.

Calder rounded on the scout. "So you know what it is?" Red Dog nodded once, as was his habit. "Good. Then you know how to kill it."

Red Dog nodded again, but this time he elaborated. "But we do not have what we need to do that."

"Well *shit*!"

"Calder, mind your mouth!"

"Or what, you'll put me on report? Go ahead, see where *that* gets you. Most likely it'll be square in the belly of that thing out there!"

Desperate, Joshua turned to the scout. "Red Dog, is there anything, anything at all we can do against this monster?"

"Now, no. In daylight we can track it and kill it, for it will not change until the moon is full again and till then it will be only a man."

"So we must hold out until dawn; about three hours from now, I'd say."

"*All* we have to do?" Calder cut in. "You say that like you're talking about a hard day's ride or clearing out stalls. Holding out against that thing's gonna be like fighting a war, and I'm here to tell you, Fancy Knife, we are *seriously* outgunned here."

The first hour passed like an eternity. The beast did not appear, and attempted no assault upon the cabin. The inaction was nearly worse than fighting a battle that they could not win. Charles and Red Dog maintained an unblinking watch at the front windows, while Ellie surveyed the rear approach through a gap in the door there. Angeline had taken a position by the hearth, where she listened for any sound of movement on the roof, while Toby, Kate and Samuel clustered together in a corner, ready to go where they were most needed.

In that hour, it slowly dawned on Joshua that their most immediate danger did not lie with the beast outside but with one of another sort right there in the cabin amongst them. Calder's eye had found Angeline shortly after he'd rolled into the cabin and his lascivious regard had grown more obvious with each passing minute. The girl became aware of the attention but did not welcome it, not that such a rebuff would have any effect on a man of Calder's ilk. Neither Charles nor Ellie noticed the discomfiting interplay, intent as they were upon the threat outside, but Joshua was certain the situation would come to a head very soon. In this he proved sadly correct.

Having his own post to man, Joshua could not maintain a constant watch over Calder, who timed his movements well so as to avoid detection until he'd sidled over to the hearth. Joshua was alerted only when Calder spoke in that oily, sneering voice of his.

"You're a real pretty little thing, ain't ya? It'd be a real shame to waste..."

"Calder, leave off," Joshua snapped as he spun from the window, rifle held low but at the ready. He could feel something inside him stretching taut and knew that it would require very little now to stress it beyond tolerance, and upon that event he would be forever changed.

"Ah, come on, I was just tryin'..."

"I know what you were trying. Leave off."

Calder's greasy, yellow-toothed smile faded into a derisive grimace of contempt. "Well, well, Fancy Knife's got a backbone after all. Too bad it didn't show up earlier when the rest of us were in the barn fighting that thing. I bet you planned it that way, didn't you? We get torn to shreds while you hide out here all nice and comfy with the womenfolk."

Calder's hand drifted out to roughly pat the cringing Angeline on the head. The hand remained there as he continued. "Did you figure on saving this for yourself?"

Joshua brought the Winchester up and in a flash had it aimed squarely between Calder's eyes. Fast as he was, the corporal was faster, fingers digging into Angeline's honey-blonde hair and pulling the girl to him as he drew a hunting knife with his free hand. Hugging the terrified young woman to him, he pressed the knife to her throat as he dragged her from the hearth.

"No reason we can't have a little fun, Sarge, if you're man enough for it."

"That will not happen, Calder; I promise you that." Joshua spoke with deadly calm, the barrel of his rifle tracking his subordinate as he reached the wall and began sliding along it to the front of the cabin. In the corner, the other three children scrambled away from the reach of this new monster approaching them.

"Why not?" Calder was saying. "These people are good as dead, probably us, too. What difference if we *enjoy* what time we got left?" The man looked to be moving for the front door.

Now Charles had his rifle up as well. "You're not taking my daughter out there," he promised flatly.

"That right? Maybe you'd like it better if I open her up right here so you can watch her bleed out. Bet it'd take a while; I can make sure it would, and maybe that thing out there'd catch a whiff and decide to come on in for a helping. Won't make any difference to me by then, but you all will get to see these kids torn up just like them in the barn."

Calder had moved in front of a small window in the side of the cabin, the flickering light of the blazing barn throwing him into hellish silhouette. It was not the most favorable of shots but Joshua calculated that he could still take it without harming the girl. That indefinable something inside him pulled tighter and tighter as the pressure of his finger on the trigger approached the point of no return, for the bullet in the rifle and the soul within the man...

Glass shattered, spewing shards into the cabin with such force that each piece was transformed into a miniature projectile capable of inflicting fatal damage. Even at that distance across the room Joshua felt a sharp, icy caress across his cheek followed by a thin warm flow of crimson. He barely noticed though, riveted as he was on the scene playing out before him.

An arm had plunged through the window, an arm that appeared manifestly *wrong* on the most fundamental level. Its entire visible length was covered with thick black fur, and there was something in the manner of its articulation that had much in common with the extremity of a dog—or a wolf. There was a hand; Joshua saw it briefly as it clamped upon Calder's throat, long, discolored talons piercing skin and drawing blood, though the damage was still insufficient to prevent the man from screaming.

And scream he did, thrashing about and stabbing with desperate energy at the arm that had ensnared him. An animalistic growl of anger and hatred issued from something outside, then the corporal's head was pulled out through the window. As he had not relinquished his hold on Angeline, the girl was in imminent danger of being drawn along to her doom as well.

This dire circumstance was averted by Red Dog, who leapt across the intervening distance to tackle the girl and wrest her from Calder's grip. The pair tumbled to the floor and Joshua lost interest in them for the moment as he served witness to Calder's fate.

The corporal did not pass quickly or easily from the confines of the cabin, for the opening that was his egress was far too small to accommodate the bulk of his body. Yet his progress continued in a series of sporadic jerks accompanied by a sickening crunch and crackle of multiple breaking bones and the endless, horrified screaming of a soul in mortal straits. The body was compressed, compacted into the dimensions of the window until at last Calder's hips collapsed inward and his legs slithered out of sight into the night.

There came the sounds of rending and snapping from right there just outside the window but no one inside dared to attempt an observation. In due course the sounds dwindled and all was silent, yet they remained frozen in place, all too aware of the palpable presence of their unnatural enemy on the other side of the wall. They remained immobile for many long minutes, the only sounds the quiet sobs of Angeline as she lay curled in Red Dog's protective grip.

At last Charles ventured, "Do you think it..."

Something flew through the broken window, striking the floor and rolling directly at Joshua. He leapt out of its path but the thing had already lost momentum and rolled to a halt, revealing its grisly nature.

It was Calder's head, eyes wide and staring into a vast abyss of unadulterated horror. Even in the brief glimpse he had of that gruesome artifact before kicking it into a dark corner Joshua could not help but note the deep puncture marks that had penetrated clear through the skull, allowing a thick flow of blood and brain tissue to emerge. Teeth marks.

A howl filled the night, startling them from the shock, a piercing sound that rose swiftly through the octaves before plunging into a basso rumble, both extremes far beyond the limits of human vocalization. Joshua anticipated the laughter that would surely follow, but in this he was grievously disappointed. What came next was guttural and as brutally mangled as the men in his command, yet chilling in its comprehensibility. Words.

"*You. All. Die. Soon.*"

Charles cried out and broke for the window, angling his approach so that he could fire through it from a position of safety. He sent off round after round through the bloodied opening until his ammunition was exhausted, with no positive result to be discerned. As the echoes of the final shot faded, they all heard the fading mockery of derisive laughter retreating into the night.

"This is a nightmare," Charles moaned, "and there's no escape from it."

"There may be." The words dragged their attention to Red Dog, who still lay in a tangled heap with Angeline.

At first glance Joshua feared that the scout had descended to Calder's despicable level, for his hand was reaching out towards Angeline's bodice, but in fact Red Dog's attention was on something far less carnal. A crucifix hung from a delicate chain around the girl's neck, having fallen out of the girl's blouse where it had previously been concealed.

"A cross?" Charles grunted, disbelieving. "A cross will protect us from that thing?"

"No," Red Dog said. "But silver will kill it, if we make bullets from this."

Charles looked uncertainly to his wife. "That cross was an heirloom from your mother..."

"And what better use for it than to defend our family?" To Red Dog, Ellie said, "Do what is necessary to end this."

The scout nodded, a glint of approval in his eyes. Retrieving the crucifix from Angeline, he set to work.

As the silver was melting in a pot over the fire, Red Dog employed what materials were at hand to create a mold of two rifle slugs, which he'd removed from their casings; he'd estimated that there would be sufficient metal to provide them with two chances at killing the beast, but only two. Beyond that they would be left without options.

It became a race, then, between the manufacture of the bullets and the advent of the creature's next assault, and it was left to them to wait out the interim with growing anxiety. At the window, Charles spoke softly so that only Joshua could hear.

"This is on my head. I should never have brought my family to this place."

"You should never have sought a better life for yourself?" Joshua whispered his retort. "For your children? This is no fault of yours; do not blame yourself. It is that evil *thing* out there that claims full responsibility and I promise you, we will not allow it to win out."

It required an hour for Red Dog to make his castings, refine them to the proper shape and mount them onto the brass shell casings. Keeping one for himself, he gave the other to Joshua.

"We will take up positions at opposite ends of the cabin," Joshua suggested as they loaded in the shells. "If we keep out of one another's line of fire we will both have a clear shot at..."

The rear door of the cabin erupted in a shower of splinters, throwing Ellie against the side wall of the cabin where she slid unconscious to the floor. A massive dark shape rocketed into the cabin, landing in a crouch atop the dining table.

This was no wolf that faced them now, but an abominable hybrid of man and beast, possessed of the worst qualities of both species.

It was manlike in that it boasted two arms rather than forelegs and appeared to be easily capable of walking upright, but the face was unmistakably lupine, the features dominated by a jutting snout filled with the yellowed, serrated teeth of a carnivore.

They had barely registered its presence when the thing launched itself from the table straight for Joshua and Red Dog. Joshua wrenched his rifle up and fired, vaguely aware of the bark of Charles' weapon as he too opened fire. His shot was taken in haste and so did not strike the beast truly, but strike it did. The silver bullet plunged into the man-thing's left shoulder and lodged there; this much Joshua saw before the creature slammed into him and the scout, sending them sprawling to the floor.

A roar of agony and rage filled the cabin, its deafening force shattering the remaining windows as a tremendous weight came down on Joshua's chest, threatening to cave in his ribs. It was on top of him, howling its fury as it clawed at its wound, digging razored talons into itself in an effort to extricate the slug, which burned into its flesh like a red-hot iron.

Red Dog scrambled for his rifle, which had been wrested from his grip by the force of the impact, but he would be too late to assist Joshua. The beast had left off its grisly surgery and now glared balefully down at Joshua, pinned helpless to the floor. Its fur-covered right arm raised, talons extended and poised to rip him to shreds.

Charles got off another shot, scoring a hit square in the center of the beast's chest, achieving no real damage but accomplishing the briefest of delays in the creature's attack, a delay Joshua determined to employ to his fullest benefit.

Red Dog had reached his rifle and required only seconds in which to bring it to bear, and Joshua could think of only one thing with which he might provide those seconds. His hand fell to the hilt of his saber, that useless decoration that had served only to hamper his movements and cause him no little amount of embarrassment, pulled the filigreed blade free of its sheath and plunged it into the vile heart of the snarling beast.

A howl of shock and—was that fear?—poured out the creature's throat to be drowned to a thick gurgle by a rising tide of blood welling forth from its mouth in a crimson torrent that splashed onto the front of Joshua's tunic. A sickening stench filled the cabin then, a malodorous amalgam of decay, excrement and burning flesh. The lupine horror slumped, pawing ineffectually at the blade that transfixed it. Its pain-filled eyes met Joshua's as a grimace of purest hatred twisted its already hideous visage.

And then Red Dog's rifle was pressed to the side of the thing's head and discharged, propelling the second silver bullet into the monstrosity's vile brain. It was thrown off Joshua and sent crashing into a crumpled, unmoving heap of abused and bloody flesh beside him.

They burned the corpse of the thing and scattered the ashes to the winds. Joshua and Red Dog were the only ones to oversee the dissolution, as no one in the Forsythe family evinced the slightest desire to participate. Joshua could not blame them; he would not have attended himself had he not felt it his duty to do so.

The remains of K Troop were interred in a secluded glade some distance from the homestead, yet near enough so that the family could properly maintain the impromptu cemetery. The men under his command had been the worst of human society, but they had given their lives protecting innocents from the depredations of an unholy monster, and so they were deserving of at least that small honor.

Joshua's hand drifted to the hilt of his saber. His father had been truly proud of his son's achievements and had spared no expense in the manufacture of the weapon, including, as it happened, having the blade plated with silver to better display the filigrees etched into it. Red Dog had assured him that it had been the saber that had struck the killing blow, but nevertheless Joshua was glad of that second bullet, dreading the depths to which his mind might have plunged had the thing spoken to him directly in those last moments of its evil life.

"What do we do now?" Red Dog wanted to know as they rode away from the Forsythe homestead the next morning.

"We return to headquarters and make a report," Joshua told him. "We engaged the raiders and wiped them out, but only the two of us survived the battle."

Red Dog nodded. "That is the best way to tell it."

They rode in silence for a time.

"Who was he?" Joshua asked at last. "Who was that thing when it walked as a man?"

The scout shrugged. "We will never know. But the world is a better place without him in it."

"Yes," Joshua agreed as he took in the fresh new day unfolding before them, "A much better place."

DRAKE TAKES A HAND

BY PETE RAWLIK

The man came out of the desert and in through the saloon doors. The town was still, the sun was high, and the shadows short. The heat shimmered in the air and even the flies had retreated from the day. He had come on foot, a wide-brimmed leather hat with a band of beads covering his head and face. A canvas duster, once brown but now faded with age covered his thin frame, his boots were snake skin, trimmed with turquoise. As he walked the dust trailed behind him hung in the air and then danced away. No one had seen him come into town, no one knew his name, no one knew he was there.

The saloon was dark, it smelled of stale drink, dust and desperation. The bartender was a portly man with thin hair and a bad mustache. He wore a shirt that might have been white once and an apron that was dishwater gray. As the stranger strolled over, the barman set up a glass and poured a shot from a bottle of rye whiskey. "Welcome stranger. What can I do for you?"

The stranger took off his hat and revealed the aged, sun-worn features beneath. He took the shot from the bar and tossed it back. It burned as it went down his throat, and his voice gasped as he slammed the glass back down on the bar. "They tell a story, a legend really, about a bar, a shit-hole bar with no customers and a card game in the back, a game in which the devil himself is the dealer."

The barman shook his head and pointed to the sign above the bar which boldly stated NO GAMBLING.

The stranger fumbled in his pocket, pulled out a sack of tobacco and some crisp white papers. He set the bag on the bar and with a skilled hand reached in and began the slow process of rolling a cigarette. "Now why is it," the stranger didn't look up from his task, "why is it, I don't believe you?"

The barman opened his mouth to speak, but as he did another door in the bar opened and a thin woman with flaxen hair and oversized breasts that were barely contained by her bustier strode in. "They've suspended play. They want drinks. Food if I can find any." There was a quiet desperation in her voice.

The stranger looked up at the bartender with a knowing grin, but the bartender shook his head. "It's not what you think. The legends, the stories they tell, they don't know the truth."

The barmaid called out urgently, a name that the stranger didn't quite catch; it could have been Eben, or Evan or even Ivan. Whatever she had said, the man behind the bar scowled, and rushed to uncork several bottles of wine and open an equal number of smokey bottles of dark, thick looking liquor. Satisfied that the drinks were well in hand, the barmaid vanished behind another door, presumably whatever passed for the saloon's kitchen. Distracted by their work, neither barman nor maid noticed as the stranger left the bar and proceeded slowly through the door from which the barmaid had appeared.

The room beyond was large, perhaps thirty feet on a side, and lined with mirrors of all shapes and sizes reflecting the weak light from the few flickering gas lamps that hung from the walls. On the wall opposite the door, a passageway marked with a sign that said GENTS led down a gloomy corridor. A few side tables sat along the walls, one by the door held a mug, a ratty old book and a half-eaten sandwich. Each side table hosted a few suspect chairs, all facing away from the center of the room, and it was the center of the room that held the stranger's attention, or at least what it was that occupied that space.

The table was a large circle, perhaps seven feet across and covered with a black table cloth that had seen better days. There were five chairs, large wing-backed things that had once been fine furniture, but had long since been worn out, re-upholstered and badly patched. The stranger noted that there was room for more. In front of each chair lay a small stack of cards that varied in number from place to place. There were more cards in the center, arranged in two stacks. One stack was face down and neatly piled, the other stack was face up, and haphazardly stacked. The backs of the cards were gray, and without embellishment, though they were creased and stained more than any other deck he had ever seen. Of the cards that sat face up, he could only see details of the top one. The background was white or cream, and held an image of a green line, a yellow curve, a blue five-pointed star, a crimson square, and a circle that was solid black. In forty years of gambling, the stranger had never seen anything like it, and he knew that he had finally found what he had been looking for.

A shuffling noise came from the gloomy corridor, and the man quickly stepped back away from the table. He found a chair along the wall, and turned it so he could sit and watch both the table and the darkened hall. He found the cigarette he had made earlier and struck a match. A figure came out of the darkness. Whatever it was that had come from the hall was not human. It stood like a man, walked like one, but it had no hair, no ears, and no lips. It had only three fingers on its short arms, and its skin was pale green and finely scaled. It glared at the man who sat next to the wall with large yellow eyes. When it opened its mouth to speak it revealed rows of tiny sharp teeth. Its voice was a hiss, its words inhuman, incomprehensible, but the stranger knew their meaning all too well, "You should not be here."

The stranger, feigning bravado, took a long drag off of his cigarette and blew smoke up into the air, and hoped that the thing couldn't sense the fear that was creeping up his spine. He had come seeking to play cards with the devil, and this thing, this reptilian thing that walked like a man, sure looked as if it fit the bill. There was a desire to run, but that was overwhelmed by his desire to learn whatever game was being played here. The boredom, the ennui, that had come to fill his life, the need to feed it, to overcome it, was stronger than any fear.

Another figure emerged from the dark and approached the table. It was short, squat, wide with a round head that was black and shiny, like a polished stone. Tufts of coarse hair fringed the thing's neck. Two large black orbs were mounted on the front of the thing's face, while a ring of six other smaller eyes wrapped round the head. Its mouth was a vertical slit, wickedly jagged. The head sat atop a round body comprised of the same shiny black material, though much of this was draped in diaphanous lace. The arms were large and multi-jointed and ended in thick clumsy looking claws. Out of the chest, another pair of arms emerged, these were smaller, more delicate and ended in an array of fine finger-like protrusions. It walked on four legs that differed little from the larger upper arms. A fat bulbous sphere of the same shiny black material, trailed behind it, attached to the rest of the beast by a thin ring of hair. That the thing knew the stranger was there was obvious, but it made no gesture or comment to acknowledge the intruder.

The stranger closed his eyes and tried to remain calm as the spider-thing approached the green scaled man and engaged him in a frenetic conversation. Although the man could not hear what was being said, both cast occasional glances in his direction. Sweat was beading on his forehead. The lifeless eyes of the spider-thing made the stranger uncomfortable, he had a subconscious urge to flee, but he swallowed whatever primal fear was bubbling up and took another drag off his cigarette. As the smoke poured out of his nostrils a melodious voice began whispering out of the corridor, and the stranger smiled as a little chinaman in orange robes and a funny hat came in. He couldn't be more than four feet tall. He was singing, the language was not one he recognized, but the man took comfort in the fact that he at least was not alone in a room full of monsters. The Asian joined his compatriots who gestured wildly. The little man peeked around the spider-thing and stared at the stranger. The stranger gave the little man a two fingered salute and a knowing smile.

The little chinaman smiled back and revealed strange peg-like teeth. He ducked back behind the spider-thing and seemed to grow angry. There was an obvious and vocal protest, but soon the little man, who was obviously not Chinese, was striding toward the stranger in a strange hopping gait. As he came closer, the stranger realized that the Asian dwarf was blind, the man's eyes were closed, and upon the lids someone had painted the semblance of irises and pupils.

The little man waddled up to the stranger and stared at him with those false eyes. "You smell like bartender and serving girl," the dwarf barked. "You speak English?"

The stranger nodded, and then realized that the gesture was useless, "I do speak English."

The dwarf harrumphed. "Who are you?" He drew in close, "Why you here?"

The stranger leaned forward. "I'm a stranger, no one you would know."

The little man leapt back. "You, a stranger? HAH! Look around you, we be far stranger than you! Why you not run when you see us? Most run."

"My name is Drake, Samuel Drake. I play cards, dice, and games of fortune. I learned a long time ago how to control my emotions, how not to let them control me. It has made me an excellent gambler, perhaps the best. I'll admit that the three of you are monstrous, and truth be told, I am shaking in my boots, but I've been around the world, I've seen the things men do to each other. I'll wager that no matter what kind of devils you are, you aren't worse than us."

The little man twisted his head to the side, wider than humanly possible. "We do not gamble here Mistah Drake. You should leave, before it is too late."

The man called Drake blew a long stream of smoke at the little man. "You play cards, not a game I know, but I would be willing to watch, willing to learn. If the rules are fair, if the stakes are right, I would like to play."

"No one watches!" hissed the serpent man angrily. "It is not permitted. You should do as Ty-Poh says! You are not ready to play; you would not, could not understand the consequences, the meaning, or the ramifications of play. Humans are not prepared for the Game of Mao."

The spider-thing was suddenly speaking as well; its voice was harsh, tinny, and low. "Zasshtythymytyquyl is correct. Your species is not prepared, not endowed; you would not suffer the consequences well. Leave! Now! Before the dealer returns."

Drake regarded the array of things before him, and sneered. "I notice none of you have said that I couldn't play."

A new voice suddenly boomed through the room, "Leave him alone Tch'tkach. We will resume play momentarily. All of you must take your places." From the corridor a strange mist poured. It was as thick a fog as Drake had ever seen, and it sparkled in the dim light. Something moved inside of it, something large, barrel-shaped with wings and tentacles. Then the shape was gone, and a fat man in a fine suit strode out of the haze. He walked clumsily to the table and sat down in front of one of the stacks of cards. Reluctantly, the other three slowly returned to the table, and took up their own positions.

Drake settled down into his chair, comfortable from his vantage point, but not unaware that there were four players and five chairs. The fat man spoke, "Do you plan on leaving Mister Drake?"

"I'll just watch for a few hands or so, if you don't mind."

The thing called Zasshtythymytyquyl shook its head. "You were warned human. No one is allowed to simply watch the Game of Mao."

"I'm afraid my saurian friend is correct Mister Drake," the dealer chided, "you cannot watch, you must play."

Drake shook his head, "In good time, I don't know the rules. Let me watch a few hands, and then I'll be ready to play."

There was a chortle from the table, which the dealer silenced with a raised finger. "I am Fifth of Five, I am the dealer, I declare the suspension over, and this Game of Mao once more in play!"

Suddenly Drake felt sick, his vision blurred, his stomach threatened, his ears popped. He didn't understand it, but somehow he was at the table, seated to the right of the dealer. "What the hell?"

The spider-thing, Tch'tkach was to his right and spoke, "Penalty, speaking without need." The dealer reached out, picked up the deck and dealt a single card in Drake's direction. It slid silently next to the stack of cards in front of him. A stack that he noticed was significantly larger than those of the other players. He started to protest, wanted to demand an explanation of the rules, but remembered what had just happened. He had already learned his first rule; that the game was played without conversation.

The dealer, who Drake thought of as Fifth, spoke once more. "I played the Fool, and declare it to be the six of strings."

The serpent whose name began with Zassht and was seated to the left of Fifth, pondered the announcement for a moment and then tossed out a card onto the pile. It was decorated with four green lines. The four of strings thought Drake, strings. Play followed suit.

Ty-Poh smiled and quickly threw out a card decorated with four blue stars. Drake smiled as he realized that play also followed value.

To his right, Tch'tkach made a strange frustrated noise. "Card." Fifth dealt him a card which he quickly grabbed and added to his hand, again he called "Card." The second card was added to his hand, and once more he called to the dealer. This time he seemed happy with what he had drawn, for the new card was quickly tossed to the discard stack. It was the eight of stars.

Drake suddenly realized that it was his play, and he struggled to gather the stack into his hand. There were twenty-two cards, five suits including blue stars, green strings, yellow curves, crimson squares and black circles. All the symbols he had seen on the card that had been sitting there while play had been suspended. A wild card of some sort. In addition to the numbered cards, Drake also held several face cards, he wanted to take the time to look at them, but instead he drew the six of stars and made ready to play it, only to pull back as Ty-Poh threw out the exact same card. Somehow play had been reversed, the eight perhaps. But more importantly, Drake now knew that there were multiple decks in play.

Zassht played a four of stars, Fifth a nine. Drake played the deuce and went unchallenged. Tch'tkach played a face card and announced "Nodens, the Prince of Stars." There was a sudden silence in the room. Everyone seemed to be staring at each other, assessing responses. Drake stared at Ty-Poh, and realized that in the mirror behind the dwarf Drake could see the little man's cards.

Suddenly the lights flickered and in the darkness Drake saw an image, a terrible vision of a monstrous titan that was at times not unlike a man striding through the sky laying waste to everything before him. Great cities fell with each step, mad auroras boiled out of the sky, the seas rolled back to make way for his presence. The very foundations of the world shook.

"Cthulhu, the Sepia Prince of Sines," uttered Ty-Poh as he threw another card onto the table. Zasht silently but quickly covered that with the nine of curves, or sines as Ty-Poh had said.

Play proceeded quickly, and Drake learned much with each card played. He learned that Fools were indeed wild, but only in suit or value, not both. He learned that if announced deuces would allow the players to speak, until the player who had thrown it played again. He learned the names of all the suits: Stars, Sines, Strings, Planes and Voids. He learned that each suit was comprised of thirteen cards. Eight cards had numbers ranging from two to ten, while four cards were faced; the Prince, the Queen, the King, and the Magi. There were also a smattering of other unsuited cards including the Fool, but also the Hound, which forced players to exchange hands clockwise, and the Librarian, a card that allowed you to see the cards of one other player. He also learned that the play of face cards, if they lingered too long, came with horrifying visions; visions of monstrous inhuman things that made that which he had seen earlier pale in comparison.

He also learned one simple and undeniable thing. They were cheating. They made a pretense of play, but any casual glance about the room revealed that the mirrors served to show everybody all the cards in play. In fact, Drake was almost sure that the glasses had been arranged for just such a purpose. At one point the barmaid, who wore a blindfold while serving the players drinks, had even gone so far as to adjust several of the mirrors so that the others could see his own hand. It was as if the entire game had been rigged against him, rigged against all of them.

Not that it mattered. Compared to the others, Drake had so many cards that finding a card to play had been relatively easy. So while the others struggled with hands of five or six, constantly drawing cards to play, Drake was quickly whittling down his own hand to a more manageable level. That is until Zassht played the seven of voids and said "Yr-Nhhngr," meekly. The reptilian humanoid waved a single card.

Ty-Poh seemed panicked, but then settled down and from his hand threw down the eight of voids. Play turned back to Zassht, and by the time he had drawn a card capable of play his hand had accumulated to eighteen cards. The process, gave Drake an idea, and he marshaled his cards, playing not the most logical or most damaging cards, but rather accumulating the most powerful. It had taken him time, but he had learned how to play the game, and realized how to win. He kept the others from seeing what he was doing by keeping his cards face down on the table.

As he shifted to this strategy, play suddenly became frenetic. The other players were forced into using cards they wouldn't have or stumbling along trying to decide which card to play. On more than one occasion the dealer called a penalty of time and fed the offending player several more cards. Face cards flew like bats out of hell, and were quickly countered by those with numbers.

Fifth played and announced "Quachil Uttaus, the Green King."

Drake stifled a laugh and countered "Mh'ithrha, the Green Prince," and then casually added "Yr-Nhhngr."

For indeed his strategy had left him with just one card.

Tch'tkach played the nine of strings, followed by Ty-Poh's nine of sines, which led to Zassht playing the eight of sines, reversing play. Drake smiled for he knew that none of them had any cards with which he could be forced to draw. The three players opposite him had accumulated a surplus of eights, and played back and forth amongst each other for five turns before Tch'tkach succumbed and had to let play move in Drake's direction.

The old spider suddenly looked wizened, old, and tired. His claws shook as he drew one card, thought better of it and then chose another. In his head Drake kept time, waiting for Fifth to penalize the player. With barely a moment to spare the player threw a card on table. "Azathoth the Black Magi," he declared.

Drake sneered and threw his own card, his last card, on the table. Time slowed, and the card spun in the air and then settled down on to the top of the pile of discards. It bore five symbols; one for each of the suits, Drake had played a Fool, a wild card.

It sat there, and all sound seemed to have been sucked out of the room. There was a pregnant pause, a kind of anti-climax that Drake didn't understand. They were waiting for something, Drake had forgotten, something important, a rule, a point of order. Drake felt panic well up inside him, and that voice that he used to count time was counting down. What had he forgotten? He needed to declare something. Wildcards needed to be declared, they could change suits or value but not both. He needed to declare the card, did it matter what it was? As soon as he declared, the game was over; the value of the card would be meaningless. Changing the card was unnecessary.

In a voice proud and defiant Samuel Drake declared "Azathoth, the Black Magi!"

Zassht hissed while Tch'tkach wailed in a high pitch squeal. Ty-Poh laughed maniacally. Fifth of Five waved his hand and silenced them all. "I am Fifth of Five, I am the dealer, I declare this Game of Mao to be over!" And with that the creature known as the Fifth of Five rose from his chair and strutted out the door that led to the bar.

The table shook, the lights flickered and Drake was plunged into a nightmare vision of the universe. From outside the galaxy he watched as a small black void at the heart of the Milky Way stirred, shuddered and then rose from its billions of years of melodic sleep. It stretched its tentacles of nightmare out and swallowed whole star systems in an instant. Billions and billions of lives were turned into fractal chaos while Samuel Drake watched and screamed in terror.

From the darkness a voice came and its light was like a beacon drawing Drake back to a rundown saloon, in a desert, on a small planet, in a star system far from the galactic core. It was the voice of the barmaid, and she cried as she spoke. "My name is Eve Clausen, I am the dealer, I declare this Game of Mao to have begun."

She dealt the cards while Drake crawled back into his chair. He sobbed as he gathered them up, "What are you doing?" He looked around, the two of them were alone, the other players had left or fled, or simply ceased to exist. Drake didn't know which.

"Penalty," she tossed another card in his direction. "I think I may be saving the world, maybe even the universe. I've sent Joe for help, we can't play alone, not for long."

Outside, Joe the bartender fled through the night, searching for others to sit at the table, but in the desert there were few to play the game, and fewer still who would volunteer. He would have to find a way to bring people to the sad little town that men had named Las Vegas. Even if players were mere mortals, the Game of Mao would continue. Under the whims of poor players, the universe might suffer, but at least it would survive. Somewhere behind him, Drake played Nyarlathotep, the prince of voids, and the lights flickered while the dealer, in search of a match, drew card after card after card after card.

THE
PUPPET MASTER
BY SAM STONE

Even though it was high noon the town was deserted as Mario rode into Oak City. His horse hesitated, rearing up as they crossed the town border. Mario took this as a good sign: he was on the right track. He held onto the reins, forcing the stallion into a short gallop until they were halfway up the high street.

There was no movement at all in any of the stores. Not that there were many: a small fabric shop, general store and a hardware shop were all that lined the main street together with the saloon, blacksmith's barn and sheriff's office. "City" was something of an exaggeration. This town was like taking a step back in time. It reminded him of all the old towns, mostly deserted now in favor of the big cities. It was hard to comprehend that New Orleans wasn't too far from here: maybe a day's ride east. He had heard many rumors on his route but even so it was odd to find this place still here, but so empty. It made him feel on edge. Though that was never a bad thing given the circumstances.

He tied up his horse outside the saloon and looked up at the balcony on the second level. The curtains were drawn. The saloon was deathly quiet but that wasn't so unusual, given the time of day. The action wouldn't happen here until after sundown. Or at least that was the usual thing in these towns. Mario wasn't so sure about Oak City though. There might never be any "action" here again.

Mario had come to Oak City looking for a girl. If Saskia was in town, this was where he was likely to find her and he was determined to find her no matter what it took.

255

At that moment a buzzard flew overhead and began to circle the town. Mario narrowed his eyes, squinting up into the sky. He watched the bird for a few seconds then unclipped his holster. *Time to get moving.*

He walked up the steps towards the traditional saloon doors and peered into the gloom over the top. The saloon was as dead inside as the town was outside. Mario pulled his gun, then pressed against one side of the swinging door with his right shoulder. The door creaked as it opened. He let his eyes adjust to the darkness before he walked all the way inside. He could see pretty well then and his eyes skittered from the bar to the stairs and over the empty tables and chairs. The old piano in the corner still had the cover up and the stool was positioned as though the pianist were still sitting there.

A floorboard groaned as he shifted his weight. He paused, looked up at the balcony above and noted that all the doors were firmly closed.

He leaned over the bar, checked that no one was lurking there, while glancing in the mirror to ensure that no one was behind him. Then he made his way up the stairs slowly, his back sliding along the wall so that he could see both the landing above and the bar area below.

At the top of the landing, Mario paused again. He could start at the end, on the last door, but who knew which one of these rooms housed Saskia? He didn't want her to realize he was there until it was too late. Making a quick decision, he opened the first door as quietly as possible. Inside he saw a whore and client, still attached, the whore on all fours, dress up around her waist, the man behind her, mid-thrust. Mario said nothing. The bodies didn't move.

He had seen this kind of thing before. It was like a paralysis, or like they were frozen in time. He walked in, got closer to the bed.

The man wore a pained smile. His eyes were half open, hips twisted in such a way that he appeared to be in the final moment of his ecstasy. His hands gripped the whore's waist in a death-like grip.

The whore's face was blank. Wiped clean of features. No eyes, lips, nose, just a smooth veneer of pale perfect wood.

Mario prodded the shallow cheeks of the man. His face began to crumble like lime whitewash subjected to intensive heat. Mario backed away. He closed the door behind him.

Saskia was here. No doubt about it now. The puppet was all the evidence he needed.

In each room he found a similar scene. The only thing that varied were the sexual positions. Sometimes the man was wood and the woman real, but most often it was the other way round. All of the humans were dead, disintegrating dried up husks that had been left to rot. They looked as though they were years dead, but Mario knew that this had all happened recently.

In the last room the set-up was more unusual. Mario noted the rich boudoir colors of reds and purples, the fancy Chinese screen that separated a bath tub from the rest of the room but what chilled him to the bone was the sight of the two men in bed with one woman. The woman was spread out on the bed, naked, hands tied to the metal headrest with purple sashes. Mario felt no sexual interest in the bare breasts: they were shrivelled like old figs. Her crumbling mouth was slightly open, while one man kneeled, his body falling to dust, above her face. His member dangled over her like tantalizing fruit that had been left on the branch too long. The other lay between her legs, his bottom raised, as though he were caught in half thrust.

Mario couldn't make sense of it at first. There were no puppets: obviously they had been active elsewhere, but why were these humans dead? There were always puppets involved in that somehow.

Mario backed away, then caught sight of himself in the mirror behind the half-drawn dressing screen. He also saw the reflection of a puppet, bent over, watching like a voyeur through the gap in the hinges.

The sight of it made the hair rise on the back of his neck. This was a new high, even for Saskia. He pulled back the screen. Anger burned in his stomach and chest. The puppet, predictably, didn't move.

Outside in the street Mario gulped in air. So she wasn't there, perhaps the damage was done already and the town was beyond saving?

Mario had a theory. The puppets were alive at night and they drained that life from the people they interacted with. He just had to find Saskia in order to prove it, and to stop this from ever happening again. The trouble was, he wasn't sure just how he was going to stop her.

Saskia had up and left him six weeks ago and she had taken something with her, something very important. Mario had to get it back. That was all he could think about.

"Hey. You."

Mario looked up. He sighed with relief as he saw the sheriff standing outside his office.

"What were you doing in the saloon? It ain't open yet."

"Sheriff, have you seen what's up there?"

The sheriff took some persuading to go inside but eventually he followed Mario into the bar. Mario waited downstairs as the man examined the rooms, it was now almost two and the afternoon was wearing on. He didn't want to be inside the saloon when the sun went down. That was when Saskia always did her work. That was when *they* lived.

"What the hell's happened here?" asked the sheriff as he descended the stairs.

Mario shook his head. His hands were trembling. This was the worst he had seen and no mistake, and he had been following her ever since this started. Saskia was getting more inventive, plus she was taking them a town at a time now. He just hoped he had arrived in time.

"Listen fella, I reckon you know what's going on. You'd better speak up or I'll be inclined to take you to the jail house."

"I don't know anything," said Mario. "I'm just passing through. Wanted a drink. I went looking for the barman but I found... that."

"Sheriff Haley?" called a voice outside. "Grant? We need you right now."

"My deputy..." Haley explained. "Wait here."

There was a creak upstairs.

"Sheriff, I'd rather come with you," said Mario. He wasn't ready to face this yet.

They went outside to find a tall, thin, young man waiting in the street.

"What is it Shane?" asked Haley.

Shane turned his head and looked down the street. Haley and Mario saw then that a small queue of people had appeared outside the sheriff's office. Mario noticed that the shops were now open and he could hear the steady tap of the blacksmith's hammer echoing down the street.

"Where did everyone come from?" asked Mario. "This place was dead not long back."

Haley shook his head. "It's a little weird. We've all been sleeping rather late recently. I can't seem to get outta bed much before noon. Fortunately neither can the rest of the town."

"Too much excitement at night?" Mario asked.

Haley said nothing, but Shane looked sick. Mario knew they had suspicions but they weren't about to discuss them with a stranger.

"What do they all want?" Haley asked Shane.

"Same as usual. Husbands and wives gone missing," said Shane.

Haley glanced up at the saloon. "I think I know where a few of them are."

Then Haley turned and walked back towards his office. His step was slow, tired, deliberate. Mario frowned.

"How long have you all been feeling... tired?" he asked Shane.

Shane turned to look at him as though he had only just noticed him. "Who are you?"

"Just arrived in town. I found the bodies."

"Bodies? What bodies?"

Mario nodded towards the saloon. Shane looked up at the balcony in front. The closed curtains did nothing to dispel the unease he was feeling. Then Shane turned and followed Haley leaving Mario alone outside the bar.

Inside the sheriff's office Mario found Haley and Shane talking to a man.

"My wife's no whore, Grant. You've known her all these years. Do you really think she'd willingly do something like that?"

Haley placed a soothing hand on the man's shoulder. "I've seen some weird stuff recently that I just can't believe. People acting out of character, going down to the saloon and taking part in things I'd never have dreamed. Hank, if Sara got tempted and went on in there, there's no telling what coulda happened. The thing is, I seen her body with my own eyes."

"I want to see..." said Hank. He tried to stand but Haley forced him back into the chair.

"It won't do you no good. Let the undertaker deal with this Hank. I promise you, you don't want this to be the way you remember your lovely wife."

Mario noticed the undertaker then, standing in the corner of the office. He looked so stereotypical, wearing a dark suit and with a sincere expression on his face as he took the sheriff's instructions and left the office, followed by Shane.

If I were making a puppet show of this story the undertaker would look just like that, thought Mario. This made him realize how tentative reality was these days. But then everything had changed so much.

"The rest of you, sit down," ordered Haley and the other people there, waiting to hear about their loved ones, sat down in unison, like puppets whose strings had just been cut.

Mario felt sick and guilty. This was all his fault. He left the sheriff's office and headed down the street. He had to find Saskia and end this. It wasn't right. These people didn't deserve this punishment, no one did.

He went to see the shop owners first. The haberdashery was a good place to start. Puppets needed clothes after all and Saskia would want them to appear as real as possible.

"Can I help you?" asked the shop keeper, a portly man in his fifties.

"I'm wondering if you've seen this woman?"

Mario pulled his pocket watch out of his waistcoat and opened it. Inside the lid was a small portrait of a petite blonde woman of around twenty. The shop keeper looked at the picture, eyes narrowing as he squinted down to see it.

"Can't say that I have. What's she to you?"

"I'm looking for her," said Mario. "She's my wife."

"Oh right. Sorry. Lots of wives going missing around these parts. No one knows what's happening, but the preacher says we have to stay strong in this darkest hour."

Mario thanked him and moved on to the general store. Inside he found a young woman and an old man serving two sluggish customers. One was a rancher collecting sacks of grain, the other was a boy buying candy sticks. When they had been served, Mario stepped forward and showed the girl Saskia's portrait.

"Never seen her," she said barely glancing at the picture.

"What about you?" he asked the old man.

"Nope," he said with a lethargic finality to his voice.

Mario walked the entire street. Everyone he spoke to said they hadn't seen Saskia, yet he knew she must be there. All the evidence pointed to her sickness and obsession taking hold. He *had* to find her before nightfall.

He walked on to the church at the far side of town. Inside he found the preacher sleeping in one of the pews.

He shook him awake. "Have you seen this girl?" he asked holding out the picture.

"Looks like a whore to me," said the preacher. "Try the saloon."

Mario resisted the urge to shoot the man in the head.

No, Saskia!

Mario heard music burst out from the saloon. It was a familiar tune, one he had heard many times. It was the melody that Saskia played when all the puppets danced on the stage. He took a step forward, then realized his feet were moving towards the saloon all of their own accord. He had to get away, before the music got to him, but first he needed to reach his horse.

The sun was going down and Mario began to panic. The puppets would be waking and Saskia would be controlling them with her music.

He felt confused for a moment. Then remembered that his horse was roped up just outside the saloon. He let the music carry him forward again. He paused at the sheriff's office and glanced through the large window. The sheriff was locking the deputy up in one cell, while he locked himself in the other. Then they exchanged keys. Both men began to dance around the cell, like marionettes on strings.

At the fabric shop, Mario saw the portly old man locking up; he had wads of thick material hanging from his ears. He glanced at Mario sadly, then he walked away from the shop, down the street, far from the saloon.

At the hardware shop he saw the old man tie the young girl's wrists and ankles. Then he placed her on a mattress, covered her with a blanket and began to tie his own feet to the leg of the counter. All this time the man's legs twitched and kicked as though he couldn't control them.

Mario reached the bar a few seconds later. There was a crowd around the door. A young man gripped the rocker that sat on the porch, his knuckles were turning white with the effort of holding himself back from the bar. Inside he could hear the voice of a girl singing now. He recognized it, so rarely used in the old days, but now Saskia had really found her voice. His heart lurched in his chest.

Then he reached his horse, hand rapidly slipping into the sack attached to the back of the saddle. He pulled out the strings and the sound of Saskia's voice receded.

It was too late to do anything now. He had to let the night unfold and keep himself safe from the spell. He turned to see the preacher dancing towards him. His face was distorted, mouth open in a silent scream. Mario felt the man's terror, even as he watched him dance, almost joyfully, up to the swing doors.

At that moment a puppet appeared. It turned its blank face out towards him. Mario was sure that the eyeless face would still see him somehow.

The preacher fell into the marionette's arms and a dance of a different sort began as the faceless thing sat him down on a chair by the piano. The doll lifted its skirt and then sat astride the man.

Mario's horse reared as the half-screams, half-cries of pleasure poured out from saloon. He stroked its mane, just as he had once stroked Saskia's hair. Then he slipped the strings up and around the animal's neck and felt the calm return to the stallion's shaking limbs. He held onto the strings, keeping the strength he needed around them both, then he mounted the horse, and rode out and away from the town with his thoughts and his memories.

His master, Federico, had taught him well. Mario manipulated the puppets with dexterity. Small though they were, they appeared to hold real life essence every time he picked up the strings.

"You have a real talent for this," Federico had said. "One day I will share all of my secrets with you."

Mario carved the puppets during the day, while Federico performed the shows at night. But sometimes he would let Mario take over during a particularly simple dance routine, and the audience never knew. Mario loved his apprenticeship with the old man, but he often wondered why Federico never taught his skills to his granddaughter, Saskia, instead. She traveled with them, making small dresses and suits for the puppets to wear. Cleaning up after them both, making edible food as they traveled over desert and wastelands between towns.

As the old man's fingers became less flexible, Mario had gone from apprentice to partner, and then eventually he had taken over the show completely while Federico and Saskia had walked the crowd, hat held out, to take money. They traveled around Mexico like this for years, scraping a living, until eventually the old man couldn't travel anymore.

After that Mario would take the show to nearby towns. Then he would return with money to help them live.

"I have to show you something," Federico said on Mario's return from yet another trip. "It is what once made me great."

By this time Federico was being nursed by Saskia, he couldn't be left alone. Mario knew that he was dying.

"Fetch me the box, Saskia," Federico said and for once Saskia hesitated to fulfill his request. "I said get me the box!"

Saskia scurried away, she was always subservient to Federico, and so Mario was surprised by her reaction to his request. She returned quickly though and she held out a wooden box to Federico.

"Thank you Saskia. You have been a good girl all this time. I now need to make sure that you are taken care of," Federico said.

"Don't grandfather," she begged. "I don't want you to leave."

The box was a rough, wooden casket carved with an S on the top. Federico now held it out to Mario, "I want you to have this. Inside is the secret that I promised to share with you. You have been like a son to me and I leave you this legacy. Promise me you will look after Saskia?"

Mario stared at Saskia as she now sat calmly on the other side of the dying man's bed. He had always loved her, but had never dared to tell her or his master.

"I will marry her," Mario said. "We will work together as always to keep the puppet show going."

Federico closed his eyes, a small tear slipped from his eye and he passed quietly away while Mario clutched the box firmly to his chest.

"Aren't you going to open it?" asked Saskia.

"I want to marry you tonight," Mario said.

Saskia said nothing, but she dutifully stood and she went to the trunk at the bottom of the bed. There she retrieved a white dress. It was beautiful and Mario knew it was something she had made herself. It was as though she had been waiting for this moment and had prepared for it. He left her to dress, while he fetched the undertaker, and then the two of them went straight to the church as Federico's body was taken away to prepare it for burial.

"This is for you," Saskia said as they stood before the priest. "You must never take it off."

She tied a cord bracelet around his wrist and Mario remembered that Federico had worn one similar for all of the time Mario had known him.

After they were married, Mario forgot about the box. It was the last thing on his mind as he took Saskia, now his wife, home. As they prepared for bed, he stowed it in the chest where he kept the parts for his puppets.

After Federico was buried they set out once more to take the puppet show all over Mexico.

A few years passed before they came to the town that changed things. Mario was happy when they had left Mexico to start their new life in New Orleans. Saskia was a good girl, easy to control, and they took the puppet show from town to town making a very good living. Mario's skill grew. He felt empowered every time he picked up the puppet strings. The marionettes did everything he wanted them to, just by the mere flick of his wrists, and so he decided to make some of them life size.

They rested in New Orleans while Mario obtained the wood and carved the new dummies. Then Saskia made the clothes. Mario had seen a picture card, taken from a cigarette packet, which showed a row of dancing girls in Paris. He asked Saskia to make the puppets look like the girls.

Then he set about making the cart they traveled in into a full size stage, with an area above where he could stand unseen and manipulate the puppets.

"Use this string," Saskia suggested as Mario laced up the first doll. It was thin and almost invisible, but incredibly strong. Mario didn't ask her where the cord came from, but he used it and hung the dolls up on the cart and began to practice the show.

Using the marionettes was easier than he thought it would be. They took on a life of their own every time Mario touched the strings. At the end of each performance, Mario could barely recall doing anything, but the dolls danced the Can Can much to the delight of the crowd.

Their reputation grew, at each new town the crowds were bigger and the money began to flow easily into the hat as Saskia went around the crowd. They traveled up and down the Mississippi and beyond.

At Dakin City, a small town that aspired to be big, Mario had left the puppet cart in the stables owned by the blacksmith, and Saskia and the puppets were in his room in the town's one small hotel. Saskia had some costume repairs to do but that day the show had been a huge success.

Mario was wired as he often was afterwards. He needed to relax, wind down and so he went to the saloon, as he sometimes did after a good day. A little whiskey and a card game was all he needed to help settle. Saskia never minded this, nor did she complain if he came back late. She was the perfect wife. All any man could ask for.

He didn't notice the tension in the air when he walked into the bar. He wasn't good with people, he only understood puppets and Saskia never made any demands of him.

"Hey Mister, you the guy with them life size puppets?" asked a man at the end of the bar.

"Yeah," said Mario. "Whiskey straight up."

The barman sloshed the amber liquid into a shot glass. Mario placed the money on the counter and slugged the drink. Then he turned around and looked at the room. This saloon was set out pretty much like any other. A few tables and chairs, one group of men with a card game in the corner, another group sat with a few of the saloon girls. The girls drank and giggled as the men refilled their glasses from a bottle in the center. Over in the corner a guy with a bald head was playing something vaguely recognizable on the piano, while on a small stage a woman sang almost in tune.

"So, these puppets... you ever use 'em for anything else?" asked the man at the end of the bar.

"What do you mean?" asked Mario. "They're just puppets."

"Yeah," laughed the man. "I caught your show, all that swirling around of skirts, frilly underwear."

Mario shrugged, he didn't understand what the man was implying but he felt strange. It was almost as though there were something dark in the air brewing.

"Where you keeping 'em then?" asked the man.

"Why?" Mario replied.

"I'd like to see one, close to."

"We have another show tomorrow, come by and I'll let you see them, and the strings and stuff."

"I'd like to see one now," said the man.

"Now Jake," said the barman. "We don't want no trouble tonight. These folks have come here for fun."

"I ain't causing no trouble," said Jake. "I just wanna see a puppet."

Mario finished his drink. He was feeling uneasy now.

"Tomorrow, buddy. Come by and I'll let you see one. 'Night gentlemen," Mario said then he left the saloon.

He went to the stables and checked on his cart and stage, making sure it was all safe, and then he returned to the room at the hotel.

Saskia was sitting in a chair by the window when he came in. She was surprised that he was back so early but she said nothing. She watched him change for bed, then he came back to her and began to stroke her hair for a while.

He liked to brush her long, blonde locks before bed sometimes. She didn't mind. It was soothing and her hair felt good afterwards. When he had finished they went to bed.

"You know I love you don't you?" he said as they curled up for sleep.

Saskia knew it was true, but she was already dozing and so didn't reply.

A few minutes later the door burst open.

"Now that's one puppet I'd like to play with," said the man called Jake as Mario sat upright in bed.

There were four men in the room, one of them was Jake. He glared past Mario at Saskia cowering under the bed covers.

"What are you doing?" yelled Mario, "Get out of here!"

But the men came in and closed the door instead. Two of them grabbed Mario, pulling him out of the room.

They held him down but he didn't care about his own safety, all he cared about was his wife. Saskia was being hurt, he had to do something. Mario twisted and turned, fought and kicked, but he couldn't get free.

Saskia would be destroyed. He couldn't have that.

He managed to pull one arm free and he hit out at one of his attackers. Then one of the men hit him so hard that Mario's head slammed back against the floor. He drifted into unconsciousness.

When he woke the men were gone. He ran up to his room and found Saskia lying listless. She was bruised and hurt and she wouldn't talk to him, or tell him what the men had done. The room was wrecked and his puppets destroyed. Some of them were covered in semen, dresses ripped from the wooden bodies, wigs torn from the smooth heads and the painted faces scarred beyond recognition. Mario felt sick. He looked at Saskia. Other than a few bruises and cuts she seemed unhurt.

"What did they do?" he insisted.

Saskia refused to speak.

As they drove away the town was quiet: the people were nowhere to be seen. Mario barely noticed. All he cared about was taking Saskia away to safety. He felt guilty: a total failure of a man who could not protect his wife. Mario had never even fired a gun in his life and didn't own one. All he could think about was that he wished he had learned.

"We'll go back to Mexico," said Mario. "I'm going to buy a gun."

"No," said Saskia. "We must carry on with the show. That is where your skill is Mario."

Mario said nothing. He wasn't used to her disagreeing with him. He couldn't face the thought that what had happened had changed their relationship in some way. He loved Saskia and would do anything to save their happy life.

"We're going back to New Orleans to make more puppets. These ones will be different Mario. This time you will open my grandfather's box."

Mario was surprised by the force in her voice. He clicked his tongue, sending the horses speeding along across the desert. As the sun rose he glanced down at his wrist and saw that the bracelet she gave him on their wedding day had gone. He felt an overwhelming sense of loss. It was as though this were the most important thing in the world. He thought it some omen that life had been irrevocably changed.

They returned to New Orleans and Mario did all that Saskia asked. He wanted to please her. Wanted to help her forget what had happened. But the one thing he shouldn't have done was open the box her grandfather gave him. That was the day when everything really changed.

Mario returned to Oak City just before dawn. The music was still drifting from the saloon but he was still holding onto the puppet cord and he had weaved it into the horse's mane.

Outside the saloon he saw the bodies of the dead entwined with puppets. A wind picked up and Mario saw one man's hat fly away. He stared down at the shrivelled face of the man. He looked more jerked beef than human, but he recognized the face nonetheless. It was the sheriff's deputy, Shane.

"I found them," said Saskia as Mario pushed open the saloon door. "They won't be hurting anyone else ever again."

She was standing by the piano. Mario looked around the room. He saw the preacher still sitting in the chair, the marionette astride him. His face looked as though all of the life and blood had been sucked from him.

"All of these people. You killed all of these innocent people," Mario couldn't think of anything else to say.

"Not innocent. These men were like those others. These women were all whores."

"What happened to you?" he asked. "We were so happy. Then all of this changed. I wanted to just forget what those..."

Mario broke down. He staggered against the bar and stood shaking until Saskia came to him. She stroked his head and put her arms around his shoulder.

"What now?" he said. "You will kill me too?"

Saskia shook her head. "I found this," she said.

Mario looked at her outstretched palm. He saw the broken remains of the cord she had placed around his wrist on their wedding day.

"You should never have removed this," she told him.

Mario's mind was a whirl of emotion, Saskia had kept this all along and he had thought it lost. His mind flashed back to the box. The one that Federico had given him, but never really explained. How he had opened it only once, the night before Saskia had disappeared with all of the puppets.

The 'S' on the lid had been important. He had known that all along and so when he had seen the heart inside, with the marionette cord tied around it, Mario had finally understood. Federico's magic lay in realms that Mario could never quite comprehend. The heart of his real granddaughter beat on inside, while the marionette copy of her walked and lived and held her memories believing she was human. This was Saskia's heart.

"Where is the heart now?" he asked.

Saskia took his hand and placed it on her chest. He could feel the slight pulse. "Where it belongs," she said. "I found the men. Aren't you happy that I killed them?"

Mario shook his head. *So many lives, Saskia.*

"I love you," she said. "Now that I have my heart I understand what that means."

Mario stroked her arm and wrist. Saskia didn't realize what he was doing until the first puppet string was tied.

"No!" she said but Mario took her other wrist and as the cord bound her she no longer had the strength to resist.

Once the puppet was restrung, Mario took the wedding bracelet and began to weave in some of the remaining cord, then he tied it once more around his own wrist. He wouldn't have to use the strings now. Saskia was his to command once more.

He looked around the saloon then turned his arm in a flowing motion. He swept his hand over the room. Saskia gasped and turned, her hands outstretched. He heard her heartbeat grow louder, filling the room as the puppet whores disintegrated. Mario knew that they would never rise again, night or day. Their mistress, Saskia, had been bound to him again and he would make sure that he never lost the cord, no matter what happened.

They went outside. The town was dead and there was nothing more he could do. He felt the regret for his uselessness once more. He would have saved them, but Saskia was more important.

"Time to go home," he said.

"Yes, Mario," said Saskia smiling.

As they rode away from Oak City, Mario smiled. He had finally learnt the lesson that Federico had really wanted to teach him. He had graduated to puppet master and he would never let the puppets get away again, particularly not Saskia. He stroked her hair as she sat in the saddle in front of him.

"Happy?" he asked.

"Yes, Mario. I love you."

Had he been facing her he might have seen the torment in her eyes. A drop of linseed oil traced a path down her face. No one really wants to give up control of themselves, not even a marionette with a human heart.

UNCLE GUNNYSACK

BY C. L. WERNER

Hard, pitiless eyes stared from behind the scraggly clump of brush, peering through the skeletal branches with a hate every bit as hot as the desert sun blazing overhead. Red hands clenched tight about the leather-wrapped stock of an old Spencer, feeling the embroidered beadwork dig into the rough flesh of palm and finger. A moment later, the watcher hesitated, savoring the sight before him, letting his heart glut itself upon the vision of vengeance soon to unfold.

Only a few dozen yards from the clump of brush, oblivious to the murderous eyes studying him, a lone man leaned over a small fire. He was a big, powerfully-built man, his blue coat struggling to contain the broad expanse of his shoulders. His bald head was shielded from the blistering sun by a battered hat, its leather brim notched and cracked.

The lurking Indian knew that hat and that coat. They were the colors of the hated pony soldiers who had broken the great tribes of the Apache and driven them from their ancestral lands. For a moment he puzzled over the deep black hue of the man's skin, but quickly overcame his curiosity. No white man, but neither was he Apache. That was all the reason the renegade needed.

The loud report of a rifle shot echoed across the rocky hills, reverberating in the arroyos and canyons. The Indian started forward from the brush, one hand already dropping to the heavy Bowie knife stuck in his wolfskin belt. He'd rob the pony soldier's corpse, but first he intended to mutilate the body so the ghost of the murdered man would be crippled in the spirit world. The Apache warrior's hand froze about the grip of his knife, his eyes going wide with confusion.

The black man was still leaning over his fire, slowly stirring the pot bubbling in the flames. The brave blinked in disbelief. It was hard enough for him to think he could have missed such an easy target, but it was impossible the soldier could have failed to hear the shot even if he hadn't been hit! The last thing the Apache was prepared for was to see his prey calmly stirring his pot. Superstitious dread flared through his heart, threatening to send him scurrying back into the hills.

It was sight of the blue coat and kepi that made the Apache re-member his courage. He wasn't about to be sent running away like a frightened child by a lone pony soldier! Maybe the fool was deaf or stupid! Either way, he wouldn't be for much longer.

Coldly, the Apache raised the Spencer to his shoulder. His finger tightened about the trigger. As he tried to shoot, however, he found himself unable to move his finger. However hard he tried, it refused to respond, refused to squeeze the trigger and send a bullet smashing into the soldier's back.

Now raw terror rushed through the brave's veins. The instinct to flee overwhelmed him. If he had been able, he would have turned and started running, not stopping until he was in the Dragoon Mountains stronghold and kneeling outside the wikiup of his tribe's medicine man.

But the Apache couldn't turn and flee. He couldn't lower his rifle, couldn't pull the trigger. He couldn't even look away as the soldier slowly rose from before the fire. His entire body was paralyzed, re-fusing to respond to him. A weird, clammy sensation was spreading through his limbs, making every nerve and tendon shudder, making each muscle spasm.

The soldier rose to his full height and now the Apache could see the man had the height to match those broad, powerful shoulders. As the man turned towards him, however, the renegade felt a new surge of terror. The man's face had been covered in paint—not the colorful patterns of war paint, but the grisly pallor of a death's head. The black of the soldier's unpainted skin formed the gaps in the pallid skull, the nasal cavity and eye sockets, the spaces between teeth and jaws.

The Apache trembled as the black giant stared at him, instantly picking him out from all the scrub and cactus littering the hill. There was a hideous lack of emotion in those eyes, an arrogant contempt that was inhuman in its cold malignance. With long, unhurried strides, the soldier climbed up towards the helpless Indian.

In his hand, the black man gripped an enormous knife, the kind of blade the Apache had seen Mexican rancheros use for chopping wood and clearing brush. Even from a distance, the renegade could see the gleam of the weapon's razored edge.

A brooding silence settled over the hills as the giant advanced, only the eerie wail of the wind through the canyons reach the frozen Apache's ears. He waited for the giant to call out, to threaten or curse at him as a white man would have, but the skull-faced ogre held his tongue. He was quieter than a slinking jaguar, his boots never making a sound as he climbed the hill, never kicking or disturbing the little gray rocks scattered in his path.

Closer now, the Apache could see that he was mistaken when he had thought this man a soldier. No pony soldier would have let himself abandon that regimented appearance his chiefs demanded of him. The giant's legs were bare above the black cavalry boots he wore, only a rough buckskin was wrapped about the man's waist, held in place by a raw snakeskin belt, the rattler's tail stuffed into its mouth and held in place by a big cactus thorn. He wore no shirt under his blue coat, his powerful chest exposed and marked with a network of slashes and scars. Tied around the giant's neck with a strip of leather was a little rabbitskin bag.

The skull-faced ogre didn't pause as he reached the Apache, didn't even look at the Spencer still clenched in the brave's frozen hands, still aimed at the black man's body. There was no change in the giant's expression, that same air of malignant contempt smoldering in his gaze.

Sunlight blazed from the machete as the black giant lifted it above his head and brought it slashing down into red flesh.

Coffin Durango stared down at what had once been a man. He'd spent most of his life in the Arizona Territory, had been raised in Tucson, met his first girl in Sahurito, buried his father in Contention, killed his first man in Wickenburgh, almost died himself in Gila Bend from a rattler bite. All that time living in the Territory, exposed to its dangers, he'd developed the common wisdom that there wasn't anything you could do to an Apache that he didn't deserve.

As he looked at the bloody thing sprawled out in the sand, Coffin realized he was wrong. He could have gone his whole life without finding out how wrong. He'd seen babies that had been thrown into stands of cactus by Apaches on the prowl, helped the cavalry pick up the pieces from a dozen burnt-out ranches and prospector camps. Yesterday, if anyone had told him he'd ever feel pity for an Apache, he'd have called them loco.

Slowly, Coffin drew the .45 from the holster nuzzled against his belly. The Apache was already killed, but the way the monster who had done this to him had left him, he'd be a long time dying. Coffin clenched his teeth as he pointed his pistol at what was left of the warrior's face. As the Indian heard the click of the hammer drawing back, Coffin fancied that the brave tried to smile with the lipless red smear beneath the wet hole where his nose should have been.

Coffin turned away from the dead Apache. He glanced up at the circling buzzards and tipped his wide-brimmed hat at the scavengers. But for them, he might never have stumbled onto the dying brave. He'd lost the trail some miles back. The mutilated Indian had put him back on the right track.

A hot wind whipped Coffin's long duster as he climbed down to the little arroyo where he'd left his horse tethered. He pulled his kerchief up over his face to block the gritty dust stirred up by that wind. His gray eyes grew hard, gleaming like bullets in the tanned leather of his face. When the hunt had started, he would have laid that sudden gust of wind down to coincidence. But time after time, the same hot, shiftless wind had risen to put him off the trail. Now he reckoned it wasn't so much coincidence as the Devil looking out for one of his own.

He'd been a lot of things in his time. A wolf-hunter in Montana, a bank-buster in California, a regulator in New Mexico, an Army scout out in the Dakotas, he'd even tried a stint as a town marshal for a time until the respectability began to grate on his sensibilities. For the past three years, he'd been making a living in Arizona as a bounty killer and he'd put a lot of vicious desperados under Boot Hill in that time. Never had he encountered a man who needed hanging more than Amos White, or as his comrades in the 10th Cavalry had named him "Uncle Gunnysack".

There were all kinds of stories about Amos White, most of which Coffin had discounted when he first heard them. The Buffalo Soldiers claimed Amos was some sort of magic-man, something they called a bokor. They said he could call up spirits to make it rain or turn milk sour or make a gun jam all on its own. When he wanted, Amos could be standing right next to you and you couldn't see him.

A few of the soldiers who hailed from the south had given Amos the name "Uncle Gunnysack", some sort of bogeyman in the folkstories down in the bayous. They claimed that Amos was seventy-three even though he looked little more than thirty. Amos, they said, had been a slave on a Louisiana plantation until he had used his hoodoo to make himself master and the plantation owner nothing but his puppet. After Emancipation, Amos had sent the plantation owner into New Orleans with a new will naming him as the sole heir to the house and lands. As soon as the old slave master had the will certified, he stepped out into the street and shot himself, screaming all the while: "Don't make me! I don't want to do it!"

If Amos had inherited a plantation, he didn't keep it long. Though now free men, Amos worked the former slaves more remorselessly than their old master, his cruelty exciting the outrage of his white neighbors. Night riders had descended upon the plantation and Amos had been lucky to escape. He'd fled north and enlisted, using the Army to hide from his many enemies.

Whatever the truth behind the villain's background, this much Coffin knew for certain. There had been a cholera epidemic at the fort, one that had ravaged the Buffalo Soldiers without mercy. Amos White had taken sick along with the others, maybe even worse. He seemed to shrivel and wither each day, but however weak he got, he would sneak out of the bunkhouse every night. A curious spy had followed him once, caught him crouched in the fort graveyard, his hands raised to the sky, his voice hissing words in a sinister whisper that set the spy's hair on end.

The epidemic at the fort grew worse after that, a hundred men were taken sick and twenty-three died before the disease was through. Yet as the other soldiers worsened, Amos White's condition improved. His body filled out again, his limbs lost the shakes, sweat no longer streamed down his skin. The army doctor had no explanation for Amos's improvement and with so many sick men to tend, little time to investigate.

It was the night that the cholera took its last victim that Amos White deserted the fort. He did so in a way that would have made Nachez turn sick with revulsion. Around midnight, Amos had stolen away from the barracks as he had every night since the epidemic began. This time, however, he didn't head for the graveyard. He snuck into the colonel's house and killed every living thing inside, right down to the colonel's three-month-old daughter. The soldiers who discovered the slaughter had been amazed that so small a body could have so much blood inside it.

That had been the start, and in the six weeks between his murders at the fort and the Apache, Amos had cut a bloody swathe across the Territory. A stage outside Red Rock, every man woman and child butchered. A mining camp in the hills near Picket Post, the victims flayed and left to dry under the desert sun. A homestead ten miles from Cottonwood. Coffin couldn't bring himself to think about what he had found there.

Amos White might have been a man once, but nothing human could do the things Coffin had seen. He was coming to believe there was something unnatural about the murderer, something obscene and unholy, something beyond mere human depravity and savagery.

The Army had posted a $300 reward for Amos White, but for the first time since he could remember, Coffin Durango didn't give a hoot about the money on the outlaw's head. This man needed killing.

It was as pure and simple as that.

Walt Prentice held his calloused hand to his forehead, trying to shield his eyes from the glare of the noonday sun. Heat shimmered from the parched terrain, creating a weird rippling miasma in the distance. On the horizon, he could see the brown slopes of the Sierra Tortillata, as desolate and forlorn as everything else in the desert.

"Something wrong, Pa?"

Walt turned at the sound of his son's voice. The boy was watering the horses. In this heat, there was no sense running the animals. They would just wear out under the sun and leave the settlers little better for the effort. The wise course was to sit out the hottest part of the day and then make a few hours before nightfall. It might take them longer to reach Casa Grande, but at least they would get there.

"Thought I saw somebody walking this way?" Walt answered, removing his hat to wipe the sweat from his forehead. He turned and walked back towards the wagon. Everything the family owned was piled onto the bed, furniture stacked into rickety tiers and lashed down with thick coils of rope, sacks of grain and seed tied to the exterior, chests of clothes and heirlooms secured beneath the box at the fore of the carriage. Walt wasn't interested in any of these. It was the serape-wrapped canteen hanging from the hook at the back that interested him.

"What would anyone be doing walking in this heat?" The question came from the woman lying inside the covered bed of the wagon. Martha Prentice had put a few pounds on her since she'd come west from Abilene, added a few wrinkles around her eyes, broadened her shape a bit after bearing three children, but to Walt she was still as pretty as when he'd first seen her behind the counter of her father's mercantile. He smiled at her, watching her fan herself and the two youngest children with one of her straw hats.

"I didn't say I saw anyone," Walt laughed. "I said I thought I saw someone." He took a long pull from the canteen and wiped the residue from his mouth with the sleeve of his plaid shirt. "I reckon it must have been the heat playing tricks."

"Maybe it was an Indian, Pa," suggested his eldest, moving to give the second of the horses a draw from the water bucket. There was a naïve excitement in Billy's voice, but Martha's breath caught in her throat at the suggestion.

Walt shrugged. "An Indian's got more sense than to be out in this heat," he reassured his family. He could tell his wife only half-believed him. Inwardly, he shared her anxiety. If Yavapai or Apache got their blood up, he didn't think there was anything that could keep them off the warpath. Certainly not something like a bit of sun. It was easy for an American to forget that these were people born and bred in the most inhospitable places in the land. They were used to everything the desert could throw at them and then some.

"We'll be in Casa Grande tomorrow," Walt told his family. "Then we'll all be so busy getting the new store ready we'll all wish we were back on the trail just loafing around."

The children brightened at his jest, but Walt could still see the concern in Martha's eyes. Calmly, so as not to alarm the children, he stepped around the wagon and retrieved the Winchester leaning against the seat. "I'll just have a look around," he told his wife, keeping his tone untroubled.

"Pa!" Billy cried out suddenly. The boy came scurrying back to the wagon from where the horses were hobbled, his eyes wide with fright.

Walt looked past his son and found himself staring at a tall, broad-shouldered black man. For a moment, he could only stare in surprise, wondering where the man had come from. It didn't seem possible he could be the same figure the settler thought he saw out in the desert. It still left the question of how he could have closed upon the settlers without being spotted.

"Shoo him off!" Martha hissed from the bed of the wagon. Walt glanced back at her, saw her hugging the youngsters to her bosom, her face pale with fear. He felt a twinge of regret flash through his heart. It was an ugly thing, that fear. She'd grown up during John Brown's bloody crusade to free the slaves, had vivid childhood memories of Brown's marauders rampaging through her town. It had left her with a deep-rooted fright of black men.

"I'll do no such thing!" Walt hissed back in an undertone. He might sympathize with his wife's fear, but he didn't accept it and wouldn't condone it. He gestured with his rifle at the keppie and blue coat the man wore. "He's a soldier, might be lost from his regiment. Maybe he was bushwhacked by renegades."

"I don't care," Martha growled back. "I don't like him."

Walt's temper bristled. "I don't care either," he said. "Doesn't matter what color his skin is, he's a soldier and I'm not going to drive him off into the desert. He might need help. Least we can do is offer to take him to Casa Grande."

Before his wife could offer further protest, Walt strode away from the wagon, walking towards the subject of their quarrel. The stranger had stopped a short distance from the horses, was just standing there biding his time, waiting for Walt to come to him. It was an attitude that gave the settler a bit of comfort. The soldier understood that his sudden appearance had given the family a bit of a surprise and was being decent enough to wait until they had overcome that surprise.

Walt shifted his grip on his Winchester, holding it by the barrel as he advanced, just to show the soldier that he wasn't afraid. "I apologize," he called out. "But you gave us a bit of a start."

He was closer now and could see just how immense the black man was. If he was much under six-six in his stockings, Walt would have been surprised. The soldier's arms were so thick around that he looked like he could strangle a steer one-handed. Walt hesitated in his march, a flicker of caution lighting inside his brain.

"How can we help you?" the settler asked. He was near enough to the soldier now that he could see the barbaric belt he wore, the bare legs and the crude buckskin that girded his loins. "I'm afraid we're on our way to Casa Grande and need those horses, if that's what you want." Walt tried to resist the feeling of suspicion that flared up inside him, tried to dismiss it as the same sort of unreasoning prejudice that afflicted his wife.

Try as he might, as much as he struggled to reason it away, Walt was afraid of this man.

"We'll tell them in Casa Grande that you're out here," Walt offered. "I'm sure they'll send somebody for you." He felt shame as the words left his mouth, but not enough shame to take them back. "We're loaded down pretty good. There's just no room for anyone else in the wagon," he added.

Until now, the soldier had stood facing the horses, acting as though he wasn't even aware of the settler. Now, he turned and glared down at Walt, glared at him with eyes that were like smoldering embers glowing from the ghoulish skull the black man had painted onto his face. The settler took a frightened step backwards, heard the gasp of fear from his wife, the terrified yelps from his youngest back in the wagon.

Walt snapped the Winchester to his shoulder, but before he could fire, a hideous numbness gripped him. His finger felt like a piece of pig-iron as he tried to pull the trigger. Struggle as he might, he couldn't squeeze off the shot and drop the approaching giant.

Uncle Gunnysack shifted his gaze from Walt to the terrified family in the wagon. The fangs of the painted skull spread wide as he smiled, transforming his face into a demonic mask of murderous malevolence. Walt struggled all the harder to bring his weapon to bear. His exertions were useless, the eerie paralysis that had stolen upon him would not abate.

The black giant looked away from the mother and children in the wagon and back at Walt. One massive paw closed about the huge machete fixed to the snakeskin belt. The settler saw the blade flash in the noonday sun. He felt it smash down as it split his skull. As he flopped against the ground, blood and brains oozing from his head, the last sounds Walt Prentice heard were the screams of his wife and children as his murderer stalked towards them.

The javelina huffed angrily at Coffin Durango as the bounty hunter approached the scene of the massacre. The pig-like scavenger slashed the ground with its paws, puffing up its brindle-hued body to make itself look more intimidating. Coffin threw a rock at the animal, sending it scurrying away, a strip of Walt Prentice's flesh still dangling from its tusks.

There was no mistaking the handiwork of Amos White. The outlaw's victims hadn't simply been murdered and mutilated. They'd been taken apart, piece by piece, each portion deliberately if not carefully cut away. Before the scavengers had come along, there might have been some sort of pattern to the way the pieces of Walt and his family had been laid out. As it was, it took Coffin several minutes to realize he was looking at the remains of three human beings; a man, a boy and a woman.

The family's abandoned wagon removed any question that what Coffin saw might be the work of renegade Indians. Far from being ransacked, it was untouched, unmarked except for the splashes of blood marking its sides. The freshness of the blood told him the atrocity was very recent. An examination of the contents of the wagon, the tiny sets of clothes, the little toys, told him that two members of the family were missing. There had been two small children in the doomed expedition.

Something close to panic closed around Coffin's heart. He thought back to Uncle Gunnysack's other rampages. There had been small children there too and the monster had performed his worst outrages against them.

It had been the same at the fort. Amos had taken his time there, too, with the colonel's infant daughter. One of the Buffalo Soldiers from the south claimed it was because Uncle Gunnysack had to pay back the old gods he had invoked to save himself from the epidemic, dark pagan spirits that could be paid only in innocent blood. In truth, Amos had become his namesake, a murderous bogeyman haunting the countryside.

Coffin studied the ground, desperately trying to spot some sign of the depraved murderer and his captives. There might still be time to save the children, but with each passing breath, he knew that the time was growing short.

The dirt was unmarked, not so much as a footprint betraying the direction Uncle Gunnysack had taken, not even a splotch of blood to give him away. After what he had done to the other victims, the marauder should be coated in their blood yet the ground gave no sign of his passing. Coffin clenched his fists in frustration. It was worse than trailing an Apache, more like trying to track a ghost than a man. Hard as he tried, the bounty killer couldn't find anything to guide him.

Then, in the distance, Coffin noticed a coyote. His skin prickled as he watched the prairie wolf and realized what it was doing. It had its head nuzzled against the ground, was licking furiously at the dirt. He'd seen coyotes do the same outside a slaughterhouse. It was exactly as though the animal was licking up blood, blood that was invisible to Coffin's eyes. Whatever filthy magic Uncle Gunnysack had used to cover his tracks, to hide his trail from the eyes of his hunter, it wasn't strong enough to fool the nose of a coyote. The beast could still smell the blood.

Coffin dug his spurs into the flanks of his horse and set off at a gallop in the direction of the coyote. It yelped and ran off as he thundered past it, but it had already done all it could for him. With a good dog, Coffin might have followed the trail, now all he could do was continue in a straight line and hope that Amos White had done the same.

The bounty hunter rode hard for the better part of an hour, until the scrub began to rise into a rocky little mesa nestled between two towers of windswept stone. Here he had his first solid evidence that his trail was true. A scrap torn from a paisley dress hanging from the thorns of a tumbleweed. The sun hadn't had time to bleach away the color, so Coffin knew it had only recently been ripped away. Grimly, he drew his .45 and checked the action, spinning the cylinder, working the hammer. Normally, he kept an empty chamber just in case his horse threw him, but now he put a sixth bullet in his gun. Coming up empty on someone like Amos White would be a hell of a lot worse than any accident.

Nudging his sturdy mustang with his spurs, Coffin set his horse to climbing the crumbly slope of the mesa. It wasn't an easy climb, and he winced at all the rocks his horse kicked loose and sent tumbling down into the scrub. He might have made more noise if he'd brought a marching band, but he doubted it. Still, if Amos wasn't close by, then he would need his horse close if he was going to have any hope of catching the depraved outlaw.

The flattened plateau of the mesa was ever more desolate than the desert below, just a field of ugly gray rocks populated by mottled lizards and some soaptree yucca. There wasn't a bush, boulder or cactus big enough to hide anything larger than a bobcat. Coffin spotted the children almost immediately. They were trussed up and lying on the ground, hogtied with bloody strips of cloth that looked like they'd probably been ripped from their mother's dress. Close beside them was a small campfire, a metal coffee pot sitting in the flames. Of the renegade murderer, there wasn't a trace.

Coffin felt an eerie chill crawl down his spine as he noticed that the fire gave off no smoke and the stink steaming up from the coffee pot struck his nose. Whatever was boiling in there sure as hell wasn't coffee.

The bounty hunter closed one hand around the grip of his pistol and dropped down from the saddle. Warily, he studied the terrain, looking for any crack or hole Amos White might be hiding in. As he cautiously advanced towards the children, Coffin kept turning around, expecting the outlaw to come at him from behind. A cold sweat that had nothing to do with the heat dripped down the bounty killer's cheeks, he could feel his heart hammering in his chest. He almost wished Uncle Gunnysack would spring his ambush and get it over with!

Anxiety collapsed into a burning rage when Coffin got close enough to have a good look at the children. They were boy and girl, neither more than six and they were in a sorry state. Their bindings were cruel in the extreme, the tethers so tight as to nearly choke them. Their faces were painted with savage patterns, and from the way the flies buzzed around the ugly red splotches, Coffin knew those patterns had been drawn in blood.

Coffin dashed to the children, leaning over them. Through the gags stuffed into their mouths, he could hear them wailing and sobbing. Strangely, they barely looked at him, but kept darting their eyes to a patch of desert a short distance away. Coffin followed the direction of their gaze.

At first, he saw nothing, but then his gray eyes narrowed, taking on the intense, murderous glare he bore when pursuing his vocation as bounty killer. There was only one thing to see, a little knot of flies buzzing around a spot about four feet off the ground.

Coffin didn't wait to puzzle out the phenomenon, didn't give his mind the chance to tell him the idea which gripped him was mad. In one smooth motion, he drew his .45, aimed and fired at a spot a foot to either side of the buzzing flies.

As the echo of his shots was carried across the desert, Coffin stared at the buzzing flies. He wasn't sure what he had expected, had just started to chide himself for his foolishness. Then, from the empty desert where the flies still buzzed, there came a peal of laughter.

Malevolent and cheerless, that roar of laughter, the voice behind it deep and bellowing as though drawn from some cavern far below the ground. Before Coffin's amazed eyes, a tall figure materialized. One instant there was nothing, in the next the hulking frame of Uncle Gunnysack stood there, glaring at him from the pits of his skull-painted face. It was like a stage curtain had been thrown back, revealing the performer lurking behind it.

Instantly, Coffin sent four more bullets smashing into the black giant. It was pure instinct that fired those shots, the hardened reflexes of the Indian fighter and frontiersman, the outlaw and the lawman. Coffin's brain could have never willingly sent those shots, for his thoughts were paralyzed with dreadful wonder at the obeah-man's impossible manifestation.

Again, Uncle Gunnysack laughed, his painted teeth peeling back in a savage leer. "They warn me of you, de Bacalou say to beware de snake-bit man. Say me hoodoo not work for de snake-bit man, that Baron Samedi, him take de snake-bit man and then let him go again." The black giant laughed again, his bellow rolling across the mesa. "Maybe de hoodoo no work de trick, but de gun not being bit by de snake and me gris-gris bag still be true!"

Coffin felt raw terror coursing through his veins. What Amos White claimed was madness, this talk of hoodoo and gris-gris! Yet he couldn't deny the evidence of his own eyes and ears. The obeah-man had materialized from nothing, had laughed as the bounty hunter emptied his pistol into him. He felt the urge to flee, to run away from this supernatural manifestation, this horrible, unnatural fiend. Only the knowledge of the fate that would befall the children kept him from fleeing for his life.

Boldly, Coffin raised his .45 and pointed it at the obeah-man's head. "Let the children go and I'll do the same for you," he growled.

Uncle Gunnysack smiled at the threat in Coffin's tone. "I'm not being afraid of de loaded gun, you thinking to scare me with de empty one?" He glanced away from the bounty hunter, looking towards the tied children. "Baron Samedi, him let me keep out of Guinee when me body take de white man's sickness. If I want to keep away from Guinee, Baron Samedi need de innocent blood. No, snake-bit man, I be keeping de little ones. They already be marked with me blood," he said, lifting his left hand through the cloud of flies buzzing around it, displaying the ugly gash running across the palm. "Baron Samedi be taking them soon."

Anger swelled up inside Coffin's breast, drowning out the fear that threatened to overwhelm him. "Of all the motherless polecats!" he snarled. Such was his rage that he didn't even flinch as Amos White drew the heavy cavalry pistol from the holster hanging from his snakeskin belt. "Go ahead, you mangy cur! You piss-licking box rustler! Draw down on a man who can't fight back!"

Amos White's eyes flashed from the depths of his face, his lip curled back in an angry snarl. Contemptuously, he tossed aside the big cavalry pistol and reached for the immense machete. The snarl melted into a sadistic grin as he pulled the huge knife and watched the sun gleam from its blade. "You be a long time dying, snake-bit man. I leave you so you can watch when Baron Samedi come for what's left of de white children."

Without further warning, the hulking obeah-man charged at Coffin. The bounty hunter tried to dodge the giant's rush, twisting to one side and swatting at his skull with the barrel of his .45. The pistol glanced off the outlaw's head, knocking his kepi into the rocks, but despite the bone-cracking force of the blow, the bald scalp wasn't so much as scratched. In the next instant, Amos White's powerful arm was wrapped around Coffin's neck, spinning the man around so that the machete could be brought to bear.

Coffin didn't try to resist the giant's pull, but instead aided it, adding to his momentum and turning himself full around. His fist lashed out, smashing into the obeah-man's painted face crackling against his nose. Unlike the blow from his gun, Coffin's fist wrought havoc upon the huge black, splashing his nose across his face. The giant recoiled, releasing the bounty hunter and trying to drive him back with dazed swipes of his machete.

The bounty hunter dashed beneath the flashing blade, driving his shoulder hard into Amos White's belly. It was like slamming against an adobe wall. The giant drove his fist into Coffin's back, almost knocking him flat. The machete came whipping around, raking across his shoulder and sending a welter of gore spurting down his arm. A kick from the obeah-man's knee sent Coffin sprawling.

"De Bacalau was being wrong," Amos White laughed as he glared down at the bounty hunter. "I being have nothing to be afraid of!"

Coffin glared back at the giant as Amos White came lunging at him again. The obeah-man's talk of spirits and magic had given the bounty hunter a crazy idea. If he couldn't fight the outlaw man to man, maybe he could fight him with magic. The obeah-man's own magic.

As Uncle Gunnysack came for him, Coffin sprang up from the ground, his hands clawing at the black giant's neck. His fingers closed around the rabbitskin bag, what Coffin thought might be the gris-gris Amos White had boasted of. Desperately, he ripped the bag from its tether, snatching it away from the obeah-man.

The black giant roared, a bestial cry of rage mixed with panic. His heavy machete came chopping down, narrowly missing Coffin's shoulder, instead slashing down along the bounty man's leg, the momentum of the attack dragging the bokor's body down after the driving blade. Coffin balled his fist and smashed it into the back of his enemy's neck, hoping to stun the killer and gain some measure of respite.

The brutal blow didn't seem to faze the hulking madman. Eyes shining with madness, Amos White swung his body full around and wrapped his powerful arms around the bounty hunter. The breath was crushed from Coffin's body in an instant as the giant's massive thews drew tight. He had seen a picture once, in some newspaper, of a huge Bolivian snake that killed by crushing its prey in its coils. As he felt his ribs groan under the obeah-man's grip, Coffin couldn't shake that awful image.

Desperately, Coffin tried to relieve the mounting pressure, but one arm was pinned at his side. Had his enemy focused upon that python-like grip, the bounty man would have been finished. But there was a panicked desperation governing the giant now. Instead of maintaining the pressure, Amos White removed one of his arms to clutch at Coffin's outstretched hand. The hand which still held the gris-gris bag.

Coffin glared into the skull-faced visage of the killer, seeing the unmistakable desperation in Amos White's eyes. Mustering the last of his strength, struggling against the powerful arm locked about him, the bounty killer managed to squirm and twist within the bokor's grip, turning around so that he faced towards the children... and the obeah-man's fire.

With a snarl almost as animalistic as Amos White's roar, Coffin hurled the gris-gris bag into the flame. At once, the hulking obeah-man cast him aside and rushed towards the fire, wailing all the while. The giant didn't hesitate for a moment when he reached the fire, but at once thrust both hands into the flames, grabbing for the gris-gris bag.

The damage, however, had been done. The magic of the gris-gris bag was broken. Before the bounty hunter's amazed eyes, the hulking black giant started to burn, smoke rising from his skin, blisters sprouting across his brawny chest and arms. The painted skull was distorted as boils erupted across the giant's visage. The black man's flesh began to flake and char, crumbling from his body as little fingers of fire burst from his own innards. In the blink of an eye, the fires grew into flames that engulfed the obeah-man.

Amos White shrieked once, a long, terrible sound, invoking the name of a power that the obeah-man had long mocked and defied. "Damballah!" he shrieked and, just for an instant, Coffin thought he could see the fiery image of a great snake coiled about the withered giant.

In the next moment, Amos White's body collapsed to the ground, crumbling into a mass of charred meat and ashy cinders. Coffin turned away from the grisly sight. If Uncle Gunnysack had really used his magic to prolong his years, then he had paid a terrible price for them.

Leaving the corruption that had once called itself Amos White to dissipate before the cleansing breath of the desert wind. Coffin Durango drew the knife from his boot and cut away the bindings from the Prentice children.

Coffin didn't understand half of what had happened to him and knew he would never understand how Amos White had been destroyed, but none of that mattered now. He wouldn't be able to turn in the cinders Amos's body had disintegrated into for the bounty, but that didn't matter either. What mattered was that two children had been redeemed from the bogeyman.

There were some things even a bounty killer couldn't put a price on.

THE BUZZARD
BY ERIC RED

The shadow of the buzzard circling overhead fell over the cowboy's hat, horse and saddle soaked with blood from the hole in his belly. He slumped in his stirrups. All around, the brutal Arizona desert faded into watery waves of heat. His gun was empty. He was out of bullets and almost out of blood. The vulture knew. It had been tailing him for hours. Just that one stupid bird. Waiting for him to die. Reminding him he would soon be dead. Real soon. His bloodshot eyes glared up at the ugly carrion bird, slowly circling. The man's parched lips twisted in a defiant sneer. "Damn you, bird, you ain't gonna get me!" The vulture didn't answer, just circled. Then it disappeared from view. God, his stomach hurt. The cowboy looked around. Only endless desert badlands, scorching white sun and pounding oven heat. At least the bird was gone. He felt he had a chance again.

Just then the vulture struck in a beat of huge, fetid wings that stunk of decay in the flapping wind they blew as the bird swooped down and ripped a piece out of his shoulder. The cowboy hollered and punched blindly at the buzzard, his fingers sinking into the mottled rubbery flesh of its scrawny neck. "Oh you miserable varmint!" he shrieked. The vulture flew away with a caw of victory, a scrap of him in its cracked beak. The struggle pitched the cowboy out of his saddle and when he hit the hard ground the searing agony from the bullet in his belly sent his screams echoing across the horizon. The man lay in the dirt catching his breath. High above, the vulture circled in its grim circumference of death.

It was mocking him. The damn bird was mocking him.

The cowboy swore he would kill it before it ate him. His whole life on the range came down to one single-minded goal. It was to survive long enough to kill this buzzard. He hated it more than any man he had ever killed, and he had killed plenty.

He'd gotten the draw on those two rustlers who'd ambushed him at the creek and dropped them before the one got off that lucky shot that punched like a fist into his intestines. The cowboy managed to crawl back into his saddle and ride off, but had used up his ammo during the gunfight. His horse had trod down the stream for a half-mile, its hooves treading through water bright with the blood of the two dead men upstream.

That was this morning. Now he lay on the ground, mortally wounded, blinking up into the sun and the black wingspan circling above him. All he had to do was get back on his horse, he told himself. The tired nag he fell off when the buzzard attacked stood but a few yards away, head slunk in the heat. The cowboy had to get to his feet. He stumbled upright in appalling pain, warm wetness from his gut wound gushing down his leather chaps onto his boots soaked with gore and sand. He staggered in a figure eight to his saddle and got there just as the horse took off, but he had a good grip on the bridle and cussing and screaming he dragged and slumped himself back on the mount.

The cowboy rode again.

The vulture still circled.

The man gave it the stink eye, keeping the buzzard in sight so it couldn't ambush him anymore. The carrion bird had been flying directly overhead as the sun rose, but now it circled at one o'clock, just out of the way from blocking the burning sun so he had to stare straight into the fiery orb to spot the bird. He couldn't do it for more than a second without looking away else he would go blind, so he had to take his eye off the vulture again and again. The buzzard knew that. It was flying near the sun on purpose so it could swoop down from the sky and attack him bleeding to death on his exhausted horse. That is what vultures did. They waited out their dying prey before the feast.

He still had some life left. The cowboy figured it was a two-day ride to Yuma. The town was due west. He could make it. In town, there would be doctors and medical supplies and they'd get the bullet out of him. There would be the bite and warmth of good whisky, the smooth touch of a woman's skin, the fragrant smell of her hair, and the clean sheets after a cool bath with the gentle water against his skin. For a few precious moments, his senses strengthened with anticipation of those simple pleasures of life.

Then his horse's hoof loudly shattered a bleached dry grinning cow skull in the dirt. It was a sound like breaking pottery that grimly reminding the cowboy of his dire situation and how his time was running out. Above, the vulture cawed, like a death rattle. "I'm still here, bird, you hear me?" The man laughed manically but he felt no humor, only doom. "You ain't gonna beat me, you ugly buzzard, nossir! I'll live long enough to spit on your grave!"

The cowboy wondered what made him hate this bird so much. It was just another mangy buzzard. He's used them for target practice. But this vulture was different. It was playing a game with him. Toying with him. The man feared it because it had his number. The cowboy had been in six gunfights and never been shot until today, and while the pain was bad, the sickening fear that his luck had run out was worse. He could die. He was dying. The bird kept reminding him of that fact, a feathered harbinger of doom that tracked him with the inescapability of death. That, or maybe he was just paranoid from loss of blood. Either way, he would kill it before it killed him. No way the cowboy was going to let the revolting scavenger eat him. He would get a proper burial when he went, yes sir. But the real reason he had to beat that bird was because it reminded him of his pending demise. Buzzards only kept company with things about to die. He was going to prove it wrong. "Damn you, bird, you ain't gonna get me!" he rasped through a raw parched throat.

The bird cawed as if in answer.

The cowboy pulled a bottle of rotgut whisky from his chaps and bit the cork out. He took a deep swig and felt the rank liquor numb his system. It helped a little. Seeing he had less than half a bottle left, he figured he better save it, so put the cork back in and pocketed the bottle.

And on they rode, man and bird, until sunset.

At dusk he made camp.

Tying off the horse in a small arroyo, the cowboy managed to build a fire before darkness fell. As the sun dropped like a red knife slash below the horizon, he spotted the circling vulture swallowed into the gathering gloom. Then it was just night and moon and glow of fire. As painfully hot as the desert was during the day, it was just as painfully cold at night, and he shivered for warmth under his blanket. He lay with his head against a log in the glimmering glow of the campfire perimeter, staring into the flames, hypnotized by the fire licks and dancing sparks, and his thoughts wandered.

The cowboy was not a religious man. He wondered if he would go to Hell. The fire made him think of Hell, if there was a Hell. Was he a bad man? He didn't know. No worse than most, he supposed. He flashed back on his early years roping cattle and breaking horses on ranches and spreads throughout Wyoming and Idaho. He should have married his sweetheart who was pretty and loved him and he could have been in her arms right now in a warm bed with a roof over his head rather than cold and alone and close to death out here in the desert. He wondered why he left her and then he remembered. He'd left because those cattlemen had beat him up and he'd ridden off to settle the score with them. When he'd found them in a corral in the next state, he had purchased his first Remington Peacemaker and drew first and they died in the dirt. It was his way; he had to get even, when he would have been better off just turning the other cheek. The cowboy realized he was looking back on his life. Isn't that what dying men did? He wanted to live, he knew that. The cowboy would change his ways. If he got out of this, when he healed up, he'd ride back to Idaho and find his sweetheart. And never leave.

The man was so tired. He couldn't keep his eyes open. He couldn't see the bird but he sure felt it. Near. Waiting for him to sleep, to lower his guard. Yeah, it was out there, alright. The fire crackled and popped, showering sparks. So tired. If only he could shut his eyes for a few minutes. No, he told himself, thats what the bird wanted. He rubbed dirt in his eyes to stay awake. It hurt like hell, and five minutes later his eyelids were drooping again. He stuck his fingers in his festering belly wound. His screams echoed across the plains. Ten minutes later sleep overcame pain and he was nodding again. He pulled out his bottle of whisky and took a long pull. The horse stood tethered to a small dead tree that looked like a stripped bone, a weary shape standing in the shadows at the edge of the meager firelight. Wood popped and crackled in the dying flames.

The cowboy heard wings. Then the sound of something landing in the darkened perimeter of the camp. His fist closed tightly on a thick, heavy branch of wood in the sand beside him. Gripping it like a club, the man carefully eased himself on his side, hugging the branch to him. He closed his eyes to narrow slits, adrenaline pumping and waking his senses. He pretended to sleep, made a snoring sound, not moving a muscle, and watched through slitted eyelids the impenetrable gloom at the edge of the campfire.

He smelled it before he saw it.

It took a long time for the vulture to appear.

But it did. Bigger than he thought it was. A giant, hulking black feathered stinking creature with a hideous disfigured and scarred rotten red face and globular yellow eyes, its hairy jagged beak cracked and razor sharp. A death bird. Death itself.

The buzzard approached him one step at a time on huge talons waddling across the sand.

Firelight gleamed demonically in its eyes.

The bird came on slowly, step by step, watching him all the time.

The cowboy feigned slumber, completely motionless, waiting until his nemesis got within reach.

It was a foot away, silhouetted in the dying firelight.

With a caw, it pecked his hand.

And the cowboy struck.

Swinging the wooden branch in both hands with all his might against the vulture's body and head, he felt bones and cartilage crack. The buzzard shrieked in a horrible high-pitched squealing agony, eyes bulging in terror and betrayal and alarm. The man hit it again and again with the bat, trying to beat it to death. Sand and dirt flew as the bird flapped its wings violently, unable to get up or get away. Its beak gaped and a grisly tongue jutted as it cawed and yelped. The horse reared in fear, pawing the air with its hooves. The cowboy was possessed with mania as he got to his knees and brutally beat the bird, hearing its body shatter as he was splattered with its blood. The pummeled buzzard met his gaze with a feral, primal hatred that matched his own. The horse was in a panic as it jumped and whinnied, straining against its bridle and reins tethering it to the tree. Suddenly, the vulture sheared its talon savagely across his belly bullet wound and the cowboy fell back, howling.

Then the bird was gone.

The man lay on the ground, curled up in pain, listening to the fading flap of wings into the sky and the wounded buzzard's cries of hurt.

He'd all but killed the thing.

It wasn't coming back tonight.

The cowboy awoke with a jolt.

Daylight burned his eyes. It was morning. Shocked he had carelessly fallen asleep, the man took quick inventory of his limbs but found himself intact except for the inflamed bullet hole. Rising up painfully, he looked around the camp.

His horse lay on its side.

Dread gripped the cowboy like a nausea in his stomach. Crawling on his hands and knees, he dragged himself through the dirt to the big animal lying prone and still in the dust, saddle askew and stirrups dangling. The sound of flies became louder. The cowboy lifted his head to look over the horse's haunches, trying to spot the rising of his animal's chest with respiration. Instead, he saw the horse's blood-covered face and tongue lolling from its gaping mouth.

Its eyes had been pecked out.

With a sickening caw, the vulture leaped up. The buzzard fixed the man in a triumphant, evil, almost human gaze. It flapped its black, rotted wings and swooped up into the sky.

The bird resumed its daily circle.

The cowboy covered his head with his hands and screamed in rage, frustration and despair in the heat and the dust, pulling out hunks of his hair at the roots. "Damn you, you miserable devil, I'm gonna kill you, you dirty filthy buzzard, I'm gonna kill you if it's the last thing I do!" He staggered to his feet, unmindful of the pain of his wound, and shook his fists at the relentlessly circling vulture. It cawed loudly in response, beating its wings.

Now on foot, the cowboy headed out into the desert wastes. He knew his hour was at hand. He could make it a mile at best, before the sun was at its height and would burn like hellfire. The man knew it would be the end of him. His legs felt like cement blocks he could barely lift. His throat was raw and constricted from thirst. Delirium embraced him and white flashes flared in front of his eyes. The buzzard had won. It would eat him.

Then the cowboy had a thought. He had matches. He could drag together some brush and scrub and light it and douse himself with the last of the whisky and set himself on fire. There would be nothing left of his roasted carcass to eat and the buzzard would go away hungry. He almost did it. He had the whisky and the matches out. Then the sun began to sear his burnt skin and he realized the long pain of immolation would be an agony too great to bear. And what if he didn't die?

So the cowboy kept walking. The shadow of the vulture swept the ground ceaselessly like the second hand of a watch. His boots churned the sand. His tired eyes met the horizon. It was blurry with heat and blank and dry as a bone. He didn't want to die like this.

Far off, something metallic glinted. He stopped walking. The gleam again. When the cowboy saw the distorted figure of the man in the distance riding towards him and heard the hoof beats he knew he wouldn't have to die today. Giving an upraised middle finger to the buzzard overhead, the man's eyes rolled up in their sockets and he passed out.

The cowboy slept for three days the doctor told him.

When he awoke on the straw mattress in the wagon, the bullet had been removed and he had been stitched up. The kindly medical man had been in the desert collecting flowers for medicinal purposes and it had been dumb luck he had been in the right place and the right time and found the injured man suffering from loss of blood, exposure and infection. Fortunately, the doctor was skilled and saved the cowboy's life.

The cowboy expressed his gratitude and offered money, which was refused.

He accepted food and water.

He felt better.

Then he asked for the bullets.

The doctor told the cowboy that he was in no condition to go back out in the desert to settle scores.

The cowboy thanked him for everything he'd done.

He paid the doctor cash for the .45's.

By noon, he had headed out on foot into the desert, fully armed.

The buzzard wasn't hard to find.

It was just sitting there.

Like it was waiting for him.

They faced one another the way adversaries did out west.

Tumbleweeds rolled.

The cowboy's hand hovered at the stock of the pistol jutting in his holster.

He fixed the vulture square in the eye.

"Draw," he chuckled, grinning.

The buzzard just watched him with its sickly yellow unblinking eyes.

The man went for his gun, grabbing the stock and sliding it out of his holster in one smooth motion with his right hand while the palm of his left hand dropped down and pressed the top of his pistol, sliding it under so the quick draw movement cocked the hammer back. He pulled the trigger with the lightest touch but the gun misfired. The .45 bullet lodged in the clogged dirt in the barrel and when it exploded the whole entire pistol flew apart in jagged shrapnel in his hand.

When he regained consciousness on his back on the ground, the last thing the cowboy saw were the yellow eyes of the vulture perched on his chest, feeding and fixing him in its victorious gaze.

It wasn't about to hurry this meal.